"HAS EDGE AND RESONANCE . . . AND REAL-LIFE 1947 GANGSTERS."
—*Kirkus Reviews*

There was a sound on the roof, creaking, then rapid footsteps. A bullet took off one of the prongs of his hand. Two more pierced the hollow aluminum cylinder that was his arm. Rabb spun around and flattened against the wall. Suddenly he remembered the .45 automatic. He ran to the hallway, picked it up off the floor, and began shooting rapidly at two forms as they burst into the living room. In seconds they lay motionless in front of the sofa.

Joshua forced himself to stand still and try to hear noise above the buzzing of the cooler vent and the blood squishing in his own ears from the wild pumping of his heart. He heard nothing. He tried the doors down the hallway. One was locked. He stood back from it and kicked it. Once. Twice. On the third kick, the thin doorjamb splintered and the door opened. He ran inside and switched on the light. The stink was suffocating. His eyes teared and nausea enveloped him again. He slumped dizzily to his knees. Someone else was there. . . .

NOTHING BUT THE TRUTH

NOTHING
BUT THE
TRUTH

▲▽✚▲▽✚▲▽✚▲▽

A JOSHUA RABB NOVEL

RICHARD PARRISH

AN ONYX BOOK

ONYX
Published by the Penguin Group
Penguin Books USA Inc., 375 Hudson Street,
New York, New York 10014, U.S.A.
Penguin Books Ltd, 27 Wrights Lane,
London W8 5TZ, England
Penguin Books Australia Ltd, Ringwood,
Victoria, Australia
Penguin Books Canada Ltd, 10 Alcorn Avenue,
Toronto, Ontario, Canada M4V 3B2
Penguin Books (N.Z.) Ltd, 182–190 Wairau Road,
Auckland 10, New Zealand

Penguin Books Ltd, Registered Offices:
Harmondsworth, Middlesex, England

Published by Onyx, an imprint of Dutton Signet,
a division of Penguin Books USA Inc.

Previously appeared in a Dutton edition.

First Onyx Printing, March, 1996
10 9 8 7 6 5 4 3 2

REGISTERED TRADEMARK—MARCA REGISTRADA

Printed in Canada

PUBLISHER'S NOTE
This is a work of fiction. Names, characters, places, and incidents either are
the product of the author's imagination or are used fictitiously, and any resem-
blance to actual persons, living or dead, events, or locales is entirely
coincidental.

Dedicated to
MICHAEL DEAN BRINK
JOSHUA BEN PARRISH
and, of course, to
PAT

"*[Charlie 'Lucky']* Luciano was inconoclastic also in that he had no qualms about working with non-Sicilians. He had in his coterie Jews such as Meyer Lansky, Louis Lepke and Bugsy Siegel, and non-Sicilian Italians such as Frank Costello, Vito Genovese, and Albert Anastasia.

"Men of my Tradition were always loath to associate with non-Sicilians. The reason for this was not bigotry but common sense. They knew that it was very difficult, if not impossible, to pass on a tradition unless one is exposed to it almost from the cradle.

△✧▽✦▽✧△

"*[In Sicily]* the Family restrained individual desire, while at the same time it provided a broader base for a Family member's activity. In America, everyone was out for himself. There was nothing holding back the individual . . . . It sapped the authority of the Father. . . . In Sicily, we referred to our leader as our Father. In America, Father became boss, Family became organization, friend became business associate, 'man of respect' became gangster.

"The lack of respect for family-based virtues—such as loyalty, trust, and honor—created the general conditions under which my Tradition deteriorated. But the specific catalyst of change was money. . . . In its pure form, my Tradition is against narcotics. We consider narcotics morally wrong. It's not a point of debate. A man wanting to trade in narcotics will be discouraged from doing so. But let's say the old Tradition is in a state of decline and cannot enforce its code. Or let's say people start believing that making money off narcotics is really no different from making money off bottling sugar water. That's when things fall apart.

▲✦▼✦▼✦▲

"By the late 1940's, New York City was like a firecracker that could go off anytime. We conservatives on the Commission viewed these developments with dismay. The Commission was supposed to alleviate such discord, but things seemed to be getting increasingly out of control.

▲✦▼✦▼✦▲

"Fay and I chose Tucson over Phoenix because we wanted a small town where no one knew me and where we could enjoy an existence far apart from that which we knew in New York.

▲✦▼✦▼✦▲

"In Tucson, some of my friends knew who I was in New York, some suspected, and some had no idea. It didn't matter. . . . I hadn't come to Tucson to subvert the town."

▲✦▼✦▼✦▲

The following excerpts are from *Little Man, Meyer Lansky and the Gangster Life,* copyright © 1991 by Robert Lacey. By permission of Little, Brown and Company.

"The problem for Ben Siegel, and for the bankroll of the new Flamingo casino, was that the players who were so energetically putting down their black, $100 chips, were almost all winning back their bets, rewagering, and then winning again. . . .

"Late in January 1947, the new Flamingo Hotel Casino closed its doors, less than a month after it had opened.

▲ + ▼ + ▼ + ▲

"On November 29, 1946, the Flamingo consortium had had to borrow more money to keep the project going. Billy Wilkerson signed for a loan of $600,000 from the Valley National Bank of Phoenix, Arizona, which had links to both Gus Greenbaum and Del E. Webb, the Phoenix contractor whose company was building the Flamingo. This brought the money paid out on the Flamingo to some $1.2 million, in addition to the price that Wilkerson had originally paid for the land—and on top of the $1.2 million, Benny Siegel had made quite substantial cash payments in order to secure restricted building materials. . . .

"With the accountable price tag for the unprofitable Flamingo at the $3 million level and rising, there was a cash flow problem.

▲ + ▼ + ▼ + ▲

"Meyer Lansky and Frank Costello gave Siegel the money he needed . . . . But as his palace in the desert reopened for business at the beginning of March 1947, Benny Siegel was under notice. This time the Flamingo would have to work—and it would have to show a profit."

The Lord, the Lord God, merciful and gracious ... who will by no means clear the guilty, visiting the sins of the fathers upon the children. ...

—Exodus 34:7

Tu ne cede malis, sed contra audentior ito.

—Virgil

CHAPTER ONE

Joshua Rabb slouched in the slightly lopsided swivel chair behind his desk and stared out the window at the parched landscape. In Tucson, he thought, in your tiny mud-floored office in the Bureau of Indian Affairs, just a couple of hundred yards from the irrigation ditch that marked the dividing line between the San Xavier del Bac Papago Indian Reservation and the white man's world, you don't get many calls from Jewish lawyers from Brooklyn named Moses Petrovich. So when you do, you can't help but get a quizzical little smile on your face and wonder what the hell a twentieth-century Moses could want with Joshua in this wilderness.

He stood up and walked to the small window, beyond which stretched seemingly endless desert desolation, almost four and a half thousand square miles of cactus and rocky hills and scrub brush composing the largest two of the three reservations of the Papago tribe. Now, in early June, southern Arizona's hottest month, the land lay scalded and faded under a pitiless sun. In August, when the monsoon rains would come again, a kaleidoscope of wildflowers would ameliorate the sepia landscape. But today, in the searing hundred nine degree heat, that gentle vision was hard to imagine.

Joshua was tall, six feet three, and a little over two hundred pounds. His brown hair was combed straight back from a widow's peak and became slightly gray at the temples. He had blue eyes, startling cerulean blue. His wife, Rachel, had described the color "like the sky next to the sea on a crisp, bright day." She also always called his smile "insouciant," a word she had picked up somewhere and loved. But since she had died in a car accident in Brooklyn while he was in a hospital in Belgium recuperating from frostbitten toes suffered at the Battle of the Bulge, no one had described his eyes quite as romantically. And since he had been shot in the lung and lost his arm in a dense forest near a concentration camp in Czechoslovakia, no one would think to describe his smile as insouciant. The sparkle had fled from his eyes, the sauciness from his smile.

He had left Brooklyn last year with his children. Hanna had been just fourteen and a half years old then and Adam eleven, but they too had lost their insouciance. First, the tragedy of their mother's death, and not long after, the terrifying shock of seeing their father carried off a hospital boat from Europe, badly maimed and tubes coming out of him all over and looking like he was going to die any minute. But he had finally healed, physically at least, and he had left the Brooklyn Veterans Hospital. After several months of practicing law again in Manhattan and developing a racking cough from the air pollution and the humidity, his doctors had told him that southern Arizona's dry, hot climate was ideal for healing pulmonary wounds. He had also suffered other wounds, much deeper and not so obvious except to his parents and his children, and these injuries too needed healing. So he accepted a job as part-time lawyer for the Bureau of Indian Affairs and Office of Land Management in Tucson, in return for which he could use his office to build a private law practice. He was also provided with a small adobe house a couple of hundred yards from the Bureau and directly across from the irrigation ditch between the Papago Indian Reservation and the rest of the universe.

In the year since he had come here, the stark and forbidding land had become instead enticing and spectacular, possessing a beauty and an allure impossible to find in the asphalt and concrete of New York City. This was his home now. In those first minutes and hours of shocked silence that had accompanied his and Hanna's and Adam's entrance into this little town, he had never thought that he would be able to say that. But it had happened. This was their home.

▲✦▽✦▽✦▲

It was ten o'clock in the morning, and the lawyer from Brooklyn named Moses Petrovich had called just an hour ago, asking for an appointment for himself and a friend, a businessman who needed some advice. The two men sat now in the straight wooden chairs in front of Joshua's desk. Moses was quite large, the other short and thin.

Edgar Hendly opened Joshua's office door and started to walk in. He stopped short. He looked hard at the face of the short, thin man. "Sorry, Joshua. I didn't know ya had anyone with ya. I'll talk to ya when yer through."

"Maybe a half hour," Joshua said.

Edgar nodded and closed the door behind him.

"I don't quite understand," Joshua said, looking from the big man to the small one.

"It's not so hard to understand. How's a New York City lawyer named Moses Petrovich going to fare in Tucson, Mr. Rabb?" the big man asked.

Joshua shrugged. "They won't elect you mayor, but you won't go to jail for it. Joshua Rabb isn't much of an improvement."

All three men laughed easily. "Well, Mr. Rabb, your modesty is laudable," said the big man. "But we're from the city, and we like to deal with *landsmen,* and you're the only Jewish lawyer in Tucson. We did some checking, and we're sure you can do a fine job."

"I appreciate the vote of confidence, Mr. Petrovich—"

"Moish, please, just call me Moish."

"Okay," Joshua smiled pleasantly. He was right. A guy called Moish didn't have a chance in Tucson. "So what can I do for you?"

"Mr. Lansky has been my friend and client for years, and he finds himself in a bit of a problem with the federal government."

Meyer Lansky nodded his head and spread his arms, splaying his fingers, showing at once his innocence and helplessness.

"A friend of his, Benny Siegel, just built a hotel in Las Vegas," Petrovich said, studying Joshua's face for a sign of recognition. "The Flamingo Hotel."

Joshua nodded. "I've read about Mr. Siegel and the Flamingo Hotel. Supposed to be the nicest one in Las Vegas. The big contractor in Phoenix built it. What's his name, Ward, Warren?"

"Webb," offered Meyer Lansky. "Del Webb." Lansky was small, short and slender, and meticulously dressed in a dull gray sharkskin suit, starched white shirt, gray wool tie, and simple black wing-tipped shoes. By contrast, Petrovich was wearing a flowered Hawaiian-type beach shirt and bright yellow pants and white suede sandals over white silk socks. Both men were in their forties.

"Right," Petrovich said. "Del Webb built it and Mr. Siegel and his partners got their financing from the Valley National Bank in Phoenix."

"Are you one of the partners?" Joshua asked. He was concentrating hard, trying quickly to put together the threads of information about the infamous Bugsy Siegel. You couldn't read the newspapers without occasionally seeing stories about the Flamingo. It was famous, reported to have cost between three and six million dollars to build, at least three times more than any other casino in Las Vegas, and also reported to be almost bankrupt.

"Me? No. But the FBI thinks that Mr. Lansky is."

"Why is the FBI interested?"

"Mr. Lansky has interests in some clubs across the line from New York City and Miami and some other places that entertain gamblers. The papers like to call them 'carpet joints'."

Mention of "carpet joints" suddenly jogged Joshua's memory of the newspaper and magazine articles he had read about Lansky. "But gambling is legal in Las Vegas, I thought."

"Right again. But anytime Mr. Lansky's name turns up, the FBI develops an interest. In this case, they think he helped provide certain restricted materials during construction."

"Like what?"

"Well, a few tons more structural steel than was authorized in the quota that Mr. Siegel was given, some decorative marble they say came from Italy. A few other things."

"I'm still not following. If Mr. Lansky isn't a partner and didn't supply these materials, how can he have any exposure?"

"Well," Petrovich said, "if he isn't and if he didn't, he won't." He smiled affably.

Joshua nodded. "Okay, so maybe he is and maybe he did, so what exactly is the problem?" He looked directly at Meyer Lansky.

"The problem is I need *tzuris* [trouble] with the FBI like I need another *tuchus*," Lansky said. "Benny's in way over his head and I got serious men looking for assurances from me about the safety of their investment. *Goyim,* not *landsmen* like us. They have no *hertzen.*" He patted his heart. "If the FBI gets into this, it's just one more knife in my guts."

Joshua nodded. Now he had made the full connection between Siegel and Lansky. He remembered reading several articles in the *New York Times,* it must have been ten, twelve years ago, that Lansky and Siegel had grown up with New York's most famous mobster, Charlie "Lucky" Luciano, and they had been partners until Luciano was sent to prison in 1936 or

1937. And he had read another article somewhere, a year or two ago, about Lansky throwing a "going-away party" for Luciano when he got out of prison and was deported to Sicily. The party had been attended by every reputed mafioso in the country.

Joshua sat back in his chair, wary and suspicious. "Well, what can I do? Have you been charged? Is an investigation going on?"

Moses Petrovich took a sheet of paper out of his briefcase and slid it across the desk. Joshua picked it up. "This is a subpoena duces tecum to a grand jury in Nevada," he said, "for Benjamin Siegel's construction records, not for Meyer Lansky."

"It's only a matter of time if they get Benny's records that they come after Mr. Lansky."

Joshua looked at the lawyer soberly. "I'm still not getting it, Moish."

Petrovich pulled a white letter-size envelope out of his briefcase. He dramatically counted out ten hundred-dollar bills and laid them on the desk. "They have brothers and sisters inside," he said, holding up the envelope. "Are you getting it better now?"

Joshua reached across the desk and picked up the money. He folded it in half and put it in his shirt pocket. "No, not really. But if you think this will help, I don't want to disappoint you." He looked amiably from one man to the other.

Lansky laughed. "I like this fuckin' guy, Moish. I like this guy."

All three men laughed. Joshua took the money out of his pocket and placed it on the desk in front of Lansky. "What do I have to do to earn Mr. Lansky's thousand?"

"No, no, no! It's not Mr. Lansky's. You got it from me. It's important you remember that." There was no humor in Petrovich's voice.

"Call me Meyer. I like you," Lansky said. "He's smart," he said, turning to Moses Petrovich, "he's a smart boy." "Smart" sounded like "smot."

Joshua smiled a friendly smile. The thousand dollars

was a huge amount of money. He had defended first-degree murder cases for much less.

"The problem is that Meyer also got a subpoena," Petrovich said. He took another sheet of paper out of his briefcase and handed it to Joshua. It was a subpoena duces tecum from the federal grand jury in Phoenix for the records of Meyer Lansky.

"Del Webb also got a subpoena for Phoenix," Petrovich said.

Joshua nodded. "Okay, I'm getting the picture." He looked at the date on the subpoena. "This is next Thursday, June 12. You'll have to bring me the records to review."

"There ain't no records," Lansky said. "My name ain't on no records for the construction of the Flamingo Hotel. That I can guarantee."

Joshua settled back in his chair. "Then why do you need me, Meyer? What's the thousand for? And why aren't you up in Phoenix hiring a lawyer?"

"I'm the kind a guy goes somewhere, suddenly everybody knows. The FBI comes sniffin'. The IRS knocks on my door. I always hire a lawyer when I go someplace so I can call when I need. I'm living here now in Tucson. My wife and me was divorced in February. She's back in New York with two of my kids, Paul and Sandra. The oldest one, Irving, I got here with me. Doctors told me this was the best place I could come for Irving, he's got some health problems. *Kenna Hurra*"—he knocked with his knuckles on the seat of the wooden chair—"he'll be all right. I bought a house over by the university, got a old friend lives near there. He has a son same age as Irving."

"So what do you want me to do about the subpoena?"

"You come with me to Phoenix next week, I'll testify, we'll come back. That's all. This ain't my first time."

Joshua looked at him soberly. "Listen, Meyer, I know you think I'm a boob from the middle of nowhere, but I lived in Brooklyn until a year ago, and I've read about you and Lucky Luciano and Bugsy

Siegel, and even out here we have newspapers and magazines. It's hardly a thousand dollars' worth of work taking a train ride with Meyer Lansky to Phoenix and back. I've got to know what this is really about."

Lansky glanced at Petrovich and raised his eyebrows. Petrovich turned to Joshua, stared hard at him for a moment, then turned back to Lansky and nodded.

"I got a big piece of the Flamingo," Lansky said. "It ain't on paper, but it's big money. Some of my associates also got big interests. I'm talking serious business here. This ain't good what's going on with the grand jury. My friends don't like that Benny got himself in trouble over bullshit." He twisted his mouth sourly. "Marble," he mouthed distastefully, "fuckin' Italian marble, shit like that." He shook his head. "It ain't good we get publicity and investigations. I got to keep the feds away from me and my associates."

Joshua nodded. "Okay. I understand. But you have to understand that I'm just a lawyer. There are rules, I follow them."

Lansky opened his eyes and hands in surprised innocence. "I ask you to do something else? No. I hire you because you got a good reputation, you're an honest guy. I need a honest guy." He pushed the stack of hundred-dollar bills across the desktop to Joshua. "Just call it a retainer, so if I need you at midnight sometime you won't resent havin' to get outta bed."

Joshua laughed. "I don't have a phone. To get me out of bed, you'll have to drive all the way out here."

"No phone?" Lansky said, disbelieving. "This is 1947 already, not the Middle Ages." He looked at Petrovich. "Fix it up, Moish. Get my Tucson lawyer a phone. My lawyer gotta be a *macher* [big shot]." Turning back to Joshua, "This I throw in extra."

"Thank you, Meyer. I'm sure my daughter will be thrilled. She can talk to her friends every night for two hours."

The three men laughed. "Give him my number, Moish," Lansky said.

Petrovich wrote on the back of one of his business cards and handed it to Joshua. "This is my number in New York. Mr. Lansky's number is here on the back."

"We'll take the train to Phoenix next Thursday morning," Lansky said, rising. "Probably be able to return in the afternoon. I'll call you in a couple days."

Joshua walked to the door of his small office. He opened it and shook hands with both men as they left. He went back to the desk, put the folded bills in his shirt pocket, and smiled broadly.

▲✦▽✦▽✦▲

A few minutes later, Edgar Hendly walked into Joshua's office. He was short and portly and had a few strands of gray hair smoothed over a pink pate. Despite the heat he wore a gray wool suit with growing sweat patches around the underarms. His white shirt was clean and starched but dulled gray with age and frayed slightly around the collar. He wore a black wool tie, anointed with a few samples of breakfast. He was the superintendent of the Bureau of Indian Affairs and had become over the last year Joshua's closest friend.

"What the hell was *he* doin' here?" he asked, looking oddly at Joshua.

"Who?"

"Meyer Lansky, that's who."

Joshua was surprised. "You know him?"

"The whole *gott damn* world knows him. There was a big spread on him a couple months back in *Life* magazine." He smiled superiorly at Joshua. "Frances keeps a bunch a magazines by the crapper. That's where I do my best readin'."

"What's he famous for?" Joshua asked.

"They call him the banker for the mob. The mob boys collect their protection money and numbers and whorehouse profits and give it to Lansky, and then he invests it in gambling joints and triples their money for them. They say he's the only one a yer tribe the mob ever let into their business. He grew up in the same neighborhood with Lucky Luciano, they were close friends."

"Well, it's no big thing. He didn't hire me to kill anybody."

"Yeah? What would ya do if he asked ya to?" Edgar smirked at Joshua.

Joshua thought for a moment and shrugged. "Ask for more money."

Edgar cackled. "So what did ol' Meyer want?"

"Sorry, Edgar. Privileged."

"Privileged, my ass!" Entreatingly, "Come on, Josh, just a hint."

"I'm going up to Phoenix with him next Thursday. That's all there is."

"Yeah, sure," Edgar said. "Just remember, don't be askin' me anythin' when there's somethin' I know and you wanna know it." Edgar left the office and his footsteps echoed down the terra-cotta-tiled hallway.

CHAPTER TWO

"**Y**'ever read *To Have and Have Not*?" the man asked. He was sitting in the passenger seat of a Chevrolet sedan, trying to stare through the darkness and the rain to find the house number for which they were looking.

"Y'ever read this, y'ever read that. What the fuck is with you?" The driver was angry and frustrated. They had been on the road for five days, driving all the way from Brooklyn to Los Angeles, taking turns at the wheel and never stopping except for gas and a piece of stale apple pie and a hamburger at the shabby diners along the way.

"Come on, Solly," chided the passenger, "don't get *meshugga* on me. We'll find the place."

"*To Have and Have Not.* Ya asshole. Next ya'll be asking me did I read the *New York Times Review a Books*. No, I'm sorry, I ain't had the opportunity lately."

"So I read when I got a little time. Jesus Chris'. I like reading a good book. Whattaya being such a shmuck about?" He squinted hard through the wet window. "Yeah, four twenty-six, that's it." He pointed at a large house set back fifty feet from the street.

The driver slowed the car and pulled into the pebbled circle drive in front of the house. It looked like some of the new parts of Long Island: wide streets, single-story houses, "ranch style" they called them, a couple of trees and a lawn in front.

There were three other cars parked in the driveway, one of them a bright red Cord, gleaming brightly in the yellow bug light shining above the front door.

"Guy knows how t' live, huh?" the driver muttered. "Ya gotta give the som bitch credit for that, he knows how t' spend his dough."

They got out of the car and ran through the rain to shelter under the front porch. They both wore black fedoras and took them off, shaking the rain off them. The driver rang the doorbell. Seconds later, the door opened a crack, then widely.

"Hey, Solly. Lou. I expected you guys ten hours ago," said the man holding the door open. He was tall and handsome, slender. His black hair was slicked back. He wore a houndstooth check brown and white wool sports coat, beige slacks, dark green alligator-skin loafers, and a cream silk shirt with a pale mauve ascot.

"Fucking rain, Benny, fucking rain," Solly said, shaking the dapper man's outstretched hand. He walked into the living room of the house, Lou behind him.

There were three women sitting on a long sofa watching a flickering TV screen. They were dressed in negligees, red, black, shiny hot pink. One was blond with Jean Harlow waves. The other two had darker hair in a softer, newer style. Two of them had cigarettes hanging out of their mouths. The third slurped on a drink and lolled back on the sofa. She looked drunk.

"What'd ya do, Benny, rent some broads from the whorehouse the spics use?" Solly looked disgusted.

"Come on, Solly. They're my own girls, work for Jack Dragna and me. They just been cooling their heels here a long time. They're bored. They'll make you happy, don't worry."

"Yeah, that blonde'll give ya a sore on yer dick, make yer brains rot," Lou said to Solly.

"Nah, they're all right. I have all my girls checked," Benny said. "Come on in the kitchen for a minute."

He walked through the living room in front of the two men. The girls looked up for an instant, appraising glances, and went back to the TV show. It was *Cash and Carry,* and one of the dark-haired girls said, pointing, "Look at that. Isn't that a riot!" A blindfolded woman was trying to feed ice cream to a blindfolded man.

Benny closed the kitchen door and looked soberly at the two men. "Frank Costello tell you what I need?"

"Sure, Benny," Solly said.

"Joe Bonanno's living in Tucson," Benny said. "He finds out, he'll kill us all."

"Nobody finds out, Benny," Solly said. "Come on, *boychik,* this is us."

Lou nodded earnestly.

"Okay, good. Meyer's living there right now too. Since he divorced Anne, he don't want to be near her in New York. Call him if you need him. We'll just make a couple scores, that's all it'll take. I had it all lined up with Charlie Luciano when he was in Havana a couple months ago. Then the fucking Cubans deported him. But he had it set up already. His people take care of Mexico. You meet his two guys a mile north of the border, near a tiny town called Newfield. Just follow the instructions I gave Frank last week. Give them the bag"—he pointed at a leather satchel on the kitchen counter—"and take what they give you up to this address in Vegas." He handed a slip of paper to Solly.

"That's all?" Solly asked.

"That's all. Two times. If it works real good, I'll talk to Charlie and Frank. Maybe we'll make it regular. The Commission has to decide."

The two men nodded.

"So you guys have a good time. The broads are paid for. They don't know who you are and don't give a shit. You can leave tomorrow morning. It'll take you probably fifteen hours to get to Tucson. Stay in a motel on the strip just before you get to the downtown, there's four or five of them, and then drive to Newfield in the morning. It's like about ten mud shacks. It'll take maybe a couple hours more. Drive west on the dirt road from Newfield and you hit another dirt road going south to the border. Then drive back north exactly one mile. Nobody's there but you. The place is deserted. I checked it out."

"No problem," Solly said. "We got all the instructions from Frank."

"Okay. See you in Vegas."

Benny walked out of the kitchen, through the living room, and out of the house. Solly and Lou went to the sofa and sat down.

The lanky girl with the drink set it down on the coffee table. She was pretty under a mask of pancake makeup and heavily rouged cupid's bow lips. She wasn't more than twenty years old.

"Benny says we should be very nice to you boys," she said, her voice a little husky from booze. "He says you're big shots."

"You just talk, or you do something more important with them big lips?" Solly said.

She giggled. "Come on, I'll show you," she said. She stood up and walked unsteadily to him, her hand outstretched. Her large breasts jiggled in the soft satin negligee. It was short and sheer, and he could see her nipples and the triangle of dark hair.

He took her hand and walked down the hallway into a bedroom. The light was on. She closed the door and leaned back against it. She pushed down the straps of the hot pink negligee, and it fell to the floor around her feet. She stepped out of the high-heeled shoes she was wearing and was still three inches taller than Solly.

He stared at her and swallowed. Her body was slim and long. Her nipples stood out firm on the summits of her large breasts. She smiled at him and licked her lips slowly, lubriciously.

"What do you like best, honey?" she said.

"Whattaya do best?" he said.

"Let's go around the world. We'll go French first."

He unzipped his pants. She knelt in front of him and pulled his flaccid penis out of his pants. "What a cute little fella," she purred. She tickled the tip with her tongue. "I didn't know you were a Jew."

"Zat a problem?"

"No, no. Benny's a Jew. It's just different. Less to suck on, know what I mean."

He slapped her hard in the face. "Ya got a lousy mouth on ya."

She fell back against the door, then got quickly on her knees again. Her eyes were a little glazed, but the slap didn't seem to faze her. "Not so rough, honey," she purred.

He was hard now. She took him in her mouth and revolved her tongue and lips on him. He began to come and he pulled out of her mouth and masturbated himself on her face. She reveled in it drunkenly, her mouth open, her tongue out, lapping at the streams on her cheeks.

"I'm gonna take a shower," he said. "I been in a car five days."

She stood up shakily and rubbed her face softly with both hands, then licked her hands. "Okay, honey, I'll be waiting," she said. She stumbled to the bed and lay down on it slowly.

Solly left the room and walked toward the closed door at the end of the hallway, which he supposed would be the bathroom. He passed a door and heard moans from inside. Louie's gettin' his ashes hauled, he thought. Louie and his books, always readin' some damn book. What the hell for? Books don't matter. Money matters. Pussy matters.

The bathroom had a built-in shower/tub, and he turned on the hot water and waited for it to get hot. He pulled up the stem on the tub faucet to convert it to a shower, but the stem was broken. He'd have to take a bath. He hated baths. Baths were for broads. His sister would take baths in the tenement where he grew up in Williamsburg. For hours she'd be locked in the bathroom. He'd have to pee in a mason jar and pour it down the sink in the kitchen.

He ran water in the tub for ten minutes, just standing and watching it dully. He was exhausted from the days in the car, able to sleep only for a few minutes at a time, during the short turns Lou took at the wheel. Lou didn't drive well. He was from a Chassidic family in Williamsburg even poorer than Solly's, and Lou hadn't learned to drive until he went to work for Lepke doing "enforcement" on gamblers who welshed on their bets with the Italians. Solly was one of the principal enforcers, and he had been lucky to escape the crackdown on what the police liked to call "Murder Incorporated," which had ultimately resulted in Lepke and several others being electrocuted on a murder conviction. After that, the most trusted of the remaining enforcers had gone to work directly for the Commission—the "Fathers," they called themselves—the heads of the seven families that made up the Chicago, Buffalo, and New York City Mafia. Frank Costello was the boss of the Commission now, having taken over the Maseria family from Charlie "Lucky" Luciano when he had been imprisoned in 1936. Luciano had been a reformer, a forward-looking visionary of crime, and he had widened the business of the families from gambling and booze and protection to include prostitution and narcotics. A couple of the old time Mustache Petes, the conservative Sicilians on the Commission like Joe Bonanno, thought that drugs and whores would tarnish the "honor" of the men of the old tradition," as he called the mafiosi. But Luciano and then Costello had prevailed.

Rivalries on the Commission were becoming common, and the Fathers were not above plotting the assassination of their rivals. So a few years ago Joe Bonanno had left New York City and bought a winter home in Tucson. His son Roberto had been living there in boarding schools since 1941.

Benny Siegel, as far as everybody knew, was the owner of record of sixty-six percent of the Flamingo, but only a few people, like Solly, were aware that Siegel's silent senior partners were Frank Costello and Meyer Lansky, who had supplied millions of dollars to the obsessed Siegel to make the Flamingo profitable. But Siegel needed more and more money, for fancy Italian marble, for solid glass walls looking out on huge swimming pools, for plush carpets and gold-leafed wood and crystal chandeliers. Solly had been to Vegas and stayed at the Flamingo. You couldn't help but be impressed. This Benny Siegel had real flair.

Frank Costello, however, wasn't impressed. He had finally told Siegel in no uncertain terms that the Commission was out of patience and low on faith, and that Benny had to raise money by himself and make the Flamingo turn a profit. By June 1947, Benny was desperate, and he had begged Costello for help. That's why Solly and Lou had been sent here. To help Benny Siegel out of a jam.

"Just stay the hell away from Joe Bananas," Costello had warned Solly. "He's from the old tradition. He finds out what you're doing, your brains'll be all over the nearest garbage can lid. And I'll tell him I don't know shit from shinola why you was out there."

Not much reassurance coming from Costello, the "Prime Minister." But what the hell could a Jew expect from Italians? You do the dirty work for the wops, and they leave you swinging in the wind if anything happens. Solly didn't like it, but that's the way it was. But as consolation the money was good, and the work was easy if you had a knack for it.

Steam rose thickly from the water as the tub filled. Solly was exhausted. He jarred himself with an effort out of his reverie, undressed, and stepped into the tub. He slid slowly down. The hot water enveloped him and made him lazy. He dozed. He awoke drowsily, not knowing how long he had been asleep, but the water was just lukewarm. He dried off slowly, pulled on his shorts and trousers, and walked lackadaisically back to the bedroom. The girl wasn't inside. The house was dark and still. He turned on the hallway light and walked into the living room. The TV was off. He went into the kitchen and turned on the light. The satchel was not on the counter. He froze for an instant, confused.

The electric clock on the nightstand said 10:10. He must have slept in the bath for almost an hour. He walked to the closed door to the other bedroom and flung it open. He turned on the light. Lou and the two whores were naked, asleep on the bed.

"Where's the bag Benny showed us in the kitchen?" Solly bellowed.

Lou sat up, rubbing his eyes. His chest and belly were blubbery and pink. "What the hell you talkin'?"

"You move the bag?" Solly demanded.

"No, uh-uh. I left it there."

"You broads, you move it?" Solly growled.

"They been with me, Sol."

"Where's 'at bitch was with me?" Solly barked, looking from the startled forty-year-old face of the peroxide blonde to the fearful teenage face of the brunette.

"I dunno," the teenager said, shaking her head vigorously, her hair loose around her face. She reached for the blanket to cover herself.

Solly grabbed the blanket and pulled it away. "Where's she live?"

"I dunno," the girl whispered, terrified. "I never seen her."

The blonde swung her legs over the side of the bed. She stood up quickly, her behind jiggling. Solly strode to her and punched her full in the face. Blood poured from her nose, and she gagged and threw up on the floor.

"Where does she live?" Solly bellowed.

"Don't touch me, don't touch me," she whimpered. "She lives near me on Normandie."

"Get dressed and take me," Solly said, his voice hard and rasping.

"You broke my nose, you son of a bitch," the blonde screamed.

Solly kicked her in the stomach, and she doubled

over and fell to her knees. "Get dressed and take me," he snarled.

She stood up uncertainly and wiped blood from her nose and mouth. She reached for her black negligee on the end of the bed and pulled it on. Blood curled from her nose down the side of her mouth and dripped off her chin onto the front of the frilly nightgown.

"You drive," Solly said to her.

"I can't," she whined. "I can hardly see."

"I'll drive," Lou said. "Get dressed. You'll come too," he said to the terrified teenager.

"Benny and his fucking broads," Solly mumbled. "Can you believe these fucking broads?"

Lou dressed. Solly went back into the bathroom and finished dressing. The teenage prostitute waited in fear, shifting from foot to foot. The blonde's nose stopped dripping blood. Solly got in the passenger seat. The girls sat in back. The blonde gave directions, and fifteen minutes later they came to a rundown area of small apartments in Hollywood.

The blonde pointed at a three-story building. "There," she said. "She lives on the third floor. That's her car out front, the Ford roadster."

Lou pulled to the curb a hundred feet away.

"I think that's her," the blonde said urgently.

A figure emerged from the darkness of the building. A tall, slender woman. There were no streetlights, but the moon was full enough to give form and shape. The woman was carrying a suitcase. She quickly walked up to the Ford roadster.

Lou floored the car away from the curb and screeched to a halt beside the Ford. The woman peered toward them. Then her mouth gaped open. Solly jumped out of the car, ran around to the driver's door of the Ford, and pulled the door open. The whore tried to slide over on the seat and out the passenger door. Solly caught her by one ankle and pulled her out of the car. He kicked her in the stomach and the face, and she lay groaning in the street. He pulled the suitcase from the rumble seat, opened it, and dumped its contents on top of her. Packs of hundred-dollar bills tied with string tumbled out. Six of them.

"This all there was?" Solly knelt beside her and spoke close to her ear.

"Yes," she gasped. "I swear to God."

"You and God are gonna get real close," he whispered. He stood up and smashed his foot down on her throat. Her head lolled to one side. Her eyes opened wide and only the whites showed.

Solly got back in the car. "Fucking cunt deserved worse," he muttered. "I shoulda made her suffer a little."

Both of the women were sobbing in the backseat.

"Shut up!" Solly hissed.

Lou drove back to the house they had left.

"Say a word, you both end up like her," Solly said from the front seat, not turning around.

"We didn't see nothin', mister," the teenager sobbed.

The women got out of the car and walked quickly into the house.

"Where we going?" Lou asked.

"I dunno," Solly said. "Maybe better head back out one-oh-one toward Bakersfield. We passed a couple motels."

Lou pulled out of the driveway.

CHAPTER THREE

Pablo Arguello had been doing this for most of the last forty years, getting out of bed before sunrise, drinking a tin cupful of coffee to keep his eyes open in the blackness of the desert, pulling on worn cowboy boots over thin socks, rolling a cigarette made of crushed milkweed leaves and inhaling deeply, eating scrambled eggs and chorizo, walking wearily—now arthritically—to the big ocotillo stave pen behind the adobe house and leading several dozen goats to their summer grazing area, a meadow of bermuda grass about five miles away, almost five thousand feet high, just a few hundred feet from Caponera Peak on the spiny western slope of the sacred Baboquivari Mountains. It would reach only eighty degrees up there during the day, not the hundred five or ten that it would be in the desert at the foot of the great mountain. And the grass was green and thick, and a spring bubbled at the western edge of the meadow.

Pablo walked down the hallway of the long house and banged his fist twice on the last door. He went into the kitchen and sat at the long mesquite plank table. His wife, Angelica, was standing at the wood-burning stove with a tin spatula pressing the fat out of the pork chorizo patties frying in the iron skillet. The kerosene lantern on the table guttered, casting dancing light around the room.

Jimmy Arguello entered the kitchen, hitching up his Levis. He closed the window near the table, and the lantern flame stood up, straight and smooth.

"You been out again all night?" Pablo said in Papago, not looking at his son.

"Not all night." He yawned loudly.

"You stink like whiskey."

"Henry bought me a couple drinks."

"I told you stay away from that place."

"Maranda was there. I went to talk to her."

Pablo shook his head and frowned. "Leave that slut alone. She's trouble."

Jimmy said nothing. It was an old speech he'd heard a hundred times since his wife had walked out on him. His mother laid plates of sausage patties and scrambled eggs in front of both of them.

Pablo and Jimmy ate silently and quickly, looking away from each other to avoid yet another argument. Pablo wiped his mouth with the back of his hand and belched. "Let's go."

They walked outside to the big pen and swung the gate open. Jimmy took the bell harness off an ocotillo stave and found the old billy goat lying in the middle of the sleeping flock. He buckled the bell around his neck and swatted him on the rump. The goat leaped up and bleated loudly, arousing the rest of the flock. They pranced out of the pen and headed toward Caponera Peak, the two herd dogs nipping and yelping at them to keep them together.

Here, just two miles from Mexico, it was a million miles from the white man's world. Pablo had experienced that world once, thirty years ago, when he joined the army and got shipped to France in a huge ship along with thousands of other boys. It was the war to end all wars, they told him. He remembered the speech Macario Antone had given to the eighteen-and nineteen-year-old boys from the Big Reservation.

They had been rounded up from all over the reservation and driven in stake trucks to the tribal headquarters in Sells. Macario Antone was there in his sergeant's uniform, and he told them that an all-Indian unit was being set up by the army to fight the Germans. It was Company F of the Fortieth Infantry Division. Pablo joined, like many of the others.

They did their basic training at Camp Kearney in San Diego and were then sent to Le Havre, France. Pablo was immediately assigned as a replacement to an all-white company dug into trenches along what seemed like at least a hundred miles of such interconnected trenches and underground bunkers, and he had shot at German soldiers for several months. He didn't really understand what it was all about, and he had never been sure why it was necessary to shoot at German soldiers. But he always remembered Macario Antone's speech about how important it was to be a patriot, to fight for the United States, so Pablo had shot in the direction he was supposed to and even got a little bronze medal to show for it. He also lost his left hand to a defective grenade, and after three months in the Veterans Hospital in Tucson, he had finally come back to his adobe house beside Vamori Wash, in the Baboquivari Valley, just a mile from the highway to Sells, which was twenty-five miles north, and Tucson still another sixty-five miles east. He had lived here ever since, as his father had, as his grandfather had, as his people had for a thousand years.

One of his two dogs began yipping, sounding like a coyote, rooting at something on the ground. The other dog joined the first, and the goats began to spread apart. Pablo hollered at the dogs to get back to work, but they were out of control. Pablo swore out loud and walked toward them in the half-light of dawn, off the well-worn path, on rocks and brittlebush, walking gingerly to avoid the cacti. He lifted his long walking stick to swing it at the dogs, and then he saw what had them so tantalized. The man on the ground was dressed in a suit. It was too early to discern colors, but it looked like a black suit. He lay on his back, his arms splayed to his sides, his eyes wide open. He was wearing no shoes. The dogs were shoving their noses into a large hole in the man's side where blood had soaked black the shirt he was wearing. The shirt looked like a white dress shirt buttoned at the neck. But the man wore no tie.

"What is it?" Jimmy called out.

"Dead man," Pablo answered matter-of-factly. He had seen at least a hundred men die, most of them packages of raw meat and blood from mortar and artillery explosions, a lot worse than this.

Jimmy walked up next to his father and stared at the body. The top edge of the sun cleared the horizon, and suddenly the darkness was dispelled. The dead man was in his early forties. He was no taller than the two Papagos, maybe five feet six or seven, but he was much heavier, probably two hundred pounds and paunchy.

"Looks like one a them Mormon missionaries," Jimmy said. "Two of 'em was up at Three Points last night in the bar, talkin' about how we was all the descendants of the lost tribe of Israel and if we stopped drinkin' and whorin' we'd be sure to go to heaven."

Pablo spat on the ground. "That where he is now? Shit. Somebody blew his balls off with a shotgun." He pointed at the man's crotch.

"Don't need no balls in heaven."

Both men chuckled maliciously.

"Better go back," Pablo said, swinging his stick at one of the dogs, which had returned to the body and was nosing in the blood puddle between the dead man's legs.

Jimmy nodded. "I'll drive into Sells and get Henry Enos."

"Stay away from the slut," Pablo called after him.

▲✛▽✛▽✛▲

For some reason the words to "Home on the Range" kept popping into Jesus Leyva's head. There were plenty of deer and antelope out here, although there had never been a buffalo within a thousand miles, maybe more. But he did feel at home here. It was his home. The Baboquivari Mountains took on distinct shapes as he drove south toward them. The main road on the Papago Reservation between Three Points and Sells was asphalt, but this road down to Newfield and the Mexican border was dirt, rutted from the last rains, and the pickup truck bounced and rattled even at thirty miles an hour. Roy Collins, the FBI agent stationed in Tucson, dozed in the passenger seat.

There was no radio in the truck, and "Chuy" Leyva sang lustily into the vast, empty desert. "Where seldom is heard, a discouraging word . . ." His deep voice filled the cab of the truck. Well, that's bullshit, isn't it? There were plenty of discouraging words out here. Words like he had heard two hours ago on the phone from Henry Enos, the BIA policeman in Sells, the capital of the huge Papago Reservation that covered half of southern Arizona. "We got us a body down at Vamori Wash," Henry had said, " 'bout two miles west a the road. Near Pablo Arguello's place. They say it looks like one a them Mormon missionaries. I'll meet you there. He been shot twice."

Leyva drove through the soft sand of Vamori Wash and turned right onto the dirt trail leading to the Arguello ranch, the only inhabited place around here for miles. It was June, and the monsoon rains hadn't yet begun, so explosions of dust trailed behind the pickup. The change of speed and the increased lurching of the truck awakened Roy Collins. He rubbed his eyes and straightened up in the seat, looking around at the bleached desert. Chuy parked beside a BIA pickup truck.

Chuy Leyva was here only because Henry Enos didn't like dealing with the FBI. Henry was the BIA chief of police here on the Big Reservation, Chuy was his counterpart on the San Xavier Del Bac Reservation, just six miles south of Tucson. The Indian police had no jurisdiction over murder cases, but Henry didn't think that was right. This was Indian land, and the FBI should stay the fuck out, he had told Leyva more than once. So whenever there was a reason to call the FBI, Henry would call Leyva instead, and Leyva would have to call the FBI.

"Hey, Chuy," Henry called out affably, slapping Leyva on the back and ignoring Roy Collins. "It's over there about fifty yards."

He led the two men to the body. It was eight o'clock, and the orange ball of the sun was high in the eastern sky. It was already almost a hundred degrees, and the body was beginning to putrefy. Collins took a small jar of Vicks out of the pocket of his baggy seersucker suit jacket and rubbed a daub of it on his upper lip. He offered it to the two Indians, who shook their heads, too macho to need to mask the smell of death.

"Anybody touch anything?" Collins asked. Henry Enos and Jimmy Arguello shook their heads.

Collins walked around the body slowly. No shoes. Black suit. Starched white dress shirt. Then he knelt on the ground by the man's head. "Two shotgun wounds," he mumbled. "One took his cock and balls off. Bled to death."

The Indians simply stood watching.

Collins pulled the suit jacket open on the man's left side. There was no label on the pocket. The other pocket was also unlabeled. He searched all of the jacket pockets. Nothing. He reached into the man's front trouser pockets. Nothing. He reached into the man's back pockets. Nothing but lint.

The FBI agent rolled the body on its side. He pulled up the jacket collar. The label had been cut off.

"Dude travels light," Collins muttered.

Jimmy Arguello snickered.

"Let's get him in the back of the pickup," Collins said to Leyva.

Chuy walked to the cab of the truck and pulled a rubberized canvas bag from under the seat. He laid it spread open next to the body, and he and Collins rolled the dead man into it.

One of the sheep dogs was yipping. The men looked

toward the sound and squinted in the sunlight. The dog was running ahead of Pablo Arguello, who was surprisingly agile and fast for his forty-seven years. Leyva and Collins shielded their eyes with their hands like visors and watched the Indian run toward them.

"Another one," Pablo gasped, breathless from running. "Up near the grazing."

"A body?" Collins said.

"No, no, alive. He been shot, but not dead. Shoulder."

"How far?" Chuy asked.

"Couple miles from here."

"How far can we get with the truck?" the FBI agent asked.

"Maybe halfway, maybe little more. Follow the arroyo until the *shahgig*."

Collins looked at Chuy Leyva. "What's he saying?"

"We can drive up Vamori Wash until it hits the canyon."

"Okay, let's go," Collins said. "This guy won't mind waiting." He looked at the body on the ground.

Chuy said something to Jimmy Arguello in Papago, and Arguello nodded solemnly. He knelt by the body and began zipping up the rubberized canvas bag around it.

Collins and Leyva got into the cab of the pickup, and Pablo Arguello got into the bed. Chuy drove jerkily over the wash bed, studded with rocks, and after about a mile they came to a deeply etched gully which transected the wash bed and created a deep canyon. They got out of the pickup, Chuy took a rolled-up canvas stretcher out of the bed, and Pablo led them on a narrow, well-worn path around the canyon and up Vamori Wash again. The air became distinctly cooler as they climbed for almost twenty minutes. Then they saw it. Another man, clad precisely as the first one. This man lay unconscious in the shade of a huge boulder. His left shoulder was covered with dried blood, but the wound didn't appear to be life-threatening.

Like the dead man, this one was short and overweight. Collins and Leyva spread the stretcher out on the ground beside him. They rolled him onto it, and he groaned but remained unconscious. Sweating and stumbling on the rocks, they carried him down the mountain and laid him in the bed of the pickup. Back near the Arguello ranch, they placed the dead man beside the wounded man and drove three hours to Tucson.

▲+▼+▼+▲

Dr. Stanley Wolfe stood over the still-clothed body, examining it closely. The autopsy room in the Pima County Coroner's office in Tucson was painted glistening white. The unpainted cement floor sloped on all sides toward a central drainpipe a foot in diameter which was directly under the surgical table. The green-robed coroner had a soft, round, pink face in a small, pudgy body. He cut through the white shirt and black trousers with a scissors.

"Help me roll him," Dr. Wolfe said.

The Indian and the FBI agent rolled the body onto its stomach. Dr. Wolfe pulled the suit jacket off and scrutinized it, then dropped it to the floor. He pulled the trousers off, looked them over closely, and dropped them on the jacket. He unbuttoned the cuffs of the dress shirt and pulled the shirt off, examining the inside of it under the high-intensity light hanging from the ceiling directly over the body.

"What's this?" the coroner said.

Roy Collins stepped to him and looked at the inside of the collar where the doctor pointed. Collins shook his head. Chuy walked up to them and peered at the collar. He screwed up his cheeks for a moment in thought.

"Looks like it could be the same kind of writing in Joshua Rabb's pocket watch," Chuy said.

"What kind?" Collins asked.

Again he pondered for a moment. "Hebrew or Yiddish, I think he told me. I could be wrong." Chuy shrugged.

"You bring the other guy's clothes?" Wolfe asked.

"Sure." Collins left the autopsy room and came back a minute later carrying a large brown paper sack. He handed it to the coroner.

Dr. Wolfe pulled out each piece of clothing, studying it under the white light. The labels had been removed from the black suit jacket and trousers and the white boxer shorts. The man's stockings were common, the shoes cheap black brogans, worn and scuffed. On the inside cuff of the left sleeve of the white dress shirt was a faded laundry mark. Wolfe squinted at it through round steel-rimmed spectacles.

"Can you make this out?" he asked.

Chuy and Collins both stepped close to the coroner.

"Can't tell," Chuy said.

"Maybe it's the same kind of writing as the other guy," Collins said.

"What condition is he in?" Wolfe asked.

"He'll make it," Collins said. "They took him into surgery, said it'd take a couple hours. But he'll be okay. May lose his arm."

"You want the cause of death on this guy?" Wolfe asked, his voice sarcastic.

"I'm not real experienced at this, Doc. But I'd guess it was loss of blood from gunshot wounds," Collins said.

"Smart. Real smart. That's why you're an FBI agent and I just cut open stiffs."

Collins winked at him. "Some guys got it, Doc. Some guys ain't."

Chuy and Roy drove to Tucson Medical Center so that they could question the injured man after his surgery. Chuy left the hospital after four fruitless hours, having learned nothing. Collins remained in the injured man's room. Chuy drove to the Bureau of Indian Affairs office on Indian Agency Road. The long low adobe building lay prostrate in the blast-furnace heat of the sun. Heat rays shimmering off the tomato red mission tile roof made the tiles appear to be dancing.

Frances Hendly was, as usual, behind her typewriter at the reception desk in the hallway, behind a sliding glass window. She glanced up briefly and nodded shortly to Chuy. He nodded back and walked down the hall to Joshua Rabb's office. He knocked on the closed door and opened it a foot. Joshua waved him in. "What's up?" he said to Chuy.

The BIA policeman pulled two bloodstained shirts out of a brown paper bag. He handled them gingerly, not wanting to touch the blood-stiffened areas. He held up the one with writing in the collar. Joshua studied it.

"It's a laundry mark," he said. "Shlomo Grushin, 315 Rutledge, in Hebrew letters. That's in Williamsburg, near where I come from. Shlomo is Hebrew for Solomon."

Chuy nodded, then turned back the cuff of the second shirt. Joshua looked at it closely. "Can't make this one out at all. Too faded." He looked at Chuy. "What happened?"

"The first shirt with all the blood got shot twice. Dead. The second one got hit in the shoulder. He's at TMC. He'll live."

"Where'd they get shot?"

"On the Big Reservation. Down below Baboquivari Peak, near Newfield."

"Not Indians?"

Chuy shook his head. "White guys. Overweight. Beards."

Joshua wrinkled his brow. "Well, Williamsburg is where the Satmar Chassidim live. Really orthodox Jews. But why would two of them be near Baboquivari Peak?"

Chuy shrugged.

The telephone rang on Joshua's desk. He answered it. "Yes, he's right here," he said, handing the receiver to Chuy. "It's Roy Collins."

Chuy told the FBI agent what was written in the collar of the shirt. Then he listened for a moment, said, "Be right there," and hung up. "Roy's staying at the hospital," he said to Joshua. "The doctor told him that while the guy was under the anesthetic, he kept mumbling 'Solly' and 'bananas.'"

Joshua shrugged. "Sodium pentothal. Even though you're anesthetized, you babble a lot. I had it for several operations in the Vets Hospital. They told me I talked up a storm."

"Roy would like you to talk to the guy, see if maybe you can find out what's going on."

"Yeah, sure. Let's go."

▲✛▼✛▼✛▲

Through months of recuperating in veterans hospitals from his own wounds, Joshua had become accustomed to the smell of hospitals. But the sight of a person in pain was something he would never get used to. The man in Room 217 was definitely in pain. Roy Collins had ordered the nurse not to give him morphine when he came out of the recovery room. The man, he told the chief ward nurse, was involved in a murder, and he wanted to question him after the operation. So the only painkiller the man had received was codeine.

Joshua walked up to the window, where Collins was standing. "You find out anything?" he asked in a whisper.

Collins shook his head. "Only his name: Lou Shiner. Acts real weird when I ask him questions, like he don't speak English."

Joshua studied the man. He was awake, lying on his back, wheezing loudly through clenched teeth. His left shoulder was heavily taped. He was covered by a sheet to his ample belly. His chest was pink and blubbery. He had a full beard of dark brown hair speckled with gray, and the hair on his head was closely cropped except for clumps of long hair at the sideburns.

"How was he dressed?" Joshua whispered.

"White dress shirt, black suit, black shoes and socks."

"Anything under the shirt?"

Collins shook his head. "No undershirt."

Joshua walked up to the man and smiled benignly.

"*Eire frent vur nit zo glicklick vie di* [your friend wasn't as lucky as you]," he said in Yiddish.

The man turned his head toward Joshua. His eyes showed deep pain. "*Er iz geshtorben?* [He's dead?]" the man said, his voice weak and gravelly. He had a rubber tube in his nose.

"*Yo, ez tut mir leid* [Yes, I'm sorry]. What happened out there?" Joshua continued in Yiddish.

"We were driving from New York to Los Angeles. Just sightseeing. We stopped for gas in some little town, I don't even know the name. Two men held us up, took the car, drove us to a remote area—" He gasped with the pain of speaking, held his breath for a moment, and let it out slowly. "It was dark. They told us to get out and start running. I got hit, but I kept running and then I crawled for as long as I could." Again a spasm came, and the man shuddered with pain.

"Where are you from?"

"Williamsburg. Solly's my brother-in-law. His father's a *shoychet* [kosher butcher], we work in the store."

"You're Satmar Chassidim?"

The man nodded.

"Okay, you rest now. I'll visit you again."

The man nodded and grimaced with pain. He squinted his eyes tightly shut.

Joshua gestured to the FBI agent to come with him into the corridor. They walked thirty feet down the hallway.

"Did you watch him being undressed?" Joshua asked.

Collins nodded.

"Just a shirt, nothing underneath?"

"Right."

Joshua shook his head and frowned. "He says he's an ultra-orthodox Jew from Williamsburg, but I never knew of one not to wear a *tallis koton,* a small prayer shawl they always wear under their shirt. He has the earlocks and the beard and the short hair, but no *tallis koton.*"

"Maybe in this heat, out in the desert, he took it off," Collins offered.

Joshua shrugged. "A real Satmar wouldn't. And he says they were both shot from behind."

Collins shook his head. "Nope, from the front. Except this guy might have been hit from the side. There's a big pattern of buckshot all over his shoulder."

"Well, I don't know what to tell you. Part of it squares, part doesn't."

"Did you ask him about 'bananas'?"

"No, I forgot." Joshua walked back into the room. The man was staring fixedly at the ceiling.

Ir hut gezugt 'bananan,' 'bananan,' a sach mol beys di operatzia. Vuss hut ir gemeynt? [You said 'bananas,' 'bananas,' repeatedly during your operation. What did you mean?]

The man's eyes opened wide. He looked frightened. "I'm in too much pain," he murmured to Joshua in Yiddish. "I have to sleep." He turned his face toward the wall.

Joshua walked out of the room again with Collins. "I'll have to come back tomorrow," he said. "He's in too much pain right now."

Collins nodded. "Something real strange going on, huh?"

Joshua shrugged. "Who knows what evil lurks in the hearts of men?"

Collins chuckled.

▲✦▽✦▽✦▲

The telephone rang on Joshua's desk, and he reached for it absently. "Hello."

"Mr. Rabb?"

"Yes."

"This is Buck Buchanan."

"Yes sir," Joshua said, straightening a little in his chair. "What can I do for you, Judge?" Robert Buchanan was the United States District Judge for southern Arizona.

"You planning to come downtown this afternoon?"

"If there's something you want to talk to me about, I will."

"I think there is. I've got a criminal case on my docket, an Indian boy named Charlie Isaiah. You been reading about it?"

"Couldn't help it. They splashed his picture all over the front page for weeks."

"Well, the grand jury indicted him last week, and I just arraigned him: kidnap, rape, and first-degree murder. I entered a plea of not guilty for him. This boy needs a lawyer, and he's indigent. I'd like to be able to appoint someone good for him. He needs all the help he can get. And I think I can dredge up from the court budget three, four hundred, maybe seven-fifty if it has to go to trial. At least you won't starve."

"Judge, you know I won't turn you down. Where is he?"

"Ollie's got him in a detention cell at the marshal's office. Come by here and look at the file first. I told Ollie to give you as much time with him as you need."

"Okay, Judge. I'll be right down."

Joshua drove to the Federal Building in downtown Tucson. The post office was on most of the first floor. On the second floor in the east wing was the federal courtroom and Judge Buchanan's chambers. On the second floor in the west wing and the rest of the first floor was the United States marshal's office.

Joshua wasn't thrilled about being asked to handle Isaiah's defense. But you didn't turn down a federal judge. And Joshua assumed that Judge Buchanan's principal thinking on the subject was not that Joshua Rabb was such a splendid lawyer—although Joshua hoped that that was at least in there somewhere—but rather that there wasn't any other lawyer in Tucson poor enough and hungry enough to agree to represent the drunk Indian who had raped and murdered Edward Carter's daughter.

The newspapers had been full of the stories for weeks. Charlie Isaiah was a young Papago who had been a used car salesman at Carter Ford. He spoke

Papago and Spanish and did pretty well selling clunkers to folks who didn't have the two and a half or three thousand dollars it took for a new car. Charlie was good-looking, tall, and slender, and he had apparently tried to date Ed Carter's seventeen-year-old daughter, Jennifer. They had gone to Tucson High School together, Charlie a year ahead of Jenny, and she had refused to go out with him. He had kidnapped her, raped her, and stabbed her in a drunken rage.

Hanna had often talked about Jenny. She had been a cheerleader like Hanna, two years ahead of Hanna, pretty and popular and very rich. She even had her own car, a new red Ford convertible. Hanna had been deeply shocked when she was killed. Jennifer wasn't exactly the angelic, pure as the driven snow super heroine depicted by J. T. Sellner in her newspaper stories, but she was a nice girl, just like most of the other girls Hanna knew, though a little snobbish and hoity-toity because she always had new clothes and new shoes.

Joshua walked down the hallway past the courtroom and entered the smoked glass door marked PRIVATE: JUDGE BUCHANAN.

The judge's secretary, an elderly woman with a squeezed face and a tight gray bun, smiled at him. "Go on in, Mr. Rabb. He's expecting you."

"Thanks, Mrs. Hawkes. You're looking mighty lovely today."

He sounded to himself like Pa Kettle, but Mrs. Hawkes basked with pleasure at the compliment.

Judge Buchanan was hunched over his huge desk, smoking a cigarette, studying a case book. He looked up at Joshua through a cirrus cloud of gray smoke and smiled. He was thin, a bit over sixty years old, and had a thick head of graying brown hair. His pale blue eyes were tired.

"How you doing, Joshua?" He stood up and held out his hand. Joshua shook it.

"Sit, sit. How's business?"

Joshua sat down in the padded leather chair. "Well, Judge, I can't tell you I'm getting rich quick out on the reservation, but it's honest work."

Buchanan nodded. "Well, there's something to be said for honest work." His eyes squinted in a wry smile. "What with what a lawyer usually has to do to make a buck." He chuckled.

Joshua nodded. "Speaking of which, why do I have the honor of being appointed for Isaiah?"

Buchanan looked at him, his face actually merry. "What other dumb prick would accept it?" He exploded with laughter, and Joshua laughed as well.

"You Jewish lawyers from back East are crazy as coots when it comes to these underdog situations. Must be in the genes. Hell, Dick Kleinfeld used to be the same way."

"Until they ran him out of town," Joshua said. "Or so I hear."

"Well, don't believe everything you hear. Ol' Dick moved to L.A., just decided to go for richer pickin's."

"Yeah, picking tar and feathers out of his butt the whole way."

Buchanan roared with laughter. Then he forced his face back into seriousness. "It's because you're a damn good lawyer, and this guy needs you. That's why I appointed you. He's about two inches from the noose."

Joshua nodded, his face sober.

Judge Buchanan handed him a file. "I set a pretrial motions hearing for next Tuesday."

"How am I going to be ready for that?"

"I'll grant you another hearing if you need it."

Joshua opened the file and read the indictment. "No facts are stated here at all," he said, frowning. "I'm going to have to move for a bill of particulars, then decide what other motions may be necessary."

Judge Buchanan shrugged. "Okay, that's fair. You're accepting this case on very short notice. I'll tell you what we'll do. I'll have Mrs. Hawkes call the U.S. attorney's office and tell them we're going to treat next Tuesday's hearing as an evidentiary hearing in lieu of a bill of particulars."

"Essert's going to love you for that."

"I'm the judge. I don't need his love."

Joshua chuckled. "Thanks."

"Okay, go on and talk to Isaiah, and bring the file back to Mrs. Hawkes when you're done."

"Yes, sir."

Joshua walked down the hallway to the west wing and down the stairway to the marshal's office. Ollie Friedkind was sitting reading a paperback novel.

"Howdy, Mr. Rabb," he said, looking up from the book. "How you been?"

"Fair to middlin', Ollie. What are you reading?"

"Oh, it's a crappy little book about this New York lawyer who moves out West and starts representin' Papago Indians and pretty soon ends up gettin' his dick shoved up his ass." He laid the novel on the desk.

"Really?" Joshua said. He looked at the cover of the novel: *The Lonesome Eagle,* by Zane Gray. "That's what it's about?"

Friedkind laughed, more like a series of honks. "Naw, I'm just pullin' yer leg."

Joshua frowned and walked upstairs behind the marshal to the detention cell. Charlie Isaiah stood leaning against the bars, staring sullenly at the marshal and then at Joshua.

"Move back," Friedkind ordered.

Isaiah moved back from the bars, then walked to the rear of the cell. Joshua went in and the marshal locked the door behind him.

"I'm Joshua Rabb." He extended his hand. "Your lawyer."

The Indian shook hands with him. "Hey, I heard of *you.* Everybody *you* represent gets lynched."

Joshua grimaced. "Not everybody. And only if they screw with me."

"Hey, man." Isaiah held up his hands in mock surrender. "Me heap good Indian."

"Glad to hear it," Joshua said. "Me heap good white guy. Why did you kill the girl?"

The smile evaporated from Isaiah's face, replaced by fear. "You my lawyer?"

Joshua nodded.

"You sound more like the prosecutor."

"I can't defend you unless you tell me what happened."

The Indian studied Joshua's face, then nodded. "Okay. I didn't kill her. Her father killed her."

Joshua had been in too many interviews, had heard too many lies from scared defendants, to be shocked or even annoyed. This was just foreplay. It would obviously take a while to get down to the truth.

"Okay, did you see him do it?"

"Yes."

"How did it happen?"

"He stabbed her four times, five times."

"Why?"

"Because he found her in bed with me."

"Where?"

"At her house, in her bedroom."

"Irate husbands usually kill the other man, not the woman."

"This wasn't her husband, it was her father. And the son of a bitch was crazy, I mean totally crazy. He kept screaming at her, 'You cheating bitch! You cheating bitch!' "

"And what were you doing all this time?"

"Being held down by her brother, then knocked silly by the old man."

Isaiah's face was drawn and fearful. Joshua paused in his rapid-fire questioning and studied him. There was no test for determining whether someone was telling the truth, no eye contact test, no sweaty palm giveaway, no flinching or looking away or flickering eyelid. Everyone was different. There was only a gut feeling you got from someone after interviewing a thousand someones, based on experience and judgment and some sixth sense. And all of this told Joshua that Charlie Isaiah was telling the truth.

"Where was her mother while all this was going on?"

"She didn't have a mother. Dead or divorced, I don't know. She never talked about it."

"And the brother didn't do anything to help her?"

He shook his head. "He outweighs me by fifty

pounds, seventy-five. He's bigger than you, plays football for the U of A, knocked me out of bed, kicked me in the ribs, put me in a chair, and held me down. Then when her father went wild and started stabbing her, he got white-faced and vomited all over me, looked like he was gonna faint. When the old man came after me, her brother wouldn't let him kill me with the knife, knocked it out of his hands." He lifted his shirt, showing Joshua several bruises on his sides and chest. "So the old bastard tried to kick me to death. I passed out, woke up in my house in bed with Jennifer next to me and an FBI guy puttin' cuffs on me."

Joshua remembered Chuy talking about going with Roy Collins to make the arrest of Charlie Isaiah. They had broken in the door and found Isaiah in bed, covered with vomit. Next to him had been Jennifer Carter, stabbed five times, any one of the wounds capable of having caused her death.

Chuy had made a remark that had simply gone over Joshua's head at the time. Now it came back to him. There had hardly been any blood, Chuy had said.

"You are in deep trouble, Charlie," Joshua said.

"Yeah, no shit," Charlie murmured.

Joshua looked in the file. "Well, I'd better get to work and find out if they have any evidence against you." His face was somber.

Charlie Isaiah stared forlornly at his feet.

CHAPTER FOUR

Joshua parked his yellow Chevrolet convertible in front of his house. He sat staring glumly at the tiny ramshackle adobe house, and thought what he could do with the ten hundred-dollar bills that Lansky had given him. They could move to a real house in Tucson. Out here across from the reservation most of the people lived in houses like this, small boxes of adobe with clattering swamp coolers on top. And on the reservation it was even worse. Many of the Papagos lived in grass and ocotillo huts, while only the richest of them had adobe homes like this one. But this was a Mexican and Indian world, and in Tucson, where the white people lived, there were real houses made of brick and stone and stucco.

The one saving grace out here was the mission. The Franciscan mission of San Xavier Del Bac was a little over a half mile away, past the irrigation ditch that was the northern border of the San Xavier Papago Reservation, and across a fallow field. The mission had been built a hundred fifty years ago by Jesuit priests from Spain and was a spectacular example of the ornate colonial architecture of Mexico. When the Jesuits had lost favor with the Spanish monarchy, they had been expelled from Mexico and their missions had been taken over by the Franciscans.

Joshua never tired of looking at it. "The white dove of the desert," the Indians called it, because it was white-painted stucco and its steeples and dome soared majestically into the air at the edge of the dusty, cactus-studded, centuries-old Indian village of Bac, which the Indians called *Wahk.*

Joshua got out of the car slowly, looking at the mission in the fading light of evening. The sun was edging behind the serrated crests of the Tucson Mountains to the west and the flat summit of Black Mountain just a couple of miles southwest of the mission. The sky over the mountains was taking on the unique pulsing orange and lavender hues of Tucson sunsets.

Twelve-year-old Adam was lying in front of the big wooden radio. He was staring at the front of the radio, shaped like a harp and covered with nubby brown cloth, listening in rapt attention to *The Scarlet Pimpernel.*

"Dad, can we get a TV set?" he asked as Joshua walked in.

"First you say, 'Hi, Dad, did you have a nice day?' "

"Hi, Dad, did you have a nice day? Can we get a TV set?"

"Where's your sister?"

"She met some guy. They went driving."

"What happened to Mark Goldberg?"

"He went to New York with his mom for the summer to visit relatives. They're going to the Catskills. His aunt has a bungalow."

"Where'd Hanna go driving?"

"I dunno. How would I know?"

Magdalena Antone came out of the kitchen wiping her hands on her apron. "I gave her some money and asked her to stop at the Mexican market and pick up some things for dinner. She should be back soon."

Joshua nodded.

"Don't worry. He looked like a very nice boy. And

he has a big new car, a Buick I think." She walked back into the kitchen.

Magdalena Antone was a twenty-two year old Papago whose grandfather had been the chief of the tribe. Under a federal program called "Acculturation," all government employees were urged to take a reservation girl as their live-in maid, the principle being that living with a white family would acculturate the girl to the ways of the white world that surrounded the reservation. Often, as in the case of Magdalena, the "acculturation girl" became a member of the family. Magdalena had attended the University of Arizona for two years before she had come back to the reservation to be close to her grandparents, both in their seventies. But her grandfather had died just two months ago, and her grandmother had moved back to her home village of Pisinimo, almost eighty miles from Tucson. So Magdalena had once again enrolled at the University of Arizona, and she was going to start summer school next Monday. She was determined to earn her bachelor's degree in education.

Joshua went into his bedroom and shut the door. He sat on the bed and kicked off his shoes. He massaged his left foot for a moment and then pulled off his tie and his suit coat and lay back on the bed. Defending a rapist and murderer last year had gotten him a shiny new convertible. Defending a gangster this year would get him what? A TV set? The down payment on a little house in Tucson? A hundred shares of General Motors stock? Hell of a way for a man to bootstrap himself up in the world.

He heard a car pull up in front of the house, and a moment later the front door slammed shut.

"Is Daddy in his room?" he heard Hanna say. Then a knock on his door. "Daddy, can I talk to you for a minute?"

He sat up on the bed. "Come in, honey."

Hanna was fifteen years old and rapidly metamorphosing from a pert and pretty kid into a genuinely dazzling beauty. She had soft brown hair loose to her shoulders, gray hyacinth eyes, and alabaster skin. Now her face was flushed pink and her eyes were wide and ingenuous with excitement.

"Daddy, Buddy wants to take me to a drive-in movie. There's a new one that was just built on Speedway. Can I go, please?"

"Who's Buddy?"

"He's this new boy I met. He just moved here from back East. He's really neat, Daddy, and he's done just about everything and been all over. He's seventeen." She was gushing with pleasure.

"Where'd you meet him?"

"Over at the Owl Drug, where all the kids go for ice cream and sodas."

Joshua pulled a pair of loafers from under the bed and slipped his feet into them. He stood up. "Aren't you planning to eat dinner?"

"Buddy wants to go to that Italian place on Fort Lowell for pizza."

"Well, bring him in so I can meet him."

Hanna looked a little crestfallen.

"You're not running around at night with some boy I've never met. You know better than that."

"Okay, I'll bring him in. But don't cross-examine him like he's a criminal."

Joshua frowned at her. "Keep it up and you won't go out on another date till you're nineteen."

"Oh, Daaaad." She smiled a sweet false smile and left the room. Joshua walked into the living room and sank onto the overstuffed sofa.

She came back into the house followed by a boy who walked with a marked limp in both legs. He had brown curly hair and dark brown eyes and delicate features. He was just a little taller than Hanna and very slender. He walked up to Joshua and held out his hand shyly.

"Nice to meet you, Mr. Rabb," he murmured.

Joshua shook his hand. "I'm glad to meet you too, Buddy. Why don't you have a seat for a minute? I'm sure Hanna can find a glass of lemonade."

"Oh, we don't want any lemonade, Dad. We're going straight over to the Italian restaurant."

"Have a seat, Buddy," Joshua said again, looking hard at Hanna.

The boy sat on the edge of the armchair. Hanna went into the kitchen and brought out a glass of lemonade. She handed it to him and smiled encouragingly.

"Are you from New York?" Joshua asked.

"Well, I was born there. But we were living in Boston."

"What brings your family to Tucson?"

The boy blushed, looking embarrassedly at Hanna and then at Joshua.

"My parents were divorced last winter, and my father decided to move here. My brother and sister are with my mother. They're living in New York."

Joshua nodded, and suddenly he remembered hearing the same story earlier in the day. "Is your real name Irving?"

The boy nodded.

Joshua swallowed. "I met your father today. He came to see me about some legal matters."

The boy's face brightened. "Oh, he said he might."

Joshua nodded. "He said you have friends here and bought a house near them."

"Yes, Mr. Bonanno. His oldest son is also seventeen. My father and Mr. Bonanno are business associates."

"Well, you two have a nice dinner," Joshua said, looking from the boy to Hanna. "But you'll have to be back early, Hanna. I promised Adam we'd all go to the observatory at the university tonight. They're having that special show on the planets that we've been wanting to see."

Adam looked up at his father in surprise. Then he looked at his sister and rolled his eyes. Don't blame me, his look told her. Fathers are weird sometimes.

Joshua stood up and extended his hand. Buddy rose quickly and shook hands. Hanna was deeply disappointed, angry, but she knew better than to argue with her father. She'd end up stewing in her room, going nowhere tonight. She and Buddy left.

"Didn't you like him, Dad?" Adam asked.

"Sure," Joshua said, smiling reassuringly. "But it's Wednesday, and I don't like Hanna staying out late on weeknights."

"Can we talk about a TV now, Dad?"

Joshua sat down wearily on the sofa.

▲+▼+▼+▲

A car pulled up outside the house an hour and a half later. Joshua waited for Hanna to come in, but he didn't hear any car doors closing. He waited several minutes, then got up and switched on the porch light. He returned to the sofa. It was almost eight-thirty, and Adam was in his bedroom listening to his own radio. Magdalena had gone back to her grandparents' house on the reservation to spend the night.

Hanna came into the house and slammed the front door. "I wish you'd stop treating me like a little girl," she said, her face angry and taut.

"Sit down, honey."

She sat down in the armchair and pouted at him.

"I'm sorry, but do you know who that boy's father is?"

She shrugged. "What do you mean?"

"He's a gambler, and he may be a racketeer."

"Oh, Dad," she chided. "I met Mr. Lansky. He's very nice. I'm sure he's not a crook."

"When did you meet him?"

"A couple of days ago, at his house."

"Did you talk to him about me?"

Hanna nodded. "Well, he asked me what you did and all, and I told him you were a lawyer."

Was that why Lansky had come to see him? Not because of his reputation or ability, but because his son had met Hanna?

"What's that limp he has?" Joshua asked.

"Something from birth, I forgot the name. That's why they came here to Tucson. There's some doctor who specializes in that certain kind of birth defect."

"Where do they live?"

"In a really nice house over by the Arizona Inn."

Joshua pursed his lips. Suddenly a lot of pieces were falling into place. One of Tucson's most famous part-time residents was Joe Bonanno, the boss of the Brooklyn Mafia. Joshua vividly remembered the newspaper stories of the so-called "Castellamarese War," when the competing Mafia families of New York had started murdering each other in the early 1930s. Joe Bonanno had emerged from the carnage as the head of the Maranzano family.

There were often stories about him in the Tucson newspapers. He lived in a reportedly opulent house in a rich area near the Arizona Inn, Tucson s most luxurious hotel. He had very important friends, the bishop of the Diocese of Tucson, a former justice of the Arizona Supreme Court, a U.S. congressman who was Bonanno's neighbor, even the chief of police. His son Roberto, whom everyone called Bobby, had been living in various boarding schools in Tucson since 1940 or 1941.

Suddenly Joshua was chilled. He remembered reading somewhere that Bonanno had the nickname Joe "Bananas."

"Did you meet Mr. Bonanno?" Joshua asked.

Hanna looked surprised. "No, but I met his son Bobby. He's Buddy's friend. They live right next to each other."

Joshua shook his head. "Jesus," he muttered to himself. "Bananas."

"What's wrong, Daddy?"

Joshua frowned. "Mr. Bonanno and Mr. Lansky are both very famous back in Brooklyn, honey. I don't think you should keep company with Buddy."

Hanna looked very soberly at her father. "Daddy, you defended a man last year who murdered a woman and her baby, and you got him off. He lives just a mile from here, and I see him all the time. I think it's awful, but you tell me that the American justice system is the highest and noblest achievement of our country. You told me that you're going to defend Charlie Isaiah, who everybody knows raped and killed my friend Jennifer Carter, but you're defending him anyway. That's what the adversary system is all about, you tell me. But now you tell me that Mr. Lansky and Mr. Bonanno, who haven't even been accused of anything, are bad people and I can't go to the movies with Buddy Lansky." She narrowed her eyes and studied her father.

"I worry about you," Joshua said.

"I worry about me too, Daddy. Every time I see Franklin Carillo I walk the other way. But Buddy Lansky is one of the nicest boys I've ever met. I really like him, and I think I'm old enough to make that judgment."

Joshua was at a loss for words. What did it say in the Bible? Thou shalt not visit the sins of the fathers on the children. Something like that anyway. Or maybe it says just the opposite? Damn! Isn't this the definition of old age, when you can't remember things you once knew very well? In a few days I'll be thirty-eight years old. What is it that Edgar says? If I ever thought I'd live this long, I'd a took better care a myself.

"Dad."

Joshua looked at Hanna.

"Are you okay?" she asked.

"Yeah, honey. Sure. I was thinking about my birthday party tomorrow night."

"It'll be a great party, Daddy. Magdalena and I are going to bake a whole bunch of different kinds of cookies." Suddenly her eyes brightened. "Can I ask Buddy to come? We'll just stay here, I promise, and you'll see he's really nice."

Joshua nodded. "Okay, honey." His voice was a little reluctant, but he tried to help it with a smile.

Hanna walked into her bedroom and closed the door. She and Magdalena had talked Joshua into letting them throw a little birthday party for him. After all, on June 11 last year, Joshua and Hanna and Adam had been in the old DeSoto, driving day after day from New York to Tucson, and his birthday had passed without notice. So this year Hanna had wanted to make him a party. In Tucson there wasn't much to do anyway. You could go to the movies—the Fox, or the Lyric, or the new Midway Drive-In—or you could go feed pigeons in Armory Park across from Carnegie Library. Or you could watch thorns grow on cholla cactus. That was about the extent of Tucson's frivolity. No beaches, as there had been back in Brooklyn, no Coney Island, no Radio City Music Hall, no Chinatown, no Dodgers and Giants and Yankees games.

In Tucson you had to rely on someone or other having a party now and then. So Hanna had invited some of the kids she knew from Tucson High, and Adam had invited a few friends from Sunnyside, and they both hoped that at least some of them would actually come. After all, summer vacation had started two weeks ago, and a lot of families left Tucson during the summer to escape the heat. But most of all, Hanna had wanted to be sure that Barbara Dubin came.

Barbara had once come over, it must have been eight or ten months ago. Joshua hadn't been home, and Barbara had sat and drank lemonade and chatted with Hanna. Hanna thought she was gorgeous, a fabulous body, shiny light brown hair in a ponytail, brown eyes with tiny flakes of yellow, and very worldly. But when Joshua came home, he was kind of distant to her. Aloof was the big word she had read that described her father's attitude to Barbara Dubin. And it wasn't so hard to understand. Joshua had been head over heels in love with Diana Thurber back then, and he wasn't the kind of man who had more than one girlfriend at the same time. Hanna had liked Barbara a whole lot better than Diana, but the choice obviously wasn't hers to make. And her father had ultimately lost them both. Barbara didn't come over again after that strained, uncomfortable afternoon. And Diana turned out to be less than the fulfillment of her father's fondest dreams. So for the last few months, her father had been alone and quite lonely, and Hanna was determined to remedy the situation. She had called Barbara two days ago and told her that her father was turning thirty-eight and she was having a birthday party for him. Barbara had been somewhat dubious, but Hanna had assured her that Joshua wasn't going out with any other woman right now.

Hanna hadn't told her father that Barbara Dubin was coming. He would have been embarrassed that Hanna had called her, and he might even have called off the party. So she decided that it was safer just to let it happen. Anyway, she couldn't be sure that Barbara would really come. Barbara told her that she was going out with a really handsome guy she met at a guest ranch where she kept her horse. The man was a banker and played polo and was from a really rich Tucson pioneer family.

Well, she'd either come or she wouldn't. Hanna had done all she could.

△♣▽♣▽♣△

It was almost ten o'clock. Joshua sat on the porch steps, a glass of Jack Daniel's in his hand, and stared into space. It was a lovely evening, a bright starry sky, seventy-five degrees, the kind of evening that made you glad to be in Tucson. A few swallows of Jack Daniel's helped you relax.

"Hittin' the sauce again, huh, boy?" Edgar Hendly said, emerging out of the darkness into the dim yellow illumination of the porch light. He and his wife, Frances, lived in an adobe house behind the Bureau of Indian Affairs, a couple of hundred yards north on Indian Agency Road. Edgar sat on the step below Joshua.

"Yeah, I'm a regular lush," Joshua said.

"Keep it up, Hanna and Adam'll be havin' to hoist ya into bed every night." He snorted. "Now come on, gimme the inside scoop on yer new boyfriend."

"Who?"

"Meyer Lansky, that's who."

"Privileged. He's my client."

"That's fine in front a others, but we're alone now, and I won't breathe a word."

"You're a real piece of work, Edgar."

"Actually, I'm two pieces a work, and if I keep on eatin' like I been doin', I'm bound to be three pieces."

Joshua laughed and took another swallow of the whiskey. "Mr. Lansky has a little problem with the FBI. They think he's a silent partner in the Flamingo Hotel in Las Vegas and that he helped supply the hotel with restricted construction materials, like structural steel and Italian marble."

Edgar stared blandly at Joshua, waiting. He nodded his head encouragingly. Joshua said nothing.

"That's it?" Edgar asked.

"That's it."

"No whores, no heroin, no murders, none a that juicy stuff?"

"Not that I know of."

"Damn! Pretty boring stuff."

Joshua nodded. "It won't make much of a movie."

"Ya ain't leadin' much of a excitamitin' life lately, are ya, Josh?"

"Excitamitin'?"

"Yip. It's one of Jimmy's words, when he was just a little boy."

Mentioning Jimmy's name precipitated a moment of leaden silence, morose stillness. Then Edgar shook it off. "He also said 'hambegurgler' for 'hamburger,'" Edgar said.

Both men laughed.

"Well, shit," Edgar drawled. "I cain't be a goin' back to Frances and tellin' her the only excitement to do with one of the biggest gangsters in America is that the gov'ment thinks he's smugglin' marble in from Italy. Hell, Frances'll lose all her respect for ya." He chuckled.

Joshua shrugged. "I like it around here when it's boring."

"By the way, did I mention Frances is pregnant?"

Joshua smiled broadly. "That's great, Edgar, that's really terrific." He slapped Edgar on the back, and the fat man beamed with pleasure. "Who's the father?" Joshua said.

Edgar guffawed. "You cocksucker!" He got up and

stretched. "Well, gotta be gettin' back. If that's all the entertainment I can get from you tonight, it wasn't even worth walkin' all the way down here."

"Well, I do have just a smidgen of news for you. Maybe it'll make your hike down here worthwhile."

"I'm all ears."

"Judge Buchanan appointed me to represent Charlie Isaiah."

"The Indin who raped and murdered Eddie Carter's little girl?"

"Allegedly."

Edgar stared at Joshua. His eyes were wide, his mouth open. His shocked look turned slowly to a smirk. "Yer one crazy som bitch. This is a fact beyond dispute. Yer a full-blowed suicidal maniac." He shook his head and strolled into the blackness.

Joshua stared across the irrigation ditch and the field at the mission. The low-voltage lights around it made it softly luminous in the deep darkness.

What do I do about Buddy Lansky? he thought. He's just seventeen, a handsome, shy boy. Do I tell him to stay away from my daughter because I suspect that his father is involved with the Mafia? Do I forbid Hanna to go on a date with him? And then what? Do I beat her up or lock her up when she goes out with him anyway? That sure doesn't work.

He took the last swallow of whiskey and set the glass on the step beside him. Coyotes began yelping in the field by the mission. Must have caught a rabbit, he thought. Then, as abruptly as they had begun, the coyote cries stopped. One of them howled mournfully, a long, lingering cry. And then total stillness pervaded the night.

I love it here, Joshua thought. I never thought I would, but I do.

▲♣▼♣▼♣▲

Meyer Lansky sat on the white satin sofa in the living room of Joe Bonanno's home. Joe brought a silver tray from the kitchen.

"Fay just made these cannolis," he said to Lansky. "Melt in your mouth."

Meyer took one dutifully, bit a small piece off one end, ate it with a great display of pleasure, and put the rest of it on the Wedgwood china plate in front of him on the cocktail table.

Bonanno flipped the silver cap open on a cut crystal decanter and poured some of the amber liquid into two Lalique snifters on the table. He handed one to Lansky.

"Salute!" Joe said, proffering a toast to Meyer. "Courvoisier VSOP, the best." He winked.

"Salute, Joe."

They both drank a sip.

"You'll have an espresso," Joe said.

It wasn't an invitation, it was a necessary part of the hospitality the Sicilians practiced. Meyer smiled and nodded. He wanted all that acid in his stomach like he needed another *loch im kopf* [hole in his head], but it was mandatory. Fay Bonanno brought in the espresso on a silver tray with a silver coffeepot and two small china cups. She poured a little Sambuca in each cup to sweeten the espresso, then twisted a curl of lemon peel and dropped a piece in each cup. She poured the espresso into the cups, placed one on the table in front of each of the men, and left the room.

The front door opened, and two young men came into the house. "Oh, hi Dad, hi Mr. Lansky," the taller boy said.

"Hello, Bobby," Meyer said, smiling and waving.

"You met my nephew Alfredo?" Bonanno said to Lansky.

"No, I haven't. Stefano's son?"

Joe nodded. "Come here, Fredo. Meet my friend Meyer Lansky. He's a good friend of your father."

Lansky remained seated while the slightly built, pleasant-looking young man walked over to the couch and held out his hand. "Nice to meet you, sir."

"Nice meeting you, Alfredo. Are you staying here?"

"I'm just in Tucson for a couple of months. I'm staying at a dude ranch on the west side of town, El

Rancho del Cerro. I had bronchitis real bad back in Buffalo. My father and Uncle Joe thought the climate out here would be good. They were right: no more cough." He smiled disarmingly. He had light brown curly hair and hazel eyes. There was something very feline about him, menacing, that made Lansky feel uncomfortable, as though behind the seemingly ingenuous smile lurked someone much less innocent and boyish.

"Stefano is getting Fredo ready to take on some real responsibility," Bonanno said, smiling approvingly. "He's a good boy, learns real good."

"Dad, we're going to get some food and then go to a late movie, okay?" Bobby said. He was tall and dark like his father.

"Sure. Here's a few bucks." Bonanno reached into his pocket, pulled out several bills, and handed them to his son. "Don't be out too late. Is bad guys out there."

The boys walked into the kitchen and closed the door.

"He doesn't look at all like Stefano," Lansky said.

"He's adopted. His father was very close to Stefano and me back in Sicily. A man, a real man. Loyal, tough. He and his wife got killed in an ambush meant for Stefano. So Stefano raise the man's son, Alfredo, as his own. Fredo is twenty-two, tough like his father was, hard. He don't look it so much, but he is a *robusto* [tough guy]."

"Bobby looks great. Getting real tall."

Bonanno nodded. "I'm happy now,' he said, sipping his espresso. "I hate it when Fay is in New York with the kids. She came out last week, and I got Sal and Elizabeth and Bobby for the whole summer. I tell you, Meyer, family is everything." He sipped the rest of the espresso with a hissing sound and set the cup down. His face hardened, and his eyes became flat. "What is this I hear from Frank Costello? He calls me, tells me two of your boys got shot near here. They had $60,000 of Benny Siegel's money, cash. They was supposed to pick up twenty kee's heroin at the border.

One of them's dead, one in the hospital. No dough, no H." He held up empty hands opened wide. "What is going on with you, Meyer?"

It was an accusation. "I didn't set it up, Joe. On my honor. It was set up by Charlie Luciano last February when he was living in Havana. Benny needs money for the Flamingo. Frank Costello told him he has to give the Commission one million by June fifteen or big trouble happens. Benny got real scared. He asked me for the dough, but I'm already out more than a million. Then he asked me could I help him set up a couple heroin scores. It goes for huge money in Vegas." Lansky held up his hands toward Bonanno in a halt gesture. "I told him I ain't into dope. Only trouble can happen with dope. But Frank was all over him for money, so Benny set up the scores with him and Charlie. Frank asked me to loan him two boys to carry the stuff. Solly and Lou, a coupla top guys. Who whacked them and why, I don't know." He looked hard at Bonanno, and he didn't like the look in Bonanno's eyes. It was you, you devious wop bastard, Meyer thought suddenly. You had Solly and Lou shot.

"Men of the old tradition don't do narcotics, Meyer."

It was the beginning to a speech that Lansky had heard many times before from the Mustache Petes on the Commission.

"Men of my tradition are fathers to their families, Meyer: we don't bring them drugs, we don't bring them whores. Look what happened to Charlie over whores. Ten years in the joint, then deported. I don't go for whores or dope."

"I don't either, Joe. You know that."

"So you tell me what's going on, Meyer. Two Yids shot in the desert near Tucson, and you here too, all of a sudden. You tell me what's going on."

Meyer shrugged and shook his head.

"It's one thing this shit happens in Brooklyn. There's plenty other guys around to blame it on. But here in Tucson, I'm it, Meyer. I'm the only one around the cops are going to visit if they figure out these Yids weren't just tourists who got robbed."

Meyer nodded. He was sure of it now. Bonanno had known beforehand what the setup was going to be, had the money and maybe the heroin stolen as well, and had Solly Grushin killed and tried to kill Lou Shiner. All to send a message to Frank Costello not to shit where Bonanno eats. Tucson was away from the volcano, far away, and Bonanno wanted his family safe and secure and insulated from the family business in Brooklyn. If Benny Siegel, another Jewboy, got himself in trouble in Las Vegas with his grandiose schemes, to hell with him. He could work it out somewhere other than southern Arizona. Or he could drop dead. Or he could even be helped to drop dead.

"I want you to find out what the hell happened," Bonanno said. "Go see Lou."

"Come on, Joe. You know if I walk into Lou's room at the hospital, the FBI will be swarming all over me." You'd like that, wouldn't you, Joe? Fuck you, you Sicilian shmuck.

"Somebody got to talk to him," Bonanno insisted.

"I'm going to find out, Joe. I hired a lawyer today who talked to Lou two days ago. He works for the Bureau of Indian Affairs, a smart Jewish boy from Brooklyn, and he speaks Yiddish. His daughter knows my son, Buddy. She was telling me how important her father is, how the FBI is using him to help investigate what happened to the two Jewish guys on the reservation. So I hired him today on a bullshit deal, nothing important, gave him more money than he's seen in months. He'll soon be telling me whatever happens with Lou, whatever Lou tells him." Meyer nodded reassuringly.

Bonanno was studying Lansky hard, his eyes squinting. "Yeah, I heard today you was out talking to this nobody lawyer when I can get you Evo DeConcini to represent you. He was on the Supreme Court, he's got real clout."

"I don't need clout, Joe. I need someone to tell me what Lou says."

Bonanno nodded. He relaxed back on the sofa. "Okay, my friend." Suddenly he was all false smiles and hospitality. "You know what you're doing. We'll speak no more of this bad business until you find out who's behind it."

Both men stood up and shook hands solemnly.

Lansky walked across Bonanno's lawn to his own house. It was a bit smaller and plainer than Bonanno's, but it too was richly appointed on the inside. A cream-colored carpet, living room drapes of a shiny, heavy gold material with golden rope tiebacks, beige crushed velvet matching sofa and chair, and a big television set. Buddy was lying on the sofa watching the *Gillette Cavalcade of Sports*. It was a heavyweight fight from Madison Square Garden. For an instant Meyer had a twinge of nostalgia for Manhattan, for going with some of the boys to the Garden on Friday nights and watching the *shvartzes* and spics and wops and micks beat the shit out of one another for fifty bucks apiece.

He sat down on the chair and said, "I thought you were going to the movies tonight with Hanna Rabb?"

Buddy shrugged his shoulders. "I thought so too, Dad. But her father wanted to take her and her brother to the university observatory. But I'm going to a party there tomorrow night. Mr. Rabb's birthday party."

"Well, that's fine. She's a beautiful girl, and Jewish even. Can you imagine finding a *yiddele* out here in the sticks. And such a nice girl too."

Children were fickle, Meyer didn't have to be reminded. He wanted Buddy to maintain this relationship for as long as necessary, at least as long as it would take to find out what Lou Shiner knew about what had happened to him and Solly. Meyer would have to report to Frank Costello.

Charlie Luciano had been Meyer's closest friend for over twenty years, so when Charlie was sent to prison, his handpicked successor as *capo di tutti capi* on the Commission, Frank Costello, had cultivated a very close friendship with Meyer. Meyer had come up in the mob world like most of the Jews. He was a *shtarke* [strong-arm man] for the Italians. He and Benny Siegel had been a team, hiring out to break strikes, enforce protection, discourage unauthorized crap games, and generally to do whatever the Italians needed doing. The wops loved to kill each other, but when it came to killing someone outside the tradition, they hired the Jews. Benny was a real *chayeh* [wild animal], and he had killed ten or twelve men. He became Meyer's closest friend after Luciano was sent away, and that made him important to the Commission. But this thing with the Flamingo Hotel was causing nothing but trouble. Benny was spending his partners' money like water, like it was his own, with nothing but a loser of a palatial hotel to show for it. Frank had asked Meyer to supply the mules for Benny to start heroin smuggling from Mexico to Vegas. It could quickly turn into a multimillion dollar business, and it looked like the only way Benny could guarantee the huge amount of money he'd borrowed from Meyer and Frank. Meyer wasn't happy with the setup, because drugs were trouble—they'd eventually awaken even the sleepiest police departments. But Frank said it had to be done, so it had to be done. You didn't tell the capo to go to hell. "Just make sure Bonanno doesn't get wind of it," he told Meyer. "Joe won't like us fuckin' around in his backyard."

But now Joe had found out. And he had sent a strong message to the Commission. He had killed Solly and tried to kill Lou. If Frank Costello had a majority of the Commission behind him in favor of the narcotics trade, it could mean war.

CHAPTER FIVE

"But it's *your* birthday, not mine," Magdalena protested.

"That doesn't matter," Joshua said. "I have everything I need. But you need a car to get to the U of A, and I want to buy you one. You've been doing most of the cooking and cleaning and looking after all of us for a year. Now it's our turn to do something for you. We're going to do everything we can to help you get that teaching degree."

Hanna beamed with pleasure. "We saw a nice little car at one of those lots. Dad brought us over there Tuesday. It's a Chevrolet, blue, and it's got one of those rumble seats. You'll love it."

"Yeah, it's got white rings around the tires," Adam said. "It's really neat."

Tears filled Magdalena's eyes and she sniffed. She burst into a radiant smile and hugged Joshua. "I'm so happy." Tears rolled down her cheeks.

They drove to the used car lot on Stone Avenue near Grant. There were about twenty vehicles, ranging from rusty ten-year-old pickup trucks to a sleek 1946 Oldsmobile. Joshua parked on the street and they walked up to the blue Chevrolet. It had a few dents in the passenger door, and the back cushion of the rumble seat had a tear in it. But Magdalena didn't see any of the defects. She couldn't stop grinning.

The used car lot owner came toward them smiling like an evangelist. He was tall and very fat and he panted when he spoke. "You folks back to see this little prize, huh?" he asked. He patted the car on the hood like a precious child. "I love this baby. Honest to God, I thought about giving it to my own daughter. She's just seventeen, needs a cute little car, but she won't need one till September, when school starts again, so I just been kind of holding it out here on the lot, know what I mean? Polish it up every day, keep it looking like new."

"Right," Joshua said. "Come on over to your office and let's talk about it." He had purposely worn his mechanical arm with a short-sleeve polo shirt. The arm hung at his side, sunlight glinting off the stainless steel prongs. Although his foot almost never bothered him anymore, he was using the cane today as well. He limped toward the office, a small mobile home. It was clammy warm inside from the wheezing evaporative cooler.

"You said you want six hundred for it," Joshua said.

The man nodded avidly. "Worth every penny."

"It's worth four hundred. Dinged up, holes in the cushions. Almost fifty thousand miles on it."

"Five hundred fifty."

"I don't have five-fifty."

"You drove up in a snazzy yellow convertible. Who you kidding?"

"Belongs to my boss. He lets me borrow it."

"Where you work?"

"Bureau of Indian Affairs, out at San Xavier."

The used car salesman frowned. "You get that overseas?" He jutted his chin toward Joshua's mechanical arm.

Joshua nodded. "Patton's Third Army, Czechoslovakia."

The man shrugged. "The missus'll kill me. I swear to God. Five hundred. Not a penny less."

Joshua pulled a roll of bills out of his pocket. He laid it on the small table. The man picked it up and counted rapidly like a bank teller. There were dozens of bills, each one fingered and crumpled and a little greasy, looking and feeling like every one had cost a pint of blood and a bucket of sweat.

"Four seventy-five?" the man said, scowling.

Joshua shrugged.

"All right, it's Christmas in June, and I'm Santa Claus." He walked to a metal filing cabinet and took out a manila file. He signed the document inside and handed it to Joshua along with a key that had been taped inside the file. "You robbed me," he grumbled. But then he smiled. "Good luck, pal."

"Thanks," Joshua said. "I really appreciate it."

He limped to Magdalena and the children. They were standing back from the car, admiring it. He handed Magdalena the key. Tears immediately filled her eyes again, and she wiped them away roughly with her hand.

"I don't know what to say," she murmured.

"Can we go with her, Dad?" Adam asked.

"Sure."

Magdalena got in the driver's seat, and Hanna and Adam squeezed in beside her. They pulled slowly out of the lot, and the car disappeared down Stone Avenue.

▲ ✦ ▽ ✦ ▽ ✦ ▲

When Barbara Dubin first walked through the front door of the Rabb house at a little after seven, every one of the high school boys whom Hanna had invited to the party turned his eyes toward her. She was obviously older than they, by five or seven years, and she was stunning. Not exactly pretty, maybe, or even cute like a lot of the girls, but like one of those high-fashion models in the magazines. Wide, high cheekbones, a strong chin, tall and slender. Her light brown hair fell softly around her tanned shoulders. They stared at her low-cut pale yellow sundress held up by a fabulous pair of tits and her nipples pressing through the clingy material of the dress. An older woman like this could mean not just making out in the backseat of the car, but going all the way. None of the high school girls went all the way, at least not until they went steady with you for a year or two, and then only if you promised to marry them when you graduated. But an older woman like Barbara Dubin? The boys had all heard the stories from their big brothers and cousins about older women. Sometimes they went all the way just for the fun of it.

But then they watched her walk up to Mr. Rabb, Hanna's father, and they watched him blush a little and look surprised, and then a big smile grew on his face, and she gave him a quick kiss on the lips, and both of their looks were like Hedy Lamarr and George Sanders in that movie *The Strange Woman* which was playing at the Lyric and everybody had seen at least twice, and the boys all realized that they didn't have a chance. Hanna Rabb's old man had this doll all to himself.

It was kind of odd going to a birthday party for somebody's father, but then, out here, you had to make do with any party that came along. And soon they ignored Mr. Rabb, because they realized that he was far too busy with the doll to do any chaperoning.

Hanna and three of her friends who didn't have telephones were busy calling everyone they knew on the new telephone. They tired of the game after running out of people to call.

Hanna had borrowed records from several of her friends, and they were playing on the Victrola in the top part of the big wooden radio. The Victrola played only one record and the arm just went scratchily around and around when it was finished, so it was Adam's job to sit beside it and change the records. He didn't go in for this stuff anyway, dancing with girls. His pal Chris Landers, who lived a couple of miles away on the other side of Martinez Hill, had ridden over on his horse, Screwy. Adam would have much preferred to get Golden Boy out of the shed and go hunt "buffalo" with Chris on the reservation, but he had promised his father that he wouldn't chase the grazing cattle anymore. And anyway, if he took off from Dad's birthday party, Hanna would get mad at him. So he sat glumly with Chris by the record player and changed records every three or four minutes.

Adam and Hanna both felt a little funny watching their father and Barbara dance. The two didn't look anything like Fred Astaire and Ginger Rogers having an almost impersonal romp on the dance floor. There was obviously nothing impersonal going on between Joshua and Barbara. Adam and Hanna had both gotten over the death of their mother and had come to grips with the fact that their father was thirty-eight, but not so old that he was past being interested in other women. But seeing him dance close with a real sultry beauty like this, seeing him acting like a teenager in the midst of a bunch of teenagers, well, it just made them both feel a little funny.

Magdalena had been having a row with Chuy lately. Apparently he had had a little too much to drink one night and had met an old girlfriend he knew from high school. The rumors that had spread around the reservation like lightning sparks leaping from tumbleweed to tumbleweed had injured Magdalena, humiliated her, and she had told him to get lost. To emphasize her unhappiness with him, she had gone out twice with Juanito Coronado, the son of the biggest American tomato importer from Mexico. Tomatoes were a multimillion-dollar cash crop for the vegetable importers in Nogales, Arizona, and the wealthy Coronado family owned a huge ranch just south of the reservation that stretched for ten miles down the Nogales Highway. They also owned the largest fleet of refrigerated produce trucks and vans in the state. The stories about Magdalena and Juanito buzzed through the reservation rumor mill with the same energy as those about Chuy and Guadalupe.

Magdalena had worked for hours, making batches of chocolate chip cookies and several cakes, and she sat now on the sofa in the living room with Juanito close beside her. He looked mortally bored. A sock hop with a bunch of teenagers to celebrate the thirty-eighth birthday of the father of one of them wasn't his idea of a great night on the town. He'd much rather have been at the Stallion Bar up on Ajo Highway howling with the cowboys and the bar girls or down in Nogales, Mexico, at the Caves, drinking tequila and dancing with the señoritas who all knew who he was and cared. Here among these gringos no one knew who he was. He was just some Mexican guy with an Indian girl. Being nondescript and ignored wasn't Juanito's style. Since Magdalena refused to leave the party, Juanito suffered through an hour of it and then left alone, angry and frustrated.

After a couple of hours, Joshua's aluminum arm got too heavy and his shoulder began to get sore. He went into his bedroom and took it off and changed from his tan linen suit and white shirt and tie into a pair of Levis and a long-sleeve blue chambray cowboy shirt. He left the empty sleeve to dangle so that he didn't look too shocking to the boys and girls. Both he and Barbara were tired of dancing, so they walked out of the house into the gentle warmth of the evening.

"Let's go for a walk," he said. "Over to the mission. It's a beautiful night."

"Don't you think we'll be missed? After all, it's *your* birthday party."

"These kids only have their minds on each other. They won't even know we're gone."

"How do we get across the irrigation ditch?" she asked.

"It's dry," he said. "Has been for weeks."

They walked down into the ditch, across the rutted, dried, and cracked bottom, and up the other side. The sound of the Victrola receded into the distance and became just disconnected sounds carried on occasional wisps of air. It was seventy degrees, and a sliver of moon cast pallid light on the rocky field. Sparse clumps of wildflowers, colorless in the darkness, sprouted next to occasional small cacti and low creosote bushes. They ambled slowly through the field. She held his hand tightly, and a couple of hundred yards into it she stopped by a long, flat rock. They looked at each other.

"It's really nice to see you," he said. "I'm sorry I was kind of rude to you the last time you came over. It was a tough time for me. I acted stupidly."

"What happened to the rich *shikse* you were hanging out with?" Her voice was just a trace catty.

He shrugged. "Turned out real bad."

"Good," she said.

"Yeah."

"Happy birthday," she said, giving him a quick kiss on the lips. Then she stood on tiptoes and kissed him longer.

"You smell terrific," he whispered.

"I don't want you to run away from me again," she said, drawing back and studying him in the moonlight. "I really don't."

He nodded.

She drew her hand away from his and pulled the bow loose on the strings around her neck that held the sundress up. The soft bodice of the dress fell around her waist.

"Jesus, you're beautiful," he whispered.

"What's Jesus have to do with this?" she said. She pulled the dress over her head and had nothing on underneath. She spread it on the rock and turned back to him. He was unsnapping the cowboy shirt and unbuttoning his Levis, urgently. She put her hand on his erection and rubbed him through his underwear.

He struggled out of his shirt, and she kissed his neck and his shoulder and the stump of his arm. She pushed his Levis and underwear down, and he kicked off his shoes and stepped on the bottoms of the Levis to pull his legs out of them.

They looked at each other in the pale glow of moonlight and they touched. She held his erection, and he put his fingers in her curly hair, into the wetness of her. She lay down on the rock and he buried his head between her legs. She rocked on his tongue and said, "God, oh God." And then she hungrily pushed him over on his back, and with her long hair on the strong, taut muscles of his stomach, she took him into her mouth and drank in the feel of him, the taste of him. Just before he came, she crawled on top of his loins and pulled him into her hard, hard, and they groaned together and he jerked into her and then held her tight to his chest in a one-armed hug.

"God," she said.

"What's God have to do with it?" he whispered.

"Everything," she murmured. "This is God."

He did not disagree, and he did not laugh. He rolled her over onto her belly and knelt behind her and lifted her buttocks toward him with his powerful arm, and he entered her again and slapped hard into her, again and again, and exploded, and she arched her back and held his hips tightly against her with both hands.

They sank to the rock and rolled on their backs, sweating, sated, then looked at each other and smiled.

"That's about the best thing that's happened to me in months," he said.

"Yeah."

They watched the moon move across the sky, not talking, just touching. It was almost ten o'clock. They dressed slowly. Barbara's dress was a little bruised from being their bedcover. They walked hand-in hand back to the house.

The music from within was quieter now, several of the cars were gone, and a few of the teenagers were standing in front of the house. Frances and Edgar Hendly were sitting on the porch steps. Edgar's always-scuffed and dusty black wingtips were the same as usual, as was his gray wool suit. Frances was wearing her broghans that looked like Buster Brown Boy Scout shoes. Her brown shirtwaist dress was plain, loose fitting, and long below the knees. Her stomach was just beginning to bulge, and it only was apparent at all because she was so thin. Her dark-brown hair was in a tight bun at the back of her head, and cosmetics, like good looks, were her natural enemy. She smiled her full-toothed smile at Joshua—her coquettish, fetching smile—which bared her big square yellow teeth and made her resemble unfortunately a braying donkey. But Joshua loved her like a sister now; what had happened to Jimmy had brought the Rabbs and the Hendlys close together. They were now one family, and Joshua no longer noticed her plainness.

Joshua and Barbara walked up to the porch steps. "Frances, Edgar, I'd like you to meet my friend Barbara."

Edgar rose up heavily. "Nice meetin' ya, ma'am," he said.

"I've heard so much about you," Barbara said. "And you, Mrs. Hendly. It's so nice to meet you." The women shook hands.

"Well, I've got to be getting back home," she said, turning to Joshua. "Don't forget dinner next Wednesday at six."

"I won't forget."

He opened her car door. She got in and drove off.

"A real beauty," Edgar said.

Joshua nodded.

"Looks like she been rode hard and put away wet," Edgar drawled. He snickered and sat back down on the step.

"Watch that vicious tongue a yourn," Frances scolded. But her lips curled up slightly with a grin.

"I guess you two was out there checkin' the stars, huh?" Edgar said, this time guffawing, his big belly bouncing up and down. "Big Dipper, Little Dipper."

"Yes. She's studying to be an astronomer at the U of A," Joshua said, his voice bland.

"Well, how nice." Frances smiled sweetly at him.

"I'd a took her for a pecker checker ya met over t' the V.A. Hospital," Edgar said.

Frances slapped her husband on the knee. "Stop that, Eddie." Turning to Joshua. "She's a lovely girl, Joshua. I'm happy to see you with someone again. Ain't good for a man to be alone all the time, just you 'n' the kids. A man needs someone for himself."

Joshua nodded. "Party's about over, I see. Hanna inside?"

"No," Frances said. "She went for a ride with that real sweet boy she was dancin' with, Buddy."

Joshua frowned. "Well, I'm going inside, get something to eat."

"Y'aint had enough?" Edgar laughed deep in his throat. Frances slapped him on the leg again, harder than the first time.

"Come on, Edgar," Joshua said. "You look like you need a cookie."

A boy and girl were kissing on the sofa in the dark living room. The adults' entrance stopped them, and they drew apart embarrassedly. They walked outside straightening their clothes. The Victrola arm was turning around and around scratching at music-less grooves. Joshua lifted it to its rest and turned it off. He turned on the radio and tuned it to a swing band playing soft dance music. He switched on the lamp on the sofa table, and Edgar and Frances sat on the sofa. The living room was empty and the kitchen dark. Joshua opened the door to Adam's room, and his son was asleep on his bed, still dressed and wearing his cowboy boots. Adam loved to sleep fully clothed. Joshua closed the door quietly. Hanna's bedroom door was closed. Magdalena must be asleep.

There were a few chocolate chip cookies left on a dish in the kitchen. Joshua took the dish into the living room and set it on the lamp table. He sat on the overstuffed chair and ate a cookie.

"I'm gonna talk to ya like family because we are family now," Frances said, looking solemnly at Joshua.

He nodded.

"I saw that man who came in to see you. I recognized him from his pitcher in *Life* magazine." She pursed her lips.

"Yes, Edgar told me about it. I didn't read the story."

"I don't think you should be representin' him against the gov'ment."

"Why not? Lawyers represent people who pay

them. Especially when the government is after you, you need a lawyer. Lansky needs a lawyer."

"But not you, Joshua. That's what I'm sayin'." She looked at him very apologetically. "Look, we been through a lot together. Edgar and me love ya. I'm gonna talk straight."

"Of course," Joshua said.

"You're the only Jew lawyer in Tucson. Me and Edgar and our kinda folks don't pay no attention, but a lotta folks do. Ya didn't make no friends over that mess with Senator Lukis and Ignacio Antone, and ya stirred up a real hornet's nest gettin' Frank Carillo off. Now Edgar tells me that yer representin' Charlie Isaiah. Well, it can only mean more trouble. But we all come to expect that kind a trouble from you. Ya got yer own code a ethics or morality, I guess, and ya sorta take to *underdogs,* I guess ya'd call em. Well, okay, that's just Joshua Rabb bein' Joshua Rabb. But this Lansky is different. I think ya'll be cuttin' yer own throat in this town representin' the biggest Jew gangster in the United States. I mean, it'd be one thing if you was writin' his will or somethin' like that, but this stuff is just poison."

Joshua knew that Frances earnestly believed what she was telling him. He rubbed his chin hard and frowned.

"I'll go you one better," he said. "That sweet, shy boy Hanna's driving around with tonight is Meyer Lansky's son."

Frances's eyes got wide.

"Yer kiddin'," Edgar said.

Joshua shook his head.

"Ya cain't have that, Joshua," Frances said, sitting forward on the edge of the couch and fixing him with a schoolmarmish scowl. "Can ya imagine what folks'll say if they hear about this?"

Joshua nodded, his face grim. "I know. But what can I do about it? I told her not to go out with that boy Mike Bowers, and look what happened. I don't think I can lock her up or punish her just for having a date with a boy, even if he's Meyer Lansky's son. I really don't know what to do. I've talked to her about it, but she likes the boy and thinks he's very nice. I can't even disagree with her. He seems like a very nice boy. What can I do?"

"Ya can beat the shit outta her and lock her in the bedroom," Edgar said, only half joking.

"I wish it was that easy," Joshua said. "Unfortunately, it isn't. I can't be with her twenty-four hours a day. I can't control who she talks to over at the soda shop. And in a couple of weeks she'll be getting her learner's permit to drive a car. When she turns sixteen in October and gets her license, she'll really be ready to spread her wings." He looked at Frances and Edgar and lifted his hand helplessly and let it drop to his lap. "I guess you raise them and hope that they learn some moral values, and then you pray a little and worry a lot."

Frances sighed deeply and shook her head in frustration.

Edgar nodded. "Well, 'nuff a this talk. Let's talk about the milkers on that cow you was out in the field with."

Joshua burst with laughter. "You got some mouth on you, Edgar."

Frances was far less amused. She fixed her husband with an accusatory stare. "I didn't know you was so interested in other women's anatomy."

"Well, I done took care a your anatomy," he said, patting her belly. "Now I gotta help Joshua."

"He's doing just fine by hisself," she said. "Come on home, mister. I'm gonna wash yer mouth out with naphtha." She stood up and Edgar followed. "It's high time you start goin' with me again to the Pentecostal church on Sundays," she said. "You need some a what that minister preaches."

Edgar looked at Joshua in mock terror. "Yes, ma'am. A little fire 'n' brimstone'll burn out my evil tongue."

"Either it will or I will," Frances said, smirking at her husband.

"See ya Monday," Edgar said.

"Yip," said Joshua, walking them to the door.

He returned to the chair and sat down heavily. He ate the last cookie distractedly. A swing band was playing music from *Carousel:* "If I Loved You," "My Boy Bill," "When You Walk Through a Storm." Is that what this was? A storm? I've been through some real storms, Joshua thought. Hell, this is just a strong wind. I've got a grand in my bedstand drawer that cures a lot of headaches, and I've got two great kids, and if the good folks around here don't like Jew lawyers representing Jew gangsters, to hell with 'em. It's not like I'm his *consigliere,* like Moish Petrovich.

He got up and switched the radio off. The station was going off the air. Suddenly the howl of a coyote shattered the night silence, and it was joined by another, and another, and then dozens more. And then the howling subsided, and there were no more sounds from outside.

Joshua sat in the overstuffed chair again, and his thoughts drifted from the war to his wife to Barbara to Hanna. He wasn't really worried about Hanna. She was fifteen, she knew right from wrong, she was strong-willed and decent. And Meyer Lansky's son wasn't going to shove a heroin-filled syringe into her arm and turn her into a junkie or murder her or make her a shill in a Las Vegas casino. Whoever his father was and whatever he did, Buddy was just a good-looking, shy teenager, doing whatever teenagers do. But there was no getting around the fact that Joe Bonanno was his father's friend, they lived next door to each other, and Joe Bonanno was a genuine Mafia hoodlum from Sicily and the Mafia boss in Brooklyn. But thou shalt not visit the sins of the fathers ... Or is it the opposite? Thou *shalt* visit ... Damn! I'll have to look that up. He got up and walked into his bedroom to get his Bible. He kept it in the bed-stand drawer. He sat on the edge of his bed and began thumbing through it. A car drove up outside. A door closed and the car drove off.

Hanna came into the house and stopped at her father's bedroom door. "Praying for my soul, Daddy?"

"Don't be a smart aleck," he said, smiling. He put the Bible back in the bed-stand. "You have a nice time?"

"Yeah, really nice. Buddy's so sweet."

Joshua studied his daughter's face. She was happy, unworried, unconcealing. He felt better.

"I really loved the party, Hanna. Thanks."

She cocked her head and eyed him amusedly. "Well, you left kind of early. I thought maybe you got bored."

He felt himself blushing. "No, Barbara and I just took a walk."

"She really looked pretty tonight."

"Yes. She's beautiful. I appreciate you inviting her. It was very thoughtful of you."

"I thought maybe you'd like to see her again."

He nodded and smiled. "Okay, honey. Better get to bed. It's almost midnight."

"Night, Daddy." She went into her bedroom and closed the door.

Joshua turned off the radio in the living room and switched off the table lamp. He closed his bedroom door behind him and undressed slowly. Turning off the light, he walked to the window. It was deeply dark outside. The light from the narrow piece of moon was blocked by clouds. The ubiquitous sound of coyotes yelping and howling were the desert's own unique symphony, and it was playing loudly tonight.

CHAPTER SIX

It was Monday morning, and Roy Collins had asked Joshua to question the man in the hospital again. When Joshua had talked to Lou Shiner for the first time, he had heard the probably false story about two sightseeing Chassidim. Last Friday he had talked to him again and heard the same story repeated three times with increasing petulance. This time Joshua waved off the story angrily.

"Herr zich ayn tzu mir. [Listen closely to me]," Joshua said in Yiddish. "I'm tired of hearing this bullshit. Neither of you guys was wearing a *tallis koton,* neither of you had a yarmulke, and none was found in the area. Don't tell me you're Satmar Chassidim. Now, what the hell were you doing on the Papago Reservation a week ago? And what does Joe Bonanno have to do with it?"

Lou Shiner's eyes grew wide. "Who the hell said anything about a guy named Bonanno?"

"Come on, *boychik,* mumbling 'bananas' has nothing to do with you wanting something to eat. You know it, the FBI knows it, and I know it. Now tell me why you were on the reservation."

Shiner stiffened and stared at the ceiling.

"Listen, don't be stupid," Joshua said in a subdued, confidential tone. "Right now you're carrying this rap all by yourself. The FBI isn't about to let you go anywhere until they figure out what you were doing and what your part was in the murder of Solomon Grushin. They're holding you on a material-witness complaint, and when you get out of here, they'll hold you indefinitely up at the federal detention center on Mount Lemmon, about forty miles from here up in the mountains in the middle of nowhere."

It wasn't true, since the FBI had absolutely no evidence of Shiner's complicity in any crime, but Joshua figured that it was worth a try.

"*Nu,* so I'll have a nice rest in the country. Like the Catskills, huh? Comedians and singers come around, give stage performances in the evening. Swing bands, dancing. Pick blueberries in the woods with some cute broad, smells like jasmine flowers."

"More like a couple of dozen Mexican wetbacks who never had a bath waiting trial for murder and robbery and rape."

"Whattaya, trying to scare me with crap like that?" Shiner's face turned sullen, his eyes flat and opaque. "I grew up with guineas and *shvartzes* trying to beat the shit outta me every day for a dime, for a fucking penny. You gonna scare me with some wetbacks?"

Joshua stared hard into the man's eyes. "What's Meyer Lansky have to do with this?"

This time Shiner's eyes betrayed obvious fear. He looked at Joshua, studied his face for a moment, then turned his eyes to the ceiling. "Fuck off," he muttered, the first words he had spoken in English.

"I thought you only spoke Yiddish," Joshua said.

Lou Shiner stared rigidly at the ceiling. Joshua left the hospital and drove back to the BIA. He called the FBI office, but Collins wasn't in. His secretary said that he was on the Big Reservation. He would probably be back later in the afternoon.

▲♦♥♦♥♦▲

The gray Plymouth was parked on a rough dirt trail exactly one mile north of the Mexican border, which was marked only by a three-strand barbed-wire fence. The trail crossed the border where the fence had been cut and parted, leaving a twenty-foot opening. There was no official port of entry down here on the Big Reservation, just an unguarded path across the border. That's why Frank Costello and Lucky Luciano had liked the setup: no border patrol, no customs officers, no cops.

"What the hell is that?" the driver of the Plymouth said, pointing with his thumb over his shoulder at the Ford stake truck coming up the road behind their car. He followed it in the rearview mirror. It stopped about thirty feet behind them.

The passenger turned around and looked. "I don't know." He reached under his Acapulco shirt and pulled a snub-nosed .38 revolver out of his shoulder holster. The driver reached under his seat and pulled out a sawed-off shotgun.

"It's supposed to be two more of the Yids in a brown Chevy," the passenger said. "This looks like a couple *melanzan'* [niggers] in a lettuce truck."

"Watch out, Tommy!" were the last words that the passenger ever spoke.

Through the rear window and the seat backs of the car came a spray of .45-caliber slugs from a Thompson submachine gun. The chests of Vincenzo Lubrazzi and Tomasso Constanzo flew into the shattered windshield of the car, followed by bits of their decimated lungs.

Jimmy Arguello lowered the submachine gun. "Let's get the bodies out of there," he said in Papago to the other Indian.

"I don't want to touch that shit," the man said.

"We have to. We got to be in the car when the guys come," Jimmy said.

"You didn't tell me you'd kill nobody." His voice was whiny.

"Come on, Joe. You think they was just going to leave if we asked them?"

"Well, you didn't tell me you was going to kill nobody. I don't want to touch those bodies."

"Come on, macho," Jimmy cajoled. "We got to get rid of these bodies and put the truck behind that hill." He pointed across the road.

"You think the other guys ain't going to notice the windows been shot out?"

"In the dark? They won't notice nothing."

Joe shrugged and breathed deeply. He walked up to the passenger door. He opened it and pulled the body out gingerly. It was covered with blood. He dragged it by the feet a hundred yards across the road behind a huge boulder. Jimmy did the same with the driver. The two Indians cleaned their hands in the sand, breathing heavily and sweating through their shirts in the late afternoon sun.

"When they coming?" Joe asked.

"Who knows?"

"You sure they're coming?"

Jimmy shrugged. "That's what happened last week. Jeep crossed over from Mexico, and a couple guys were waiting for it in the same spot. They got some packages from the Jeep, then five minutes later they got shot two, three miles from here. Jaime saw the whole thing. The guys we just killed in the gray Plymouth was waiting on the road and pulled the other car over and shot them."

"What the hell for?"

Jimmy shook his head. "For the car and the dope, man. But what the hell's going on, I don't know. One of the guys these two was trying to kill got away, crawled away in the dark. That's the one my old man found up by the canyon. Guy must've crawled till he collapsed."

"How come Jaime saw it happen?"

"That's his job," Jimmy answered. "Him and Harry Long Ears sit down by the border on their asses making sure everything's right. Every couple hours they scout the hills on horseback. That's what the boss pays them for."

"Who? I thought this was your deal."

"You got too many thoughts, Joey. I told you yesterday, you stick with me, you make more dough in an hour than you seen all year. How do you think you was going to do that, by sitting in the mission all day long and praying?" He looked menacingly at Joe Valenzuela. "You chickening out on me?"

Joe backed up just a step. "No, no, Jimmy. I'm okay. You know me twenty years. I was just wondering is all."

"Stop wondering." Jimmy turned around to walk back to the truck. The first bullet caught him just below the left eye and knocked him on his back. The second went into his stomach and ricocheted off his spine into his heart. Joe Valenzuela also lay on the ground, supine, his arms splayed to his side, with two bullet holes in his chest.

The two men in black suits walked quickly back to their brown Chevrolet sedan and got into the front seat. They sat tensely, staring out the windshield.

"What the hell's going on?" Jake Haberman asked, looking at the driver.

Saul Blaustein shook his head and shrugged, gripping the steering wheel tightly. His face was grim. "Let's go back to Tucson and call Meyer."

Jake studied Saul's face. "You don't think we should wait and pick up the H like we're supposed to?"

"I don't think we should do shit around here. This place is crazy. That's two of the Commission *shtarkes* back there. I recognized them. Tommy somebody and the other guy I seen around the neighborhood a lot, Vinnie Lubrazzi. I'm telling you, they're muscle for one of the fathers, And Solly and Lou got hit last week. Something crazy is going on."

Jake nodded. "Yeah, all right. Let's get the fuck out of here."

"We get the plates off the car and truck first, find the registrations," Saul said.

He took a screwdriver out of the glove compartment. He removed the license plates from the truck. Jake got the registration from the leather pouch taped to the steering column. They did the same to the gray Plymouth. It was just getting dark as they began the drive to Tucson.

▲✣▼✣▼✣▲

"Meyer?" Saul said into the receiver of the pay telephone.

"Saul?"

"Yeah."

"What number?"

"Seven-nine-five-four-eight."

"Wait, I'll call in five minutes," Lansky said. He put on his gray suit jacket and a panama hat and left his house. He walked to the filling station at the corner of Grant and Campbell and dialed the number.

"Crazy shit going on, Meyer."

"Tell me."

"We get down there, we head for the place. We get there, there's an empty stake truck and a car all shot up, blood all over the place. We follow the drag marks, there's two Papago Indians or Mexicans—who the hell can tell the difference?—and they just killed two guys, Vinnie Lubrazzi and another guy, Tommy something. I seen him around plenty with Vinnie."

"Tommy Constanzo? Jesus Christ, what is this shit? They're a couple of wop soldiers, belong to the Commission."

"I know."

Silence. Meyer couldn't think, his mind a jumble of conflicting thoughts. "You know who they worked for specifically?"

"No," Saul answered.

"Bonanno? You think Bonanno?"

"I don't know, Meyer."

"What about the greasers? What were they doing?"

"Beats the hell outta me."

Silence again. "All right," Meyer said. "We got to blow this off for a while till we straighten it out. You stay put at the motel. I'll call Vegas, tell Benny he's

going to have to raise money someway else till we find
out what's going on and settle it."

"Frank Costello don't get his dough, he's gonna be
ready to kill."

"Can't be helped. Got to hold off for a while." Lansky hung up and walked back to his house.

▲ ✛ ▽ ✛ ▽ ✛ ▲

The bodies of the four dead men weren't discovered
on the Big Reservation until Tuesday morning, so by
the time Roy Collins and Chuy Leyva arrived at noon,
they were swollen, putrid balloons inflating in the
hundred-five-degree heat. The stake truck still had the
keys in the ignition, so they loaded the bodies in the
back, and Roy Collins drove to the coroner's office in
downtown Tucson. Chuy drove the BIA pickup over
the choppy dirt road to Pablo Arguello's ranch. He
parked in front of the goat pen until the old man came
down the mountain and had penned his flock. It was
almost five o'clock.

They sat at the kitchen table, drinking Angelica Arguello's homemade saguaro wine. After the first para-
lyzing shock of hearing what had happened, the old
woman stood up shakily from the table gasping with
tears and left the kitchen. Pablo sat silently, stunned,
not able fully to focus on the death of his only son.
He had four daughters, all married and settled in their
own homes, three in Ajo and one in Sells, but his only
son had just been murdered. It was almost more than
he could bear. How much must one endure in this
life? he thought through a cloud of turgid memories:
the killing in the war, the loss of his hand, the twelve-
hour days, seven days a week, three hundred sixty-
three days a year herding goats—every day except
Christmas and Easter, which he spent at Mission San
Xavier del Bac in Tucson—all to have his only son
murdered and left like garbage for the vultures. And
now cut up like dog food on some white doctor's table.

"Pablo. Pablo," Chuy said repeatedly, staring into

the old man's eyes, trying to bring him out of his shock.

Finally Pablo heard. He looked vacantly at Chuy, then blinked hard and focused on him as though he realized for the first time that Chuy was sitting across his kitchen table.

"I've got to know why he was there," Chuy said in Papago. "And do you know who he was with?"

Pablo slowly shook his head. "Yesterday he left early from the summer grazing. He said he had to go to Three Points. I told him all the time, stay away from that slut. But he couldn't."

"Who?"

"Maranda. Jimmy's wife. She walked out on him two months ago."

"I didn't know he was married."

"Yeah, just three months ago. She's a beauty, but she's a fucking whore. Long as he gave her money for whiskey all the time, she was okay. Angelica couldn't get her to help with nothing around here. Always drunk. Then suddenly she up'n left. Just like that." He snapped his fingers.

"Where'd Jimmy get all the money?"

Pablo wrinkled his brow and shrugged. "Before he came back here with Maranda three months ago, he was working in Nogales at the vegetable distributors'. Drove a truck."

"Working for who?"

Pablo shook his head. "One of them. Don't know."

"Did he ever have a stake truck around here?"

"Yeah. Lots of times. I ask him. He says he borrows it from a white guy in Sells."

"Where is Maranda from?"

Pablo shook his head. "I don't know. She's a Papago from Sonora, Imuris or Magdalena, I think."

"Do you know where she is now?"

Again the old man shrugged. "Maybe at that bar in Three Points, at the junction of Highway Two Eighty-Six. That's where Jimmy went looking for her."

As Pablo mentioned his son's name, tears began streaming down his cheeks.

"Okay, my friend," Chuy said, rising. "You can get Jimmy tomorrow.

Pablo put his head on his folded arms and wept.

By the time Chuy reached the bar in Three Points, over an hour and a half later, it was dark. The bar was in an old, small Quonset hut. The dozen men inside and the several women and the bartender were all Papagos, but Three Points was off the reservation on state land, and Chuy's BIA badge didn't mean anything here. His questions were met with baleful stares and resentful silence. He left after a few frustrating minutes and drove back to Tucson.

CHAPTER SEVEN

Judge Buchanan walked into the courtroom and took his seat in the high-back leather chair behind the elevated bench. He put on his eyeglasses and opened the file in front of him.

"This is the time set for the hearing of pretrial motions in the matter of *United States versus Charlie Isaiah.* Announce your appearances."

Tim Essert stood up at the long table next to the jury box. "Tim Essert, assistant U.S. attorney, for the government, Your Honor."

Joshua stood at the other table. "Joshua Rabb for the defendant, Charlie Isaiah, who is present with me at the defense table, Your Honor." He sat down next to the Indian. Isaiah was dressed in federal detention center garb, a faded air force jumpsuit and unlaced combat boots. His ankles were chained eight inches apart.

"Mr. Rabb," the judge said, "you have moved this court to compel the United States attorney to provide you with a bill of particulars, setting forth the precise facts upon which it bases the indictment against your client. Since this is a capital case, it is essential to afford the defendant every opportunity properly and fully to defend himself. For that reason I have scheduled this hearing, which I intend to be utilized by you as a means of acquiring the particulars of this matter." The judge settled back in his chair. "Let's go, Mr. Essert."

"The government calls Edward Carter," Tim Essert said. Essert was of medium height, thin, brown hair slicked back and pomaded, wearing an expensive beige linen suit, a crisply starched white shirt, and a chic royal blue silk tie. He smiled toothily around the room at the numerous spectators and nodded to J. T. Sellner, a middle-aged reporter for Tucson's morning newspaper.

The bailiff left the courtroom and returned a moment later with Edward Carter behind him. Carter held up his right hand at the clerk's desk, placed his left hand on a Bible, and swore to tell the truth. He was over six feet tall, paunchy, with well-tended waves of thick gray hair. His nose was a little veiny and bumpy, and his eyes were quite bloodshot. He looked to Joshua like the quintessential barroom buddy, a garrulous, back-slapping fellow who could down a few straight shots, tell some off-color stories, and charm you into buying a rusted old hulk with no hubcaps, thinking you were getting a collector's bonanza.

"State your name and address, please," Tim Essert said.

"Edward Carter, 327 West Hampton." He nodded toward the judge.

Buchanan nodded back. "Sorry to see you under these circumstances, Eddie," he said.

Carter sniffed.

"Your occupation?"

"I own Carter Ford, down on Stone Avenue."

"It was your daughter who Charlie Isaiah murdered, is that correct, sir?"

Joshua shot up out of his chair. "Objection, Your Honor. Assuming facts not in evidence."

"Yes," Judge Buchanan said, leaning forward over the bench and looking at Essert. "Let's not put the cart before the horse, Timmy. The jury is the one who decides whether she was murdered by the defendant."

"Was Jennifer Carter your daughter?" Essert asked.

Carter gulped and swallowed. "Yes."

"When did you last see her alive?"

"The day she was murdered." He gulped and swallowed. "She came by the dealership to say hello. It was four o'clock, maybe five."

"Did you see anything unusual happen?"

Joshua shot up again, "Objection, Your Honor."

Buchanan leaned forward again, looking quizzically at Joshua. "What's the objection, Mr. Rabb?"

"Calls for speculation and a narrative answer."

The judge frowned and pursed his lips. "Well, this isn't a course in Wittgenstein's logical positivism, Mr. Rabb. I can understand the question. Did you understand the question, Eddie?" he asked, swiveling in his chair toward the witness.

"Yes," Carter answered. "I saw Charlie Isaiah push her into his car and drive away fast."

"Do you see this man in the courtroom?" Essert asked.

"Yes." Carter pointed at the defense table.

"May the record reflect that the witness has identified the defendant, Your Honor?" Essert said.

"So noted," Buchanan said.

"Did you know Charlie Isaiah at the time?"

"Yes. He worked for me, had been for a year. Sold used cars. He's good-looking, speaks Papago, Spanish. Did real well with those people."

"Was he dating your daughter?"

Carter's face blanched, and he sucked in his cheeks. "No, of course not," he said harshly. "She was a nice girl." Tears came to his eyes, and he sniffed.

Joshua stood up. "Move to strike as nonresponsive, Your Honor."

Buchanan grimaced at him. He lifted his arm and waved his wrist down several times. Joshua sat down.

"Go on," the judge said to Essert.

"Did you ever hear from anyone that your daughter was dating the defendant?"

Joshua shot up again. "Your Honor, I—"

"Hold it, Mr. Rabb." Judge Buchanan shut him off abruptly. He uncoiled from deep in his large leather chair and fixed Joshua with a stare. "I know that the U.S. attorney is eliciting hearsay, and I know how displeased the lawbook writers get when they use that term. But I am a grown man, Mr. Rabb, and I can hear such things without having my thoughts twisted or my soul perverted. Now, this is a hearing to provide you your bill of particulars, Mr. Rabb, not a trial. There's no jury, there's no danger that Mr. Isaiah is going to be found guilty of anything, and I think we'll move this thing along a whole lot smoother if you quit wearing the finish off that old oak chair and just let Timmy ask his questions." He stared at Joshua and Joshua sat down slowly. Several of the forty or fifty spectators snickered and guffawed. J. T. Sellner scratched rapidly with her pen on a steno pad.

"On the other hand, Mr. Essert," Judge Buchanan continued, turning to the United States attorney, "there's no reason in the world for you to be asking very seriously objectionable questions one after the other like a poorly aimed machine gun. Let's get on with it."

"Yes, sir," Essert said. He turned to Carter. "What did you do after you saw your daughter kidnapped?"

Joshua gripped the arm of his chair and gritted his teeth, but he stayed seated. Judge Buchanan held up his hand toward Essert in a halt gesture. Then he looked at Joshua.

"Very commendable, Mr. Rabb. Laudable restraint." He turned to Essert. "You can either ask a straight question, Mr. Essert, or I'll let Mr. Rabb have a go at him."

Essert swallowed and nodded. "My apologies to the court."

"I don't want your apologies. I just want you to ask permissible questions to elicit admissible evidence concerning the particulars of this crime. Try it one more time, Mr. Essert."

"Did you observe your daughter being kidnapped, Mr. Carter?" Essert asked.

Joshua stood up at the defense table. "How can the court continue to indulge this prosecutorial misconduct, Your Honor?"

Buchanan speared him with a disgusted glare. He banged his gavel on the bench. "Okay, let's take a five-minute recess. I'll see you two gentlemen in chambers." He stalked off the bench through the doorway to his office. Essert followed him closely. Joshua waited ten seconds and then joined the procession.

"I guess you two boys don't like each other so much, huh?" the judge said, standing behind his desk and glowering at the two lawyers. Neither of them responded.

"You keep this up, I'm going to hold both of you in contempt and throw you into Ollie Friedkind's holding cell for an hour or two. Whichever one comes out alive wins the case." He looked harshly from Rabb to Essert.

"Let me hear you say something, boys."

Joshua grimaced. "I apologize, Your Honor. I'll just sit with my mouth shut."

"Sorry, Your Honor," Essert said. "I've known Eddie Carter for almost ten years, since I bought my first car from him. This case really got to me."

"I've known him for fifteen years," the judge spat back. "But out in that courtroom I'm a judge, not an old drinking buddy. And out there you better start acting like a lawyer."

"Yes, sir," Essert mumbled.

"Are we ready?" Buchanan asked.

Both men nodded.

They walked back into the courtroom. Judge Buchanan settled into his chair. "Let's go," he said, glancing at Essert.

"What did you do after you saw your daughter driving away in Charlie Isaiah's car, Mr. Carter?" Essert asked.

"I telephoned the sheriff's department, told them that my daughter'd been kidnapped."

"No further questions." Essert sat down.

"You have a son, Philip, is that correct?" Joshua asked, remaining seated.

Edward Carter flinched. "Yes."

"How old is he?"

"He's twenty-one."

"He's a big fellow, plays guard for the University of Arizona football team, I understand."

"Yes."

"Was he with you when this happened?"

Carter shook his head slowly.

"Where is Jennifer's mother, Mr. Carter?" Joshua asked.

Judge Buchanan fixed Joshua with a warning frown. "This better be relevant, Mr. Rabb."

Joshua nodded.

Carter shrugged. "She left five years ago. I don't know."

"Just up and left one day?"

Carter swallowed. "Yeah."

"Jennifer would have been, let's see, twelve years old at the time?"

Carter nodded.

"You have to answer audibly, Eddie," Judge Buchanan said.

"Yes. She was twelve."

"Had your wife ever seen you engaging in incest with your daughter?"

Tim Essert leaped out of his chair roaring, "Objection! Objection!"

Buchanan held up his hand and silenced Essert with a stare. He looked soberly at Joshua and studied him. "You better be going somewhere that is relevant to this case," he said quietly. "If that question is only to get my heart beating faster, you succeeded admirably. But you're the one going to need artificial respiration when I get through with you."

"Your Honor, I will make a personal avowal to the court that this is not only relevant evidence, but it is absolutely critical to this case."

The judge stared hard at Joshua and gritted his

teeth. He turned to Carter and said gently, "Go ahead and answer the question, Eddie."

Carter's face was flushed, and tears rolled down his cheeks. "You son of a bitch," he gasped, looking at Joshua. "Nothing dirty like that ever happened."

"No further questions," Joshua said.

The judge looked at the United States attorney.

Essert said, "No redirect."

"You're excused," the judge said. Carter walked off the witness stand, staring viciously at Joshua.

"Special Agent Roy Collins of the Federal Bureau of Investigation," Essert announced.

The bailiff brought Collins forward to be sworn. He took the stand and testified that he had been with the FBI for eleven years and investigated over fifty deaths by stabbing. He had discovered Jennifer lying in bed, dead, next to Charlie Isaiah, who was dead drunk.

Joshua had just three questions on cross-examination. "How many times had Jennifer been stabbed?"

"Five times."

"How much blood was in the bed?"

"Very little. Just a few spots."

"Did you, in your experience investigating stabbing deaths, find this unusual?"

"Yes, very. She had been stabbed in the heart and in the artery under the collarbone. There should have been a huge amount of blood."

"Thank you, Agent Collins," Joshua said, sitting down.

"We call Dr. Stanley Wolfe, Pima County coroner," Essert announced.

The pathologist was sworn and took the stand.

"Dr. Wolfe," Essert said, "did you perform an autopsy on the body of Jennifer Carter?"

"Yes, sir, I did."

"And what was the cause of death?"

"She bled to death from five stab wounds. In my judgment any one of the wounds would have been fatal."

"Did you determine how much blood she had in her body at the time of the autopsy?"

He opened the manila file he had brought to the stand, flipped a couple of pages, and read for a moment. "That's extremely difficult to do," he responded, "since blood does not flow freely in the body after the heart ceases to function. But I can say with clinical certainty that she had lost at least half of her blood, some six pints, given her body weight."

"No further questions," Essert announced.

"Mr. Rabb?" Judge Buchanan said.

"No questions, Your Honor."

The coroner left the stand.

"Anything more?" Judge Buchanan said.

"May I be heard on a motion, Your Honor?" Joshua said, rising at the defense table.

"Very well," Buchanan said, settling back in his chair.

"I would ask this court to order that a search warrant be issued for the automobiles belonging to Edward Carter and his son, Philip, and that a warrant be issued for the Carter home. I believe that justice requires that this court determine whether the murder of Jennifer Carter took place at the Carter home and the body was transported to the reservation in one of the Carter vehicles."

Tim Essert stood up and looked disgustedly at Joshua. "There is no credible evidence to suggest any such scenario, Your Honor. The government strongly objects." He sat down.

Buchanan took out his pocket watch and wound it for a moment. He snapped open the hunting case and examined the face, then closed it, snapped it open, and closed it again and put it back in his vest pocket. He leaned forward over the desk.

"Mr. Rabb, I'm sure that you are aware that I do not have the power to issue a search warrant. The only authority I have by law is to approve or deny an application for a search warrant submitted to me by a law enforcement officer. In other words, Mr. Rabb, only the U.S. attorney or Agent Collins can make application." He turned toward Essert. "Well, Timmy, what do you think? Do you think that the interests of justice would be served by acceding to Mr. Rabb's request?"

Essert stood up. "I do not, Your Honor. The evidence against the defendant is overwhelming. Maybe he didn't kill her in his house, just brought her there afterward. But him lying next to her in his own bed is pretty good evidence of murder." He sat down.

Buchanan pursed his lips and shrugged. "Well, I can't argue too much with that analysis, although I have to say that in a capital case it behooves the government to look under every rock they can find to guarantee that justice is done." He stared at Essert. Essert simply sat, looking straight ahead, unmoving.

Buchanan shook his head slowly and frowned. He wrote something in the file on his desk, then looked at Joshua and said, "I do not have the power to grant your request, Mr. Rabb. This case will be set for a trial to a jury three weeks from this day." He banged his gavel and left the bench.

Tim Essert walked quickly out of the courtroom. Charlie Isaiah sat glumly at Joshua's side. "What now?" he asked.

Joshua shook his head. "Well, I'll try Roy Collins. But if Essert orders him not to do it, he won't, and we're screwed."

"You mean I'm screwed," Isaiah muttered.

Joshua nodded and looked away. Ollie Friedkind led the Indian from the defense table.

CHAPTER EIGHT

"Mr. Bonanno, I'd like you to come downtown to my office," Roy Collins said, standing at Joe Bonanno's front door. "I have a few questions to ask you about some bodies that we've found on the Papago Reservation."

Bonanno's face was bland, innocent. "Bodies? Why you want to talk to me?"

"Routine investigation, Mr. Bonanno."

Chuy Leyva stood beside Collins. It was Wednesday morning. Chuy had no authority off the reservation, but Roy had asked him to come along and look mean. Just that. Chuy was over six feet, athletic and muscular, very dark, black eyes, uniformed in Levis and a khaki short-sleeve shirt with a fancy polished brass badge, and a Single-Action Army .45 Colt strapped to a low-slung "gunslinger" holster on his hip. Bonanno was used to dealing with cops, but not like Chuy. Roy Collins was decidedly more nondescript than the Indian and could hardly be perceived as threatening: much shorter than Chuy, a baggy seersucker suit, a blond butch haircut, soft brown eyes in a round, boyish face. He figured that bringing Chuy along might provide a nice touch of intimidation.

"You got a warrant to arrest?"

"No, sir, I have no warrant. I just want to ask you some questions."

"When you have a warrant, you come back," Bonanno said. "But you better have big evidence I did something. Otherwise my lawyer is going to rip your dick off, feed it to his parrot." He closed the front door.

Collins lingered just a moment, angry, then walked back to his car with Chuy. "We scared the shit out of him," Chuy said, looking wryly at the FBI agent.

Collins nodded, then laughed. "Yeah, had him pissing in his pants."

Both men laughed. They drove away from Bonanno's house.

"What now?" Chuy asked.

"He's going to leave his house and make a call from one of the pay phones at the Standard Oil gas station on Grant and Campbell, or in front of the Texas Company station on Speedway."

"How do you know?"

"We know a lot about Padre Giuseppi." Roy pulled the car to the curb at the corner of Elm and Campbell, switched off the engine, and adjusted the rearview mirror so that he could watch the front of Bonanno's house.

"The special agent here before me put a tap in on ol' Joey's phone, but the bastard never makes business calls from his house, only from pay phones. But it's too dangerous for us to tap all five of them between the two filling stations. Wouldn't help anyway. We brought in a lip-reader with a telescope one time. He couldn't make out a word. Said it was either Italian or Sicilian—"

Collins stopped abruptly and fixed his eyes hard on the rearview mirror. "There he is. He's crossing the lawn, going to the next house. Knocking on the door. He's inside."

"Who's the neighbor?"

Collins shook his head and shrugged. "Haven't got a clue. But we better find out."

They remained parked, waiting. Ten minutes later,

Bonanno came out and began walking down Elm Street toward the corner of Campbell. He was eighty yards away.

"Let's go," Collins said. He started the car and pulled around the corner. He parked facing Campbell in the parking lot next to Saints Peter and Paul Catholic Church. It gave them a view of Campbell from the Standard Oil station at Grant Road to the north, to Speedway Boulevard and the Texas Company gas station to the south. There were several other cars in the church lot. Roy and Chuy slid down in the seats almost below window level.

Bonanno rounded the corner and walked into the church rectory. Chuy looked at Roy. "Something new?"

Roy nodded. "I heard that Father Greene is his buddy. Maybe it's true."

They waited fifteen minutes, and Bonanno did not come out.

"We're just wasting our time," Roy said. He started his car and drove Chuy back to the BIA. Neither of them had noticed a short, slightly built man in a gray suit turn the same corner and walk north on Campbell to the Standard Oil station.

Lansky stood at one of the three black telephone boxes. "Joe wants to meet," he said into the receiver.

"Where?" Frank Costello asked.

"The Park Avenue Sheraton, same as last time. The small dining room at lunch. He wants to fly in tomorrow morning, leave by evening."

"Shit," Frank Costello murmured. "I can't get them all together in that short time. Gagliano is in the Virgin Islands. Profaci is sick, flu. He was in the hospital for a while. I don't know."

"Joe's mad as hell, Frank. Says it's got to stop. Says he wants the whole Commission or he goes to the mattresses. We're shitting where he eats."

"What the fuck is going on there, Meyer? Two of your boys, and now Vinnie and Tommy."

"I don't know, Frank. I can't figure it. But it's got to be Joe. None of the other fathers would interfere.

Now we got Mexicans or Papagos in on the deal. Maybe Joe's got a connect. I don't know. But he's the only one it could be. The FBI just paid him a visit. I tell you, Frankie, Joe's ready to kill, he's gone nuts."

"Okay, okay. Tell him I'll do my best. We'll at least have four of the fathers."

▲ + ▼ + ▼ + ▲

Collins had driven Chuy Leyva back to the BIA and stopped into Joshua Rabb's office to ask him to have one more go at Lou Shiner. Roy told him what had just happened with Bonanno and mentioned him going into the house just to the west of Bonanno's. Joshua told him that the house belonged to Meyer Lansky.

"You know the guy?" Collins was surprised.

"He's my client. He's been subpoenaed to appear in front of a federal grand jury in Phoenix tomorrow. They're investigating the construction of the Flamingo Hotel in Las Vegas, whether the contractor used restricted building materials."

"He's involved with the Flamingo?"

"He's my client, Roy. I can't talk about it."

Collins pursed his lips. "Well, I guess you must know what his connect is with Bonanno?"

Joshua shrugged. "Just what I read in the papers. They say he's involved with the Mafia, supposed to be their banker."

Roy nodded. "I'll have to talk to our office in New York, find out what the hell they think is going on out here."

Chuy walked into Joshua's office and sat down next to Collins.

"You have any luck tracing the truck and the Plymouth?" Joshua asked, looking from Chuy to Roy.

"No," Collins said. "The serial number was filed off the engine block of the car, so it's a dead end. We traced the truck to a leasing company that leased it from the—wait a second." Collins reached in his coat pocket and pulled out a small spiral notebook. He leafed through the pages. "The Cooperativa Agricultura Mexicana in Nogales, Mexico. Chuy's going to go down there Friday and check on it."

Chuy nodded. "I hope it's one of Juanito Coronado's companies."

"You want me to try one more time with Lou Shiner?" Joshua asked.

"Right," said Collins. "I got a material-witness warrant on him from Judge Buchanan. I can hold him for ten days, then I have to show cause whether I've come up with additional evidence sufficient to keep the hold on him. I went out to the hospital earlier this afternoon and ankle-chained him to the bed. I got his attention this time."

Joshua laughed. "Yeah, I imagine that would do it."

"I didn't tell him there's a ten-day limit on the warrant. I told him we'd hold him up at the federal detention center on Mount Lemmon till his pecker dried up and fell off if he didn't open up. He asked for a lawyer. I told him to get fucked and instructed the nursing staff to keep him away from phones."

Joshua glanced at his wristwatch. "Well, I've got a date tonight." He grinned a bit sheepishly at Leyva and Collins. "Going over to a young lady's house for dinner. Six o'clock. Doesn't give me much time."

"Well, just give it a shot. We got five bodies and one wounded man on the Big Res in one week, four dead white men. That story about being tourists is bullshit. Shiner's got to know by now that nobody's going to believe him. If he thinks he's going to be indicted all by himself, maybe he'll say something."

"Why hasn't it hit the papers?" Joshua asked.

"I'm keeping a lid on it," Collins answered. "Don't want any reporters fishing around. They'll find out that the warrant expires in ten days, and Shiner'll clam up."

"Why don't we sweat him?" Chuy asked.

"The bastard still has tubes sticking out of every hole. A kidney infection or some damn thing. If he dies, Judge Buchanan might be offended."

"Can't imagine why," Joshua said.

Collins snickered.

"Speaking of Judge Buchanan," Joshua said, looking at Collins, "I had a little problem in court yesterday."

"Little problem?" Roy said, rolling his eyes. "For you it may be little. For Isaiah it's big, real big."

"He didn't kill her."

"Yeah, Tim Essert called me this morning and told me what you did in court yesterday." He shrugged. "I been at a lot of murder scenes. This sure looked like one to me."

"Her father murdered her."

Collins laughed. "You haven't one piece of evidence to prove it."

"No blood was found at the scene."

"That just means it happened somewhere else. How the hell do you leap from that fact to Eddie Carter murdering his own daughter?"

"Because that's what Charlie Isaiah told me and I believe him."

Collins snorted. "If you'd have seen him when Chuy and I arrested him, you'd be talking differently. He was drunk, and he was mean. Didn't show any emotion over the body next to him."

Chuy nodded in agreement.

"Well, all I want to do is prove it one way or the other. I need to have warrants for the Carter home and automobiles."

Collins shook his head. "Tim said no. Period. I don't have the authority to apply for a warrant without his permission, even if I believed this bullshit about Eddie Carter. Which I don't."

Joshua swallowed down his frustration. He shook his head slowly. "Shit. This is a mean world for an Indian," he muttered.

Collins said nothing. Chuy sat stolidly.

"All right, I better go," Joshua said. "Can't be late for dinner at Barbara's."

▲✦▼✦▼✦▲

Lou Shiner's attitude hadn't softened. "You think it'll be better for me if I spill my guts?" he said to

Joshua. "I'll end up with my asshole in my mouth lying in a ditch under a thousand pounds of horseshit."

"The feds are going to keep you locked up till you're an old man," Joshua said.

"Doss iz narishkeit, boychik [That's ridiculous, pal]," Shiner said. "Soon as I get to a phone and call Moish Petrovich, I'm outta here. You guys ain't got nothing to hold me on."

"You know Moish?"

"Everybody where I'm from knows Moish."

"He's Meyer Lansky's attorney."

"And a hundred other guys. He's from the neighborhood, that's all. He knows us, we know him. We go to shul together, eat bialys and whitefish at Minsky's Deli, swim at Brighton Beach. That makes us all criminals? You been out in the sticks so long you're beginning to think like a fucking goy."

"I swam at Brighton Beach too. But I didn't have Moish Petrovich for my lawyer."

Shiner looked earnestly at Joshua and nodded. He spoke in English. "All right, *boychik,* you want the truth?"

"That would be nice."

"The truth is, by you guys I get slapped around a little, and then you gotta toin me loose." He mimicked a Yiddish accent. "By anybody else I get dead. That's the truth. So get ya goyishe ass outta heah and tell the noice I need a nice cup borsht *oon a shtickel pumpernickel.* Dat vould be nice." He turned his face to the ceiling and shut his eyes.

Joshua drove quickly up Campbell Avenue to the foothills and Barbara Dubin's sprawling redbrick ranch-style home overlooking Tucson. It was almost six-thirty when he parked the car in the driveway and knocked on the front door.

"I thought you forgot," Barbara said to him as she opened the door.

"Never," he said. He was wearing his gray sharkskin double-breasted suit, just like all the movie stars were wearing in the movies lately, and he had on the new tie from Goldberg's Department Store that Hanna and

Adam and Magdalena had bought him for his birthday. It was royal blue silk with a bunch of teardrop-shaped bright red splotches on it.

"Lovely," she said, admiring his tie.

"You look beautiful," he said. She was wearing a hot pink jersey halter top tied in front and a pair of raw silk harem pants.

She closed the front door, and they walked down the hallway to the living room. Joshua had met Barbara's mother months ago, also here at dinner, and she greeted him warmly, with slightly slurred speech. She stood up and shook his hand, holding an old fashioned glass in her left hand. She was tall and shapely and had carefully permed bleached blond hair in a Mae West style that was long out of fashion. Her face was thin and drawn and heavily made up. She wore tight-fitting sparkly silver pedal pushers, gold lamé spike heels, and a fitted white satin sleeveless top.

She sat on the sofa and patted the cushion next to her. "Sit down, Joshua. Hal isn't home yet, had to work late again. We have a little time to get acquainted before dinner. We didn't have that opportunity when you were here last, did we, dear?" She looked at her daughter.

Barbara forced a smile at her mother and glanced apologetically at Joshua. "No, Mother," she said. "Last time Joshua was here just for dinner, and you weren't feeling too good."

"Pardon my daughter, Joshua," Rebecca Dubin said, her voice haughty. "She thinks I drink too much."

Joshua sat on the sofa several feet from her.

"Get Joshua a drink, dear."

"Can I get you something, Joshua?" Barbara asked.

"Do you have Jack Daniel's?"

She nodded.

"And a little bit of soda," he said.

Barbara walked to the sidebar, poured the bourbon in a tumbler, added soda from a siphon, and brought it to him.

"Cheers," her mother said, lifting her glass.

"Cheers," Joshua said.

They both drank. Barbara sat on the sofa between her mother and Joshua. Rebecca Dubin cast an injured glance at her daughter, then looked at Joshua.

"I hadn't noticed before that you had only one arm," Rebecca said.

Barbara rolled her eyes at Joshua. He lifted his aluminum left arm and worked the prongs that constituted his left hand. "Yes, I lost the arm in the war."

"Ooh, you must tell me the story sometime. I bet it's awfully exciting."

He smiled dutifully and nodded. The telephone rang on the end table. "Get that, will you, dear?" Rebecca said to her daughter. She turned to Joshua. "Probably my husband saying he's very sorry but he can't be home till late," she said. "I think he's got some *shikse* stashed away. But what's to worry? At least it keeps him away from me." She cackled drunkenly.

"It's for you," Barbara said, looking at Joshua.

Joshua was surprised. He got up from the sofa, walked to the end table, and took the receiver from Barbara.

"Yes?" he said.

It was Roy Collins. "Sorry to bother you, Joshua. I got the telephone number from Hanna."

"What's wrong?" Joshua was immediately worried.

"Nothing with your family. I'm sorry to scare you. It's Lou Shiner. He's dead."

"Dead? I just saw him a half hour ago."

"Yes, dead. They say it's suicide. He apparently pulled the tubes out of his nose and pecker and got some morphine out of the drug cabinet at the nurses' station when nobody was there, and he overdosed."

Joshua was stunned. "Nonsense. The guy was cold as ice. He wouldn't have shot himself up dead."

"Well, he's sure cold as ice now."

"You at the hospital?"

"Right. Did he say anything to you?"

"No, same as the other times."

"Was he afraid of anybody? Did he think anybody would come after him?"

Joshua thought for a moment. "The only time he showed fear was when I mentioned Bonanno. Then he clammed up. Nothing else."

"Okay. Sorry to bother you."

Joshua hung up the telephone and looked apologetically at Barbara. "I'm sorry. Business."

"Sounds like serious business."

He nodded. He sat on the end of the sofa, as far from Rebecca as he could get.

"So what is it exactly that you do, Mr. Rabb?" Rebecca Dubin asked. She peered at him closely, a woman looking for a good cut of filet mignon at the butcher shop.

"I'm a lawyer. I work part-time for the Bureau of Indian Affairs, and the rest of the time I'm building a private practice."

"Making a living?"

"Mother," Barbara chided sternly.

"Yeah, a living. But it'll get better."

"He's had some very big criminal cases," Barbara said defensively.

"Anything big now?" Rebecca persisted.

"Meyer Lansky just hired me to do some work for him." Joshua knew that he should keep his mouth shut, but the needling was bothering him. He was a thirty-eight-year-old lawyer with an aluminum arm, four missing toes, a yellow Chevy, a mud hut that didn't even belong to him, and two children. Not much of a prospect for a wealthy beauty like Barbara Dubin.

Rebecca's eyes opened wide. "Lansky's here, in Tucson?"

Joshua nodded.

"Pay up your life insurance," she said, laughing wickedly. "The only business that gangster is good for is funeral parlors. We paid protection to that *gonnif* for years, *er zoll zein in drerd* [he should be buried]."

"Okay, Mother," Barbara said, getting up and taking her mother by the hand. "Let's check on the roast." She pulled Rebecca off the couch. The drink sloshed in Rebecca's hand. She followed her daughter unsteadily into the kitchen.

A few minutes later, Barbara emerged alone. She sat on the sofa next to Joshua.

"I'm sorry, Josh. Mom is not usually this bad."

"It's okay. She's just wondering why in hell you're with me." He looked thoughtfully at her. "I wonder too."

"I like you a lot." She shrugged. "You have, I don't know, I guess more *depth* than most of the men I meet."

"I'm not complaining, mind you."

She laughed. "I'm not complaining either." She leaned over and kissed him on the cheek.

He turned toward her and smiled. "We can go out to eat, if you'd rather."

"No, it's okay. The roast is done. It's setting. Daddy will probably be home in a minute."

"Where were we?" Rebecca said, coming out of the kitchen.

The front door opened and Hal Dubin came in. He was short and fat, wearing a red silk shirt and a white silk suit, a black silk tie, and black suede loafers. He smiled broadly at Joshua as he got up from the sofa.

"Welcome, welcome," Hal said, ebulliently shaking Joshua's hand. "It took a helluva long time to get you back heah. You got somethin' bettah going than my little goil?"

Joshua shook his head. "Impossible."

"That what I like t' heah!" Hal said, slapping Joshua on the back.

"*Nu,* dinner, what? We gonna starve the guy?" Hal said, turning to Barbara.

"No, Daddy, don't worry. He'll live. Go sit down in the dining room and we'll start dinner."

"Foist I wash," he said. "Come, you too," he said to Joshua. He led the way into the kitchen. On the window ledge above the sink was a silver cup. He took it, filled it with water, poured the water over his hands, one at a time, and wiped them off with a clean dish towel as he murmured a Hebrew prayer. Joshua hadn't done the hand-washing ritual since his last dinner at his parents apartment in Brighton Beach, and he suddenly felt a pang of nostalgia. Here in Tucson, in the middle of nowhere. He washed his hands the same way, recited the short prayer, took the cloth from Hal, and dried his hands. It was improper to speak between the hand washing and the prayer that started the meal, the prayer over the bread. They walked to the dining room table. Hal recited the prayer and passed a piece of pumpernickel to Barbara, Rebecca, and Joshua. They all sat down.

"You know where I was all afternoon?" he said to Joshua.

Joshua shook his head.

"Tucson Merchants Association."

Joshua stared blankly at him.

"All the big shots in town, Goldberg's Department Store, the Flying Y Dude Ranch, the big restaurants downtown. All the Tucson *machers* [big shots]."

Joshua nodded.

"You know what bug they got up their ass?"

Joshua shook his head.

"Sales taxes." He looked at Joshua and frowned. "First the goddamn state puts a tax on everything. Now the goddamn county wants to hang another percent or two on us. Going to hurt our business. We might have to sue."

"That's very interesting, Daddy," Barbara said. "Why don't we talk about something interesting?"

"Don't be a *shlemiel*," he said to her. "I'm talking big money for some lawyer to bring a lawsuit on behalf of the association against the county. Twenty, twenty-five bucks an hour. For Joshua this *is* something interesting, damn interesting."

Joshua nodded. "Only trouble is, nobody hired me."

"Yeah, well, there is that little obstacle. But who knows, maybe the county will go ahead with the tax thing, and maybe the association really will sue." He smiled at Joshua. "You been thinking about that house I got for rent up on Speedway? Remember, I talked to you about it?"

Joshua nodded. "I'd love to look at it."

Hal winked victoriously at his daughter. Then suddenly he remembered something. "Uh-oh," he said, glancing at his watch. "I got to eat fast. *Special Agent* is on the radio at eight. I never miss *Special Agent.*"

They all finished dinner hurriedly, and Hal wiped his mouth with his napkin. "Want to listen with me?" he said to Joshua.

"Now, Daddy. Don't be dragging Joshua off to listen to the dumb old radio. I think Joshua and I will go for a drive."

He shrugged, shook hands with Joshua, and left the dining room. Rebecca had fallen asleep in her chair, snoring lightly.

"Come on, let's get out of here while we can," Barbara whispered.

They put the top down on Joshua's convertible and drove up Campbell Avenue to where it dead-ended on a dirt road at the crest of a hill. The view over Tucson's twinkling lights was stunning. He parked. It was a warm, breezeless night.

She snuggled against him and unzipped his trousers. "Ooh, look at Mr. Racehorse," she whispered.

Two hours later, she buttoned the last button of her blouse. "That was great," she said. "I'm starving. You want to eat something?"

"You must have a short memory."

Her laugh was lushly lascivious.

▲✦▽✦▽✦▲

Hanna was waiting up for Joshua when he returned home after ten. "Hi, Daddy," she said, "can we have a little talk?"

"Sure, honey." He sat beside her on the sofa. "Why such a long face?"

"I was over at the soda shop this afternoon. One of the kids had the morning paper. Did you see it?"

He shook his head.

"There was a big story in it about you and Charlie Isaiah and the hearing in court."

"I wish you wouldn't read that stuff, honey."

"I'm a big girl, Daddy. The story said that you said

Charlie was her steady boyfriend and that you accused Jennifer's father of having sex with her and killing her out of jealousy when he found her with Charlie." Her face was sour.

Joshua nodded. "Things like that happen, honey."

"Well, I don't know about her father. Jennifer never said anything like that. But I guess she wouldn't. But I don't think that Jennifer ever went out with Charlie."

Joshua stared at Hanna. He wrinkled his brow and screwed up his cheeks. "What?"

"We weren't best friends or anything, but I knew Jenny pretty well. She mostly went out with Jerry Hawkins, sometimes with Terry Hempstead. I never even saw her talk to Charlie."

Joshua thought for a moment. "Well, Charlie graduated last year, before we even came to Tucson. There's no reason for you to have seen them together."

"Daddy," she chided him, "don't you think if he was her steady for a year I'd have seen him pick her up after school, even once? And the other kids said the same thing. They never heard that she was going with Charlie."

"Maybe she was hiding it, figuring that no one would approve."

"Come on, Daddy. I saw his picture in the paper last week. He's beautiful. Why would she hide it?"

"Because he's a Papago Indian."

She shook her head crossly. "That may mean something to you older people, but it doesn't mean anything to us. Maybe she'd hide it from her father, but not from any of us."

He stared at Hanna and felt sick. Goddamn it, he thought. What now? Had Charlie Isaiah murdered Jennifer Carter? He breathed deeply and squinted his eyes shut. And I'm standing up in open court and accusing her father of incest? He opened his eyes and took another deep breath.

"Okay, honey. Thanks for telling me."

"Night, Daddy," Hanna said, walking into her bedroom and closing the door.

▲✦▽✦▽✦▲

"*Buon giorno, Padre Giuseppi,*" Albert Anastasia said. He knelt on one knee and kissed the back of Bonanno's left hand, like a supplicant kissing the pope's hand. Anastasia was close to Frank Costello, but he wasn't a father. So he was not allowed into the highest-level meetings that the Commission held, like this one. He had taken over what was left of Murder Incorporated after Louis Lepke's execution, and he was now in charge of the Commission muscle. So he and two of his closest soldiers were guarding the entrance to the small dining room of the Park Sheraton Hotel in Manhattan.

Bonanno had left Tucson at one o'clock in the morning. The plane had arrived at Idlewild an hour late, and it was now after two o'clock. The four men inside the dining room appeared fidgety and strained.

Steffano Maggadino, the father from Buffalo and Joe Bonanno's cousin, embraced Joe warmly. They exchanged greetings and family good wishes effusively in Sicilian. Then Bonanno and Joe Profaci and Vince Mangano, old and close friends, went through the same greeting ceremony of the men of tradition. Frank Costello's greetings were more subdued. He was not Sicilian, and he lacked the same decades-long relationship as the other fathers. After a half hour of small talk and family talk, the five men sat down at a small, round dining table set with Wedgwood china, Baccarat crystal, and Gorham silver. The meal was prepared in the small, private kitchen next to the dining room by Costello's two personal cooks and served by them.

They ate the shrimp cocktails noisily without speaking, letting the mood of the meeting shift from the joviality of the greetings a few moments ago to the business at hand.

"There is a serious breach of honor going on where my family lives," Joe Bonanno said in English. Since Luciano had taken over the Commission almost fifteen years ago, meetings had always been conducted in English, because Luciano didn't speak Sicilian and his

Italian was far from fluent. It was a custom that had survived even after Luciano had been imprisoned and the faces on the Commission changed. The newer men, especially the subordinates, born and reared in the United States, had Americanized the Commission. They were street toughs, thugs, unlike the men of the old tradition. Bonanno had graduated from the Merchant Marine Academy of Sicily. He had a classical education, spoke cultured Italian, and loved to read and quote the Latin poets. Among the newer fathers and their subordinates, he was an antique.

Bonanno looked around at the others and continued. "In the last week one of Meyer Lansky's men and two of Anastasia's have been murdered. Another of Lansky's is in the hospital with shotgun pellets in his shoulder."

"He is saying anything?" Profaci asked.

"*Omerta* [silence]," Bonanno said, wiping his open hand over his mouth. "Not to worry. But that is not the point. The point is that I bring my beloved wife and children to Tucson, Arizona. They should live in anonymity and safety, not like here in the volcano. And now you send men to deal in heroin, and the FBI is banging on my door wanting to know why I am killing people." Bonanno spoke softly and steadily, as he always did, but his eyes were dancing flames, and his voice cracked with emotion. "There are five men dead, more bodies than is in Tucson in funeral parlors for a whole year, and it is me the FBI looks to for answers." He struck his chest with his closed fist.

The men ate quietly for a few moments. Small bites, tasting nothing, the pleasure of the fine meal lost entirely in the gravity of Bonanno's implicit accusation.

"The killings is not us, Joe," Frank Costello said. He put his hand histrionically over his heart, and his face became the countenance of St. Luke healing the sick. "We had to help Benny with the Flamingo. Just a couple heroin deals, a quick million. Benny's in trouble, Joe, I don't have to tell you. Meyer and I personally gave him a million. The Commission helped him put together another two million. Now every day it's 'more money, more money.' He's a Jew, Joey, what can I tell you?" Costello nodded knowingly, and the men around the table looked at each other and rolled their eyes in agreement.

"But killing was not in the deal, Joey. No way." Costello looked earnestly at Bonanno and repeated, "No way. It ain't any of us, Joey."

Bonanno looked around at the others, and they each nodded solemnly.

"Meyer?" Bonanno asked, again searching the faces of the other fathers.

Costello threw up his hands dramatically. "He swears to me no, Joey. I talked to Charlie in Sicily, and Charlie called him. He swore to Charlie no. If Meyer tells Charlie Luciano and Frank Costello no, then it's no. Period."

Bonanno frowned and nodded grimly. "Then what? If it's none of us, then who?"

"Maybe Indians or Mexicans," Costello said, taking a big bite of veal piccante now that the heaviness of the confrontation had dissipated. "Maybe we stepped on somebody's toes, they thought we was trying to move in on their business out there. Maybe they don't even know who we are. They're just a bunch of fucking greasers and spics without honor or tradition." His face reddened, and anger muddied his eyes. "I'm sending Albert Anastasia and Tommy Lucchese out there to find out what's going on."

The men around the table nodded in approval, except Joe Bonanno. "No, no, no," he said. "The FBI sees Albert or Tommy, they pull me in without waiting two seconds. No, you cannot send anyone that is so well known. But I will think of a way for Meyer and me to find out. He got two guys with him in Tucson. I got some friends too. I handle it myself." It was much less an assertion than a request.

Bonanno looked at Steffano Maggadino. Steffano nodded in approval. Vince Mangano and Joe Profaci also nodded. Frank Costello held up his hand.

"No vendetta with any of us, Padre Giuseppi. Your word as a man of honor."

Bonanno responded slowly, soberly. "I come here as a man of the old tradition, Padre Francesco, as a man who honors the ways of our families, and I tell you from my heart that as long as you respect my family and do not endanger me or them, you have nothing to worry from me. We have all spoken in honor, nothing but the truth?" He looked around the table, and the other men nodded solemnly.

"Then there is no vendetta," he continued. "There will only be a strong discipline for those who are responsible."

▲+▼+▼+▲

At midnight Bonanno arrived in Tucson. He was met at the airport by Julius Lovello and Lorenzo Viti, two close friends who had moved to Tucson with the Bonanno family and whose only duty was to protect them.

"Did everything go well, Don Peppino?" Lorenzo asked. He and Big Julie were in the front seat of the touring Packard, Bonanno alone in the rear.

"Yes, they want peace. And Frank Costello tells me it ain't Meyer Lansky behind this."

Big Julie looked over his shoulder at Bonanno. "You believe Frank is being straight on this, Don Peppino? Maybe Lansky and Bugsy Siegel decided to freelance."

"*No io so* [I don't know]," Bonanno growled, his shoulders tensing. "*Ma io scopriro* [But I will find out]."

"That fucking Maggadino is a snake, Don Peppino," Lorenzo Viti said. "I don't care he's your cousin. He's jealous of you."

"I know," murmured Bonnano. "But we don't go to the mats until we are sure."

CHAPTER NINE

Joshua stood on the single platform at the Southern Pacific depot waiting for the train to Phoenix. Meyer Lansky joined him on the platform just a minute before the train pulled out at seven o'clock. They shook hands, exchanged brief greetings, and took seats across from each other in an almost empty coach car. The rest of the ninety cars were carrying grapefruit from Yuma to Chicago.

"Lou Shiner is dead," Joshua said casually. He watched for a reaction from Lansky. There was none.

"Who?"

"Knock off the act, Meyer. Lou Shiner."

Lansky stared out the window as the train gathered speed. He was silent for a minute. "Okay," he said finally. "I did know Lou. He worked for friends of mine."

"For the Mafia," Joshua said.

Lansky fixed him with a harsh glare. "Friends, just *friends*," he said. He shook a finger at Joshua. "Don't fuck with me." For the first time his eyes were flat and menacing.

They rode in silence for ten minutes.

"How did he die?" Lansky asked. "I thought his wound wasn't so bad."

"It wasn't. He overdosed on morphine."

Lansky flinched. "Louie? Morphine? *Er hut nit gehobt keyn gevoinheit* [He didn't have a habit]."

Joshua shrugged. *"Ver vays fun gevoinheiten* [Who knows from habits]. All I said was he died of an overdose."

Lansky gritted his teeth. His cheek muscles stood out like peach pits.

"Why don't you tell me what's going on, Meyer?"

Lansky swallowed and breathed deeply. "Look, what do you need to know more than I told you? I gave you a grand to do next to nothing. This ain't enough? You know the song from *On Your Toes,* that Broadway show: 'Fools rush in where angels dare not tread,' something like that. Take the advice. Don't rush in."

"That's the musical with *Slaughter on Tenth Avenue,* isn't it?" Joshua said.

Lansky shook his head disgustedly. "You ain't getting it. I don't know why you just ain't getting it."

"Anyway, that's not the song from *On Your Toes.* It's a quote from Alexander Pope. *On Your Toes* doesn't have the 'where angels dare to tread' stuff."

"You're a real smart boy," Lansky muttered. "Your mother must be proud. Such a mouth on you, such *saychel* [brains]." He tapped his forefinger on his temple.

Joshua didn't look at him. He stared out the window at the cactus and palo verde trees and endless sand. They rode in silence for a half hour.

"Listen, Joshua." Lansky's voice was solemn, his look sincere. "I didn't know Lou died. I really didn't. And so help me God, I had nothing to do with it. This is *emmiss* [the truth], on my mother's grave, I swear it."

Joshua studied him and nodded. "All right, I believe you. But what were he and his pal Solly doing on the reservation?"

"I'm going to tell you the truth, so help me." Lansky put his hand on his heart. "These boys I knew. I don't hide that. You're too smart to buy into bullshit, so I'm talking straight. I knew these boys. They're from the neighborhood, but they never worked for me. They worked for some friends. Why they're here? Maybe Joe Bonanno knows. Maybe it ain't even to do with Joe. I don't know. I really don't know. But one thing you learn in my business, you keep your nose out of other people's business."

"What's Bonanno's business?"

Lansky looked at Joshua and frowned. "Listen to me, smart boy, listen good to me. Don't be a shmuck. You don't want to have a pair of balls no more to keep your putz company? You tired of living, you want your kids should be orphans? Keep asking these questions. That's all you gotta do. Just keep asking questions about Joe and Solly and Lou. Me you can ask." He leaned forward in his seat and looked earnestly at Joshua. "Me, I'm your friend, so help me God. But don't ask these questions no more from somebody else." He held up his forefinger and wagged it, cautioning. "Them *gedillah pippicks* [big shots] back East hear you been asking questions, even God can't help you."

The conductor walked through the car. "Casa Grande next station stop. Casa Grande next." He went into the adjoining car.

The train slowed and stopped at a cement platform with a small yellow wooden shack at one end. No one was waiting to get on the train.

"This is my stop," Joshua said. He stood up, reached into his shirt pocket, and withdrew the ten folded hundred-dollar bills that Lansky had given him a week ago. He threw them on the empty seat next to Lansky.

"Hire somebody else, Meyer. I don't sell my soul for a few lousy dollars."

The look Lansky gave him was acidic. "You have such a pure soul?"

Joshua stepped onto the empty platform and watched the train pull away. He walked to the end of the platform to the yellow clapboard shack with the sign STATIONMASTER. Inside was a bare room with a desk, chair, telegraph, telephone, and a very thin man reading a newspaper.

"When is the next train to Tucson?" Joshua asked.

The man looked up, bored. He looked at a large clock on the wall. "The *Limited* in a hour. Ya wannit?"

"Yes."

"I gotta put out a flag on the track, otherwise it don't stop. Two dollars seventy-five cents."

Joshua reached in his pants pocket and pulled out three crumpled dollar bills. The man opened the desk drawer, threw them inside, and handed Joshua a quarter from a coin tray. He laboriously wrote out a ticket and handed it to Joshua.

The waiting bench on the platform was a two-by-twelve plank propped up by cinder blocks. Joshua sat down on it and stared glumly at the desert. A jackrabbit stood up and pricked its ears, then scampered behind a creosote bush. The sun was well up in the sky, although it was only eight o'clock, and it was already at least ninety degrees. It shined obliquely through the angular branches of the mesquite trees and cast jagged shadows on the parched, cracked earth.

You are a regular hero of moral rectitude, Joshua thought, a giant of decency. You are in the world's dirtiest business, where you make money by getting criminals off from suffering any consequences for the most horrific crimes, and you hand a thousand dollars back to Meyer Lansky and tell him to drop dead. And as far as you know, he hasn't done a thing wrong. And what if he did? Is he different than Charlie Isaiah or Frank Carillo? Hell no! You are a genius of dumb, you are a shmuck of epic proportions, you are a self-righteous jerk. All you had to do for the goddamn guy was sit outside a grand jury room and look concerned while he sat inside and answered questions about Italian marble and structural steel. But you are too clean to represent him. You defend rapists and killers but not Lansky. When you get to heaven, God himself will throw his arms around you and welcome you with a kiss on both cheeks. *"Boychik,"* He'll say, "have a nice piece fruit. Have a peach, a nice pear. I just got these oranges at the A&P. Sweet, like you never tasted. From Miami. Take one, keep one for later, you shouldn't get hungry, *kenna hurra.*"

Joshua stared morosely at the short freight train pulling into the station. The skinny stationmaster was standing on the platform, holding a clipboard and counting cars.

"This going to Phoenix?" Joshua asked, walking up to the man.

"Yeah."

"Can I get there on this?" Joshua handed him the ticket to Tucson.

The man shrugged. "Yeah, why not."

Joshua boarded the only passenger car. It was empty. An hour later, he walked from the Phoenix train depot to the Federal Building. It was nine-thirty, the grand jury session was at ten, and Meyer Lansky sat outside the jury room in a dimly lit corridor on a high-back walnut bench. Joshua sat down beside him.

"You take the wrong train?" Lansky said.

"You are entitled to the best legal representation money can buy," Joshua said.

Lansky laughed. "Here," he said, handing him the thousand dollars. "I love a man with an idealistic turn of mind. You can't trust a man who just loves money. Never know what the fuck he's gonna do. But a man with ideals? Now, there's a man who can be relied on."

Joshua let the comment pass. Maybe Meyer even meant it as a compliment.

"So how do we play it, Counselor?"

"I'm not allowed in the grand jury room with you," Joshua said.

"Yeah, I know."

"You've gone through this before?"

Lansky nodded. "Twice."

"How did you handle it?"

"Even though you're not allowed in there with me,

I'm entitled to consult with my attorney. So after every question I excuse myself and come out here and we consult." He laughed. "After four or five hours they'll get tired of the routine."

Joshua nodded. "Sounds okay. You going to take the Fifth?"

Lansky shrugged. "I doubt it. They got nothing on me. All they can possibly know is that I had a piece of the El Cortez Hotel in Vegas and got $62,500 when it sold. I rolled it over into the Flamingo. They may have learned that much from Billy Wilkerson. He testified two weeks ago, but he ain't such a good friend I can ask him. He owns the Cafe Trocadero and Ciro's on Sunset Strip in Hollywood. Strictly legit. He bought the land for the Flamingo and started the construction and then ran into money problems. He sold two-thirds of the project to me and Benny and some partners for $650,000. Billy and Benny have been negotiating for a complete buyout of Billy's third, but Benny got a little upset and it ain't settled yet."

"Who are the other partners?" Joshua asked.

"The only ones I think that Billy would know are the guys actually running the Flamingo, Davie Berman, Willie Alderman, and Morrie Rosen." He thought for a moment. "Also Gus Greenbaum, he's a bookmaker from here in Phoenix, and Moe Sedway, he's an old friend of Benny's and mine from New York. That's all that Billy Wilkerson would know."

"There are others?"

Lansky shrugged. "Who knows?"

"How about restricted materials?"

"I had nothing to do with the construction. That was all Benny's. I got no idea. If that's all this investigation is really about, it'll only take ten minutes."

The door to the grand jury room opened, and a young man came out. He was about thirty years old, medium height and slender, dressed in a gray linen suit, white starched shirt, and burgundy and white polka-dotted bow tie.

"One of you gentlemen Meyer Lansky?" he asked, walking up to the bench.

Joshua stood up. "This is Mr. Lansky. I'm Joshua Rabb, Mr. Lansky's attorney from Tucson." He extended his hand.

"I'm Mike Brink," the man said, shaking Joshua's hand and eyeing the other steel-pronged hand jutting out from Joshua's blue suit jacket. "No weapons allowed in here," Brink said, laughing.

Joshua smiled.

"I'm the assistant United States attorney," Brink said, becoming serious-faced and turning toward Lansky. "I'll be conducting the grand jury investigation and asking most of the questions. Some of the grand jurors may also ask questions, especially the foreman." Brink grinned disarmingly. "He's a loud-mouthed prick, fancies himself J. Edgar Hoover."

Lansky wasn't amused or disarmed. "What's the purpose of the investigation, Mr. Brink?"

A boyish kid-next-door grin spread over Mike Brink's face, but his dark brown eyes remained flat. "The Flamingo, Mr. Lansky. Anything and everything to do with the Flamingo."

"What are you jerking my chain for?" Lansky muttered. "I don't know shit."

"In a couple of minutes you'll be under oath, Mr. Lansky. You tell that to the grand jury." Brink kept smiling, a fixed plastic smile, and walked back into the grand jury room. A moment later, an elderly woman holding a stenographic pad opened the door a crack, looked out into the corridor, and said, "Mr. Lansky, please."

Meyer Lansky walked into the grand jury room. Five minutes later, he came out and sat on the bench next to Joshua. "They swore me in and read me a bunch of federal statutes on restricted building materials, trading with former Axis nations, some crap about use of structural steel. They also read some tax statutes. Then the U.S. attorney asked me to state my name." He looked blandly at Joshua.

"So?"

"So I told him I have to consult with my attorney."

He forced a tight-lipped, brief smile. "So what do I do, Counselor?"

"My legal advice to you, Mr. Lansky, is that you provide that information."

"All right, Counselor, I'll follow your advice. Do I tell him both first and last name? Do I give him my middle name?"

"What exactly was the question?"

"He said, 'State your name, please.' "

Joshua considered that for a moment, pursing his lips and pondering. "I think that the question calls for your entire name."

Lansky nodded. He walked back into the grand jury room. Two minutes later, he came out again and sat down next to Joshua. "Now he wants to know where I live."

"What's the exact question?"

" 'What is your home address?' "

"What's the answer?"

"Well, I got an apartment in the City. I got a house in Hallandale, Florida. I got a house in Tucson. They're all my homes."

"Ask him to clarify the question."

Lansky walked back into the grand jury room. Two minutes later, he returned to the bench next to Joshua. "He says he wants the addresses of all places I consider to be my home."

"Well, that's explicit enough. Answer the question."

Lansky returned to the grand jury room. Five minutes later, he came out again and sat on the bench. "I shoulda worn my Keds," he said. "I feel like I'm running a marathon." He chuckled. "Now he wants to know, 'Do I have any business interests in Las Vegas?' " I told him I had to consult with my attorney again. He got pissed off and threatened to hold me in contempt and charge me with obstruction of justice."

"He can't do that," Joshua said. "All he can do is take you in front of a federal judge and ask him to hold you in contempt. But don't worry, what we're doing is perfectly legal. Brink knows that."

"I ain't worried," Lansky said, looking bored. "I don't get worried so easy."

"Ask him to define what he means by 'business interests.' "

Lansky nodded and returned to the grand jury room. He rejoined Joshua on the bench five minutes later. "He started screaming that I know perfectly well what 'business interests' means and that he's going to hold me in contempt."

"Did he define 'business interests'?"

"No."

"Ask him to define 'business interests.' "

"The guy's really getting nuts in there."

"Well, this is your ball game, Meyer. If you want to cut the bullshit, you can just answer the questions. It's up to you. But there's nothing illegal about what we're doing."

"I know," Lansky said, smiling wearily. "We'll keep up the consultation routine. It can't get around that Meyer Lansky is an easy touch." He got up and strolled leisurely back into the grand jury room.

By the time the grand jury recessed for lunch, Meyer had described the nature of his holdings in the Flamingo Hotel: one hundred shares of stock. He and Joshua ate greasy barbecued beef sandwiches at a pool hall on Washington Street. They shot two games of eight ball. Joshua discovered that the steel prongs made an excellent rest for the cue as long as he stroked the ball smoothly and didn't jerk the cue.

After the second game they sat at a small table in the rear of the pool hall.

"What are they really after?" Joshua asked.

"I think they think that the Flamingo is owned by shady characters from back East and Benny's just the front. They got all the loan documents from the Valley National Bank in Phoenix. I think they're really trying to find out who the silent partners are."

"Did you have anything to do with the loan?"

"Absolutely nothing."

Joshua nodded. "Okay, let's get back. They must be getting tired of it by now."

They returned to the bench outside the grand jury room a few minutes before one o'clock. The routine resumed and dragged on for another two hours. Finally Lansky came out, didn't sit down and said, "They've had enough. Brink is about to have a stroke." He laughed.

They walked to the train station and caught the four o'clock to Tucson. They sat staring out the window, saying nothing for over an hour.

"What they're really after is where Benny got the money for the hotel," Lansky said, looking grim-faced. "That's what they're really after. They put together some figures, the loans from the bank and the down stroke from Wilkerson and the construction costs, and they realize that there's about three million accountable dollars in the deal and maybe twice that much has actually been spent. So they figure there must be some silent partners in the deal, bad guys, guys who would, God forbid, not report their holdings to the IRS."

"You think this is a tax-evasion investigation?"

Lansky nodded, his face sour. "Ever since they got Al Capone, it's their favorite gimmick. I think they're after Benny for evasion, and if they squeeze him hard enough, up'll jump some Jew or Italian bad guy. Then this Mike Brink'll run for governor of Arizona. Another Tom Dewey. He put Charlie Luciano in prison and got elected governor of New York." He frowned and shook his head. "Fuckin' Benny. He spends sixteen times more money than he reports. They'll squeeze him till his eyes bulge and his tongue turns purple." Lansky rubbed his mouth hard. "Benny wouldn't be so happy in prison. He'd probably tell them something just to get out. If he don't get laid constantly, he gets crazy."

"He'll get laid all he wants in prison," Joshua said.

Lansky snorted. "I don't mean that kind. Benny likes pussy, not a couple *shvartzes* holding him down on the floor and sticking it to him."

"When is his subpoena for, for the grand jury in Nevada?"

Lansky grimaced. "June twenty-three." He stared out the window, dismissing further conversation. "June fuckin' twenty-three," he muttered under his breath.

▲ + ▽ + ▽ + ▲

Joshua didn't get home until well after six o'clock. Magdalena had made Indian fry bread and chile colorado, and they sat around the chipped Formica table in the kitchen and ate dinner.

"I've got a date Saturday night," Hanna said.

Joshua nodded. "Buddy Lansky?"

She shook her head.

"Somebody new?" Joshua took care not to show too much pleasure.

She nodded.

"You going to tell me, or I have to guess?"

"Bobby," she said.

"Okay, that's nice, dear. Bobby who?"

"Bonanno," Adam said, looking victorious.

Joshua stopped chewing, his fork suspended in air. He glared at Hanna, and she ate silently, her head down, concentrating on the food on her plate.

"It's time for you to visit Grandma and Grandpa in Brooklyn," Joshua said, his voice hoarse with anger.

"Okay, Daddy," Hanna said very sweetly. "Bobby is going back to New York next month too. He's going to visit his cousins in Brooklyn for a while."

"You cannot go out on a date with Bobby Bonanno."

"Why not?"

"Because his father is one of the Mafia bosses of New York."

"What's that have to do with Bobby?"

Joshua didn't feel much like getting into a theoretical discussion with Hanna about the Mafia, but screaming at her didn't seem to be very useful. He spoke to her more calmly than he felt. "Well, I guess it has to do with environment. A boy who lives in such a family all his life is sure to become part of it and its way of life, the same as you and Adam are part of the Rabb family and our way of life."

"Daddy," Hanna said, looking at her father soberly. "Bobby has been living in Tucson since he was nine years old. He's lived here all by himself in boarding schools, and his parents only started coming here a couple of years ago for a few months a year. So he really hasn't even lived with his family for eight years. His way of life is parochial schools and boarding schools. And he's very nice, Daddy, you'll really like him."

Joshua sat back in his chair. He put his fork on his plate. He was on the verge of exploding. "In most things now I will let you decide what to do, Hanna." He spoke very quietly, trying to keep his anger from erupting. "You are fifteen and a young woman. I can't be with you every minute of the day. But in this matter of Buddy Lansky and the Bonanno boy, I will make the decision. You will not go out on a date with either of them. And that's all there is to it. I've spent all day with Buddy's father. He is a hoodlum, a gangster, plain and simple. I don't want you around him or his family. And as for Bobby Bonanno, his father is a gangland boss. Crime is his business just like lawyering is mine. These are not boys that a fifteen-year-old girl hangs around with."

Hanna gritted her teeth and remained silent. She knew better than to get into an argument with her father over boys. She'd end up being restricted to her room. And after what had happened with Billy Bowers. . . . She shuddered with the memory. Well, Daddy had been right that time, couldn't argue about that. But this was different, at least she thought it was, and maybe she could convince her father of it. But it would take time.

Actually, Bobby Bonanno hadn't asked her out on a date for Saturday night. But he would, she just knew it. He was big and handsome with shiny seal-brown hair and dark brown eyes, and she could tell that he really was attracted to her. They had spent the morning together with Bobby's cousin Alfredo and Buddy and a couple of other of their friends at the Owl Drug, where they got sodas, and then at Armory Park, across from the Carnegie Library, where there was a little carnival going on, a monkey grinder and some Mexican mariachis and dancers and a small Ferris wheel and a hot dog and cotton-candy stand. In the afternoon they had all gone over to El Rancho del Cerro, where Alfredo was staying, and they had played Ping-Pong and shuffleboard and volleyball and had a really great time. They had all decided to go back to the carnival Saturday afternoon and then go swimming in the big pool at El Rancho del Cerro. She was sure that Bobby would ask her out for a date. He had a big black Cadillac convertible and lots of money to spend. And she really liked him. She liked Buddy too, but not in the same way. More as a friend.

"Okay, Daddy," she said, her voice and face unemotional. She got up from the table and went to her bedroom, shutting the door softly.

Joshua looked in frustration at Magdalena. "Okay, Daddy? What the hell is going on here? Nothing is ever okay with Queen Hanna."

Magdalena laughed. "Maybe she's growing up. Maybe she's going to take your advice."

"She's just being sneaky," Adam said.

"Thank you, Master Rabb, for that altruistic assessment of your sister's conduct."

Adam wrinkled his nose. "What's altaristic mean?"

"Haven't you got something to do?"

"I'm meeting Chris over at the reservoir."

"Well, isn't it time to go?"

Adam frowned and got up. "Bye, Dad. Bye, Magdalena. Been nice knowing you all and being part of the great Rabb family." He walked out the kitchen door.

"I'm a man blessed with family riches," Joshua muttered. He looked sourly at Magdalena.

"Yes, more than most," she said brightly. "Well, I've got to get the dishes done. Juanito's picking me up at seven." She got up from the table and began stacking the plates and silverware.

"What's going on with you and Chuy?" Joshua asked, happy to think about something else.

She shook her head, and her voice was tinged with sadness. "I guess he likes Guadalupe Padilla better than me. She puts out for any man who gets close enough to sniff her."

"Come on, Magda. He's in love with you. He drank a little too much, made one mistake. Don't lose him over that. 'Let him who has not sinned . . .' "

She frowned at Joshua. "Listen, Mr. Philosopher, this isn't just being catty. He really hurt me. I went to the market yesterday, and Jana Higaldo and Virginia Enos snickered at me."

"Those two old yentas snicker at anybody about anything. Ignore them and anybody else like them."

Magdalena sat down on the chair, and her shoulders slumped. Tears misted her eyes. "I don't know what to do."

"Do you like this Juanito Coronado?"

"Not really. He's spoiled and he loves himself. But he spends plenty of money and has a nice car, and he's a lot of fun." She looked at Joshua, and tears rolled down her cheeks. "But he's no Chuy Leyva."

Joshua took her hand on the table. "I'm bringing Chuy over for dinner Saturday night. Okay?"

She sniffed, and her eyes brightened. "Okay. But make it your idea. I don't want him to think I'm running after him."

"Don't worry, I'll handle it like a real *shadchan*."

"A what?"

"Matchmaker."

"Good luck." She smiled.

CHAPTER TEN

"Whattaya, some kinda moron?" Edgar Hendly said, looking oddly at Joshua.

"It's a living, Edgar. That's all there is to it. I'm making a whole hundred twenty-eight dollars a month working for you. What the hell do you want me to do, let my kids starve to death? I have to make a living, and Meyer Lansky's a paying client. End of story."

"But such a piece a shit?" Edgar looked disgusted. "Cain't ya find someone else to overcharge?"

"Sure. Send me some Papago drunk who's been arrested for raping and murdering a sweet seventeen-year-old white girl. You like that better?"

"Yer in a lousy business," Edgar said.

"This is real news. I'll call the newspapers."

"Ya don't have to call them. J.T. is gonna call you for sure." He held up the morning newspaper with the headlines FIVE MURDERS ON PAPAGO RES, and a two-column story by J. T. Sellner with a long paragraph about Joshua Rabb helping the FBI with the investigation, and him being the last person to have seen Louis Shiner alive before he died mysteriously of a morphine overdose administered into his carotid artery. "The corpse showed signs of severe bruising on both arms," the story quoted Coroner Wolfe, "indicating the high probability that the injection had not been voluntary."

Joshua had read the story twice at breakfast earlier, almost gagging when he read the part about himself. "J.T. doesn't like me very much," he said, shrugging. "What can I tell you?"

"She's gonna like you a whole helluva lot less when she finds out you was up in Phoenix yesterday at a federal grand jury, bein' the mouthpiece for one a the biggest gangsters in the country. Can you imagine what that story's gonna look like?"

Randy Stevens knocked on the doorjamb and walked into Joshua's office. He was stocky, average height, and had thinning blond hair and pale blue eyes. He was the chief deputy county attorney for Pima County, and Joshua had tried several cases against him. They had become friends. Randy had a newspaper folded under his arm. He shook hands with Edgar and sat in the chair beside him, facing Joshua's desk.

"To what do I owe this unsurpassed honor?" Joshua said.

"Read about you this morning over my bacon and eggs." He waved the newspaper in the air. "Just about puked."

"Didn't do much for my digestion either," Joshua said.

"I got a call from Mike Brink yesterday afternoon," Randy said. "You heard of him?"

Joshua nodded.

"He was real thrilled the way you jerked him around at the grand jury."

"Just doing my job."

Randy nodded and frowned. "Yeah, that's what I told him. He's sure one of your admirers."

Edgar smirked at Joshua. "Yeah, one a many, that's fer damn sure. Mr. Rabb is becomin' down right famous for bein' the champion a the poor 'n' down-trodden."

Joshua gritted his teeth and said nothing.

"Did you know that this Lansky bought a house next to Joe Bonanno?" Randy asked.

"Ya don't say." Edgar chortled, delighted with the latest tidbit.

Joshua stared Edgar into silence, then said, "Yes, I know that."

"And there's hardly any doubt that what's been going on on the Big Reservation has something to do with Bonanno," Randy said.

Joshua shrugged.

"Fools rush in, baby. Fools rush in," Randy said.

"Funny," Joshua said. "This is the second time I've heard that in two days."

"Don't make so light of it," Randy said. "This is a sleepy little town. We'd like these gangsters to go back to New York and do their shit there, not here."

"Then why don't you go tell them, Randy? Why are you wasting your valuable time jawing with me? I have no influence with these folks, and I don't think I ought to be telling them where you'd like them to live. But you don't need my permission to tell them yourself."

"Mike Brink wanted to know did I have any evidence that you were working *with* these guys, not just their attorney."

"Lansky's attorney, not Bonanno's," Joshua corrected him.

"Right, right. Slip of the tongue. I told him, no, you're no mobster, just a poor dumb jerk trying to make a buck."

"Thanks for the vote of confidence."

Randy shook his head. "Actually, I told him you're the best damn criminal lawyer in Tucson, and if you're representing Lansky, poor Mike had a nuclear war on his hands."

Joshua smiled slowly. "I appreciate that."

"Well, he didn't," Randy said. "He said no one-armed Jew is going to try to rip him a new asshole and get away with it."

Joshua stopped smiling. Randy looked at him seriously. "Take it real careful with guys like that," Randy said. "Some prosecutors think they're doing God's work going after bad guys, and they figure that defense lawyers are tools of the devil and ought to be beaten to death for the good of society."

"Is Mike Brink one of them?"

Randy shrugged. "I don't know. Met him a couple of times up in Phoenix. We were both on carriers in the Pacific. He was navy, I was marines, so it gave us something to shoot the bull about. Seems like a nice enough guy. But he was sure as hell hopping mad yesterday."

Joshua nodded. "Well, I wish I could make all you prosecutors happy, but that's not the way this system works."

"Here's another newspaper so you can send a clipping to your folks back home," Randy said, laying the paper on Joshua's desk. "They'll love it."

"You're a true friend," Joshua said.

Randy turned to Edgar. "By the way, I heard Frances was expecting. Congratulations."

"Damn!" Edgar slapped his knee. "News a my sexual prowess travels this town like wildfire."

"I didn't say anything about *your* sexual prowess," Randy said.

"You two guys been talkin'?" Edgar peered at each of them and chortled. Joshua and Randy laughed.

▲+▼+▼+▲

Joshua asked Chuy to go with him to the Isaiah house on the reservation to search it and look for evidence. It had been abandoned since Charlie's arrest, the door hanging open from the broken jamb. But it didn't appear to have been looted. No one else lived there, since Charlie's father had died of tuberculosis three years ago and his mother was living with Charlie's oldest sister and her family at Cowlic on the

Big Reservation. Charlie's three older brothers were gone from the reservation.

There was nothing that struck Joshua as particularly noteworthy inside the house. The sheet had been taken off the bed and brought with the body to the coroner. The knife had been embedded in Jennifer's sternum, and it was too covered with blood to have retained any fingerprints.

They walked slowly around outside the house in widening circles. It was surrounded with low tufts of browning bear grass, thick clumps of hummingbird trumpets and scarlet penstemon, and scattered wild Mexican primrose, some lavender, some pale red. Between the patches of flowers and grass were broad areas of bone-dry dirt, cracked and curled on the edges like old leather. It hadn't rained in over a month, and much of the dirt had turned powdery. About fifty yards behind the house, Chuy stopped short. He pointed at a puddle-shaped rust-colored spot in the grayish tan earth. It was perhaps six feet around, uneven around the edges, darker in the middle.

"Six pints of blood?" Chuy said, looking at Joshua.

Joshua frowned. "I'll get a piece of paper out of my car. Wait here."

He walked to his car, got a sheet of paper out of a clipboard, and returned to Chuy. They gouged out a few chunks of the earth with a stick and wrapped it loosely in the paper. They walked back toward Joshua's car. He stopped in front of Isaiah's Ford and looked inside. There were no apparent bloodstains on the front or back seats. He put the paper in his car, opened the trunk, took out a short crowbar, and went over to Isaiah's car. One quick pry sprung the trunk. It contained an old spare and some dirty work clothes. Nothing else. Joshua was relieved.

They drove silently to the coroner's office in the Pima County Courthouse. Joshua asked Stan Wolfe to test the earth samples for blood and type, if possible, against Jennifer Carter's blood type. Then he got back in the car with Chuy.

"I got Philip Carter's address from the university student affairs dean," Joshua said. "He lives in a dorm in the stadium."

"You think I ought to be going with you?" Chuy asked.

"Why not?"

"Well, it isn't exactly official BIA business, and I'm in uniform."

"That's why I want you with me. Put the fear of God in him."

"You think that's fair?"

"I think he stood by while his father killed his sister. I don't think that was fair."

They drove to the dormitory on the ground floor of the east wing of the football stadium and parked in the lot. The fourth room from the entrance had the name P. CARTER penciled on a piece of scrap paper taped to the doorjamb. The door was open and a large fan was whirring on the floor, aimed toward the bed. A young man was lying on the bed reading an *Esquire* magazine.

"You Philip Carter?" Joshua asked.

The young man put down the magazine slowly, swung his legs around, and put his feet on the floor. "Yeah?"

"My name is Joshua Rabb. This is Sergeant Leyva."

Carter's eyes flicked toward Chuy and quickly back to Joshua. "My dad told me what you did in court, you son of a bitch."

"What's wrong with what I did in court?"

"You accused my father of forcing Jenny to—to—to do things." Philip's mouth was twisted viciously.

"In court the truth has to come out," Joshua said, keeping his voice hard and accusatory. "Dirty little family secrets can't be kept." He narrowed his eyes at the young man. "We know that's why your mother left. She couldn't take it anymore."

Carter stood up from the bed and walked toward Joshua. He was the same height, but some sixty pounds heavier. None of it looked like fat.

Chuy stepped forward and growled, "Hold it there, sonny."

Carter studied Chuy and stopped six feet from Joshua. He sat back down on the bed. "You seen my mother?"

Pay dirt, Joshua thought to himself. By God, it worked. He shook his head.

"How did you know?"

Joshua was almost there. He softened his voice. "Jenny told some friends of hers," he lied. "My daughter, Hanna, was a real close friend of hers."

Carter's eyes flickered and tears came to them. He sniffed and rubbed his hand across his eyes. "I never knew about it till last month. Just a week before she died. She couldn't stand it any longer. She came over here and told me." He began to cry. Tears spilled from his eyes. He covered his face with his hands and muttered, "Goddamn, Goddamn, Goddamn." He recovered his composure after a few minutes and stared at the floor between his legs.

"I tried to help her," he mumbled. "I went over to the house the next afternoon. My father was there. I confronted him. Jenny was in her room." He looked up at Joshua and sighed deeply.

"And you held down Charlie Isaiah," Joshua said quietly.

Carter's face shot up. He looked quizzically at Joshua. "What the hell does Charlie Isaiah have to do with it?"

"You held him down while your father stabbed your sister."

"What are you, nuts?" Philip Carter stared in shock at Joshua. "What the fuck kind of bullshit is that?" There was no more timorousness in his face, his voice. He stood up and tightened his hands into fists.

Chuy put his hand on the butt of his revolver. Carter looked at him, swallowed, and stayed where he was.

"You watched while your father murdered your sister," Joshua persisted. "Then you helped him take her body to the reservation and frame Charlie Isaiah."

He shook his head, a look of disbelief on his face. "Is that where you've been heading with all of this?" He stared hard at Joshua. "That's crazy. Jenny never had anything to do with that Indian. She was too much of a snob to go out with an Indian."

Joshua had lost control of the boy. His defense was slipping away. He needed desperately to get this young man to tell the truth.

"We're having a search warrant issued this afternoon," he lied. "The FBI is searching your sister's room for blood. With as much blood as she lost when she was stabbed, the chemicals they use will find it, even if it's been scrubbed and scrubbed."

Carter sat down on the bed. His voice was calm. "There's nothing there. My dad didn't kill Jenny, at least not in the way you're saying. He should be shot for what he did to her, but he didn't kill her, just ruined her life." He lay back on the bed and covered his eyes with his forearm. His body shook with sobs.

Joshua looked at Chuy and grimaced. They walked back to Joshua's car and got in. He sat tensely in the driver's seat, staring straight ahead.

"Well, where are we now?" Chuy asked.

Joshua shook his head.

"You still believe Charlie Isaiah."

Joshua looked at Chuy and shrugged his shoulders slowly. "It was a good story," he said, his voice muffled. "And he tells it real well."

They sat silently for another minute. The heat in the car was scalding. It was at least a hundred ten degrees, and there was no wind stirring. A huge Aleppo pine tree in the parking lot gave off a sharp resinous odor, as though it were melting. The tips of its needles were sunburned to a dull rust color. Joshua's shirt was stuck to his back, and perspiration streamed down his face. Chuy appeared to be dry.

"How do you keep from sweating on a day like this?" Joshua said.

Chuy looked at him. "It's the one great talent God gave the Papagos, so we make good ditch diggers and bricklayers. We can take a lot of sun."

Joshua nodded. "Out here that's a damn good talent to have."

"I'd rather have a Ph.D. in engineering," Chuy said.

They sat silently for a few more moments.

"Well," Joshua said, "I guess we'd better go see Edward Carter."

"You anxious to get yourself killed?"

Joshua shrugged. "What else can I do? If I can't break down Philip or his father, Charlie Isaiah's going to die."

Chuy nodded. "That's what ought to happen."

"Charlie was telling the truth about the incest."

"Just a wild guess, a lie that turned out to be true," Chuy said. "At least that part of it."

Joshua gritted his teeth, his face grim. He started the car, pulled out of the lot, and drove to Carter Ford. It covered an entire block of Stone Avenue, just a mile from downtown Tucson. Two salesmen beamed great smiles of joy and gladness when Joshua and Chuy parked on the street in front of the dealership and walked toward the picture window–enclosed showroom.

"Can I help you boys?" said one of the salesmen, his face covered with teeth and good fellowship.

"Is Edward Carter here?" Joshua asked.

The brilliant smile ebbed. "Yeah. In there at the end of the hallway."

It was windy inside the showroom. Humid air from the evaporative cooler whipped out of several vents. The moisture made the narrow hallway smell like mildew. Joshua walked to the end of the hall. A plastic plaque on the door read: EDDIE CARTER, YOUR BEST FRIEND FOR A FORD. Joshua knocked.

"Come," boomed a voice.

Joshua and Chuy entered the small office. Carter was behind the desk, another man in front of it. The other man began beaming his toothy smile.

"What're you doing here?" Carter growled.

The other man saw the vitriol in Carter's face and the sober faces of Joshua and Chuy. He edged out of his chair and backed out of the room into the hallway, closing the door behind him.

"Leave that fucking door open," Carter bellowed. "These bastards ain't staying."

The door swung open. The other man fled. Joshua sat in one of the two chairs in front of the desk. Chuy remained standing, his hand resting easily on the butt of his gun.

"We just talked to your son, Philip," Joshua said. "He told us what happened."

Carter's eyes were bloodshot. His swollen jowls hung down like a Boston bulldog. He was wearing a starched white long-sleeved shirt and a plain bright red silk tie. The moisture from the evaporative cooler had wilted the collar and cuffs of the shirt into masses of wrinkles, and it made him appear disheveled.

"Philip don't know shit."

"Jennifer told him about you forcing her to have sex with you."

Carter's face darkened. His jowls appeared literally to hang lower. "I lost my daughter, you son of a bitch, you scum, you—you . . ." he sputtered. He jabbed his finger at Joshua and started screaming. "How'd you like to lose your daughter, see her with a knife sticking out of her chest?"

"Philip told us he held Charlie Isaiah down while you stabbed her."

The baleful look on Edward Carter's face changed to disgust. "You are a dangerous motherfucker. But you just overplayed your hand. Get out of here before I call the cops."

"He's the cops," Joshua said, jutting his chin toward Chuy.

Carter looked annoyedly at Chuy. "He's a fuckin' greaser cop. He touches that gun in here, both you assholes are going to jail."

Chuy's hand came off his revolver. He folded his arms over his chest.

"You be off this property in ten seconds, asshole, or I call the police, have you arrested for trespassing."

Joshua breathed deeply to repress his anger. He got

up and walked out of the office, followed by Chuy. They got into Joshua's car, did a U-turn, and drove south.

"You were terrific," Chuy said.

Joshua looked over at him. They both laughed, short, nervous laughter.

"I had to try," Joshua said.

"What now?"

He shook his head. "I don't know. Wait for the coroner's report on the dirt we brought him. If it's Jennifer's blood type, I guess Charlie Isaiah's story falls to pieces."

"What if it isn't?"

Joshua shrugged. "I don't know. I just don't know."

They drove to the BIA. Joshua went into his small office with the army surplus olive drab metal desk and navy surplus battleship gray metal bookshelves and stared out the smeary window, seeing nothing. He had to talk to Charlie Isaiah again, try to determine if he was lying. The first time he had been convinced that the Indian boy was innocent. But the evidence did not support the conclusion. The evidence was mounting against him. The now certain fact that Edward Carter had forced his daughter into an incestuous relationship did not prove that he had murdered her. Being a reprehensible pig didn't make him a killer.

He picked up the telephone and dialed Judge Buchanan's office. "Hello, Mrs. Hawkes. This is Joshua Rabb. Judge in?"

A moment later, the judge came on the line.

"Your Honor, I need an order permitting me to interview Charlie Isaiah up at the detention center."

"It'll be ready when you get here."

"Thank you, sir." Times had certainly changed since Joshua had represented Ignacio Antone a year ago. Getting into the detention center to interview Ignacio had been something like being under fire at the Battle of the Bulge.

He walked out to his car and laboriously put down the convertible top. He stopped downtown and picked up the court order. His head cooked for a half hour, until he got a few miles up the Santa Catalina Mountains, but the rushing air felt refreshing and dried him off. The federal detention center was located an hour farther up the mountain at a logging camp a few miles below the town of Summerhaven, almost at the summit of Mount Lemmon. It was eighty-six hundred feet high up here and just eighty degrees. Huge blue cypress trees and Douglas fir and ponderosa pines swayed in the gentle breezes of the mountaintop. Joshua turned onto the dirt road leading to the detention center. He parked in front of the chain-link fence surrounding several barracks and walked into the guard shack by the entry gate.

"What's up, buddy?" the guard said. He was sitting on a wood slat chair next to a small wooden table.

Joshua handed him the court order. The guard read it, pulled a clipboard off a nail in the wall, located the name, and picked up the walkie-talkie on the table. He pushed a button and adjusted the squelch to suppress the static.

"Hey, Marty," he said into the mouthpiece. "Send Charlie Isaiah over to the visitors' area. He's in slot twenty-three, barrack four. Over."

"Roger" came the staticky response.

"There." The guard pointed to a barbed-wire enclosure around several picnic tables. He walked outside with Joshua, unlocked the chain-link gate, and Joshua walked through the compound to the visiting area. He sat on a bench by a rough redwood picnic table and waited. Charlie Isaiah came into the area ten minutes later. His black hair was covered with fine sawdust, and his faded blue jumpsuit was beige with wood chips.

"Been working in the mill," he said, sitting across from Joshua.

"How are they treating you?"

"Okay, no problems."

"Good."

"What's up, Mr. Rabb?"

Joshua breathed deeply, studying Isaiah closely. "I'm having a tough time getting evidence in your favor. No one seems to know that you were dating Jennifer. And I can't find any evidence that she was murdered in her own home."

Isaiah looked frightened. "Well, uh, uh, lots of the students at Tucson High must have seen us together," he stammered. "We were together lots of times."

Joshua shook his head.

"How about blood in the cars, in her room? You said you were going to get a search warrant."

"I can't. I just can't get one."

A look of grave terror clouded his eyes. "You can't let them do this to me, Mr. Rabb. I didn't do it. I wouldn't ever have hurt Jenny. I loved her. We loved each other." He began to cry.

Joshua felt sick. He couldn't help it, he was deeply convinced that Charlie Isaiah was telling the truth. But he had no words of comfort for the handsome Indian boy. He felt enervated, impotent. He sat still, waiting for Isaiah to stop crying.

"Look, Charlie, I believe you. But you've got to give me some leads. I need to have the name of at least one of Jennifer's friends who saw you together. Ten would be a lot better."

Isaiah looked haunted. He stared at his hands, then rubbed his eyes and looked ashamedly at Joshua. "I'm sorry, Mr. Rabb. I'm so damn scared."

"I know, Charlie," Joshua said gently. "But think hard. Who saw you on a date together?"

He gritted his teeth and shook his head slowly. "I don't know," he murmured, tears again coming to his eyes. "She was so afraid of her father, she never let anyone see us together. We didn't even go to movies or Johnny's Drive-In. We'd just meet downtown after dark over at Armory Park or she'd drive out to the reservation." He stopped and thought for a minute. "There was one girl, yeah. Jenny came out to the reservation one time with her friend Cindy. Hansen or Danson. Yeah, yeah, that's it, Cindy Danson." His face brightened.

"Good," Joshua said, feeling a little better. "Anyone else? Think hard."

Charlie sighed deeply and shook his head. "I'm just too shook up to think right now. I'll think about it."

"Okay," Joshua said. "Just take it easy. Don't do anything stupid up here. The trial's coming up in two weeks. I've got a lot of work to do."

Charlie nodded and smiled, an infectious, attractive smile. "I trust you, Mr. Rabb." They shook hands.

Joshua walked across the compound to the gate, waited impatiently for the guard to fiddle with the padlock and let him out, and drove quickly down the mountain to Tucson. He went directly to the Tucson Unified School District headquarters building, a Quonset hut next to Tucson High School. He asked if there was any record on a Cindy or Cynthia Danson. The elderly woman looked through one filing cabinet, said, "Not a current student," then looked through another cabinet in the rear of the office. She pulled out a dog-eared manila file and opened it. "Graduated from Tucson High, June 1946. She lived at 1417 East Turner with her mother. Father killed in the war. That's all we have."

"Thanks," Joshua said.

He went outside to his car and drove quickly two blocks north to Turner Street and turned east, nine blocks, ten blocks to 1417, a small whitewashed stucco house with a dead patch of Bermuda lawn in front. A FOR SALE OR RENT sign was pounded into the ground next to the mailbox. He walked to the front door. It was locked. He peered through the foot square of smudged glass. There was no furniture in the living room, no table or chairs or icebox or stove in the kitchen just beyond it. He felt defeated. He got into the car and drove to a gas station two blocks away. He paged through the telephone book and found no listing for Danson. He put a nickel in the phone, asked for information, and asked the operator for the number for Danson, "could be -son, maybe -sen," he said. There was no listing.

He drove home slowly, pondering what to do next. Hanna was with Magdalena in the kitchen preparing dinner.

"No, Daddy. I never heard of anyone named Cindy Danson."

"Will you ask around, all your friends?"

"Sure, Daddy."

He walked listlessly into the living room.

"By the way, Daddy," Hanna said, coming out of the kitchen wiping her hands in her apron. "Dr. Wolfe called. He said he tried to test what you brought him earlier today, but he couldn't get any positive reaction. He said it had been exposed to the open air and heat too long. Is that important?"

Joshua nodded. He sat on the couch and wondered miserably what it was going to be like watching an innocent man be gassed.

▲✛▼✛▼✛▲

The truck that had been found behind the Plymouth at Newfield had carried registration to a Mexican company called Cooperativa Agricultura Mexicana. Chuy Leyva was hoping that it would lead to Juanito Coronado. Wouldn't that be great! Arrest the son of a bitch for conspiracy to smuggle heroin and throw him in the detention center, a long way from Magdalena.

Chuy drove across the border into Nogales, through the American and Mexican checkpoints, without being stopped. The car searches took place on entering the United States, not leaving it. He parked on Calle Obregon across from the small cinder-block building that housed all national ministries represented in this backwater town in Mexico's northernmost state of Sonora.

Like the great majority of Papagos, Chuy had relatives in several Sonoran towns and spoke Spanish fluently. Roy Collins had loaned him the government car the FBI employees used, an unmarked and unobtrusive black Dodge with regular Arizona license plates. Chuy was dressed like the average Papago farmer from any of the small villages in Sonora and Arizona: Levis, scuffed cowboy boots, a plaid cowboy shirt, and a straw cowboy hat.

He walked down the dirt-floored hallway of the Oficinas del Gobierno Federale and came to the door marked AGRICULTURA. Five minutes later, he emerged with the address and name of the president of Cooperativa Agricultura Mexicana. The company was located on Calle Obregon in an office building next to Banamex, the major Mexican bank. It was only a block away, and Chuy walked to it. The building was an old one, built of adobe brick with two filthy windows in front. He opened the wood plank door and stepped inside. A candle was burning on a small desk, and an aged man was sitting at it in a straight-back wooden chair. He peered over thick glasses at Chuy.

The truck, the old man said, was leased to a company in Nogales, Arizona, Commodity In.porters, Inc. He scrutinized Chuy. "Why are so many people interested in that truck?" he asked.

Chuy looked at him oddly. "What?"

"Two other men were in here yesterday afternoon asking about the same truck."

"What did they look like? Do you know who they were?"

"Norteamericanos," he answered. *"Trajes* [suits], *corbatas* [ties], *parecido a dos George Rafts en una de las peliculas Americanas* [like two George Rafts in one of those American movies]." He winked knowledgeably at Chuy, like a true connoisseur of gangster films. "You know, hats down over their eyes." He demonstrated with his hand, pulling an invisible snap-brimmed fedora down low on his forehead. His mouth opened wide in a toothless smile. *"Gorilas* [tough guys]."

Chuy nodded, his face exhibiting none of the mirth of the old man. "What did they want to know?"

"Same as you. Who owned it. Address."

"You told them?"

"Yes, sure. Why not?"

"What is the address of Commodity Importers?"

The old man opened a desk drawer, pulled out a ledger book, and flipped through the pages. He laboriously wrote out an address on the back of an opened envelope on the desk, tore off the piece of paper, and handed it to Chuy.

"Gracias, viejo," Chuy said and left the small building. He looked around, almost expecting to see two gangsters in black felt hats sitting across the street in a gray Plymouth. No one was there. He walked back to his car. He drove back to the border, and the American inspector examined his driver's license.

"You American?" the inspector asked, eyeing Chuy suspiciously.

"Born and bred," Chuy said.

"This your car?" the inspector asked, as though he didn't expect a greaser like this to own a car newer than 1934, with rusted dents and steam coming from the radiator cap.

Chuy reached into the glove compartment and handed the registration to the border patrolman in his soiled green uniform, the buttons tugging over his paunch. The patrolman studied the registration, looked oddly at Chuy, and handed it back to him.

"Shit, I applied for the Bureau," the man said. "They tol' me I didn't have the qualifications. Shit!" He spat on the ground. "But they take you?" He glared at Chuy, then turned on his heel and went back into the guard shack.

Chuy drove to Calle Codorniz, which wound high up a hill, affording a panoramic view of the tiny towns of Nogales, Arizona, and across the border to Nogales, Sonora. There were a few modest residences along the dirt road, but the address of Commodity Importers, or where the company should have been if it actually existed, was an acre of mesquite trees and palo verdes and thick brittlebushes in full bloom with their bright yellow daisy-like flowers. Chuy got out of the car and walked slowly around the empty lot. It was pleasant here, elevation over four thousand feet, maybe ninety degrees, with a marvelous view of the Santa Rita Mountains to the north and the Pinito Mountains to the south, and the sparkling Santa Cruz River flowing from the Pinitos through the center of both border towns until it disappeared underground some twenty miles into Arizona. Along the west bank of the river just below the hill he was on, Chuy could see the corrugated tin roofs of produce warehouses glinting hotly in the late afternoon sun. The warehouses stretched for two miles, surrounded by stake trucks and vans and refrigerated trucks. Behind the warehouses on the river side was a Southern Pacific railroad spur that went through a chain-link fence at the border and continued unhindered into Mexico, linking it with the Mexican railway system, Ferrocarril Sudpacifico.

Juanito Coronado had been on Chuy's mind for days now, not only because he was bird-dogging Chuy's girl, but because his family had the largest produce-importing business in southern Arizona and therefore controlled the largest number of trucks. Chuy had several times amused himself with the thought of discovering the prick smuggling heroin and shooting him or maybe just breaking his neck. As he looked down at the warehouse roofs, he once again smiled at the possibility. Then Magdalena would come back to him. He had made a mistake with Guadalupe Padilla. He'd run into her at the Tres Amigos bar on South Sixth Avenue one Thursday night. He and his brother Solomon had gone there after supper for a couple of beers, Guadalupe was there, and Chuy hadn't seen her in two or three years. They had gone out a few times in high school in Sells, and she had been very popular with the boys because she had far fewer inhibitions about sex than the average girl. But so what? Chuy wasn't the only one, and it wasn't right for a boy to be a virgin much after his sixteenth birthday.

When Chuy had gotten out of the marine corps a couple of years ago and returned to his family's farm on the Big Reservation, he had gone out with Guadalupe a few more times. After all, a man had needs. And so did some women. But it had never been love, just lust. And then he ran into her at the Tres Amigos, and she told him about how she had married a Mexican vaquero who worked on a ranch down by Sahuarita. Then she started crying, telling Chuy about how her husband had run off with some *puta* he picked up in a bar. Chuy felt sorry for her. And the comfort she needed, and the comfort he wanted her to have, after five shots of Four Roses and five beer chasers, had apparently been obvious enough to some of the other people at the bar that rumors had started immediately after Chuy and Guadalupe left together.

Well, it just plain hadn't been worth it. He was in love with Magdalena. She was gorgeous, like one of those phony Indian maidens in that Jeanette MacDonald–Nelson Eddy movie. But Magdalena wasn't phony. She was educated, she was classy, and she was Macario Antone's granddaughter, a former chief of the Papago tribe and its most influential elder until his death just a few months ago. And Chuy had screwed up his relationship with Magdalena pretty damn completely. Two weeks ago he had been certain that she would marry him. They hadn't discussed it, but he was sure that she would. But now? Now she wouldn't even talk to him. He had come like a penitent to the Rabb house three times, and she had slammed the door in his face. He had gone to the *siwani's* [chief medicine man's] house across from Mission San Xavier del Bac, and he had refused to intercede for him. "You young people work it out yourselves," he had said. "And practice keeping your pecker in your pants."

Chuy got back into his car and drove down the hill to the produce warehouses. The first long warehouse had no sign on it or in front. Some twenty men loaded crates into half as many stake trucks at a loading dock. The second warehouse shed was closed, and no one was on the dock. Twenty empty vans and stake trucks were parked by it. The third shed was twice as wide as the first two. At least forty men loaded boxes into about fifteen refrigerated trucks. The sign facing the highway read AMERICAN PRODUCE DISTRIBUTORS, INC., F. CORONADO, PRES.

It was almost six o'clock. Chuy parked his car among a long row of cars across the highway from the warehouse. He didn't really have a reason, didn't know what he was going to do, but he felt defeated. He had failed to trace the truck to anyone real. And now, suddenly, the pent-up frustrations of the last two weeks had caught up with him. He wanted to do something, virtually anything, to get Magdalena back, to get Juanito Coronado out of the picture. He sat stiffly behind the wheel of the car and pondered what to do.

Two men walked down the steps of the warehouse loading dock. They were dressed differently than the workmen on the dock. These two were wearing light colored slacks and what looked like silk shirts. As they walked toward the cars parked beside the highway, Chuy recognized Juanito Coronado. He had been pointed out to Chuy two or three times in bars. "There's the richest Mexican in Arizona," they would say. "All he does is drink and fuck." And then they would wink and shake their heads at their own poor fortune, that they didn't have rich fathers and weren't able to lead such a life of luxurious dissipation.

Chuy slid down in the seat. The two men went to a black Cadillac convertible, with the top down, parked at the end of the row. They pulled out on the highway and drove toward Mexico. Juanito was driving. Chuy pulled out, two hundred yards behind, and followed.

Coronado drove his car slowly through the border station and waved to the Mexican guard. Chuy followed a long distance behind. He entered Mexico again. There were almost no cars on the road. The Cadillac turned right on Canal Street. A mile down the street was a cluster of bars, the Nogales whorehouse district. Coronado parked his car in front of the largest of the bars, with a garish green neon sign over the entrance, WAIKIKI BALLROOM, and a yellow neon outline of a palm tree hanging next to the sign. Dozens of men were on the front porches of the whorehouses, milling about with drinks in their hands. Some of them were Mexicans, saluting the end of the work week. Many were Americans, University of Arizona boys and older high school boys from Tucson. Just a couple of miles away, you couldn't drink legally until you were twenty-one, and it was almost impossible to find a girl to do what these girls would, and these didn't want you to marry them, and they didn't charge more than a dollar. Mecca.

Chuy parked in front of the B-29 Club, across the street from the Waikiki. He watched Juanito and the other man walk into the whorehouse. If he followed them, would either of them know who he was? He doubted it. There was no reason for anyone to have pointed him out to Juanito Coronado.

Chuy got out of his car and walked across the street to the Waikiki. It was not yet dark, hardly six o'clock, and already at least fifty men and women were inside sitting at the small bar tables surrounding a large dance floor. In the middle was a trio of musicians, two guitarists and a trumpeter, playing raucous Mexican songs.

Juanito Coronado and the other man were sitting in one of the eight booths against the south wall of the room. It had ceiling-to-floor draw curtains, open now. One of the bar girls walked up to the table and greeted them both like old friends. She was wearing a tight black elasticized skirt so short that the nude bottoms of her buttocks were uncovered. Her blouse was a well-filled black velvet halter top. Another girl came to the table and sat next to Juanito. She was a very slender bleached blonde and young, no more than seventeen or eighteen. She wore only a gaily colored scarf tied around her breasts and the same kind of skimpy black skirt covering a six-inch band of flesh below her navel and above her pubic hair.

Juanito unzipped his trousers. The girl beside him put her hands on his lap, then leaned over and sucked on him until he came. When he ejaculated, he threw his hands into the air and snapped his fingers and hooted like a mariachi, then loudly sang, *"Cu cu ru cu cu, paloma-a, ai, yai, yai, cu cu ru cu cu-uh, palo-o-ma-a."* The whore standing by the table clapped her hands and laughed delightedly, as did the man sitting across the booth and several other patrons at nearby tables.

Chuy had many times been in bars such as this, not only in Nogales but also in the Philippines and Okinawa. This was fairly mild entertainment for such places, and you really couldn't see anything the girl was doing, just her head bobbing in Juanito's lap.

Now the girl standing beside the table climbed onto it, knelt on her hands and knees, and pointed her behind to the man across from Juanito. The man was about twenty or so, thin and fair-haired. He busied himself with the girl squatting on the table, sucking avidly between her legs. This was a much more visible performance than the first, and when the girl groaned and squirmed, it elicited clapping and cheering from much of the crowd.

A woman of twenty-five or -six walked into the middle of the ballroom floor. She was voluptuous and dark, probably a Yaqui Indian, leading a donkey by a six-foot hackamore rein. The only thing she wore were gold lamé spike heels and a silver crucifix around her neck. The musicians played a fanfare for her, and a spotlight shone on her and the donkey.

A man hooted, "Yai, yai, yai, yai," jumped up from a small table by the dance floor, and started dancing in front of the girl and the donkey. A mock flamenco dance by a drunk vaquero. It was Chuy's brother, Solomon. Chuy swallowed and stared, sickened by the sight. Two bouncers took Solomon by the arms and set him back in his chair at the table. He hooted again but didn't leave the chair.

Solomon had been back on the Leyva ranch on the Big Reservation in San Miguel for a year now, working cattle as he had done for many years before he went into the army in 1941. In the army he had spent over three years at various fronts, and after that a year in Phoenix trying to find a job. The Leyva family ranch had enough cattle to provide a good living for Chuy's mother and two younger sisters, so Solomon had left Phoenix a year ago and returned to the ranch, embittered by his failure in the white man's world. Chuy's mother had told Chuy that she was worried about her eldest son, that he drank too much, that he was gone to Nogales almost every weekend, drinking and whoring, that he had become taciturn and moody.

Chuy wanted to run to him, to pull him out of this place and sober him up. But he couldn't. He couldn't make a scene here. He couldn't risk being recognized by anyone. He would probably end up in the bottom of an irrigation ditch. So he got up from the table and left the Waikiki Ballroom.

He drove back through the border, wasn't hassled by the border patrolman, and angrily pushed the car to sixty miles per hour on the road to Tucson. At Sahuarita, about twenty miles south of Tucson, he passed a sign suspended between two poles thirty feet apart, over a gateless ranch entrance. RANCHO CIELITO LINDO in huge letters, and below that, in much smaller letters, FILBERTO CORONADO Y FAMILIA.

He was filled with frustration, smarting at the wasted hours in Nogales, at the dead end in identifying the lessee of the truck. And mostly he was depressed and sickened by seeing his brother Solomon that way. He slowed the car as he passed the ranch and stopped on the highway shoulder. He backed up slowly in the gathering darkness. It was almost seven-thirty. He swung the car around and drove slowly over the clattering cattle grating.

What the hell am I doing? he thought. This is the way a dumb Indian gets his brains blown out. Trespassing on a ranch, in the dark, nobody knows where I am. Nobody will ever find my body, just the vultures and the Gila monsters.

He breathed deeply, trying to push away the pain and pointlessness of the day. He stopped the car, turned it around, and drove back to his small house on the San Xavier Reservation. He sat in the kitchen, drank four beers, and listened to *The Fat Man, This Is Your FBI, Break the Bank,* and *The Adventures of Ozzie and Harriet.* He became increasingly restive and annoyed with himself for letting Juanito steal his girl. Flushed with the bravado provided by the beer, he drove over to the Rabb house to see Magdalena.

She and Hanna were sitting on the porch steps, in

the puddle of illumination provided by the dim yellow bug light.

"Hi, Chuy," Hanna said as he walked to the steps. "Time for me to go to bed." It was only a little after ten on a Friday night, but neither Chuy nor Magdalena urged her to stay.

"You're not going to slam the door in my face?" Chuy said to Magdalena.

"Have you been drinking?"

He softened his voice, not wanting Magdalena to go inside. He sat on the steps, not too close to her. "Just a few beers. I promise I'll be a good boy."

"That'll be something new."

"You should talk, going out with that Mexican jackass."

"I don't let him touch me," she said quietly. "Not like you and Lupe."

"You really don't let him touch you?"

She looked hard at him. "Of course not."

He moved closer to her on the step, two feet from her. "I'm sorry, Magda. I've never been more sorry about anything in my life. I got drunk, it just happened."

"What if it *just happened* with me? How would you feel then?"

"That's different."

"Why's it different?"

"You're a woman."

"Come on, Chuy! You're talking like our fathers and grandfathers. One way for the girls, one way for the boys. It just doesn't work that way anymore. This is 1947, not 1927. If you expect me to be faithful to you, I expect the same."

He leaned over and kissed her on the cheek. She didn't recoil. He slid next to her. "I'll never touch another girl in my whole life, I swear it."

She turned to him and kissed him, lightly at first, then harder. Their breathing was fast, aroused. He held her tightly, then caressed both her breasts softly with his hands. She was wearing a T-shirt. She didn't stop him.

"I want to marry you," he whispered.

She pulled back from him a little, enough to scrutinize his face. She put her hands over his on her breasts and pressed them to her. "Is that just booze talking?"

"No. I love you. I want you to marry me. I can't go through another two weeks like the last two."

They kissed hard and wrapped their arms around each other. "Come back to my house," he whispered in her ear.

She stiffened a little, then pulled away from him. "Not tonight. Joshua would like you to come to dinner tomorrow night. If you still feel the same way, tell Joshua you want to marry me.

He looked at her soberly. "What time is dinner?"

"Six."

"I'll be here."

She smiled and nodded.

"You sure you want to let me go home and waste this?" He put her hand on his erection.

She rubbed it through his Levi's, then pulled her hand away. "There's more where that came from, I hope."

"Me too," he said. They kissed again and held each other closely.

They were sitting on the porch an hour later, holding hands, when Joshua parked his Chevrolet convertible next to Magdalena's roadster in front of the house. He got out of the car and called out, "Well, I see you two are back like you ought to be. It's about time."

He walked up to the porch steps and sat on the lower one, below Chuy and Magdalena.

"You look like you've been rolled," Chuy said.

Joshua stared at him, then looked at himself. His shirt was part in, part out of his trousers. His left sleeve wasn't pinned up as it would normally have been if he weren't wearing his arm. It was simply dangling. He had one sock on, one sock off. His hair hung down on his forehead.

"Oh, sorry," he said, a bit sheepish. "I didn't expect to run into anyone. I've been out with Barbara."

"Did you have a nice time?" Magdalena asked.

"Apparently," Chuy said and laughed.

Joshua grinned, a little uncomfortably. "I asked Barbara to come to dinner tomorrow night," he said to Magdalena. "Is that all right?"

"Yes, sure. Chuy's also coming." She looked coyly at Joshua, and he smiled.

"By the way," Joshua said, turning to Chuy, "you turn up anything in Nogales?"

He shook his head. "Dead end, like we figured. I got the address for the truck lessee, but it was phony, an empty lot."

"Got any ideas?"

"Yeah, one," Chuy answered. "I'm going to talk to Juanito Coronado. His old man runs the biggest trucking business down at the border. He might know something."

"Great. Well, time for beddy-bye," Joshua said. He got up off the porch step and went into the house.

▲✛▽✛▽✛▲

Hanna took the bus to the Owl Drug near Tucson High School at a little after one o'clock Saturday afternoon, as she had told Bobby Bonanno she would. She had her bathing suit rolled tightly in her purse, hoping that they would end up at the swimming pool at the dude ranch where Alfredo was staying. Hanna's friend Tracy Stiller was at the Owl Drug. She was also a cheerleader like Hanna. Jean Borland, one of the pom-pom girls, was there too. Hanna asked the girls if they knew Cindy Danson. Tracy said that she did, that Cindy had graduated a year ago, and that she and her mother had left town. Where? Tracy didn't know, but she'd ask around.

Jean's boyfriend, Doug Marks, drove up in his jalopy. A few minutes later, Buddy Lansky came in. He sat down beside Hanna at the counter and ordered a hot fudge sundae.

"I don't know where Bobby is," he said to Hanna. "I banged on the front door for five minutes, but no one answered. His car was parked outside, but it looked like nobody was home." He shrugged. "He'll probably come by later."

Hanna was disappointed. They stayed at the Owl Drug until another wave of teenagers came in, needing counter space, and then they drove over to Armory Park in Buddy's car. It wasn't much fun without Bobby, and Hanna was crestfallen that he hadn't shown up. She could have sworn that he liked her. She sat glumly on a bench feeding popcorn to pigeons.

"What's wrong?" Buddy asked.

She shrugged. "Nothin'."

"Looks like somethin' to me." He sat down beside her on the bench.

"I thought Bobby was going to come," she said, staring at two squabbling pigeons.

"Yeah, I figured that was what was bothering you."

"Oh, it's not bothering me," she said quickly. "I was just wondering why he didn't come."

"Let's go over to his house and see if he's there," Buddy said.

She looked seriously at him. "Hey, we could do that, just to see if there's anything wrong."

Buddy nodded and grinned at her. "I wish you liked *me* that much."

"I do, only different," she said. She smiled at him self-consciously.

"Yeah, it's the difference that's the problem." He got up and called over to Doug Marks, standing in line with Jean and Tracy at the cotton candy wagon. "Hey Doug, Hanna and me are going over to Bobby's house. Want to come?"

"Naw, we'll stay here," Doug called back.

They drove to the Bonanno house. In front of it, parked at the curb, was a long black Cadillac limousine. Parked behind the Cadillac was a Packard. A black-uniformed man carried suitcases out of the house and put them in the trunk of the limousine.

Buddy parked down the street in front of his own house. Hanna got out of the car and started walking toward the front door of the Bonanno house. Suddenly from the backseat of the limousine, Bobby Bonanno came running toward her.

"Hanna," he called out.

He startled her, and she turned around abruptly to him. Then she smiled. "Hi, Bobby. We were waiting for you at the park."

Lorenzo Viti came running out the front door, a revolver in his hand. Joe Bonanno and Alfredo Maggadino were behind him.

"Okay, Lorenzo, it's okay," Bobby said, holding up his hand.

"You shouldn't be out here," Lorenzo said. "You *padre* told you, is dangerous."

"You are Hanna?" Joe Bonanno said, walking up to them, a look of relief on his face.

She nodded.

"You are a very pretty girl. I am sorry, Roberto must go for a while to our home in New York."

"Dad, let me talk to Hanna alone for a minute. Just a minute."

Joe Bonanno studied his wristwatch. *"Bene, un' minut'."* He turned to Hanna. "The plane will not wait." He shrugged and smiled pleasantly at her.

"My mother and sister and brother are in the car," Bobby said to her. "Let's walk down to the church."

"Alfredo, andi con mi figlio," Joe Bonanno said.

"Si, zio Giuseppe."

Alfredo winked at Bobby and followed behind him and Hanna. Buddy Lansky was standing by the driver's door of his car. Big Julie Lovello and two other men came out of the Bonanno house and surrounded the Bonanno limousine.

"God, what's happening?" Hanna asked.

"I'm sorry, Hanna. My father got a call this morning. Someone said there's a contract on him and all of the family."

"A contract?"

"Yes. Someone has been paid to kill us."

She stopped walking and stared at him in disbelief. "What? Are you kidding?"

He shook his head. "I wish I was. But my dad's got some enemies."

"But why would they hurt you? Or your mother?"

"That's the way they operate. They don't want any family left to carry on a vendetta, to get even."

"Who is it?"

"We don't know. My dad's going to try to find out." He took her arm. "Come on, I just have a few minutes. Come down to the church with me."

They walked quickly down the street and into Saints Peter and Paul Church. It was dark inside, illuminated only by a large chandelier and dozens of offertory candles. They stood in a rear corner of the nave. Alfredo stood ten feet away, his back to them, watching the entrance.

"I wish I could stay, Hanna," he whispered to her. He put his hands on her arms and stepped close to her.

"Me too," she whispered. She tilted her face up and they kissed.

"I'll come back as soon as I can," he whispered.

"Va, Roberto, va subito. El aereo," his cousin Alfredo whispered.

"I've got to go," Bobby whispered. He kissed her quickly again. "I'll call you."

They left the church and walked briskly to the limousine. Bobby got in the back. Lorenzo Viti got into the driver's seat and pulled quickly away. Joe Bonanno was surrounded now by his nephew Alfredo and the other three men. Bonanno walked up to Hanna.

"Use discretion," he said quietly, inclining his head slightly toward Buddy Lansky, standing at the front door of his house. "There is much that is puzzling with these people." He walked into his house, and the three men followed.

Hanna walked up to Buddy. "Do you know what's going on?" she asked.

He shook his head slowly, a look of fear in his eyes. "Come on in. I'm going to call my father."

"Where is he?"

"In Las Vegas, at the Flamingo. He's one of the owners.

She followed him into the house, and he went directly to the telephone on the end table by the sofa in the living room and called the Flamingo. His father wasn't in his room or the administrative offices, so he left word that he would be home by five o'clock, for his father to call him then, and hung up.

"Come on, I'll take you home," he said to Hanna. His eyes twitched nervously. "I've got to be back by five."

"Mr. Bonanno said I have to use *discretion* with your family. He said you were all *puzzling*. What's that mean?"

Buddy's face showed obvious pain. "I didn't even know that my dad was involved with those people till I read it in the papers one day. It was on the front page of the *New York Times* that my dad was tied in with the Mafia. My dad swore to me it was a lie." He looked at Hanna and his eyes were teary. "I didn't want to go back to my school, so I changed schools. Then we moved out here, and I thought it would be better. But look who we moved next to."

They walked outside to Buddy's car, got in, and drove silently to the corner of Valencia Road and Indian Agency Road.

"I better walk from here," Hanna said. "If my dad sees you, he'll have a conniption fit and lock me in my room for three years."

She walked home, mulling over whether to tell her father what had just happened outside the Bonanno house. She decided not to. If Bobby came back, she wanted to go out with him. But if her father found out about today, he'd never permit her to see him, no matter what. It was best to just keep her mouth shut. Nothing bad had happened anyway. Just talk.

▲+▽+▽+▲

Saul Blaustein answered the telephone in the motel room. "Yeah?"

"Call me five minutes," Meyer Lansky said. "Las Vegas, the Flamingo casino. A pay phone, number 73922." He hung up.

Saul and Jacob Haberman walked out of the Desert Palms Motel on Tucson's "strip," the "Miracle Mile," and walked to the gas station at the south end of the block. Saul picked up the receiver of the pay telephone, put in a nickel, and waited for the operator. Then he put in two dollars in quarters. A moment later, he heard Lansky's familiar voice.

"We gotta help Benny," Lansky said. "Frank's talking about killing him."

"What the hell we gonna do, Meyer? If the Commission wants him dead, we'll end up in the same grave if we get in the way."

"He don't want him dead, goddamn it! He just wants his million dollars. We gotta help Benny."

"How?"

"Yesterday I sent a package down to the Greyhound terminal in Tucson. It'll be there twelve o'clock noon. It's the dough for another transaction with the guys Charlie Luciano set up in Mexico. They're delivering two hundred kee's. Enough H to buy Benny's way outta this mess. We don't help him, he's finished. I told Frank we have the stuff up here tomorrow. He says okay."

"I thought you wasn't gonna get involved in this shit, Meyer."

"I thought too. But that's how it is. Benny's my best friend, over thirty years. I ain't gonna abandon him now."

"Okay, okay." When Meyer Lansky gave an order, you didn't argue, you carried it out. "Whatta we do?"

"Go down to the same place. A Jeep comes over. That's all. You get it, drive it up here."

"Look what happened to Lou and Solly."

"They got careless. Don't be careless. Go in two cars. Jake can stay behind you all the time."

"Yeah, yeah, awright. We'll make it happen. I'll call you when we got it."

He and Jake drove over to Mac's Cars on South

Sixth Avenue. They bought a 1941 Ford sedan for $500. It was a little banged up, but it ran well. They got to the bus station at about twelve-thirty and picked up the small package. Inside was $75,000 in hundred-dollar bills. They drove to the Ajo Highway, staying about a hundred yards apart on the deserted road, which went from south-central Tucson to Three Points, then through the entire Big Reservation and its capital, Sells, to the copper-mining city of Ajo, ninety miles west of Tucson. They turned south on the dirt road from Sells, leading to the Mexican border, and an hour later, Saul drove up to the border gate, backtracked down the road exactly a mile, and waited. Jake pulled the Ford sedan off the road into the desert and parked it behind a mesquite-covered knoll. He took a short-barreled .30-caliber carbine out of a hard rectangular case, screwed a telescopic sight onto it, and walked up the knoll. He knelt behind a thick mesquite trunk and pointed the rifle at Saul's car, adjusting the sight until the car, fifty yards away, was perfectly clear.

It was a boiling hot day. A ferocious sun burned down through a pellucid powder blue sky. When you looked around the desert on a day like this, Jake thought, it appeared that everything was still, dead. But close to the ground, by a mesquite tree, kneeling on a smooth, flat stone, the desert teemed with life. Tiny little bugs ran up and down the rough, scaly bark of the tree. Ants crawled around on the ground, big red ants, carrying food in their jaws and crawling down several holes surrounded by symmetrical mounds of fresh, moist dirt. A gopher stood twenty feet away, staring in his direction, sniffing the wind. Mosquitoes buzzed around close to Jake's head. A hawk was circling in the sky above, and suddenly it swept to the ground and swooped immediately upward again, screeching harshly.

You didn't see this kind of stuff in Brooklyn, but then again, maybe you never really looked. Williamsburg and Bed-Stuy weren't exactly the kinds of places that made a nature lover out of you.

He saw an old army Jeep drive slowly toward Saul's car. The Mexican delivering the shit. It crept up to the brown Chevy and stopped. Jake looked behind him down the long dirt road. No one, no cars, not even a puff of dust for miles. So far, so good. No troubles like what happened last week.

A shot rang out, shattering the desert peace. He jerked his head toward the sound. The man from the jeep pulled Saul out of the car and laid his body on the ground. He pulled Saul's shoes off, tied the shoelaces together, and slung them over his shoulder.

"What the—," Jake muttered under his breath. He sighted his rifle on the man and pulled the trigger gently. The man flew backward and sprawled on the ground. Jake ran down the knoll, got into the Ford, and drove up behind the brown Chevy.

Saul was dead, shot in the left temple. Jake immediately recognized the man from the Jeep. He wasn't a Mexican. He was an Italian killer named Spinelli, Martin or Marvin or something, yeah, that's it, "Mad Marvin" they called him because he was crazy like Mad Dog Coll, the legendary Mafia hitman whom they all modeled themselves after. For a dollar he'd kill anybody, no questions asked.

Jesus Christ! What the hell was going on? Mad Marvin worked for the Commission. Jake was sure of it. He had heard that Marvin was big in Murder Incorporated, always hanging out with Albert Anastasia, that they were close friends. What was he doing killing Saul in podunk Arizona?

He walked over to the jeep, but there was no heroin inside. He went back to the brown Chevy and got the package of money. He'd leave Saul and the Chevy. Neither of them could be identified. Saul wore clothes with no labels. The car engine serial number had been filed off two weeks ago, before they left Brooklyn. But he couldn't leave the Ford. They had just bought it in Tucson, and Jake had had to show his driver's license to the salesman for the bill of sale.

He took a rock and crushed the face of Mad Marvin. Let him go to hell looking like the pile of shit he really was. Then he drove rapidly up the dirt road toward Sells, raising immense billows of dust on the baked and rutted ground.

▲✦▽✦▽✦▲

"He did what?" Meyer Lansky asked.

"He took his shoes off and slung them over his shoulder."

"Maybe he liked the shoes. Were they alligator, what?"

"No, Meyer, just those black wingtips he always wore, must've been two years old, all run down at the heels."

"Your three minutes are up," the operator said. "Please deposit one dollar and thirty cents for the next three minutes."

Jake put the coins into the pay phone.

Meyer's heart was beating hard, banging against his chest wall. It could be just a coincidence. Mad Marvin was as crazy as they came. But what if it wasn't? Oh my God, oh my God. "Do you know whether Solly or Lou had their shoes taken off?"

Jake thought for a minute. "I don't know. Why? You think it was Mad Marvin shot them?"

"No, but I once heard a guy talking about taking off the shoes."

"Who?"

"Listen, Jake, you go where nobody knows you. I mean, nobody. Then call me. We got a big, big problem."

For the first time in his life Jake heard fear in Meyer Lansky's voice. "You think Bonanno? Meyer, you think it's Joe Bonanno?"

"Call me ten sharp tomorrow morning, Tucson, 43792." Lansky hung up.

▲✦▽✦▽✦▲

Joshua was sitting on the couch reading *Siddhartha*. Adam was on the floor in his usual position in front of the radio. The telephone rang on the lamp table next to the sofa. Joshua hadn't yet become comfortable with a telephone interrupting him at home. It annoyed him. He picked up the receiver.

"Hello."

"Joshua?"

"Speaking."

"This is Meyer Lansky."

"You don't know what a pleasure it is for me to hear your voice."

"Yer a cute guy."

Joshua chuckled politely.

"I got a question for you. It's a serious question."

"I never thought there was much about you that was anything but serious."

"It's about Solly Grushin."

Joshua stiffened. "Yeah, that's pretty serious."

"You saw the body?"

"I was at the autopsy."

"Was he wearing shoes?"

Joshua sat thinking for a moment. "He had socks on. They didn't find his shoes."

Turbid silence hung heavy on the telephone line.

"*Gott in himmel* [God in heaven]," Meyer said. "*Mir hobben a veltkrieg* [we have a world war]." His voice was sepulchral.

"*Vuss gibt mit dir, Meyer* [What's up with you]?" Joshua had never before heard such evident fear in anyone's voice. "*Vuss iz gevayn* [What happened]?"

Joshua heard Lansky breathing deeply, composing himself. After a moment he said, "*Es iz gevayn a mol a lange* [once upon a time]. My mother used to start her stories like that. She'd read me fairy tales, you know, 'Once upon a time there lived a handsome prince and a beautiful milkmaid.' *Vay iz mir. Es vur a bessere tzeit* [It was a better time]." He hung up the phone.

Joshua stared at the receiver, buzzing now with the dial tone.

"Was that Grandma?" Adam asked.

"Why?"

"You always talk Jewish with Grandma."

"No, just a client," Joshua said slowly, hanging up the receiver. "Just a client."

▲+▼+▼+▲

Hanna got home at a little before five o'clock. Magdalena had two chickens roasting in the oven and a large pot of asparagus simmering on the stove. Hanna peeled a sack of potatoes, and then she set the kitchen table, even covering it with the white tablecloth that Magdalena had washed and ironed.

Joshua and Adam were in the living room. Adam was listening to the radio. His father was reading *Siddhartha* again. Herman Hesse had won the Nobel prize for peace last year, and *Siddhartha* was his best-known work. It hadn't been translated into English yet, so Joshua was reading it in German. His father had been a high school German teacher in Brooklyn for thirty years, and Joshua had been reared speaking German and Yiddish as well as English at home.

Siddhartha was magnificent prose, lofty, lyrical. Joshua was completely absorbed in it.

"Dad, you been thinking about a TV set?" Adam said.

"Huh?"

"You know, we were talking about a TV set."

"Oh, yeah. Well, I haven't had a chance to think about it." He returned to his book.

Minutes later. "Chris's dad said they were getting one."

"One what?"

"You know, a TV set."

"Oh, that's nice. You can watch his."

Adam ignored the brush-off. He pulled a crumpled piece of paper out of his pants pocket and read, "It's an RCA model 630TS. Chris's dad wrote it down for me." He held up the piece of paper for his father to see. "He said it's a real good one. It has a ten-inch picture, and it only costs $350."

"Only?" Joshua said.

"Yeah, he said most of the others cost a lot more, so $350 isn't much."

"What's Chris's father do, print money?"

"Naw, he's a superintendent down at the mines."

"Well, then he can afford it a lot better than I can. Lawyers don't make much money." He got up from the couch. "I'd better put on my arm." He walked into his bedroom and closed the door. He had put the thousand dollars into his savings account at the Bank of Douglas yesterday. That way it wouldn't burn a hole in his pocket. Anyway, he had figured it out and decided that a TV set wasn't worth the money. He had looked at them at Goldberg's Department Store, and the RCA for $350 was touted by the salesman as the best for less. But it wasn't even as good as going to a movie, if you really wanted entertainment. A movie cost twenty-five cents. If he and Hanna and Adam went to a movie every Sunday, they could go for nine full years for the three hundred fifty bucks. Spending it on a TV set would be a waste.

Joshua sat on his bed for a half hour, escaping from Adam, reading *Siddhartha*. Then he strapped on his arm and changed into a long-sleeve dark blue cowboy shirt, freshly laundered Levis, and his tan loafers. As he went into the living room and sat on the sofa, Magdalena emerged from the bathroom. She looked like a dusky oriental princess, black almond eyes slightly slanted, high cheekbones and a strong chin, and sparkling ebony hair pulled back in a single thick braid that reached halfway down her back. She had a lovely figure, tall and slender, and she was wearing a pale pink sundress that showed it off enticingly.

"Chuy's a lucky man," Joshua said.

Magdalena looked at him and smiled. She walked over to the couch and kissed him on the cheek. "Thanks. I hope last night wasn't just beer talk."

"It wasn't. He'll be down on his knees as soon as he sees you."

She giggled brightly and went into her and Hanna's bedroom.

A car drove up and parked in front of the house.

Adam ran to the front window to see who it was. "Mrs. Dubin," he announced.

"Miss," Joshua said.

Adam opened the door for her, and she came into the living room. She was breathtaking, a true fashion model's face and figure. Joshua stood up, feeling a little awkward and self-conscious, wondering again for a fleeting instant what a twenty-five-year-old beauty like this found so attractive about a thirty-eight-year-old gimp like him. And then, like always, he suffered a twinge of guilt, thinking of his children's mother. But when Barbara came to him and took his hand and stood on tiptoes and kissed him briefly on the lips and looked deeply into his eyes, every thought fled.

Chuy arrived just moments later, dressed smartly in a silver-belly felt Stetson and a plaid cowboy shirt and Levis and a new pair of tan calfskin boots. Like all Papagos, he felt that it was insulting to the host to remove his hat indoors, like taking off your shoes and displaying smelly socks, so he sat at the dinner table wearing his hat.

Hanna, though much younger than the other women at the table, looked almost as old. This wasn't her night, and she was troubled over what had happened this afternoon at the Bonanno house, so she had her soft brown hair in two pigtails and was wearing a simple white shirtdress.

"I feel like I'm sitting in the casting room for an MGM movie," Joshua said, looking around at the three women. "All of you are wasted here in the desert."

Hanna giggled. Magdalena smiled. Barbara said, "You have the slickest line of bullshit I've ever heard."

All of them laughed.

The telephone rang. Adam jumped up from the table and ran into the living room to answer it. It was still a new and exotic toy. He came back into the kitchen a moment later.

"It's for you, Dad."

Joshua looked up, annoyed. "Damn telephone is a

nuisance. I liked it better when nobody could bother us at home." He got up and went into the living room. After a few minutes, he returned to the table but didn't sit down.

"That was Edgar Hendly. Roy Collins called him from Three Points. Pablo Arguello found two more dead men on the Big Reservation near the same place as the others, Vamori Wash." He looked grimly at Chuy. "Edgar wants you and me to pick him up and drive out there right now. Chief Romero is with Collins. He's called a tribal council meeting for nine o'clock tonight in Sells, and he wants us there. We'll stay overnight at the BIA office there."

Chuy grimaced and threw his napkin down on his dinner plate. "I'm sorry, honey," he said, turning to Magdalena.

She nodded, looking sadly at him. He got up from the table and waited while Joshua put some clothing and his Dopp kit in a small overnight bag. Joshua came out of the bedroom.

"Now, you both are staying home tonight, right?" he said, looking from Adam to Hanna.

"Yes, Daddy," Hanna said.

Adam nodded.

"Good. I don't want to have to worry about you. It'll take us a couple of hours to get to Sells, and I'll call you when I get to the BIA." He looked at Chuy. "Did they fix the telephone wire yet?"

Chuy shrugged.

"Well, I'll call if I can," Joshua said. "Anyway, I'll be back by ten o'clock tomorrow morning at the latest, and I'll see both of you then, right?"

Hanna and Adam nodded.

"Don't worry, Joshua," Magdalena said. "I'll be here with them all the time."

Joshua and Chuy walked out the front door and got into Chuy's BIA pickup truck.

Barbara and Magdalena stood on the porch and watched them drive away. "Get a load of that," Barbara said. "He'd rather be with a dead body than my body. And a man to boot. Doesn't say much for me, does it?" She chuckled maliciously.

"Doesn't say much for him," Magdalena said. They both laughed.

▲✦▽✦▽✦▲

Chuy picked up Edgar, standing by the road in front of the BIA, holding a small carpet bag.

"Chief Romero's fit to be tied," Edgar said. "He says between the Jews and the Eyetalians, cain't no Indin do a honest day's work smugglin' heroin."

Joshua looked askance at him.

Edgar laughed. "Just kiddin', just kiddin'. But this shit's really gettin' bad. Eight people dead in one *gott damn* week. It's the Third World War out there on the res." He grimaced, no more laughter in his voice.

They drove west on Ajo Highway. The culvert at Coyote Creek had finally been repaired, so the trip was faster than it had been for the last couple of years. But the telephone pole that had been repaired just a short while ago, Joshua thought, was down again, and the two lines had snapped. He'd get it repaired as soon as they got back. It annoyed him to be cut off from his family like this, but then again, the last time he had come out here they hadn't even had a telephone, so they would have been cut off with or without the lines being repaired. Don't let yourself become addicted to newfangled gadgets, he chided himself. Be self-reliant.

They got to Sells at eight-thirty. The entire town was just two blocks long, consisting mostly of adobe and tin and tar-paper shacks. There was a wood plank sidewalk on the side of the street where the BIA office was, because when it rained, the street became viscous with mud. The BIA office was a small redbrick building with a sign painted on the front window that read FEDERAL GOVERNMENT: BIA, OLM, IHS.

Roy Collins was parked in front of it. It was dark, and there were no streetlights and very few lights from the other buildings. Edgar unlocked the front door and switched on the fluorescent ceiling tubes. They brightened slowly. In the small anteroom, it was at least ninety-five degrees.

"Lemme turn on the cooler, get some air stirred up in here," Edgar said.

The three men followed him into the large office, and Edgar switched on two wall switches. The evaporative cooler began clattering and blew hot air from the vents.

"Take it a minute to soak the pads," Edgar said. "Then it'll get cooler."

All of the men's shirts were moist with perspiration. They stood still in front of the vents, trying to dry off.

"I got the bodies over at the icehouse behind Sam's Cafe," Roy Collins said.

"Bad enough ole Sam serves dog and cat meat in his tacos," Edgar drawled. "Now yer *really* gonna have to be careful."

They all exploded with laughter. They stood still and silent for another five minutes while the cool air blew on them.

Refreshed, Chuy said, "Better go have a look."

They walked down the rough wooden plank sidewalk a half block to Sam's Cafe. They went down the alley beside it into the wooden shack where Sam stored his perishable foods. It was cold inside. Roy pulled a bead chain, and an overhead bulb lit up the shack dimly. There were large blocks of ice stacked against the wall, and in front of them were crates of tomatoes and lettuce. The melt off the ice seeped into the dirt floor, and it was muddy mush. Roy opened the door of the large steel freezer box. Two sides of beef hung from hooks. A three-hundred-pound hog lay frozen next to two bodies, one atop the other on the narrow floor.

"Pablo found them when he was driving his goats this afternoon," Roy said. "They'd been dragged off the road about fifty yards into the desert. There was a brown Chevy with no serial number and no plates. There was a U.S. Army Jeep with no plates. The stars were painted over on the doors. This guy"—he pointed at the one on top—"had no shoes on. They were tied together on the ground by the Chevy. He's got a hole in his temple surrounded by burns. The other guy's got a clean hole square in the middle of his chest. Guy on top is circumcised. Other guy's got a foreskin longer than Edgar's dick."

"How d'ya know 'bout my dick?" Edgar said. "Ya been talkin' to the girls down at the Catalina Hotel?"

Roy chuckled. He turned to Joshua. "Looks like the same as the others," he said. "One Jewish guy, one not. I think we got a full-blown Mafia war going on here right in the middle of the res."

Joshua nodded. "I guess it's time to talk seriously to Mr. Bonanno."

"Yeah, and that guy you represent, Meyer Lansky," Roy said. "I talked to the Bureau chief in New York City. He says Lansky's real cagey and publicity-shy, but they think he's as big as Lucky Luciano used to be, even more powerful than Joe Bonanno."

Joshua nodded and frowned. That meant that whoever or whatever Meyer was afraid of had to be very dangerous. And here was another dead Jew with no shoes on his feet. Just like the first shooting, and precisely what Meyer had asked him about when he had called earlier in the day.

"I'll get a couple of bags and wrap these guys up," Chuy said. "We'll have to leave them here till tomorrow morning when we go back."

"Yeah, I'll help you," Roy said. They left the icehouse, and Edgar and Joshua walked up the sidewalk to the Papago Tribal Council Headquarters, a small wooden building. Inside, by a long, chipped Formica-topped table, surrounded by folding metal chairs, stood eight Indians. Chief Francisco Romero was in the middle of the men. He was an old man with pure white hair like ermine fur spilling about his shoulders. He had glistening black eyes and sweat-shiny deep brown leathery skin. He was short and gaunt, dressed like all the others in a plaid cowboy shirt, Levi's, and scuffed, dusty cowboy boots.

He smiled broadly at Joshua. "It's good to see you again, my friend," he said, holding his hand out.

Joshua shook it. "How've you been, Francisco? I heard you were sick."

"Yeah, yeah. Nothing serious, just pneumonia. But everything better now."

"Good," Joshua said.

"You know other council members," the chief said.

Joshua nodded to them, and they nodded back, stiff and wary.

Edgar shook hands with Romero. "Nice to see ya again, Chief. Sorry it has to be under these circumstances. Any a the other boys comin'?"

Romero shook his head. "Couldn't get here on this short notice. Too far away for them. But we got quorum."

Edgar rolled his eyes and turned to Joshua. "Don't ya just love it when he uses them big official-type words?"

"Ignore him, Francisco," Joshua said. "He just saw a couple of dead men, and he's not thinking too clearly."

Romero snorted. "Yeah, I hear one of them has a cock on him longer than Edgar's leg."

Edgar laughed. Joshua grinned at the chief.

The men sat down at the long table. Levity disappeared from the chief's face.

"What in hell going on down here?" Romero asked, looking from Joshua to Edgar. "White men shooting each other. Two of our own murdered last week." He squinted at Edgar.

"Well," Edgar said, "we think your two boys didn't like the white guys hornin' in on the heroin trade. And we think there's some kind of turf war goin' on to control the smugglin'. But we ain't got a handle on it yet. Roy Collins and Chuy Leyva's workin' on it day 'n' night."

Romero scowled. "We don't want read in papers about our people involved in narcotics. Not good for us. We got enough prejudice."

"I know that, Chief. We're doin' what we can to

keep a lid on it. We don't want any trouble for your people either." Edgar's voice and expression were sincere.

Romero nodded and his face relaxed.

"I talked to Harry Coyle in Washington yesterday," Edgar continued. "He says about the only way to get control over the situation is to fence the whole damn border and put a border-crossin' station down there by Newfield where all this shit's happenin'. But we ain't got the money for it. It'd have to be appropriated by Congress and prob'ly take a year, year 'n' a half, before it ever even got off the ground."

Francisco's face soured. "We don't want fence." He looked around at the other Indians, and they stared sternly at Edgar. "Our people live here and in Sonora long before there is border, long before there is United States. We no want fence."

"We know that, Francisco. But how the hell else can we get a handle on this thing?"

"We think is best idea we set up our own patrol, maybe twenty of our boys with guns, patrol the border down by Newfield."

Edgar's jaw tightened, and he shook his head slowly. "Uh-uh, Chief. I cain't be havin' none a that. You think the press'll be bad if there's stories about Indins smugglin' dope, whattaya think it'll look like if the Indins get into a *gott damn* war with Jews 'n' Eyetalians? J. T. Sellner'll have it on the front page of every newspaper in the country. She'd love it." He scowled at Romero. "I think you'd best let us handle it."

"Well, maybe I not be able to control it. We got plenty young men think the government is bunch of crooks, does nothing for us. They think we have right to protect our own nation."

Edgar pursed his lips and swallowed back his bile. "Now listen, Francisco," he said, his voice low and angry. "You better kick ass and take names with them young bucks who wanna have a little shootin' match with the white boys. It ain't gonna happen and me sit back and let it. I damn well guarantee ya we're gonna take care of this problem and take care of it fast." He shook his finger at Romero for emphasis. "Just let us handle it."

"Then do it, Mr. Superintendent," Chief Romero growled. "More of this shit happens, *we* take care of it." He stood up abruptly and stared hostilely at Edgar.

Edgar stood up slowly, as did Joshua.

"Nice meetin' with you boys," Edgar drawled. He walked out of the building.

Joshua shook hands with the chief. "We'll do our best," he said. "You have my word on it."

Romero nodded, his face receptive, his eyes no longer wary.

CHAPTER ELEVEN

Meyer Lansky stood in front of the pay phone inside the Southern Pacific railroad depot in Tucson. It was ten o'clock Sunday morning, and he had just gotten back to Tucson from Las Vegas an hour ago. He had immediately telephoned Buddy and told him to come downtown at eleven-thirty, to meet him at the Cattleman's Hotel Restaurant. It was the most crowded restaurant in town, day or night. Then he went straight from the train station to the Hotel Geronimo, a small, out-of-the-way hotel on Pennington Street, and rented a room. He walked back to the railroad station and got to the pay phones at 9:54, stood in front of the one with the number 43792, and waited for Jake's call. It rang at 10:02.

"Meyer?"

"Where you at?"

"South Tucson, little dive down by the fairgrounds."

"Meet me at the Cattleman's Hotel Restaurant as soon as you can. I'll walk over there now."

Meyer hung up and walked the three blocks to Tucson's finest hotel, the Cattleman's. It was a white-plastered skyscraper six stories high, Tucson's tallest building except for the Valley National Bank a block south of it. Meyer was dressed not to be noticed, a short-sleeve pale yellow sports shirt, tan linen slacks, brown brogans. He sat down at a booth in the rear of the restaurant and ordered toast and coffee. He studied the other patrons and decided that he hadn't been followed. He hadn't told any of his Flamingo partners that he was coming back to Tucson. And if the FBI or his back East pals had bugged his home telephone, they would be expecting him here at eleven-thirty, not at ten-thirty. He sat drinking coffee for ten minutes.

Jake Haberman walked into the restaurant. He was dressed in a dull gray suit, a white shirt and blue and white polka-dotted tie, and dusty wingtips, just an average Tucson businessman. He sat down and nodded at Meyer. The waitress came to the table, and he ordered coffee.

"I think I know what's going on," Meyer said, his voice just above a whisper.

Jake's face was stolid. He leaned over the table toward Lansky, listening closely.

"It's Costello."

Jake furrowed his brow and squinted, then looked skeptical. "Frank?"

Meyer nodded.

"Why?"

"He don't want Benny to pay him back. He don't want Benny to get the H and pay off enough dough to keep the Commission happy."

"Why not?"

"He takes Benny's twelve and a half percent if Benny don't make the payments. Frank figures like I do, that with good management, in a couple years Benny's piece is worth ten times, twenty times, the three million bucks. But Frank thinks that for that to happen, Benny's got to be cut out of it. He's ruining it."

Jake gritted his teeth, his eyes muddy with fear.

"Vinnie and Tomasso were Albert Anastasia's boys," Meyer continued. "That means they really worked for Frank. So what were they doing down at the border by Newfield?" He stared at Jake. Jake shrugged.

"They was there to make sure you and Saul didn't get the heroin," Meyer said, "just like they done with Solly and Lou. That's why Mad Marvin was there too."

"You mean Costello sent them out here to *keep us* from bringing the H up to Benny? That's ridiculous. You're saying Frank Costello planned the whole thing?"

"Exactly. It's perfect. Nobody thinks Frank is involved, Benny misses the deadline, Frank takes Benny's piece of the casino, and the Commission sends Benny to never-never land."

Jake thought for a minute. "Why would a couple greasers whack Vinnie and Tomasso?"

"Probably just part of Frank's plan, how to fuck up everybody's mind, make everybody think there's a three-way turf war going on down there. Jews, wops, greasers, then nobody can point the finger at Frank. Everybody thinks the Jews are killing the wops and the greasers are killing everybody."

"You really sure? How did you figure this?"

"The shoes."

"What shoes?"

"Taking the shoes off. Twelve, fourteen years ago, when Frank was muscle for Charlie Luciano, he did a couple favors for Charlie. He used to joke about it. He'd take the guy's shoes off, joke that the guy'd soon be getting blisters walking on hot coals in hell."

Jake shook his head and scowled. "It just don't sound right, Meyer. Frank Costello doing all this shit just to get Benny's piece of the action? Hell, Frank's the capo. Why don't he just have Benny killed? All this other shit is too fuckin' complicated, like it's somebody else trying to make it look like Frank."

Meyer shrugged. "Well, I'll tell you what. Whoever the hell it is, it's getting too fuckin' dangerous around here."

"This I can't disagree," Jake muttered. "I don't need no more of this shit, Meyer."

He nodded, his face grim. "Yeah, me either. It's over. Poor Benny. He fucked around too much, push, push, push. I tried to call him, tell him to wise up, but he wasn't at his house, must be shacked up with that whore of his somewhere in Beverly Hills. I hope he's having a helluva time. It's gonna have to last him." He grimaced and shook his head.

"What are we going to do, Meyer?"

"We're getting outta here, back to the city. I had enough of this fuckin' place."

Jacob Haberman nodded solemnly.

"Buddy's coming here in a half hour. He'll be driving the Buick. Wait for him. Don't scare him, just tell him you're both going to pick me up at the Geronimo. Then we're driving back to New York."

"You don't even want to stop by the house, pick up some clothes?"

"Nothing. What we need, we buy. We ain't got much stuff here anyway."

"What I do with the Ford?" He pointed out the picture window of the restaurant at the car parked at the curb. "The bill of sale's in my name, my New York driver's license number is on it. I leave it out there, the cops gonna trace it."

Lansky thought for a moment. "Drive it three blocks south of here, park it on South Fourth Avenue, and leave the keys in the ignition. It'll be gone in two hours, be sold in Mexico before dark tonight. No questions asked." Meyer got up, threw a dollar on the table, and left the restaurant.

▲+▼+▼+▲

It was just after ten o'clock Sunday morning. Joshua and Roy Collins had gotten back from Sells an hour ago, dropped the bodies at the coroner's office, and driven back to Joshua's house. Hanna and Adam were lying on the floor in the living room, listening to the radio. Magdalena was in the kitchen studying, a pile of textbooks on the table.

Joshua and Roy walked out on the porch. They

were both extremely frustrated. More bodies, and they had nothing but vague suspicions about who was causing it and why.

"I'm going to call Meyer Lansky and hear what he has to say about this," Joshua said. "I'm his lawyer. I guess I have the right to talk to my client whenever I want."

Roy waited on the porch while Joshua went inside. A few minutes later, Joshua came out.

"Tried three times. Busy signal."

"Why don't we go over and talk to him? Then we can go next door and talk to Bonanno. Maybe we can squeeze something out of one of those bastards."

Joshua shrugged. "Not much else to try, is there?"

He opened the front door, told Hanna and Adam that he would be back in an hour or so, and got into his Chevy with Roy. They drove to Elm Street and parked in front of Joe Bonanno's house. They went first to Meyer Lansky's front door. Joshua knocked. A moment later Buddy Lansky opened it.

"Hi, Mr. Rabb."

"Hi, Buddy. Is your dad home?"

"No, sir. He's still in Las Vegas. I'm not expecting him back for a few days at least."

"If he calls, would you ask him to give me a ring?"

"Sure, Mr. Rabb." Buddy closed the door and leaned back against it, his heart beating wildly. His father had just called from the station and told him to meet him at the Cattleman's Hotel at eleven-thirty. He had also cautioned Buddy not to talk to anyone. Buddy was Meyer Lansky's son. He didn't have to be told twice.

Joshua and Roy walked across the lawn to Joe Bonanno's front door. Roy knocked on the door. Big Julie Lovello opened it a moment later. Big Julie had come by his name—at least—honestly. He was Joshua's height and at least fifty pounds heavier, some of it muscle, the rest of it collected around his girth in a great bloated gut. He had a dour, meaty face with bloodhound jowls and thick curly hair unnaturally black for his fifty or more years.

"Is Mr. Bonanno home?" Roy asked.

"He at mass. Sunday mornings he at mass."

"Where?"

Big Julie jutted his chin toward Saints Peter and Paul at the end of the street.

"Bene, bene, grazie," Roy said, mimicking a thick Italian accent.

They walked toward the church, and as they reached it people began coming out the front doors. Roy and Joshua waited on the corner of Elm Street, and a moment later Joe Bonanno emerged and came walking toward them, three bodyguards close around him.

Bonanno stopped in front of Collins. He was taller than the FBI agent and thinner. His graying hair was full and wavy. He was wearing an obviously expensive navy blue wool sharkskin suit, tailored beautifully, over a soft white cotton shirt and burgundy and royal blue-striped silk tie. His shoes were soft kidskin shining in the sun.

"You ain't got no respect, Mr. FBI man," Joe said gruffly. "I been in church. I ain't been kill nobody."

"There have been two more murders on the reservation, Mr. Bonanno. Another Jewish guy, we think, and one who looks like one of yours."

"He was wearing my photograph in a locket around his neck?" Bonanno drawled. "Or maybe he was wearing dog tags said he belong to me?"

The man next to him snickered. The two others stood still, unflinching.

"This is not me," Bonanno said, his voice harsh, his face losing its color. "This is not me. I told you last week. I don't do drugs. I don't permit drugs. I am a man of honor of a very old tradition, Mr. FBI man, and everybody know I ain't involved."

"Who is?" Roy asked.

"How the hell I know?" Joe asked, angry now. "Every two-bit greaser bastard in Tucson steals a battery is my fault?" He looked quizzically at Joshua. "FBI now hires men with steel hands? Times are changing."

"This is Joshua Rabb. He's the legal-affairs officer for the Papago Reservation."

Bonanno's face softened. He smiled at Joshua, appraising him openly. "My Roberto say your daughter is one in a million, Mr. Rabb."

"Bobby?"

"That's what he goes by. These children don't like Italian names."

"Yes, Hanna said he's very handsome and very nice. I'm sorry I haven't met him."

Bonanno beamed. "Well, he's back East visiting relatives now, but he come back soon."

So that's why Hanna was so compliant yesterday, Joshua thought. Bobby had already gone back East. Joshua was relieved at the news, yet at the same time more concerned about Hanna's actual state of mind.

"We've got a big problem by the Mexican border, Mr. Bonanno," Joshua said. "It has to be related to heroin smuggling. There's no other reason for white men to be getting shot down there."

"Maybe they're hunters," Bonanno said, a grin fleeting over his lips. "Maybe they forgot to wear red hats."

Joshua ignored the remark. "Mr. Bonanno, this looks like a turf war, apparently between Jews and Italians from New York. We don't accuse you of having anything to do with it, but surely you can make inquiries and see where it's coming from. I'm sure you don't like this happening in your own backyard any more than we do."

Bonanno nodded pleasantly. "You see, Lorenzo," he said, turning to the man next to him, "they think I am *importante,* they think I am somebody I ain't." Turning back to Joshua. "I tell you, Mr. Indian lawyer, I know nothing. I got no way to find out nothing. I am a businessman, I own a dairy farm in New York. *Finito.*"

"Mr. Bonanno," Joshua said, his voice harder, "I was born in Brooklyn, I lived there until June of last year, except for a few years in the army. I have read about you for fifteen years. I know who you are and what you do. And as long as you keep it in Brooklyn, we don't give a shit."

Collins nodded in agreement.

"But this war on the reservation has to stop," Joshua said, his voice now harsh.

Bonanno stared back at him. "You a tough guy, huh? I bet you are one very tough guy. Probably could rip somebody's face off with that hand, huh?" He looked at the steel prongs sticking out of the sleeve of Joshua's cowboy shirt. He turned to the man next to him. "Huh, Lorenzo, *che tu credi,* huh [what do you think]? You think he's a tough guy?"

Lorenzo was no more than thirty-five years old, shorter than Bonanno and very thin. His face was gaunt, and he was almost completely bald except for a fringe of brown hair. He stared truculently at Joshua, unblinking.

"Well, nice chatting with you gentlemen," Bonanno said. He walked past them, followed by his three bodyguards.

Joshua and Roy stared after them. "We really impressed him," Joshua said.

"Yeah," Roy said, his eyelids twitching. "For the second time. I could get real impatient."

They walked slowly back to Roy's car.

▲✦▽✦▽✦▲

Joe Bonanno walked to the Standard Oil gasoline station on Grant Road. Big Julie Lovello and Lorenzo Viti walked on either side of him. Behind them were Donatello Luna and Harve Penny, two lieutenants brought in last week from Brooklyn.

It took Bonanno almost fifteen minutes, placing calls to five different New York telephone numbers, before he finally reached Frank Costello.

"Frankie, I hear someone wants me dead," he said calmly.

There was a moment's hesitation, then, "What? What kind of bullshit is that, Joey?"

"Someone called and told Big Julie yesterday afternoon."

"It's bullshit, Joe. You getting paranoid there. Too much sun?"

"Don't give me none of that crap, Frankie. I'm telling you, it's Meyer. I never did trust them fuckin' Yids. They ain't like us, Frankie. They're scum, no loyalty. Meyer and Benny are happy as pigs in shit with this heroin business from Mexico. They must think I'm going to interfere. Now two more guys got killed out here, Saul Blaustein and Mad Marvin. I thought Marvin been working for you?" The question had just a hint of accusation.

There was silence for a moment. Then, softly, as though guarding his voice from being overheard, Costello said, "No, Joey. He used to. Then he went to work for Lansky, couple months ago." He paused to let this sink in. "I been talking to the fathers, and we think you're right. We think Meyer and Benny are off on their own. Charlie Luciano and me told them just two deals, then we see if it should become more. It's up to the Commission. But it looks like they ain't happy with that. Benny suddenly sees big bucks, wants to make it his own regular business. They're whackin' everyone who gets in their way."

Bonanno breathed deeply, suppressing his anger. "I got to put a end to it, Frankie. The FBI is at my door second time over this. They think all the bodies on the reservation is my doing. If I don't stop Meyer and Benny, I am in big trouble here. I don't want no trouble, Frankie."

Costello sat back from the telephone receiver, and the sides of his mouth curled in a smile. He coughed and forced a frown, hoping that it was reflected in his voice, hoping that it held the proper timbre of sadness and tragic inevitability.

"I tol' Benny," Frank said, "I tol' Benny, I said over and over, Benny, I said, don't shit where Padre Guiseppe eats. But, Benny, all he thinks about is money 'n' pussy, Joey, money 'n' pussy." A sigh. "Meyer couldn't talk sense to him neither. Listen,

Joey, what can I tell you, that cunt Virginia turned Benny into a pussy-whipped *pagliaccio* [clown], *pazzo* [crazy], *pazzo*. And Meyer? What can I say, I tol' Charlie Luciano a hundred times when push comes to shove, you can't trust the Jews. They ain't like us. They got no tradition. They're like fuckin' *melanzan'* from Harlem, sticking together, fuck everybody gets in their way." Deep reluctance, sadness over a friendship turned sour, the loneliness of the commander. Uneasy lies the head that wears the crown, but the painful decision must be made. "You handle it, Joey. You do what you gotta do. Nobody on the Commission raises a peep. You hear me, Padre Giuseppi?"

"Si, Padre Francesco. Grazie."

Frank Costello smiled broadly and hung up the telephone. He roared with delighted laughter and slapped both of his thighs.

▲✢▼✢▼✢▲

"This *mazzochrist'* [Christ-killer] Lansky wants me dead," Joe Bonanno whispered hoarsely. "Him and that whoremonger Bugsy Siegel. They are doing this." He looked from Lorenzo to Big Julie. They sat close together on the sofa in Bonanno's living room. The two other bodyguards stood together on the other side of the living room, out of earshot.

"We gotta stop him, Don Peppino," Lorenzo said.

"Lansky's in Vegas, I think," Joe said. "We can't get him there. And Siegel, who knows what whore's bed he's groveling in?" He thought for a moment. "We got to stop these bastards. Meyer brought in two more of his boys from Williamsburg last week. I saw them next door. Jacob somebody and the other I didn't recognize. But this Jacob is a real *animale,* a real *uccisore* [killer], one of Lepke's boys from the old days."

"Yeah, I know him," Big Julie said. "The other guy too I know. Saul Blaustein. He's Lansky's personal muscle."

"We got to put an end to this shit on the reservation," Joe growled. "It's too close."

"We go down there, have a talk to Lansky's boys, whoever he sends as mules this time," Big Julie said. "They're bound to try another run, tomorrow, the next day. Lansky and Siegel will keep trying. They want the dough."

Lorenzo snorted. "This little Indian town Newfield is looking suddenly like Grand Central Station. More New Yorkers in one week than they seen in five hundred years. There's already eight bodies down there. Two more of us show up, they gonna call out the air force to bomb our car."

Bonanno scowled and nodded. "What else can we do?"

Lorenzo shrugged.

"Maybe instead of going down to the border, you stay up in Sells at the turnoff," Joe said. "There's plenty more cars there. You'll recognize these guys. Stay back, they won't recognize you, they won't be looking, at least not in Sells. Discourage them way up north of the border."

Lorenzo nodded. *"Bene, bene."*

"Andiamo [let's go]," Big Julie said. Joe walked them to the door and watched them get in the black Dodge sedan.

They stopped for gas at the Texas Oil Company filling station on Speedway. They also picked up an Arizona map. Joe had lived in Tucson on and off for years now, so he knew southern Arizona well. But Big Julie and Lorenzo were newcomers. They both lived on the Bonanno estate on Long Island and had never been to Tucson. Here Joe wasn't supposed to need bodyguards.

Lorenzo drove west on the Ajo Highway. An hour and a half later they drove slowly through Sells. There were perhaps a half dozen cars driving around the town and twice as many trucks. They drove south on the dirt road toward Newfield for five miles, and Lorenzo parked on the side of the road in a cluster of palo verde trees. He and Big Julie both got out to stretch their legs. Lorenzo walked behind one of the trees to take a piss. He was almost done wetting down the tree trunk when the .22 slug from Big Julie's revolver entered his skull just behind and below his right ear and ricocheted around in his brain. Lorenzo dropped soundlessly, almost bloodlessly, to the ground. Big Julie undressed him and dragged his body several hundred yards into the desert and rolled it down into a deep wash. There were already three vultures circling overhead. Lorenzo would be dinner for them and the coyotes. No one would ever find anything but parched bones, if even that, in this endless wasteland.

It was well over a hundred degrees, and the wind was coming up strongly. It was two o'clock in the afternoon, and Big Julie was sweating profusely. He rolled Lorenzo's clothing in a ball and put it in a brown paper bag he had brought along in the car. Back in Tucson, he tossed the clothes into the Salvation Army bin on the Nogales Highway. He drove to a small motel a few miles out of Tucson toward Nogales and spent the night there. He didn't need any change of clothes or his shaving gear. He wasn't going to look crisp and fresh and dapper when he drove to Joe Bonanno's house and told him that he and Lorenzo had been ambushed by Saul and Jacob, and that Lorenzo had been killed.

▲✛▽✛▽✛▲

Virginia Hill wasn't with Benny Siegel at her home in Beverly Hills. She and Benny had had one of their violent arguments, and she had flown off to Chicago to spend a few days with Joe Epstein, an elderly professional gambler and a very old friend of hers, who loved Virginia's blow jobs and traded hundred-dollar bills for them.

Benny was sitting in the living room on a chintz-covered sofa reading the *Los Angeles Times* after dinner. Someone rested a .30-caliber carbine on the latticework of a rose-covered arbor outside the living room window. The first of nine shots hit Benny in the left eye, another the bridge of his nose, another shattered a vertebra in his neck. The impact of the slugs blew his right eye fifteen feet across the room.

▲♣▽♣♣♦▽♣▲

Several days later, Joe Bonanno stood at the pay phone in the gas station a few blocks from his house. Big Julie Lovello stood nearby, looking warily around. Bonanno called Frank Costello at his office in Manhattan. After a few moments of muffled conversation, he hung up the phone.

"Where's Meyer gone?" Joe Bonanno asked Big Julie.

Julie shrugged. "Ain't seen him in over a week."

"Well, I guess he's either in Vegas putting the hotel in order or in New York hiding from me."

Big Julie nodded. "Whattaya gonna do?"

"I'm going to think hard on this," Joe said. "I got to plan something very special for Meyer. Frank Costello tells me that he just confirmed that Meyer put a contract out on me, had Lorenzo killed. I loved Lorenzo like a son." Joe's eyes became moist, and he sniffed. His voice cracked with emotion. "Meyer showed very bad judgment, very bad."

Julie nodded and swallowed hard to suppress a smile.

CHAPTER TWELVE

It was Wednesday afternoon. Almost two uneventful weeks had passed. Joshua came home from work a little early, and Hanna told him that none of her friends knew where Cindy Danson had moved. Cindy's best friend had been Tina Haggerty, and Tina didn't even know. Tina had remembered that Cindy's mother had once talked about going "back East," but just where they actually went was anyone's guess.

Joshua had once again pressed Hanna about Jennifer's relationship with boys, and Hanna said that she had talked to just about half of the girls in Jenny's class, anybody that might know anything about it, and everyone thought that Jenny had been going with Jerry Hawkins, at least for the whole second semester. Jerry was working as a gas station attendant at his father's Standard Oil Station at Stone and Speedway.

Joshua was going to Barbara Dubin's house for dinner. They had been together almost every night for two weeks, meeting downtown, going out to dinner or a movie, several times making love in Joshua's car. But he hadn't been back to the Dubin house in weeks. He left early so he could stop for gas at the Standard station. The young man who pumped the gas was wearing a greasy green uniform shirt with the name patch JERRY over his left pocket. Joshua got out of the car.

"Are you Jerry Hawkins?"

He looked up, surprised. "Sure am."

"I'm Joshua Rabb, Hanna's father." He paused. "I'm defending Charlie Isaiah."

Hawkins nodded. "Yeah, I know. I heard."

"I'm sorry about what happened to Jennifer. It was awful. But I have to make sure the right guy gets convicted."

Hawkins's face was sour. "They got the right guy. That Indian Charlie Isaiah. Two years ago he asked Jenny to go out. Twice. She told him she was going with me. But I used to see the way he looked at her. Then he graduated, and I never saw him around anymore. Jenny said he was selling used cars to greasers for her old man."

"Could Jenny have gone out with him and not told you?"

"Not in the last six months. We got pinned last Christmas, I gave her my lavaliere. We were together all the time. She used to drive me home from school every day almost. We'd be there until six or seven, a lot of times later. My mother really loved her, thought she was beautiful, always said she wished she'd had a daughter like Jenny instead of just two sons. Jenny was a flirt sometimes, but she wouldn't be going out with Charlie Isaiah anyway, and I would have known about it if she was going out with anybody but me."

Joshua nodded.

"You want me to check your oil?"

"No, Jerry. It's all right. I appreciate you talking to me about this."

He shrugged. "It's okay, Mr. Rabb." He looked at Joshua with deep sadness in his eyes. "But don't be getting him off. Charlie Isaiah doesn't deserve to get off."

"I have to do my job, Jerry. Which means that if there's a legal way to get him off, that's what I'll do."

The boy frowned. Joshua handed him three dollars. Jerry fished in his pocket and handed the change to Joshua.

"I don't understand how it *can* be legal to get a killer off," Jerry muttered. He walked into the garage, wiping his hands on a greasy red shop rag.

Joshua drove the entire way to Barbara's house wondering what he had left undone, whom he could interview, how he could get the evidence he needed to defend Isaiah. The trial was next Tuesday, and the way things were stacking up, it would last for only three hours, and the jury wouldn't deliberate for more than fifteen minutes before they convicted him. Maybe they would be right to convict him. But Joshua still didn't think so. He was convinced that Charlie was innocent.

The burden of representing an innocent man bore heavily on him. It was easy to represent someone who was guilty. Then you did your job and performed professionally and didn't take it home with you. But defending an innocent man was a terrible responsibility. It haunted you constantly. It wouldn't let you digest your food. It wouldn't let you sleep. It didn't happen very often, thank God. It had happened to him just once in the last six years, and it had ended very badly. That once was all he needed.

He parked beside the Dubin house in the foothills of the Catalina Mountains. It was a little after six, and the sun still had an hour and a half to go before it slid behind the Tucson Mountains. It was hot, well over a hundred degrees, and it wouldn't get below eighty-five tonight. The red roses in the three clay pots by the rustic mesquite slat door were incongruously gay and perky in all this heat. Joshua scowled at them. "Why do you look so damn happy?" he mumbled.

The door opened. "Well, the stranger," Hal Dubin said. He held out his hand and shook Joshua's. "Come on in, come on in. Sit down, what are you drinking? What's your druthers, as the rubes say out here, huh?"

They went into the living room and Joshua sat down on the cream-colored satin sofa. The carpet was thick pile in a complementary pale cream color. Sliding glass doors revealed a large patio of flagstone surrounding a small swimming pool. The house was built on a lot cut into a gently sloping hill, and the hill rose dramatically behind the patio, constituting its rear wall. The two times that Joshua had been here before, he hadn't really taken notice of how beautiful it was. None of the elegant furniture looked like it had come out of Dubin's own furniture showroom. The quality of furniture he carried was for much poorer people than he obviously was.

"Jack Daniel's and soda," Joshua said, sitting down on the edge of the sofa.

"Yeah, yeah, you been a real stranger." Hal Dubin kept up a constant stream of chatter. "Hey, you see that movie *The Stranger?*" He handed Joshua the drink and lifted his own glass in a toast. "You shouldn't be a stranger." He drank a gulp and stood in front of Joshua. "Orson Welles, he plays the Nazi *mamzer,* marries a girl in Connecticut, she don't know, it's got Edward G. Robinson, Loretta Young. They should all rot in hell, the Germans, eh! But I guess you know that even better than me, huh?" He glanced at Joshua's arm. "So I been reading about you in the papers. The *goyim* out here really love you, huh? Make you a real folk hero." He burst into laughter.

Joshua smiled.

"Don't let him talk your ear off, Joshua," Barbara said, coming into the room. She walked over and gave him a brief kiss on the cheek. Then she went to the bar to fix a drink. She was wearing hot pink silk baggy shorts and a natural raw silk bustier. Around her neck was a heavy link gold necklace that looked real, and her hammered gold earrings, two inches long, looked like they had small clusters of genuine emeralds in the center.

"Dinner's almost ready," she said. "Pork roast and creamed spinach."

"We only do kosher around here," Hal said, beaming at Joshua.

Joshua laughed.

"Just kidding," she said, sitting beside him on the sofa. "Roast lamb and spring potatoes."

"What's spring potatoes?" her father asked.

"Ones that have been in the pantry since March," she said.

Her father roared with laughter. "They grow little feet on them?"

"Don't worry, I cut them off."

He laughed again. "Is this a girl, huh? Is this a beauty?" he said, looking at Joshua.

He nodded. "Yes. A beautiful girl."

"Like Loretta Young she swept into the room. You see that? Loretta Young never did a better entrance."

"Be careful what you say, Daddy. Loretta Young's ex-husband called her a "chocolate-covered black widow spider.'"

Hal erupted again with laughter. "Is this a girl?" he said to Joshua. "What a girl."

"My mother left for Brooklyn yesterday," Barbara said. "She was sorry she couldn't be here tonight."

"Yes, a pity," Joshua said.

"She's staying in my sister Clara's bungalow at the Grand Mountain Hotel in the Catskills," Hal said. "She goes back most summers, doesn't like Tucson's heat." He shrugged. "I miss her a lot when she's gone."

"That's very sweet, Daddy. I'll tell Mom when she calls. She'll be so pleased."

Hal gave his daughter a sarcastic, forced grin. *"Nu,* so what's with you?" he said, sitting on the rose satin upholstered chair. He looked pointedly at Joshua. "You thought about that offer I made you for the house on Speedway?"

Joshua nodded. "Well, I've never even seen it, and you didn't talk price. But sure, I'm interested."

"Good, good. Barbara has the key. The electric is on. You go see it after dinner."

"Okay, sure," Joshua said.

Barbara leaped up from the sofa and ran into the kitchen. A pungent odor of burning meat began to permeate the living room.

"Such a fabulous cook she ain't," Hal confided, his voice confidential. "Like her mother, *kenna hurra*, she isn't what you'd call so domestic." He shrugged. "But a good girl, in here." He put his hand over his heart. "A *kaporeh oif* cooking [the hell with cooking]," he said. "A *shvartze* you can hire for cooking, a spic, but a girl with a *hertz* like Barbara? One in a million. *Ayshes chayil mi yimtzo* [A woman of valor, who can find]?" He looked at Joshua and winked. He nodded his head gravely. *"Nu?"*

Barbara came out of the kitchen looking embarrassed. "I'm so sorry. I forgot all about it. It's a little on the done side."

"You mean it's a charcoal briquette," her father said gaily.

She frowned, abashed.

"Nu, so much for Loretta Young," Hal said. "You see before you Barbara Dubin. One in a million." He smiled at his daughter. "Okay, listen, you two kids go somewhere to eat. I'll eat a *bissel* gefilte fish, some horseradish. Clears my sinuses. You go, go." He stood up from the chair.

"Come, Joshua, Daddy's right. We can get a bite in a restaurant." She held out her hand. He took it and stood up from the couch.

"See you some other time, Joshua. She'll take a few lessons in French cooking." Hal laughed and opened the front door for them.

They got into Joshua's car. "I'm really sorry about dinner," he said.

She turned to him, a wry smile on her lips. "Are you kidding? Do you know how hard it is to burn lamb? I thought the damn thing would never burn. Finally I turned it up to four hundred." She laughed.

"You are genuinely incorrigible," he said, smiling at her.

"Is that good?"

"In you it's good."

She put her hand on his thigh. "I'm starving."

"Where do you want to go? Italian, Mexican, Chinese?"

"Let's eat Mexican."

"Sure," he said. "I know a fabulous place."

He drove to the El Charro Restaurant in downtown Tucson. Carlotta Flores greeted him happily. Her husband, Ray, waved from the kitchen. "The usual?" he called out.

"The usual," Joshua said.

"What's that?" Barbara asked.

"The best food in the world, other than Jewish salami, of course. It's *carne seca burros,* enchilada style. You ever have it?"

She shook her head. "But I'll try anything once."

The food came, along with Tecate beer, and it was delicious. They ate quickly and hungrily, eager for the rest of the evening.

Joshua drove to the modest-looking two-story house on Speedway Boulevard near Fourth Avenue. It was redbrick with a peaked shingle roof. A dormer window was under the V of the roof in the center. The second story had a long picture window in front. A gardener had obviously been keeping the yard up, since there was a thriving green Bermuda lawn and small manicured patches of orange marigolds and multicolored snapdragons and ice plants under a broad Chinese elm tree.

The front door opened into a vestibule with a small sitting room to the left and a receptionist's desk to the right. The inner door led to a spacious secretarial area in front of a room with double doors. The floor was oak planks. Beyond the double doors was a large office with a rear window looking out over a backyard of pink-and-lavender flowering crepe myrtle trees and a dense mulberry tree.

A wooden stairway with a polished walnut railing curved up to the second floor. It was carpeted in a beige shag. The center room was a spacious living room. Behind it was an open kitchen and dining area. On one side were the master bedroom and a large bathroom. On the other side were two smaller bedrooms with a small bathroom between them. A narrow stairway led to the dormer.

"This is terrific," Joshua said, looking out the living room picture window. "It didn't look nearly so nice from the outside."

"Yeah, Daddy picked it up last year. The owner died, didn't have any children. The estate sold it."

"It's really beautiful," Joshua said. "Magdalena and Hanna would each have their own bedrooms. Adam could have the dormer bedroom upstairs." He looked around eagerly. "How much does your father want for it?"

"Oh, I'm sure he'd rent it for a hundred a month." Joshua nodded. "I could handle that."

She stepped to him and looked into his eyes, her face serious, her eyes glistening. "He doesn't want to sell it. He wants me to have it as a wedding present."

Joshua studied her face. She was beautiful. He put his hand lightly on her waist and slid it up her side.

She stepped back from him. "No. We're not going to do that. I think I gave in to you too fast. You don't take me seriously."

He shook his head. "Maybe the first time," he said softly. "I was kind of surprised, I guess. But not now. If you love someone, that's just a natural part of it."

"I love you, Joshua."

He blinked and stared at her. "I love you too," he whispered.

"And I don't go to bed with every man I know on the first date."

"Second?" he said, his eyes smiling.

"Sometimes even third," she drawled.

She stepped on tiptoes and kissed him on the lips. There were tears in her eyes.

"What's wrong?" he said to her gently.

"I don't know. I feel crazy. I guess I'm about to get my period." She sniffed, and tears rolled off the tip of her chin.

He wiped her cheeks tenderly with his fingertips.

"I want you to love me," she whispered. "Not just want to make love to me."

He nuzzled her cheek. "I do," he whispered.

She sniffled again and looked deeply into his eyes.

She took his hand, and they walked into the master bedroom. There was a double bed against the wall. The mattress was bare.

"We've never tried it in a bed," he said. "Is it the same as a rock or a car?"

She smiled at him. "Let's see."

The bustier fastened by two buttons between her breasts. She removed it in a second. She put it on the end of the mattress. She unbuttoned and unzipped her shorts and pulled her panties off with them. She lay down in the middle of the mattress and crooked her finger at him.

He pulled the short-sleeve polo shirt off and placed it on the end of the mattress. He kicked off his loafers and unbuttoned his Levi's and pushed them and his underwear down and stepped out of them. He sat on the edge of the bed and pulled off his socks. He had left his arm at home, since he had expected that they were going to end up together like this, somewhere, and the arm would only be in the way.

He felt her lips on the small of his back. Then her arm slid around his waist and she took him in her slender fingers. He lay back and they embraced.

Afterward, they lay quietly, perspiring in the heat of the early evening. She got up and switched on the cooler, and a noisy breeze came through the vent. In a few minutes it was cool. It was pitch black in the room. She got up again and pulled back the curtains on the big window. A few lights from the houses across the street cast a dull glow into the room.

He rolled her over gently and kissed her buttocks. "You have a great big beautiful magnificent ass," he whispered.

"Don't call it big," she said.

"You have a skinny little beautiful magnificent ass," he whispered.

"That's much better," she said.

She rolled over on her back and drew him on top of her. "I want Hanna and Adam to like me," she said. "I want them to be comfortable with me."

"They are. Remember, it was Hanna who invited you to my birthday party."

"No, I mean really comfortable. I want them to think of me as a mom."

"Well, you're only ten years older than Hanna. Let's try for big sister." He kissed her, wanting nothing else in the world at this precise instant but to stay this way forever.

CHAPTER THIRTEEN

When Joshua had opened the newspaper last Saturday morning, he had gaped at the front-page story about Benjamin Siegel's untimely demise. "Bugsy Siegel certainly didn't invent gambling or Las Vegas," the story said, "but he put them in the forefront of everyone's mind. His Flamingo Hotel was the very definition of the fashionable casino."

Joshua had telephoned Meyer Lansky. It was not yet seven o'clock in the morning, but no one had been home. Odd. Now, a week later, Meyer still hadn't turned up, and Hanna hadn't seen Buddy since the day that Bobby Bonanno had left.

Things had quieted down completely on the reservation. No more bodies and no more abandoned cars and trucks. The turf war was apparently over, and Bonanno was here but Lansky wasn't. Did it mean that the smuggling was over? Who had won, Bonanno or Lansky?

▲+▼+▼+▲

Roy Collins walked into Joshua's office at the BIA. He was munching a shiny green apple. "Great," he said. "Granny Smith from Washington. My wife got them over at the El Rancho Market."

Joshua looked up from the work order he was filling out, to get the telephone lines by Coyote Creek repaired for the third time. Every time the winds came up, they blew down a couple of poles like toothpicks. The Office of Land Management needed to put up cement poles there.

Roy sat down. "I located Meyer Lansky."

"Where?"

"In New York. FBI field office in Manhattan says he's living in an apartment on Central Park West overlooking the park. They think Bonanno won, that Lansky's lying low."

"Did Bonanno's boys do Ben Siegel?"

Collins shrugged. "Who'll ever know? Let's just be grateful that whoever did it and why, it looks like it ended the problems here on the Big Res."

Joshua nodded. "Chuy went down to Sahuarita yesterday and talked to Filberto Coronado. He says he never heard of a company called Cooperativa Agricultura Mexicana, and that his own company owns all of their own trucks except the reefers, which they lease from Evergreen."

"What's Evergreen?"

"It's a Southern Pacific railroad wholly owned subsidiary which owns all the refrigerated railway cars and leases them back to SP. Something to do with tax gimmicks. Anyway, it also owns refrigerated trucks and leases them to the produce importers so they can load perishables directly from the railway sidings and cut down loading and demurrage time."

Roy raised his eyebrows and wrinkled his forehead. "You sound like a vegetable expert all of a sudden."

"Chuy says old man Coronado knows his business. Nice guy. Talked to Chuy for a couple of hours. Kept on filling his glass with margaritas. He almost hit three telephone poles driving back up here yesterday evening."

Roy laughed.

Chuy looked in at the doorway. "Frances says that Edgar wants to see us."

Joshua shrugged. "So why doesn't he come down here?"

"Maybe because *he's* the superintendent and *we* work for *him*," Chuy said.

"Oh yeah," Joshua said. "I almost forgot." He laughed.

"Do I get to come too?" Roy said.

"Why not?" Joshua said. "Frances can bring in a pitcher of lemonade and we'll have a party."

Edgar's face was drawn. His forehead was beaded with perspiration. The three men sat on the burgundy leather-covered armchairs in his office, in front of the huge walnut desk.

"I thought this shit was over," Edgar said.

"What?" Joshua asked.

"The *gott damn* heroin smugglin', that's what," Edgar answered.

"What happened?" Roy asked.

"Forty kilograms of pure Mexican heroin was just seized at the California agricultural inspection station across from the Arizona border at Yuma. A couple of Mexicans driving produce stake trucks. It was under the floorboards in the cabs. Their trip certificates showed that they both came up through the Nogales border crossing. There were two other seizures earlier this week." Edgar frowned. "Harry Coyle just called me from Washington, wants to know what the hell is goin' on down here. He says there's more Mexican brown showin' up in New York and Philadelphia the last week than in the whole previous history of the world." He looked gloomily at Joshua. "He chewed my ass for ten minutes, said I gotta get this shit under control."

Joshua nodded. "Chuy and Roy have been working on it."

"Too *gott damn* slow," Edgar muttered, his teeth clenched. "Gotta go fast on this thing, 'fore he chews alla way through to bone."

"Long way to go, Edgar," Joshua said.

Edgar snorted. "Okay, this is priority. We gotta do it fast. Harry wants a report next Monday. Anybody got any ideas?"

Chuy frowned and shrugged. "I've been mulling over a plan for a while. If you put me on it full-time, I think I can do it. My mother and brother Solomon live in San Miguel. That's just three miles north of Newfield, less than five miles from the Mexican border. We have a small cattle ranch there. Nobody will notice if I go back to my mother's place for a while, help her and my brother fix the fences, patch the barn roof. I'm going to try to get my brother to infiltrate the smuggling outfit. He's a Papago, bitter against the whites, no money. Perfect for them. If we can get information on when the dope is coming through Nogales, we can seize it and cripple their operation through Nogales. They'll have to move it, and the only logical secondary route is through Newfield on the Big Reservation, the one the Italians and Jews were using. That crossing is a hell of a lot easier for us to police."

"I'm not quite following," Edgar said. "There's a hunnerd produce trucks through the border ever' day. We'd need Patton's whole damn Third Army to search 'em all."

"Not if we have somebody well enough placed to give us inside information on when it's coming and on which trucks."

Edgar nodded. "Yeah, okay. But how ya gonna get Solomon into that position?"

Chuy shrugged. "I don't know. You have a better idea?"

Edgar shook his head.

"Let's let him try," Joshua said.

Roy Collins shrugged. "Yeah, why not?"

"Okay, give it a whirl," Edgar said. "And I hope yer brother don't get his balls blowed off."

Chuy winced.

▲♣▽♣♣▽♣▲

Solomon Leyva lived on the small ranch with his mother and two unmarried sisters, both teenagers. He was built like Chuy, strong and tall, but his face was covered with small acne scars, giving him a decidedly meaner appearance. Solomon was two years older than Chuy and had spent over three years in the army. He had seen action from North Africa to Sicily to Italy to the Normandy invasion to the liberation of Paris. In Paris he had been stabbed in the stomach by a whore in a brothel and been awarded the Purple Heart. The citation read: "Wounded by Vichy sympathizer." The stab wound hadn't been serious, but the subsequent peritonitis was. He had spent a month in the U.S. Army Hospital at Orly before being sent home. He had lived the next year in Phoenix, hand to mouth, trying to find a job with some kind of future, but it had been a futile quest. There were no jobs for acne-scarred Papagos, unless cleaning toilets in flophouse hotels for rent and two squares a day qualified as one.

A year ago he had returned to the Big Reservation, to the home he had grown up in. His sense of despair was palpable, and he had taken to going up to Three Points on weekends, to the bar at the crossroads, and drowning his sorrows in Four Roses and Jim Beam. But this cost too much money, and after a while he started going to Nogales, Mexico, instead.

It took about the same time to drive there, almost two hours, but the amenities in Nogales were much preferable for a Papago with very little money. A whiskey sour with strong rotgut Mexican whiskey was only ten cents, and a whore named Linda, who was his regular, was only twenty-five cents. Sometimes she didn't even charge.

Linda lived with her brother, Manuel, in a tiny shack on the steep hill above Canal Street, and she had been on her own since being orphaned at the age of seven. Her brother had been just four years old. By the age of fourteen, five years ago, she had grown up enough to work at the Waikiki Ballroom, and she had provided the school uniforms and money sufficient for shoes and school books so that her brother could get an education and stay out of trouble. But now at the age of sixteen, Manuel had dropped out of school and was hanging out by the border, smoking marijuana, occasionally robbing tourists, often earning five dollars just for riding atop the tomato and lettuce trucks that were so common going through the border crossing. The owner of Linda's whorehouse had gotten him a job.

It was to help unload the produce at the Coronado warehouse on the Arizona side. He was issued an important-looking identification card that he flashed at the American border inspectors, and they never hassled him. The reason why he was so highly paid for less than a day's work was that it was his job to make sure that the small packages wrapped in butcher paper at the bottom of the load always got to just one of the warehouse men, a big Mexican nicknamed "Fat Henry." Manuel suspected that the packages contained heroin, but who cared? It was damn good money for damn little work. He would often brag to Solomon that he could make more money in two easy workdays guarding Mexican brown than Solomon could make in a week of sixteen-hour days getting bowlegged on a rank horse chasing stray cattle out of arroyos.

▲+▽+▽+▲

Chuy arrived at the Leyva ranch in the afternoon. His teenage sisters were in Phoenix, boarding at the Indian School there. His brother was out with the cattle, and his mother was baking bread in the earthen oven outside on the *vato*.

Chuy put his duffel bag in his old room. He asked his mother where Solomon was likely to be, and she said that he had the cattle up on the hills just below Lalo Peak, in a pasture with a pond on its south side. It was about four miles to the east over rough terrain. Chuy had tended the cattle in the same place for many years, and he knew that the pickup truck could make it most of the way.

He bridled and saddled a horse, tied it by a longe

line to the rear bumper of the pickup; drove slowly over the rocky desert to the Baboquivari foothills, then up the hills until a ravine barred his way. He mounted the elderly buckskin and rode up to the pasture. Solomon's horse was grazing on the Bermuda grass along with about a hundred cows and calves. Solomon was sitting against a broad-trunked mesquite tree, his eyes closed, his straw cowboy hat beside him on the ground.

Chuy rode up to him and dismounted. He loosened his horse's girth and removed the bridle. The horse walked off to graze.

Solomon squinted up at his brother, framed against the late afternoon sun. *"Sha: p a'i masma* [How have you been]?" he said.

"Manya 'ash 'i s-ape [I'm fine]," Chuy answered. *"Sha p 'e-wua* [What are you doing]?"

"Anyi 'an ko:s kui wecho [I was sleeping under the mesquite]."

Chuy laughed. "I can see that," he said in Papago. "But it looks like some rain may be coming this way. We'd better round them up and start back."

Solomon squinted up at the small white cumulus clouds. "Okay, but I don't think it'll rain." He stood up and rubbed his temples.

"You look like shit," Chuy said.

"Thanks, brother." He looked at Chuy sourly. "Just a little hangover."

"When are you going to get a grip on yourself?"

Solomon didn't answer. He picked up his hat and bridle from the ground and walked slowly toward his grazing sorrel mare. Chuy put the bridle back on his torpid buckskin gelding and tightened the cinch. Both men mounted and easily rounded up the cattle, which began to meander down the hill toward the Leyva ranch, having done this enough times to know their way and need hardly any prodding.

Chuy cantered up to Solomon and slowed to a walk, staying next to him. "I've got a big job for you. Maybe it can get you out of here."

Solomon looked over, interested. His eyes were

bloodshot and face pinched because of the throbbing in his temples. "I'm listening."

"There's been heroin smuggling going on in Nogales and down here by the crossing below Newfield."

Solomon nodded.

"I want you to help Joshua Rabb and Roy Collins and me put an end to it."

He shrugged. "It's not happening down here. They just had some trouble with some gringos trying to take over. The trouble is over."

Chuy stared at him. "How do you know about this?"

"I know."

"You involved?"

"Hell, no! You know me better than that."

"Then how?"

Solomon hesitated. "Girl I stay with in Nogales has a brother. He tells me about it."

"A whore from Canal Street?"

Solomon looked sharply at Chuy, then gritted his teeth and looked away, saying nothing.

"Mom says every weekend you're down there drinking and whoring."

"Ain't none of her business. I ain't a kid. I'm twenty-seven. I do what I want."

"One of these days she'll stick a knife in your back and steal your wallet."

Solomon stared harshly at his brother. "Linda's not like that. She and her brother been on their own since she was a kid, can't read or write. What the hell's she supposed to do, be a doctor?"

Chuy studied his brother. "You in love with this Linda?"

Solomon stared back at Chuy and looked hotly away. He spurred his horse and trotted forward. Chuy joined him a minute later.

"Okay, Solomon, okay. It's none of my business. Be careful."

"So what do you have in mind?"

"Do you think you can get in on the smuggling operation?"

Solomon snorted. "So some gringo cop can stick a knife in my back?"

"No, on the level. We've got to find out who's controlling the traffic."

Solomon laughed. "You think a few of us gonna put a stop to a million-dollar business? You nuts or something? It goes through Nogales on produce trucks. Those families, whoever's doing it—maybe all of them—will have us dead and fed to the coyotes in ten minutes."

"Not if we do it my way."

"What's your way?"

"If we can stop enough of the trucks it's coming in on at the border in Nogales and confiscate the heroin and the trucks, they'll move the operation. Probably here to Newfield. It's a little out of the way, less convenient than Nogales, but there's no border station and no patrolmen. Then we'll bring a bunch of Customs officers and border patrolmen over here and put an end to it in a hurry."

Solomon listened closely and nodded. "Maybe, but there's a hundred trucks up through Nogales a day. You'd need the whole damn Seventh Cavalry to search them all."

"True," Chuy said, "but not if we had good inside information on when it's coming through and on which trucks."

Solomon looked intently at his brother. "And what do I get, besides a .38 slug between my eyes?"

"We need another BIA policeman at San Xavier. I'll talk to Edgar Hendly. If you can do this for us, you'll be the man for the job."

Solomon sat a little straighter in the saddle. "Not bad," he drawled. "That wouldn't be so bad."

"You think you can get inside?"

Solomon nodded his head slowly. He pursed his lips and thought for a moment. Then he nodded again. "I don't need to get inside. I may know a way."

"Okay, it's yours. Do it your way. How fast can you get on it? I told Edgar I'd try to have it set up in a month."

"I may be able to set it up in two or three days."

Chuy studied Solomon. "Okay."

"We got to hire somebody to honcho these cattle while I'm gone," Solomon said. "Diego Morales, I think."

"We'll go over to the Morales place after dinner," Chuy said.

▲+▼+▼+▲

Solomon drove to Nogales the next morning. Chuy had already left an hour earlier. Solomon parked on the southern end of Calle Obregon and walked back toward the border. Manuel Rodriguez was in the place he usually was, standing in front of a trinket bazaar a block from the border. He was with three friends of his, boys his age or younger, and they looked warily at Solomon. He memorized their faces.

"Como va, Manuel?" Solomon said to Linda's brother.

Manuel nodded at him and shrugged. "What you doing here? It's Sunday. Ain't you gotta be back on yer ranch?"

"Got tired of cows, *amigo*. Can't take that shit no more. Gotta get a honest job."

The four boys snickered.

"We got one this afternoon. Make five bucks each. But I don't know I can get you on."

Solomon shrugged. "You ask, huh? Right now I go see your sister."

Two of the boys chuckled maliciously until Manuel silenced them with his eyes.

Solomon walked back to his 1939 Ford pickup. He drove across the border into Arizona and parked behind Bracker's department store. It was a half block from the border. He walked up the street to a small park beside the Southern Pacific depot and sat on a wooden bench. He had the walkie-talkie that Chuy had given him. Chuy was a mile north, across the road from the produce warehouses, also with a walkie-talkie. Three carloads of border patrolmen were parked by the highway another half mile north, in a grove of sycamore trees beside the Santa Cruz River.

Two hours later, a tomato truck came across the border with one of the boys he had seen with Manuel sitting on the top. Solomon transmitted the license plate number to Chuy. Fifteen more trucks went by before another of the boys appeared, riding atop a load of lettuce. Solomon radioed the plate number. Several trucks went by, some with boys or men on the load, some without, but Solomon didn't recognize any of them. Then came a stake truck with Manuel Rodriguez aboard, and immediately following it was a truck carrying the last of the four boys whom Solomon recognized. Solomon transmitted the two plate numbers. Then he drove back into Mexico, to Linda's shack on the hill above the whorehouses.

It was Linda's night off, and she had never seen Solomon when she wasn't working and drunk or well on her way. She was pleased to see him, and a smile lit her face with more animation than he had seen in her before. When she wasn't drunk, when she wasn't painted with pancake makeup so thick it literally masked her face, she was pretty. Not a matinee idol, not a fairy princess, just a pretty nineteen-year-old girl with freckles on the bridge of her nose and anxious brown eyes, hungry for affection.

They went to a movie. A few minutes after they returned to the shack, Manuel came in and excitedly told them what had happened. Four loads of heroin going through Nogales had been seized by cops at the Coronado warehouse. They had surrounded four specific trucks as they were reaching the end of the unloading. The drivers had been arrested along with the drugs, charged with smuggling, but no one else had been arrested. One of the trucks had had thirty kee's on it, the others twenty each. Manuel spoke very excitedly. This had been a great day. He couldn't remember ever having had so much fun.

The next day, the same thing happened. Of the hundred twenty-five produce trucks through the border, four of them had the riders on top whom Solomon recognized. The four trucks were searched at the Coronado warehouse, and well over a hundred kilograms of heroin were seized.

Fat Henry had pulled Manuel over and asked him how it was happening. Two days in a row meant somebody was talking, the fat man said, but so many people were involved in the smuggling operation that it was next to impossible to find out who. Fat Henry didn't believe that it was one of the four boys. He had used boys from Nogales many times before, and they had never snitched. But the smuggling was going to stop, Fat Henry said, at least for now, at least for Nogales. They had lost eight drivers, eight trucks, and two hundred fifteen kilograms of heroin in just two days. Luckily, the drivers didn't even know that they had been carrying heroin, Fat Henry said, so "my boss, he won't have to pay no money for lawyers to keep the drivers' mouths shut. They get real expensive." Fat Henry sucked in his cheeks and looked thoughtfully at Manuel. "You wanna be a driver? We gonna have trouble finding drivers for a while."

Not around here, Manuel told him. Too dangerous, man. He didn't bother to tell Fat Henry that he had never driven anything but a motorbike—well, and an old Ford a couple of times, but never a truck.

It's okay, Fat Henry said. We ain't gonna use Nogales. We gonna have to take it through the Pjacate Mountains and then through the unmarked crossing near Newfield in Arizona. Another driver will take over in Newfield, and there'll be someone else to pick up Manuel and bring him back to Nogales. Pay will be a hundred pesos for each trip.

Manuel was delighted with the promotion. He gushed to Linda and Solomon how slick he'd been in negotiating a higher price. He was going to get two hundred pesos. That's more than Linda earned in two whole months, having to shell out most of her money for drinks and to the owner of the Waikiki for the privilege of working there.

Solomon appeared to get drunk as he always did and pointedly paid little attention to Manuel. He grumbled sourly about having to go back to the ranch in the morning. He had never told Linda and Manuel where he was from. They knew that he was a Papago, but as far as they knew, he might live anywhere in Arizona, just like the Sonoran Papagos, who had no reservation. They didn't know such places as Indian reservations existed, and while Manuel could read a little, neither of them had ever seen a map of anywhere.

Solomon left at five o'clock Tuesday morning, when the first rays of the sun outlined the serrated Nogales hills. He marveled at how well Chuy's plan had worked. But what would they do now? The border patrol could seize some more heroin at Newfield, and they could arrest Manuel and the other boys too, if the others were also going to be drivers. But then what? New boys would take over after the smuggling ceased for a few weeks, boys whom Solomon wouldn't recognize, and they'd ship a load or two through Nogales, tentatively at first, and then the smuggling would be back to full speed ahead. So what would ultimately be accomplished, other than throwing Manuel in federal prison? Solomon didn't want that. He was in love with Linda, whore or not. He loved her. And he wouldn't let her brother go to prison because of him. Her life had been bitter enough already. She didn't need that.

She was devoutly Catholic and said her rosary every morning when she awoke. Jesus had loved the sinners even more than the righteous, she always said, for he was the savior, and in saving the souls of the sinners he had carried out his appointed sacred mission on earth. Above her head was a picture of Mary Magdalene, torn from some old missal that she couldn't read. But Mary Magdalene was the proof that even a prostitute could be the favorite lamb of the son of God. It didn't matter what Linda had to do to make money. God knew that her soul was pure, her heart good.

Solomon was not very religious himself. Too many drunk Franciscan friars at the missions, too many venal nuns at the schools and clinics. But he recognized genuine piety when he saw it. Linda was a pious girl. She had an unsullied soul. He was in love with her, and he would not be the cause of her brother's being sent to prison.

Solomon slowed the car and stopped. He was twenty miles west on the road to Newfield. He turned around and drove back to Nogales, through the border crossing, and up to the San Xavier Reservation. He got to Chuy's house at seven-thirty. Chuy was in the pen beside the house feeding his two goats.

"What are you doing here?" Chuy asked, studying Solomon's somber face. "Something go wrong?"

"No, it all went your way, perfect. The smuggling is going to stop through Nogales. They're going to send it through Newfield just like you figured."

Chuy clapped his hands. "I knew it!" he said. He looked at Solomon's frown. "So what's the problem?"

"We can't do the plan the way you originally set it up."

"Why not?"

"Do we have to watch the goats shit while we talk? This is serious."

"Okay, okay," Chuy said. "Come on in the house. I got some coffee made."

Solomon sat down on a short stool at the folding card table in the kitchen. Chuy poured steaming coffee into a stoneware mug and set it in front of his brother. Solomon picked it up, steadying it with both hands, and drank.

"So why can't we do it my way?" Chuy asked.

"Because if you bust Manuel Rodriguez and put him in prison, I'm going to lose his sister, Linda."

Chuy studied his brother sourly. "You mean the whore you've been living with in Nogales?"

"Don't call Linda a whore."

"What the hell should I call her, Solomon, an angel? Why don't you get your goddamn brains out of your dick!"

"Listen, little brother," Solomon muttered. "You become a cop, suddenly you're God's personal altar boy. I've been your brother for twenty-five years. I know you. You don't have any right to preach to me. Linda's a good girl. I'm going to marry her."

Chuy stared at Solomon. "You serious?"

"Yes. I'm bringing her up here to live with me."

Chuy grimaced. "You tell Mom?"

Solomon shook his head. "But when she meets Linda she'll love her. And you don't have to fill in any details."

Chuy sighed. Then he shrugged. "Listen, if she's what you need, I'm all for her. That's the truth."

"You got two bedrooms here. Can we stay here until we get our own place? The López place down by the Santa Cruz is empty, abandoned since the old man died. It's on tribal land. I can fix it up. It'll take a few weeks, then we'll move into it."

Chuy nodded. "Okay, sure. Stay here as long as you need."

"Thanks," Solomon said. "Thanks very much. And how about that job as a BIA cop?"

"I think I can swing it."

"Okay." Solomon nodded.

"So what about Manuel?"

"I don't want him going to the joint. Linda would never forgive me."

Chuy sat back on the wood slat folding chair and thought about it. "There is a way."

Solomon waited.

"If he works for me. If he's willing to testify. Then he gets immunity from prosecution. But he has to get up in federal court and testify against the people he knows about."

Solomon rubbed his chin. "So instead of going to the joint, he gets killed. Not much of a trade-off."

"No, he doesn't have to die. The network is down in Mexico. He can live up here, be pretty safe, as long as he's careful."

Solomon shook his head doubtfully. "Too damn risky for him."

"Listen, big brother, this boy got into his problems all by himself. If he drives a load through the border, we can bust him and put him in Terminal Island or

McNeil Island for ten years. He's the criminal, not us. If he wants to make a deal, there's some risk involved. It can't be avoided. But I doubt that the Mexicans are going to send anyone up here to kill a kid. It isn't worth it for them."

Solomon breathed deeply. "What do we have to do?"

"Have you at least talked to Manuel about it?"

Solomon shook his head. "He'd tell me to get fucked."

"Then we have to bust him with a load. After a few days up at Mount Lemmon in the detention center he'll be begging us to make a deal. How old is he?"

"Sixteen."

"Yeah, a sixteen-year-old boy up there doesn't stand a chance. After he gets punked a few times, he'll do anything to get out."

Solomon flinched. "Hell of a way to have to do it."

"He should have gotten an honest job."

"Okay, how do we set it up?"

"We'll have to talk to Joshua Rabb. He'll fix it with Roy Collins and the U.S. attorney."

"Okay, let's do it," Solomon said. "I'll go down to Nogales this afternoon and bring Linda back with me."

Chuy nodded. He glanced at his watch. "Joshua will be over at federal court. He's got Charlie Isaiah's trial today. I've got to testify. You might as well come and watch. If you're going to be a cop, you'd better see what happens at a trial firsthand."

"What's going to be with Charlie Isaiah?"

"Charlie's going to the happy hunting grounds."

Solomon frowned. "Did he do it?"

Chuy nodded. "Yeah, he did it."

They left the house, got into Chuy's pickup, and drove to the federal courthouse. The trial had started at eight o'clock, and the jurors had already been selected and were sitting in the box. The U.S. attorney was asking a witness questions. Chuy and Solomon sat in the last row of the crowded courtroom.

CHAPTER FOURTEEN

The witness on the stand was Edward Carter. He was being questioned very deferentially by Assistant United States Attorney Tim Essert.

"When was it that you first hired the defendant, Charlie Isaiah, to work at your Ford dealership, Mr. Carter?"

"When he graduated from Tucson High, about a year ago."

"Had he been your daughter's friend in high school?"

Carter shrugged. "I don't know. I doubt it."

"Do you know if she went out on dates with him?"

Carter squirmed in his chair. "Well, I sure don't think that she would have."

"If the defendant claims that your daughter was sweet on him, will he be lying?"

"Oh, yes!" Carter spat out, his face twisted sourly. "Jennifer wouldn't never fall for a—a—" he stammered, trying to find the right word "—*person* like him. She was a cheerleader, she was real popular. She didn't have to go out on dates with *them*."

Essert walked to the clerk's desk and picked up a

small hunting knife with a yellow paper tag hanging from it. He laid it on the flat rail in front of the witness stand.

"That is the knife that both the government and the defense have stipulated was the murder weapon. Does it belong to you?"

"No, sir."

"To your son?"

"No, sir."

"Had you ever seen it before I showed it to you prior to this trial?"

Carter shook his head. "Absolutely not."

"Okay, now, Mr. Carter, let me take you back to that day that she was killed. Do you remember that day?"

Carter nodded.

"You have to answer audibly, Eddie," Essert said, "so the court reporter can record your answers."

Carter sniffed. "Oh yeah, sorry. I remember that day."

"Did you see her that day?"

"Sure."

"When did you last see her?"

"I guess about four or five in the afternoon."

"What was she doing when you last saw her?"

"Charlie Isaiah was pushing her into his car."

"Did she appear willing?"

"No, absolutely not."

"How can you be so sure?"

"Because she stumbled and fell on her knees, and then Charlie grabbed her real rough, and she was crying."

The courtroom was hushed. There were at least two hundred spectators, and not a single one made a sound. The sensation was electric. Even Joshua, sitting at the defense table next to Charlie Isaiah and trying to look calm and unconcerned, could feel the tension in the courtroom. It would get much worse. He willed himself to look unconcerned. Don't ever let the jury see you sweat. He crossed his legs nonchalantly and stared straight ahead at the witness.

"What did you do, Mr. Carter?"

Carter rubbed his eyes hard. His voice came hoarsely. "I ran after them, but they were too far away. Charlie pushed her in the car and drove off. I ran back to the office and called the sheriff's department, told them that my daughter'd just been kidnapped." His voice broke and he sobbed for a moment. Then his crying subsided. He took a handkerchief from the breast pocket of his navy blue suit jacket and dabbed his eyes.

"Your witness," Essert said, sitting down.

Joshua limped around the table, and stood at the far end of the walnut railing separating the jury from the rest of the room. In serious criminal cases he always wore his black wool suit and vest and his gold pocket watch. He thought it made him look funereal, like he was in mourning. His voice was deep and sonorous. He had the black ebony wood cane with him, was walking with a pronounced limp, and he had shined up his stainless-steel prongs with a steel wool pad so that they gleamed under the high fluorescent lights of the courtroom.

"You told the jury a moment ago that Jennifer wouldn't fall for a *person* like Charlie, that she didn't have to go out with *them*. What did you mean?"

Carter shrugged. "Well, you know, a Papago Indian."

"Did she have something against Papagos?"

"No, I mean, I guess not. But a nice girl don't go out on dates with them." He shrugged his shoulders and glanced at the jury as though nothing could be more obvious.

"Are you *certain* that she was not going out with Charlie?"

"Yeah, I'm certain." Carter's manner had become more rigid. He was getting annoyed. "Yeah, she wouldn't do that. She was going out mostly with a nice kid, Jerry Hawkins."

"Did you find your daughter in bed with Charlie Isaiah?"

The spectators broke into whispers and gasps. Judge

Buchanan rapped his gavel and waited for silence. "Did you hear the question, Eddie?" Buchanan asked gently.

"Yeah, sure I did," Carter said, his face flushed. He swallowed hard. "No, I never did. Jennifer never did."

"How long had you been carrying on a sexual relationship with your own daughter?" Joshua asked in a very soft voice, so that everyone except the closest jurors had to strain and concentrate to hear him.

"You filthy son of a bitch," bellowed Ed Carter, standing up in the witness stand. He jabbed his finger toward Joshua, who stood perfectly still, as before, at the end of the jury box. The spectators and the jury were silent, shocked.

Essert leaped up from his chair. "I object to this disgraceful, unethical conduct by this lawyer."

Judge Buchanan rapped his gavel again. "Eddie, I'm afraid that you're going to have to sit down and answer these questions." He waited until Carter sank back into the oak swivel chair. Essert sat down slowly. "That is, of course," Buchanan continued, his face severe, "if you will absolutely avow to the court, Mr. Rabb, that you will present direct evidence to support the allegation you've just made."

"I will do precisely that, Your Honor," Joshua said in a strong voice.

"Very well, Mr. Rabb. Be very careful," the judge said, settling back into his chair.

"I never touched Jennifer, not in that way," Carter yelled at Joshua. "Never. God, she was my daughter." His voice became choked, and he sobbed again for a moment.

"You have a son named Philip, is that correct?"

"Yes."

"He is a twenty-one-year-old student at the University of Arizona, plays guard for the football team?"

"That's right."

"Big, strapping fellow, maybe two hundred fifty pounds."

"Yes."

"Did you find Jennifer in bed with Charlie Isaiah

and murder your daughter in a jealous rage while your son held Isaiah down?"

Ed Carter's face became deep red. His eyes bulged out. He held tightly to the armrests of the chair as if to restrain himself from springing out of it. "No," he gasped.

"Just one more question, Mr. Carter. Do you know of any reason or motive whatsoever for Charlie Isaiah, in broad daylight, in front of his place of work where everyone knew him, to kidnap your daughter in his own car and drive off and murder her right in his own home?"

Carter breathed deeply to calm himself. He slowly shook his head. "No. He was crazy is all I can think. Just plain crazy."

Joshua limped slowly to the defense table and sat down. Carter left the witness stand and the courtroom.

"Government calls Roy Collins," Essert said.

Roy came into the courtroom behind the bailiff, was sworn by the court clerk, and took the stand.

"You are Special Agent Roy Collins of the Federal Bureau of Investigation?"

"Yes, sir."

"How long have you been so employed?"

"Eleven years."

"How many deaths by stabbing have you personally investigated?"

"At least fifty."

"Did you investigate the death of Jennifer Carter?"

"Yes."

"Please tell the jury how you became involved."

"The sheriff's department dispatcher called the FBI office, since the sheriff doesn't have jurisdiction on the Indian reservation. My secretary called me on the car phone. She said there was a reported kidnapping by a Papago Indian named Charlie Isaiah. She said the sheriff's department had an all-points bulletin out for him and the girl, and they wanted me to head over to the reservation and see if he was there. They gave me a description of his car, but they didn't know a home address. A lot of the places on the reservation have no addresses."

"What did you do then, Agent Collins?"

"I drove out to the Bureau of Indian Affairs to see if Jesus Leyva was there. He's the Indian policeman for San Xavier, and he knows his way around the reservation and where most of the folks live. He was in his office. He accompanied me to Charlie Isaiah's house. Isaiah's car was outside."

"Please continue, Agent Collins."

"The door was locked. Chuy broke it in. He's a lot bigger than I am. We went inside. Charlie Isaiah was in the bedroom, on the bed, the girl was beside him."

"What condition was the girl in?"

"She was dead. She had multiple stab wounds. A small hunting knife was embedded in her sternum."

"And the defendant?"

"He was passed out, dead drunk. Covered with vomit, blood all over his shirt and hands and Levi's."

"Did you take the defendant into custody?"

"Yes, of course."

"Did he make any statements?"

"No, he was just real mean, like he was still half drunk. He resisted arrest, and it took both Leyva and me to restrain him and get him in my car. He passed out again."

"Thank you, Agent Collins." Essert sat down.

Joshua remained seated. "You said that Charlie was covered with blood?"

"Yes."

"How about Jennifer Carter?"

"Yes, she was covered with blood."

"Was there a bedsheet on the bed?"

"Yes."

"Was there blood on the sheet?"

"Just a few drops."

"What did that indicate to you?"

"That she had not been stabbed in the bed."

A murmur arose among the spectators. Joshua waited for it to subside. "Did you ever determine where she had been killed?"

"No."

"With Charlie in the stuporously intoxicated state that you have testified to, how is it possible for him to have carried or dragged a dead woman into bed?"

"Objection," Essert said. "Conjecture."

Judge Buchanan raised his eyebrows, pursed his lips, and pondered for a moment. "No, I'm going to allow it. Overruled. Go ahead and answer."

"Anything is possible, Mr. Rabb. I've seen some awfully strange things happen in my eleven years with the Bureau. Frankly, I don't know how he did it. But he did it. Maybe he wasn't nearly as drunk as he was acting. I really don't know."

"Is it possible that someone else killed Jennifer, beat up Charlie, and put them both in that bed?"

Collins shrugged. "Again, Mr. Rabb, anything is possible. But if the question is whether it is *probable,* my answer is that it's terribly *improbable.* I've seen plenty of murder scenes, more than three hundred, I think, and there's hardly a one that you couldn't look at and look at and dream up all kinds of theories. But my experience is that the simplest explanation is virtually always the correct one. When I see a drunk covered with blood and a body next to him covered with blood, and a hunting knife embedded in the body, I find it hard not to come to the conclusion that the drunk had something very substantial to do with putting the knife there."

"Did you check out the interior of Charlie's car to determine if there were bloodstains in it?"

"Yes, I did, but I didn't find any."

"How about bloodstains from the car to the front door?"

"Just a few small spots on the porch."

"Were there any inside the house, but not in the bedroom?"

"Yes, there were some fresh spots, not puddles, just spots."

"Large enough for Jennifer to have been stabbed there?"

"Not in my judgment."

"Did you ever check inside Jennifer's bedroom at home or in her father's or brother's or her own car to determine if there were traces of her blood there?"

"No, sir, I did not."

"Why is that?"

Essert was quickly to his feet, his face pinched. "I object most strenuously, Judge. This is improper."

"On what grounds are you objecting?" Judge Buchanan asked.

"It's irrelevant, Judge. We had the murderer, and we had the murder weapon."

"Overruled," Buchanan said.

"Why didn't you search the Carter vehicles or their house, Agent Collins?"

"Because such a search would have required a warrant, and Mr. Essert would have had to apply to the court for it, and he refused."

There was stirring among the spectators. Joshua sat still, milked it, and waited for quiet.

"That's all I have, Your Honor," he said.

"Government calls Jesus Leyva," Essert said.

Collins left the stand. Chuy was sworn and sat down. After the preliminary questions, Essert asked, "You helped Mr. Rabb investigate this matter at one point, isn't that true?"

"Yes, sir."

"You found a big puddle by the defendant's house that looked like blood, didn't you?"

"Objection, Your Honor, leading," Joshua said.

"Yes," said the judge. "Rephrase the question."

"What did Mr. Rabb ask you to do?"

"He asked me to go with him to Isaiah's house to search for evidence, both inside and outside."

"Did you find anything that you believed might be of evidentiary value?"

"Yes. Near the house I found a big rust-colored spot, maybe six feet around, that was dried. It looked to both of us like it might be blood. We took a few samples of the dirt over to the coroner's office."

"Thank you."

"I have no questions for this witness on cross, Your

Honor," Joshua said. "But I will be calling him in my case, so I would ask the court not to excuse him from the subpoena."

"You hear that, Officer Leyva?" Judge Buchanan asked.

"Yes, sir. I'll stay in the courtroom."

Essert rose. "Government calls Dr. Stanley Wolfe."

Essert introduced the Pima County coroner and his qualifications to the jury through a series of questions. Then he moved quickly to the important testimony.

"Did you perform an autopsy on Jennifer Carter?"

"Yes."

"What was her cause of death?"

"She bled to death from five stab wounds. In my judgment, any one of them would have been fatal."

"Thank you, sir."

Joshua rose at the table. "Did you determine how much blood she had in her body at the time of the autopsy?"

Dr. Wolfe opened the manila file he had brought to the stand, flipped a couple of pages, and read for a moment. "I believe that she had lost at least half of her blood, probably about six pints."

"Did you determine her blood type?"

"Yes, type O."

"Can you determine whether dried blood is human and what type it is?"

"We can determine that it is blood with the benzidine test, and that it's human blood with the precipitin test. But when the blood is dried and over twenty-four hours old, the precipitin test isn't completely reliable, and even if it's positive, we sometimes can't type the blood."

"Did I bring to your office some samples of dried dirt?"

"Yes, you did. A couple of weeks ago."

"What did I ask you to do?"

"To test for the presence of blood, and if I could determine that it was blood, to test for type."

"And did you do that, Dr. Wolfe?"

"Yes. But the dried fluid that had caused the dirt

to take on a rust color was so old and so decomposed by exposure to sunlight and the elements that I could not even determine whether it was blood."

"Thank you, Dr. Wolfe. That's all I have."

"Could it have been blood?" Essert asked.

Dr. Wolfe shrugged. "Sure. And it could have been grape juice or wine or God knows what."

Essert frowned. "Nothing further, Your Honor."

"Government rests, Your Honor," Essert said.

"Very well," said the judge. "You may begin your case in chief, Mr. Rabb."

"Thank you, Your Honor. Defense calls Philip Carter."

The tall, stocky young man stood up in the back of the courtroom and came forward to the clerk. He raised his hand, was sworn, and took the stand.

"You are Philip Carter, son of Edward Carter, brother of the victim in this case, Jennifer?"

"Yes." His voice was thin.

"You have been subpoenaed by me, is that correct?"

"Correct."

"And you have sat through this entire trial so far?"

"Yes."

"You heard me accuse your father of engaging in incest with your sister and of killing her when he flew into a jealous rage upon finding her in bed with Charlie Isaiah?"

Philip Carter flinched and swallowed hard. He looked angrily at Joshua. "Yeah, I heard it."

"And you heard your father swear on the witness stand that it wasn't true?"

"Yes."

Joshua stood up and limped around the table. He stopped about five feet in front of the young man and fixed him with a hard glare. "Your father was lying, wasn't he?"

Carter's face reddened and his lips quivered. His eyes became bloodshot and he began to hyperventilate. "No, he wasn't lying." He squeezed the words out of a constricted throat.

"You remember that I came to visit you at your dorm?"

"Yes."

"And you admitted to me that your sister had told you that your father had forced her into a sexual relationship."

Carter gritted his teeth and his lips blanched. "You damn liar. You can't say things like that in court."

Joshua stepped two feet closer to Philip. "You did admit that to me, didn't you?"

Carter shook his head slowly, then vigorously.

"You must answer audibly, sir," Judge Buchanan said.

"No," Carter hissed.

Joshua limped slowly back to his chair, clacking his cane dramatically on the wooden floor, and sat down. "Nothing further."

"No questions," Essert announced.

"Re-call Jesus Leyva," said Joshua.

Chuy took the stand again.

"You're still under oath, Officer Leyva," the judge said.

Chuy nodded.

"You were with me that evening when I visited Philip Carter in his dormitory room?"

"Yes, you asked me to accompany you."

"Did you hear Philip Carter admit that his sister had just a month before come to him and told him that her father had forced her into an incestuous affair?"

"Yes."

A loud murmur went up among the spectators. There was considerable moving around and shoes shuffling on the floor. Judge Buchanan rapped his gavel and gazed around sternly.

"Your witness," Joshua said, looking over at Essert.

"You work for Mr. Rabb, don't you?" Essert asked.

"Not exactly. I work for Mr. Hendly, he's the BIA superintendent. Both Mr. Rabb and I work for him."

"But Mr. Rabb is your superior?"

Chuy shrugged. "No, I don't think so. I work under

the superintendent's orders. Mr. Rabb is the legal officer."

"You're a very close friend of Mr. Rabb's?"

"That's true."

"You're a Papago Indian."

Chuy smiled. "Yes."

"Charlie Isaiah is a Papago being defended by Mr. Rabb."

"I most strongly object, Your Honor," Joshua said, standing up. "This line of questioning is purely meant to discredit Officer Leyva, and he was Mr. Essert's own witness. It is improper for him to impeach his own witness."

Judge Buchanan frowned and leaned forward over the bench. "Well, in this instance, Mr. Rabb, Mr. Leyva is your witness, and I think that Mr. Essert is not violating the rule. You'll have your opportunity on re-direct to repair any damage. The objection is overruled."

Essert was full of steam now. He stood up at his table and bellowed his question: "You are a Papago, Charlie Isaiah is a Papago being defended by your very close friend and fellow employee of the BIA, Joshua Rabb. Is that true, Mr. Leyva?"

"Yes, it is true. But I would not lie on this witness stand for either of them."

"The jury will be the judge of that," intoned Tim Essert in full voice. He sat down slowly.

"Nothing, Your Honor," Joshua said.

Chuy walked to the back of the courtroom and sat down next to Solomon. Solomon's face was etched with bitterness. He looked at his brother and shook his head. "Somebody ought to tear that gringo bastard's face off," he muttered.

"Mr. Rabb?" Judge Buchanan said.

"Your Honor, our next witness is Charlie Isaiah."

There was audible shuffling and whispering among the spectators as Charlie was sworn by the clerk and took the stand. He was wearing the jumpsuit uniform of the federal detention center prisoners, but he was not handcuffed. United States Marshal Ollie

Friedkind, who had been sitting in a chair behind the defense table, walked to the clerk's table next to the witness stand and sat down on a short stool next to the table.

Charlie had the constitutional right not to take the stand and testify and be cross-examined. And if he chose not to, the United States attorney could neither call him as a witness nor make an issue to the jury of the defendant's silence. But in a case like this, where the difference between life and death depended heavily on the ability of the defendant himself to convince the jury that he simply was not the kind of person to have committed such a heinous crime, it was essential that the defendant testify.

"State your name, please," Joshua said.

"Charlie Isaiah."

"And where do you live, Charlie?"

"At San Xavier, about a mile from the mission."

Joshua got up slowly from the table, as though his war wounds were causing him pain, and limped to the end of the jury railing. His deliberate movements and clacking cane brought all of the jurors' faces toward him. He looked as austere and solemn as he could, a Presbyterian minister at a tragic funeral for a friend killed in an accident not of his causing.

Many people thought that defense attorneys were phonies for using these tactics. But in Joshua's judgment it was not unnecessary phoniness. It was critical for the defense attorney to attempt to counteract the aura of "officialness" that surrounded the prosecution. The prosecutor was called the United States attorney, as though he bore the entire future safety and strength of the nation and its citizenry on his willing but over-burdened shoulders. The law enforcement officers were either "FBI Special Agents" straight out of the popular radio shows, or uniformed officers with black shiny boots and bright gold badges. In contrast, sitting opposite this array of officialdom and legitimacy was the defendant, dressed in a faded denim air force surplus jumpsuit with a big black P stenciled on the back, a pair of scuffed brown ankle-high work boots with no laces—lest this villain use the laces to throttle any innocent maiden who should venture too close—and a burly uniformed United States marshal always close at hand to make sure that the treacherous defendant did not run amuck in a murderous rampage. The government set this stage purely for its benefit. Joshua deeply believed, as did most of his fellow criminal defense attorneys, that the defendant deserved to try to reset the stage as much as possible to even his chances. A trial, after all, was supposed to be a quest for truth in which the defendant was presumed to be innocent.

"Now, Charlie, tell the jury your background."

"Yes, sir." He turned toward the jury, frightened, his voice hesitant, and spoke directly to them as Joshua had instructed him to. "I was born on the San Xavier Reservation. My father got killed in a ranching accident fifteen years ago. He was gored by a bull. My mom died of TB just a couple of years ago, and me and my older sister lived together until she got married last year. Then she moved to Ajo. I went to the convent school at the mission through the sixth grade, Sunnyside through the eighth, and graduated from Tucson High in May last year."

"How'd you do in school, Charlie?" Joshua asked. Make it friendly, conversational. Always call him "Charlie," like you're talking to a pal. The U.S. attorney would call him "Mr. Isaiah" and refer to him as "the defendant," to distance him from sweet little Jennifer and her grand old dad Eddie Carter and the good folks on the jury.

"I did okay. Got pretty good grades. Wasn't so good in math, you know. But I did okay." He grinned sheepishly. What average kid likes to talk to grown-ups about his grades?

"How did you come to be employed at Carter Ford?"

"Well, Jennifer Carter told me her father was looking for someone to be a salesman who spoke Papago and Spanish, and I went over there and talked to him.

He put me on temporary for a couple of weeks, and then when I sold some cars, he hired me full-time."

"Did you know Jennifer Carter well?"

The jury became completely still, intense. The simple stuff was over. The real stuff was coming.

"Yes, sir." He swallowed, obviously saddened by the memory. "I met her when I was still at Tucson High, she was a year behind me. I went out with her."

"You mean on dates?"

"Well, not exactly the usual kind. She said her dad hated Papagos and greasers, wouldn't let her go on dates with them. So she'd go out with her girlfriend Cindy and tell her dad she was going to the movies or something, and then Cindy would take her to meet me. Then when she got her own car, she'd come by herself."

"How many times did you meet her like that?"

He shrugged. "I don't know, maybe a hundred, maybe more. It was for two years before her father killed her."

There was absolute silence among the spectators. The jurors' faces were riveted on Charlie.

"Did Jennifer and you have an intimate relationship?"

He swallowed and sighed. "Yes. We loved each other. She started coming out to my house on the reservation, and a few months after I graduated, we went to bed together. Then a lot of times. I wanted to marry her, but she was real scared of her father."

"Did she ever tell you that her father forced her to have sex with him?"

"No, sir. I never knew that."

"Do you remember what happened on the day that Jennifer was murdered?"

Charlie looked at his hands, and tears rolled off his cheeks. He sniffed and swallowed and caught his breath. "Yes, I remember," he said in a hoarse whisper.

"Please tell the jury."

Again he turned toward the jury. "I wasn't working that afternoon. I was supposed to work six to nine in the evening. Jennifer and I were together, we went to a movie. It got out about three o'clock. She said she needed to get something at her house—you know, it's just a few blocks from downtown—and that her father was never home from work early. We went over there and I went up to the second floor, to her bedroom with her, and we started making out, you know, and then we got into bed—" He stopped and shuddered, and tears once again streamed down his cheeks.

Joshua said nothing, letting the boy's weeping and the jurors' rapt attention create painful suspense.

Charlie was talking to his hands in his lap now, his voice just above a whisper. "And then suddenly her dad and her brother were both there. I don't know why. But suddenly they were there, and her dad had a hunting knife, and he was screaming at her, 'You cheating bitch! You cheating bitch!' over and over, and he started stabbing her, and her brother dragged me out of bed and beat me up and threw me into a big cloth chair, and her dad came after me with the knife, but her brother wouldn't let him kill me. And then he kicked me. . . . I guess I passed out. The next thing I knew I was next to her in bed in my house and the cops were dragging me off the bed."

Joshua stood rigidly still. Two minutes passed. Three. Charlie Isaiah wept loudly. He wiped his eyes with his hands and sniffed. Joshua limped heavily back to the defense table and let himself sink onto the oak chair.

"Agent Roy Collins has testified that you were covered with vomit and dead drunk. Is that true?"

"No, sir. I hadn't been drinking at all. I don't drink. And the vomit was from Phil Carter. When he saw his father murder his sister, he vomited all over me."

Joshua paused for a moment and stared solemnly at Charlie. "You have sworn on the Bible to tell us nothing but the truth, so help you God?"

Charlie nodded. "Yes."

"Is what you just told us the absolute truth?"

Charlie nodded his head vigorously. He looked intently at the jurors and then back at Joshua Rabb. "Yes, sir. I swear it."

"Thank you, Charlie," Joshua said. He looked at Judge Buchanan. "That's all I have, Your Honor."

"Mr. Essert, you may cross-examine," said the judge.

Essert stood up slowly, a look of disgust on his face. "Mr. Isaiah, is there a single human being in the entire world who can verify any of the story you have just told us about Jennifer Carter?"

"Yes. Cindy Danson."

"And where is she?" Essert looked dramatically around the courtroom.

"I don't know. She moved."

"Mr. Isaiah, in this whole year you were still going to Tucson High and dating Jennifer Carter, is there even one other fellow student you know of who ever saw you together with her?"

"There must be, but I don't know."

"You say you were with her a hundred or more times in two years, yet no one but this girl who has disappeared can verify your story?"

Charlie swallowed. He said nothing.

"Please answer my question, Mr. Isaiah."

"Yes, I guess so," he said quietly.

Essert walked to the clerk's table, picked up the hunting knife with the attached tag, and laid it on the flat railing in front of Charlie. "This is the knife you murdered Jennifer Carter with, isn't it?"

"Absolutely not. I never seen it before."

"Are you a heroin user, Mr. Isaiah?"

Joshua squinted at Essert. This was out of left field. Joshua hadn't seen any signs of addiction, nose dripping, constant sniffling, tracks on the arms. But of course, he hadn't seen Charlie until almost two weeks after he had been arrested. By then the tracks would have disappeared. But not the other signs, and he would have been in withdrawal. What the hell was Essert pulling?

"No, I never used heroin," Charlie answered.

Essert picked up a manila folder off his desk. He took out a large photograph and brought it forward to the clerk. The clerk wrote on the back of it and handed it back to him. Essert laid the photograph next to the hunting knife on the flat rail in front of Charlie Isaiah.

"Is this a photograph of you?"

Charlie looked at it and hesitated. Then, in a small voice, "Yes."

"Move the admission of government's exhibit number two, Your Honor," Essert said.

"Have you seen it, Mr. Rabb?" Judge Buchanan asked.

Joshua shook his head casually, remaining in his chair. Stay calm. Don't fall off the chair in a dead faint.

"Show it to defense counsel, Mr. Essert."

Tim Essert brought it to Joshua and handed it to him. He stood staring at Joshua with a pleasant smile on his face.

Joshua studied the photo. It was of Charlie Isaiah at the detention center, probably shortly after his arrest. He was holding his arms up toward the camera, apparently at someone's command. He was dressed in a T-shirt covered with bloodstains and other stains, no doubt the vomit that had been described, and extending from both of his inner elbows almost to his wrists were long black lines. They could have been streaks of blood and vomit. But they looked much more like what junkies called "snakes," the bruised tracks that heroin commonly caused in the veins into which it was injected. Joshua felt like jumping out of his chair and rushing to the stand and demanding an explanation from Charlie. But instead he sat impassively at the defense table. Any sign of shock that the jurors read in Joshua's face spelled conviction for Charlie Isaiah. Joshua had long trained himself never to appear surprised or rattled in front of a jury.

Joshua nodded nonchalantly and handed the photograph back to Essert.

"Government's two is admitted," Judge Buchanan said.

Essert spun around abruptly to face Charlie. "You

were high on heroin when you murdered Jennifer Carter, weren't you, Mr. Isaiah?" he roared.

"No," Charlie said meekly.

Essert walked back to the table and sat down. He nodded at Judge Buchanan.

"Re-direct, Mr. Rabb?" the judge asked.

"There is blood all over you in that photograph, Charlie. And the other stuff is vomit, is that right?" Joshua asked.

"Yes, sir."

Joshua stood up and limped to the witness stand. He held up the photograph and displayed it to the jurors. He walked up to the railing and held it before them to give them all an opportunity to see it, turning it this way and that to give every juror his fill, making a strong show of not being afraid for them to examine it closely, because Charlie Isaiah had absolutely nothing to fear from it.

"What are those marks on your arms, Charlie?" Joshua asked. Charlie shook his head. "Must be blood. I had it all over me.

"Joshua walked back to the clerk's table and laid the photo on it. He went back to his chair and sat down.

"Are you a heroin user, Charlie?"

"No."

"Did you ever use heroin?"

"Never."

"Are you telling the truth, Charlie?"

"I swear to God I am." He turned toward the jurors, his face a plea for mercy. "I swear to God I am."

"Did you murder Jennifer Carter?"

Charlie shook his head vigorously. Tears came to his eyes. "No, sir," he said.

▲✛▼✛▼✛▲

Joshua sat in his chair at the defense table and felt that if he tried to stand up his legs wouldn't hold him. The courtroom was empty, silent. Charlie's tears were still on the table where he had laid his head and sobbed when the jury had returned and rendered its verdict. "Don't let them kill me, Mr. Rabb," he had whimpered. But it was not under Joshua's control. The jurors had filed out, not looking at anyone. They almost never looked at anyone after a guilty verdict. Then Judge Buchanan had passed sentence in a somber voice, his face melancholy and drained of its normal color.

Joshua didn't know for certain whether he felt so terrible because a man he believed to be innocent was going to be executed, or because he had somehow become addicted to hopeless causes. He hoped that the latter was not the case. It sometimes happened to lawyers, that they were almost inexorably drawn to causes for underdogs because it made them feel noble and righteous. Joshua didn't admire such lawyers. The practice of criminal law required a profound belief in the right of every person, no matter how base or debased, to defend himself from the overwhelming power of the government when it sought to convict him of a crime. But when that belief, that commitment to justice, became an unreasoning repugnance by a lawyer against "the system," a battle by the lawyer against "the establishment" and a need for him to buck it, oppose it, revile it mindlessly, then the practice of law became a weapon against society or a tool for dishonorable self-aggrandizement, and the quest for justice became a Hollywood movie. It sometimes happened. Joshua hoped it was not happening to him. He had interviewed dozens of men charged with serious crimes. He was neither gullible nor foolish. He just plain believed that Charlie Isaiah was telling the truth.

But what about the snakes on Charlie's arms? They had been the most persuasive evidence that Charlie was lying. But were they heroin tracks? Or were they really just streaks of blood and vomit, as Charlie had sworn, as Joshua had avowed to the jurors in his closing argument?

"We'll appeal," Joshua had said. But his face had revealed nothing but defeat, and his voice was tinny and hollow, devoid of reassurance. Charlie had wept.

CHAPTER FIFTEEN

Joe Bonanno was still in New York. He had called his closest friend, Joe Profaci, and told him that Meyer Lansky was causing him great grief by persisting in narcotics trafficking in Bonanno's backyard. Now that Benny Siegel had been taken care of and was no longer a problem for anyone, Joe said, he was convinced that Lansky had a contract on him so that he wouldn't be able to interfere with the drug smuggling.

Profaci had listened to Bonanno's ranting and simply dismissed it out of hand. Meyer was a gambler, a carpet joint man, not a dope dealer. And Meyer needed the goodwill of the Commission fathers too much to have one of them killed. It had to be someone else. Who? The possibilities were unfortunately endless among the men of tradition.

Profaci had worked for over a week to broker a meeting between Lansky and Bonanno, to put the talk of going to the mats to rest, to try to bring peace to the volcano that was raging in New York City. Bonanno agreed to come to Manhattan to meet with Lansky.

Meyer's apartment on Central Park West had a

beautiful view of the park through a huge picture window in the spacious living room. It was in a very fashionable and expensive Art Deco building on Ninetieth Street. But no one was enjoying the view at the moment.

Meyer was livid with rage. He stared malignantly at Joe Bonanno. "You come into my house, you accuse me of schemes against you. Who the fuck you talking to?"

Joe winced. No one talked to him like this. Jake Haberman stood by the sliding doors to the veranda with his right hand in his suit coat pocket holding the gun he had brandished openly just a few minutes earlier. Donatello Luna stood next to the sofa on which Joe and Meyer were sitting uneasily. Both Bonanno and Luna had been patted down at the door to Meyer's apartment before being allowed to enter, and Luna had been disarmed. Bonanno was humiliated. No Yid should ever treat a father this way.

"I talked to Frank Costello," Joe hissed. "He says he thinks you and Benny was freelancing and that you're still running dope through the border on your own.

"That's horseshit, Joe. Y'unnerstand? Pure horseshit. You hear me what I'm saying, Joe? I'm gonna tell you something. I didn't have nothing to do with the whole deal from the first. It was all Benny and Frank Costello. I just loaned them a couple mules to carry the shit. Now all of a sudden there's a goddamn war going on and you tell me I caused it. Who the hell is doing what to who, huh? It's horseshit, y' hear me talking? Joe Profaci knows I got clean hands."

Bonanno studied Lansky's face, and he believed the little man. Profaci was right. Whatever was happening, Lansky wasn't behind it. Maybe even Costello was involved. "What is going on?" he mumbled, looking at Donatello Luna.

Luna rolled his eyes and shrugged. "Big Julie said it was him shot Lorenzo." He pointed at Jake Haberman. "Big Julie says they was ambushed by him and Saul Blaustein."

"Jake didn't do nothing, Padre Giuseppe," Meyer said. "You hear me talking to you? He didn't do nothing. Y'unnerstand? And Saul was murdered even before Lorenzo. Big Julie is lying to you. He's lying, Padre Giuseppe. Somebody turned him against you. You go back to Frank, you tell him what I say to you. Somebody's trying to start a war, but it ain't me." Meyer thumped his open hand against his chest.

Joe rubbed his chin hard and shook his head. "*Son averen una tresca contro mi* [They are intriguing against me]," he said hoarsely.

Meyer had been close enough to the Italians for thirty-five years to understand. He nodded. "As God is my witness, Joe," he put his hand over his heart, "I don't know what's been going on, but it ain't me."

"Then who?" Bonanno growled, his face distorted with hatred.

"I only hear things," Lansky said slowly and carefully. "I don't know nothing for sure." He paused. "There is rumors about Frank Costello."

Bonanno stared at him oddly. "Rumors? Costello himself? What kind of bullshit is this?"

Meyer looked earnestly at Bonanno. "They say him and Charlie Luciano want to keep the deal going, running dope through the Papago reservation. Frank already has plenty of markets, here, Philly, Brooklyn, Newark. Charlie has the contacts in Mexico."

Bonanno swallowed and narrowed his eyes at Lansky.

"*Emmiss,* I swear on my mother's grave, Joe. This is what I hear."

"Why I don't hear *nothing*?"

"You been in Tucson, Joe, out of touch. You stay here in New York, you hear these things just like me."

"You can find out, Meyer. You was Charlie's best friend for thirty years."

Meyer shook his head gravely. "I called him, Joe. He told me stay out of this shit. That's it. I don't ask no more questions. Listen to me, Joe. Charlie's changed. He ain't the same Charlie. Ten years in the joint, now living like a peasant in Sicily." He shrugged.

"It's only money that matters anymore, Joe. Only money."

Bonanno sighed deeply and stood up. Lansky stood, and the men shook hands solemnly. "We are at peace, Meyer. We are at peace, on my honor. I will find out who the *escrementi* is that does this to us. *Tu ne cede malis, sed contra audentior ito* [Yield thou not to adversity, but press on the more bravely]."

The Latin was well beyond Meyer, but he smiled and nodded sagely, glad to have Bonanno's avowal. Bonanno left the apartment, Donatello Luna close on his heels.

"Bring Big Julie to me," Joe said through gritted teeth.

"Yes, Don Peppino. But he went to Montreal just two days ago. I'm sure he ain't back on Long Island yet."

"Good, good. I want Fay and the children on the first airplane back to Tucson. Call your brother. Tell him, drive them to the airport, go with them. I don't know who Julie's working for, and I don't want my family here when he gets back."

"Yes, Don Peppino."

Donatello drove the big touring Packard across the Williamsburg Bridge and pulled up to an apartment owned by the Bonanno family on Nostrand Avenue in Brooklyn. Joe waited in the car while Luna made a telephone call to the Long Island estate, to his brother Michael. He got back in the Packard and drove to the sprawling house near Hampton Bays. A fog was rolling in off the Atlantic, presaging a summer storm.

Michael Luna had already taken Fay and the children to Idlewild. It was safer to wait for the airplane among all those people than to stay one more minute on Long Island.

▲✛▼✛▼✛▲

Joe Bonanno waited restlessly for Big Julie at the Long Island estate for three days, but he had disappeared. He had gone to Montreal to check on labor

unrest at a mozzarella plant owned by the Bonanno
family there, and he had simply disappeared after he
had hospitalized two of the troublemakers who were
trying to incite a strike for higher wages. Maybe some
of the workers had dealt with him as he had with
them. Or maybe he had heard a rumor about the
peace conference between Joe and Meyer Lansky and
realized that he was in jeopardy. Whatever the reason,
however, he didn't return to Long Island.

Joe was frustrated and uncomfortable. Big Julie was
a formidable killer. Working for someone else, with
the intimate knowledge he had gained over the years
of the Bonanno family, made him a fearsome *avvers-
ario*. A *voltagabbana* [turncoat] was far more dangerous than a simple enemy.

The only thing to do was to talk to Frank Costello
himself. But it couldn't be at a Commission meeting.
If Joe caused the *capo di tutti capi* to lose face in front
of the other fathers, Joe's guts would be smeared like
dogshit all over a Brooklyn gutter. The meeting had
to be private, informal, and attended by enough of
Bonanno's soldiers to guarantee his safety.

Joe Profaci once again acted as intermediary. Frank
liked to have dinner at the Taste of Calabria restaurant in the Bronx. But it was too close to Costello's
base of support, too embedded in his own neighborhood, to be agreeable to Bonanno. Bonanno recom-
mended Pasquale's Kitchen on the border between
Williamsburg and Bedford Stuyvesant. But it was too
deeply ensconsed in Bonanno's old neighborhood to
be acceptable to Costello. Finally after an afternoon
of traded telephone calls, the dinner was to be at
Shmulik's Delicatessen on the Lower East Side of
Manhattan, a Jewish neighborhood neutral to both
Mafia fathers.

When Joe got there at eleven in the evening, he
entered the almost empty restaurant in the middle of
six men. The seventh, Donatello Luna, led the group.
They walked up to a small round table in the rear.
Frank Costello was sitting with Tommy Lucchese and

Albert Anastasia. Four other men stood behind Costello.

Joe sat down at the table across from Costello. Anastasia and Lucchese stood up and backed away.

"*Tu hai tanti sicarii, Francesco* [You have many hired guns]," Bonanno said. He strained to smile.

"*Et tu, Brute,*" Costello responded, returning the smile.

"I like a man who steeps himself in classic literature," Joe said.

"*Grazie mille,* Don Peppino. So what can I do for you?"

"You can first ask your *assassini* to stand back a little from the table. It is warm in here with all this breath."

Costello flicked his hand off the table and jutted his chin toward Anastasia. All of the thirteen lieutenants went to other tables and booths to sit.

"Now tell me, Don Peppino, what troubles you so?" Frank Costello leaned over the table and spoke barely above a whisper.

"The drug trafficking where I live must cease. No more," Bonanno whispered. He drew his forefinger across his neck. "And I want to know who put out the contract on me."

Costello looked hard at Bonanno for a moment, then his face softened. "I am sorry, Don Peppino, I have let this go too far. Charlie set up the deal for Benny. But Benny was *un' culo* [an asshole]. *Pazz', pazz' completamente.*" He pointed to his temple and made a circular movement with his forefinger. "But that is over. Unfortunately, he had someone helping him with the Mexicans who is not under the control of the Commission. And this *serpente* is now on his own. I have talked to him. Joe Profaci talked to him. Your cousin Stefano talked, begged him—Don Peppino, listen what I tell you. Stefano *begged* him he should come back home, or at least move the operation to California or Texas. But we couldn't do nothing." He sat back in his chair, looking defeated.

"Nothing. This *mamaluta*, this wild man, ain't got no respect for the fathers."

"What are you talking?" Bonanno was having trouble keeping his voice calm and low. "What are you saying? That you can't control him? You sent there Mad Marvin, you sent there Tomasso Constanzo and Vincenzo Lubrazzi. You tell me you can't do nothing more?" The last question was a hiss.

Frank held up a calming hand. "That was before, Don Peppino." A soothing, confidential whisper. "That was business, Commission business. As God is my witness. We had to take care of Ben Siegel, we had a very big problem." He shook his head sadly from side to side. "Marvin, Tommy, Vinnie. May God rest their souls." He crossed himself. "But I tell you, Joe, I tell you on the soul of my beloved daughter, may God strike me dead, I tell you this is not me that is scheming against you. This is a *rinnegato* [renegade]. You gotta handle him yourself."

"So who?"

"Alfredo Maggadino," Costello whispered barely audibly.

Joe Bonanno sat back in his chair, a look of shock twisting his face. "My nephew Alfredo. I change his shitty diapers when he's a baby. I give him licorice when he's this big." He held his hand out below the table. "I treat him like a son, like my own Roberto, like Roberto's big brother. He made his bones with me. With *me*, Padre Francesco, with *me*. Like a son." He looked profoundly shocked, wounded.

"Nobody could have been a better friend, Don Peppino. Nobody could have been better *famiglia*."

Bonanno sighed deeply. "He stays for the last two months at the El Rancho del Cerro, it's a dude ranch on the west side of Tucson. I have him to my house, he eats by me, sometimes he sleeps." He shook his head in disbelief.

"*Giovani di oggi* [The young people of today]," Frank Costello said, his voice wistful. "They got no honor, Don Peppino." His voice trailed off, and he shook his head sadly. "They got no respect for the old tradition."

▲+▽+▽+▲

The next day Joe Bonanno left Long Island. Donatello drove him in the touring Packard to Tucson. They arrived on Wednesday afternoon the first week in July in a thunderstorm so intense that it blackened the skies and rendered the windshield wipers virtually useless. The lawn in front of the abandoned Lansky house had died, and the pelting rain turned it into a huge puddle of mud spilling onto the rich green grass in front of the Bonanno house. Joe had to chide himself to put it out of his mind, to not let it annoy him. Remember who is the enemy, he thought to himself over and over again. Do not dissipate your strength on extraneous distractions.

Fay and thirteen-year-old Elizabeth were delighted to have him home. Sal, the baby, was in the crib in his room taking a nap. Roberto was off somewhere. Usually in the afternoons he was at the Owl Drug by Tucson High. Michael Luna had the Cadillac over at the Texas Oil station getting it worked on. Things were calm and quiet. This was Tucson, not the volcano.

Fay had kept the eight morning newspapers that had been delivered to the house since she returned. Joe was always very conscientious about keeping up with Tucson news, who was who, who was doing what, what was most on everybody's mind in this sleepy town.

The articles that most arrested his attention were from yesterday's and today's newspapers. Yesterday's paper had a long article about the trial of Charlie Isaiah starting in federal court that morning. It regaled every known fact concerning the murder of Jennifer Carter, and it gave a long description of Isaiah's family, what was known of his short life, and the details of his arrest. There were several paragraphs about Joshua Rabb, the New York lawyer who had been appointed to defend Isaiah. The same lawyer who had defended Ignacio Antone and Franklin Carillo last year. Bonanno read the story with interest. He knew about Carillo, since the trial had taken place just last winter when the Bonannos were in Tucson. But the Antone trial had been last summer, when they had been on their farm in upstate New York, and Bonanno had not known the details until now.

This morning's paper carried J. T. Sellner's story of Isaiah's trial on the front page. Before the trial had started, Judge Buchanan had denied Joshua Rabb's motion for continuance, because Rabb could not assure the judge that there was a genuine probability that he could locate Cynthia Danson at all, let alone within a reasonable period of time.

The trial had not lasted long. Rabb had accused Edward Carter of incest. Carter had broken down on the stand and wept uncontrollably for several minutes:

> Then he pointed a shaking finger at the leering defense attorney and accused him of the most "grotesque scheme of lies and innuendos to get a killer off. I never touched my daughter," Mr. Carter choked out, "except in tenderness and a father's love."
>
> Mr. Rabb tried the same tactic with Philip Carter, the twenty-one-year-old brother of the victim, who has starred on the University of Arizona football team for three seasons. The young collegian also vigorously denied knowing anything or even hearing anything about such infamy. After Philip Carter left the stand, Charlie Isaiah testified. His story was that he had been in bed with Jennifer Carter in her own house, that her father and brother had discovered them, and that Edward Carter had murdered his own daughter while Philip held Isaiah down.
>
> Assistant U.S. Attorney Tim Essert then revealed the clinching piece of evidence against Isaiah. It was a photograph taken of him at the Mount Lemmon Detention Center shortly after his arrest, which clearly showed heroin tracks on the insides of his arms. Mr. Rabb desperately tried to convince the

jury that they were streaks of blood, and that Isaiah never used heroin.

The jury was clearly unimpeded by these disgraceful defense tactics. It took only thirty-seven minutes for the twelve men to find Charlie Isaiah guilty of murder, kidnapping, and rape. Mr. Rabb renewed his motion for continuance by asking for a mistrial, because he had not been given adequate opportunity to locate a critical witness. Judge Buchanan denied the various defense maneuvers. He sentenced Charlie Isaiah to be executed on December 10, 1947, and told Rabb that if in the interim he discovered Cynthia Danson or any other important witness, the execution would be stayed and a new evidentiary hearing would be granted on an application for a writ of habeas corpus.

Joe Bonanno put down the newspaper. This Joshua Rabb was an interesting man. He was willing to incur the wrath of an entire community to defend an Indian man accused of murdering a white seventeen-year-old cheerleader at Tucson High. That took a pair of *culones* between his legs the size of *bocci*. A tough guy this Rabb. A very tough guy. One must be careful around such a man.

CHAPTER SIXTEEN

Joshua sat in the kitchen reading the newspaper story about yesterday's trial, and he had no appetite for the sausage and scrambled eggs lying on the plate in front of him. Magdalena tiptoed out of the kitchen. Hanna took one look at her father's face and walked quickly outside to throw corn kernels in the chicken coop attached to the west end of the house, where some sixty White Rock chickens squabbled and fluttered over breakfast. Adam, not so attuned to the sensitivities of old people, had the radio in the living room turned up high enough to hear while he ate breakfast at the table. After Joshua had stared at him for a full minute, he finally looked up, startled, gauged the look in his father's eyes, and left the house quickly through the kitchen door.

Joshua got up heavily from the table, slung his seersucker suit coat over his shoulder, holding it by his forefinger crooked in the collar, and walked slowly to the BIA. The ammoniac stink of the chicken coops wafted up Indian Agency Road on the sluggish morning breeze and made his eyes tear. For the first time in weeks he caught himself really limping and wished that he had brought along his cane. Adam and his pal Chris were currying their horses, tethered to the hitching post in front of the shed behind the Rabb house. Another day for the cavalry, Joshua thought.

"Don't let me hear that you've been chasing any cows, Adam," Joshua called out.

"We don't do that anymore, Dad. That's kid stuff," Adam called back.

It was only nine in the morning, but it was at least a hundred degrees already. Joshua went into the BIA, smiled as pleasantly as he could at Frances Hendly sitting in the reception area behind the smeary glass window, and walked down the corridor to his office at the end. Roy Collins and Chuy Leyva were both sitting in front of his desk waiting for him.

"You don't look too happy," Collins said.

"I've been thinking how you can make me happier," Joshua said.

"I'm not into any of that kinky shit," Collins quipped.

Chuy laughed. Joshua smiled. "You been taking lessons from Edgar?" he said.

"A true poet, that Edgar," Roy said. "So what's on your mind?"

"Send a TWIX or a cable or however you do it to all of the FBI field offices and ask them to locate a Cynthia Danson, eighteen years old, formerly of Tucson."

"You still riding that horse?" Roy's voice was sarcastic. Joshua nodded.

Well, I don't guess Tim Essert has any say over that," Roy said. "Okay, I'll do it. Now that he's won the case, it shouldn't make him too crazy."

"Good. Thanks. I really appreciate it."

"No sweat," Roy said. "Matter of fact, I'll do it right now before we leave."

"Where we going?" Joshua asked.

"Chuy's brother, Solomon, set up the drug deal in Newfield. The three of us are going to handle it."

"Don't you think we ought to get the border patrol or Customs in on it?" Joshua asked.

Chuy shook his head. "No, all that movement is bound to be noticed down there, and it'll blow the whole setup. We can handle it. The heroin will be coming over the border in a day or two for sure. I don't know how many loads. But at least one."

"Good. We going down there today?"

"Yeah," Chuy said. "We'll leave in an hour." He hesitated. "Solomon's got a girl with him."

Joshua shrugged. "So?"

"It's the mule's sister."

Joshua considered that for a moment. "Is there a problem? Is she involved?"

"No, no. But it's real touchy. Solomon wants to marry the girl."

Joshua nodded. "Let me see if I can guess what's coming. We can't arrest the brother because Solomon's girlfriend would be pissed off. So we have to turn him."

Chuy shrugged. "Good guess."

Joshua shook his head. "How in hell are we going to do that?"

"Well," Chuy said, "I think if we bust him and put him in the Mount Lemmon Detention Center for a couple of days, he'll be begging us to cooperate. He's good-looking, sixteen years old, not big."

"Real nice," Joshua said. "Throw him in there to get sodomized so he comes our way?"

Chuy nodded. "It's the best idea that I can come up with."

"Well, to get him immunity, the U.S. attorney has to go along with it." Joshua turned toward Roy. "Did you talk to that scumbag Essert?"

Roy nodded. "Yeah. I caught him yesterday after the trial. He'll get the grand jury to grant immunity. He was so elated about kicking your ass that he would've agreed to anything."

Joshua threw him a finger. "Thanks, pal."

Collins gritted his teeth to keep from laughing. Chuy was straight-faced.

"Okay, I'll go home and get some clothes," Joshua said. "Pick me up in an hour."

Joshua walked home. He changed into Levis and a pair of Keds high-top black sneakers. He couldn't wear boots because of the missing toes on his left foot. He pulled on a faded blue cotton chambray work shirt. The final touch was a straw cowboy hat. He put several changes of clothes in a small valise. He took the Smith & Wesson .45 revolver out of the nightstand, made sure it was loaded, and put it under Magdalena's pillow. She slept on a foam mattress on the floor beside Hanna's bed.

He heard the chickens squawking in the pen next to the little house. He walked outside to the coop. Magdalena was inside throwing handfuls of sweet feed to the chickens.

"I'll be gone for a few days," Joshua said.

She looked up. "What happened?"

"Nothing, nothing. But Chuy and Roy Collins and I are going down to Chuy's mother's place in San Miguel and stay for a while. Chuy thinks we can put an end to the heroin smuggling that's coming up through the border at Newfield."

"That's dangerous. You think you ought to be involved?" She looked at his steel hand.

"Either me and the other two handle it quietly now, or we'll scare them underground and most likely lose our chance."

She nodded reluctantly.

"The telephone wire is down again," he said. "I won't be able to call. But I'll be back in three or four days at the most. I put the gun under your pillow."

"You think there'll be any trouble here?"

He shook his head. "But it's there just in case. And if Bobby Bonanno or Buddy Lansky comes by, Hanna is not to go out with them."

She frowned. "I'll tell her, and I'll do my best. But I can't tie her to the bedpost."

Joshua knew that she was right. The best thing to do would be to go over to Lansky's and Bonanno's homes, confront both Meyer—if he had returned yet—and Joe, and ask them to leave Hanna out of their milieu. A father's request to two fathers. Rude?

Overly protective? Maybe. Uncalled for? No. Hanna was a fifteen-year-old girl who could set any seventeen-year-old boy's heart beating like a high-tempo metronome, and her father had the right to some say as to whom she dated.

"Okay," he said to Magdalena. "I'm going to go see Mr. Lansky and Mr. Bonanno and ask them to tell their sons to leave Hanna alone."

Magdalena's eyes opened wide. "Do you think that's wise?"

Joshua shrugged in frustration. "Give me a better idea."

She thought for a moment. "My cousin lives in Topawa, about fifteen miles north of San Miguel. She and her husband have a real big place. Hanna and Adam and I could stay there. We'll be just twenty minutes from you instead of three hours. And no one will know we're there."

Joshua nodded. "Okay, that's a good idea." He went inside and telephoned Barbara. She was disappointed that they wouldn't be able to be together for a few days, and she wanted to go with him. Not wanting to worry her, he told her that he was meeting Edgar in Sells on a construction matter, and they were staying at the BIA office, and there simply wasn't any privacy for her there. He promised to call her as soon as he returned.

Chuy drove up with Roy in the BIA pickup. He got out of the truck and walked up to Magdalena. Joshua got his valise, came out, and laid it in the bed of the truck. There were three rifle cases with FBI stenciled in black on the khaki canvas. There was a long wooden crate with BROWNING A.R.—FBI painted on it, and beside it were six steel cans of ammunition. Joshua got into the cab, and Roy handed him a .45 Colt automatic in a black leather shoulder holster.

"I thought this would be the easiest thing for you to use," he said.

"Good."

Chuy got into the driver's seat. "That's great that

Magda and the kids will be in Topawa," he said. "We can check on them every day."

"What?" Roy asked.

"They're going to stay in Topawa with Magdalena's cousin while we're in San Miguel," Joshua said. "We'll only be fifteen miles apart."

△✚▽✚▽✚△

Topawa was close enough to the tribal headquarters in Sells that it had gotten electricity and running water over a year ago. Erma Baltos, Magdalena's cousin, was the mother of four small children. Her husband, Humberto, a Mexican American originally from Phoenix, worked as the chief agent for the feed-lot cooperative that pooled and marketed the cattle from the Big Reservation as well as from most of the white-owned ranches of the Ajo Valley and Buckeye Valley all the way up to West Phoenix. The Baltos family was wealthy by reservation standards, and their large redbrick house reflected it.

Magdalena and Hanna took an empty bedroom with bunk beds in it. Adam got his own room, a small storeroom with a cot. They all went outside to the *vato,* a porch with a saguaro rib roof propped up by mesquite poles. Erma was baking bread in the large earthen oven, although she had a gas stove inside the house.

Adam walked over to the barn. There were seven horses in stalls and several sawhorses covered with all kinds of riding equipment. Adam had never had a hand-tooled leather western saddle like these, and he admired them covetously. A couple of them were of plain leather, but the rest were embossed with flower designs and basket weaves and silver conchos holding leather thong ties.

Erma came into the barn. "You want to ride?" she said, smiling broadly at Adam.

"Yeah, I'd love to."

"Take the roan." She pointed at the reddish gelding

in the third stall. "He's real calm, won't get you in trouble."

"Can I use one of these saddles?" he asked.

"Sure. Use that one." She pointed at the oak-tanned saddle with a beautiful flower design. "It belongs to my husband, but he doesn't use it much. He likes stock saddles better. They have a deeper seat."

She left the barn, and Adam saddled the roan and put the bridle on him that had been hanging on the gatepost of his stall. He led the horse outside and swung into the saddle. He dug his boot heels into the horse's belly, and it began cantering easily. He was soon out of sight.

▲✦▽✦▽✦▲

Chuy's mother's house in San Miguel was almost exactly what Joshua had expected, having lived next to the San Xavier Reservation for a year now. It was larger than most of the houses on San Xavier, but it was otherwise the same: adobe brick, low ceilings, no running water or electricity, two outhouses behind a low hill, a large kitchen and several small bedrooms, and a *vato* outside. The *vato* was where most of the family activity took place, around a long dining table of rough pine planks, chairs of bent ocotillo staves with cowhide seats and backs, and a great earthen stove where all of the baking was done. The water well and hand pump was behind the stove. It hardly ever rained here, and the coldest it got, even in the dead of winter, was forty degrees, and then only in the darkest hours of the morning. Now in early July it was cooler out here in the *vato* in the evening than it was inside the house.

Solomon drove up to the house early in the evening. Chuy, his mother, Joshua, and Roy were sitting at the table on the *vato* eating baby back beef ribs and drinking lemonade.

Solomon introduced Linda in Spanish. He looked a little embarrassed, and she was so timid that she hardly looked up. Chuy was surprised and very pleased. She was a slender, freckle-faced girl, cute and shy, and obviously very happy to be here with Solomon.

Maria Leyva was pleased that her older son had found a woman. A man needed a woman, and Solomon had been lonely and at loose ends for years. He used to go with her to San Xavier mission almost every Sunday morning for mass. But lately he had been spending most weekends in Nogales drinking and whoring, and he was turning into a pagan, a bum. But now he had a sweet girl. Thank God, she thought. *Madre de Dios,* thank you for answering my prayers. She crossed herself while no one was looking, then took Linda by the hand and led her into the house to Solomon's room and helped her unpack the small suitcase. The house had been so lonely with her daughters away in Phoenix at the boarding school. A woman needed to have daughters around her. Sons were okay, but a daughter, nothing substituted for a daughter. She hugged Linda, and the girl was so overwhelmed and relieved that she wept.

"You will be my daughter," Maria Leyva said, holding both of the girl's hands. "I will take care of you, and you will take care of Solomon." They hugged warmly, and Linda cried happily.

▲✛▽✛▽✛▲

"Does she know what's going to happen?" Chuy asked.

Solomon nodded. "As long as he doesn't get put in prison, she's all for it."

"Do you know for sure when Manuel is coming up with a load?"

"No. But I think tomorrow. When Linda and I left, Manuel was there. She told him she was coming to the ranch with me. He said he'd be fine, that he had a big job beginning tomorrow." Solomon shrugged. "Either tomorrow or pretty soon."

"What's the logistics?" Roy asked.

"There are a couple of hills down by Newfield beside the dirt road," Chuy said. "We'll be able to see all the way to the border and well beyond. We'll take two vehicles, me and Solomon in one, you and Joshua in the other. Get up on the hills and wait. When the exchange goes down, we bust them. If there's no exchange, if Manuel just keeps on driving, we stop him up near Sells. If there's going to be an exchange or substitute driver, it should occur before Sells. Too much possibility of traffic in Sells or on the road either to Ajo or Tucson."

Roy nodded.

▲✦▽✦▽✦▲

At about seven o'clock in the evening, Magdalena drove up to the Leyva ranch and parked in front of the *vato*. The sun was almost to the horizon in the west, and it had cooled off to about ninety degrees. The men were sitting at the long table playing five-card stud. Adam sat down next to his father. Magdalena and Hanna sat on a bench beside the earthen oven, where Maria Leyva and Linda were baking bread.

"Can I play, Dad?" Adam asked.

"Know how?" Joshua asked, examining his hand.

"Sure. You keep pairs or three of a kind or your highest card and get rid of the rest."

"Here, play this hand." Joshua gave Adam his cards. "I'm going to read a little while there's still some light left." He walked into the house, got *Siddhartha* out of the bedroom, and came back to the *vato*.

Chuy and Magdalena strolled hand in hand away from the house and over the small knoll to the east.

"Daddy, can we go driving?" Hanna said. She had just gotten her learner's permit a week ago.

Joshua was bored and restless, and he put the book on the table. "Sure. But Magdalena has the key."

"Uh-uh," Hanna said, holding up a small key ring.

She got in behind the wheel. Joshua sat in the passenger seat. Hanna started the car, ground the gears putting it in reverse, and let the clutch out too quickly.

The car stalled. She turned the key again, forgetting to depress the clutch, and the engine screeched. She grimaced, looked apologetically at her tight-jawed father, and started the engine properly. She backed the car slowly and jerkily away from the *vato,* put it in first, and headed for the road. The car lurched when she shifted into second and again into third, but then the ride was smooth, and Joshua relaxed. The convertible top was down and the rushing air felt refreshing. There were no other cars on the road, and they drove thirty-five miles an hour toward Sells.

"Bobby Bonanno is back," Hanna said, concentrating on the road.

Joshua looked over at her. "Since when?"

"A couple of weeks."

Silence for a minute. "His father back?"

She nodded. "Last Wednesday."

He breathed deeply, trying to quell his rising anger.

"I know you don't like Bobby," Hanna said softly, "but I don't think you're being fair."

Joshua swallowed hard. "Why don't you stop the car so we can talk without going over a cliff?"

She looked around. "There aren't any cliffs."

"Stop the car," he said, his voice low.

She pulled off the side of the road, forgot to put the clutch in, and the car stalled and jerked to a stop.

He got out of the car. "Let's walk. Take the key."

She got out of the car and walked with him up the side of a gentle hill on the east side of the road. There was a broad granite boulder under a thick palo verde tree. He sat down facing the car and the setting sun. She sat down next to him.

"Where have I failed?" he said.

She pursed her lips and studied him. "Don't tell me." She held her hand up and pondered dramatically for a moment. "That's it! Spencer Tracy in *Boys Town.*"

He frowned at her. "And you're Mickey Rooney."

"Nope. I'm much too tall."

The sunset was a pastel light show. A sky filled with

wispy clouds took on undulating hues of magenta and azure and yellow.

"Do you have any idea why we've had to come out here?" He studied her soberly.

She shook her head. "Magdalena just said BIA business for a few days."

"It's because of Bobby's father."

She looked at him oddly. "What?"

"Roy Collins believes that Bonanno is involved in some way with the heroin smuggling that has been going on around here and Nogales. Nothing like that could happen this close to Joe Bonanno without him knowing about it and approving it."

She shook her head. "How can you say that about him when you don't even know him? It's just not like you, Daddy."

"Honey, I hate to say this to you, but you're being very naive. I look at you and I see a grown woman. But I talk to you and I know you're still a girl." He took her hand and held it. "You know what Mark Twain said? He said that he left home when he was nineteen, and he was disgusted how dumb his parents were. And when he returned at twenty-three, he was surprised at how much they had learned."

She pulled her hand away and wrapped her hands around her knees. She was wearing Levi's and a faded red cowboy shirt. She fiddled with the snaps on one of her sleeves, then stared angrily at the sunset.

"There are some things I'm better at than you are, honey." Joshua spoke as gently as he could. "One of them is making judgments about people. I've been doing it a lot longer than you. I have much more experience at it."

"But it's not Bobby you're making a judgment about, Daddy. It's his father. But it's only Bobby I want to go out with." She put her chin on her knees and stared morosely ahead.

Joshua felt numb. He had no arguments left and was deeply frustrated. This is how it is when your daughter leaves the nest, he thought. She has her own wings, she can catch her own worms, and off she goes while you sit in the nest and hope that she won't hit a tree or mistake a rattlesnake for a worm or get shot by a hunter. What can you do to protect your baby, your fledgling?

They sat silently, absorbed in their own thoughts.

It is depressing having these conversations with myself, he thought. I used to think about Rachel. I used to brood about the war and the concentration camp in Czechoslovakia. Bad dreams haunted my sleep at night. Bad memories sprung to my mind at odd and unexpected times during the day. And I couldn't do a thing about it. But time actually began to heal me, and I have much fewer dreams now. So now that I have whipped most of those dragons, I have a whole new set. When do I get to stop having to slay dragons every day? I am tired of fighting all the time. I am tired of having to fight with my daughter to get her to see just a little of what I see so plainly. Why is life an interminable battlefield? Why is it so full of pain?

I just want to declare a truce, to sit on a mountain-top somewhere, this hilltop even, and cross my legs and stare into the horizon, and leave everything else behind. Like Siddhartha. Get rid of the things that own you, get rid of the relationships that ensnare you. Seek nirvana.

Wouldn't that be nice. Just leave all the pain behind.

But I cannot just immerse myself in me and abandon my daughter, who needs me even though she doesn't know it. And I have a son who needs me, and hasn't yet reached the point where he thinks I'm a dumb shit. That'll take another year or two. And I have a lady who I think really loves me. And I love her too. And I am not a man who can be alone, just sitting on a mountain or beside a stream. I need a woman. I need to have someone to share with.

The sun finished its descent behind the hills far to the west. They sat watching it with unseeing eyes.

Darkness would come quickly in the desert. He stood up, feeling deeply depressed. Hanna stood up next to him.

"Daddy, I love you," she said very quietly. She turned to him and hugged him tightly.

Tears fell down his cheeks and wet her hair.

▲✦▽✦▽✦▲

The next day dawned darkly. Pregnant black cumulus clouds lightened to ominous slate gray as the sun rose. At five-thirty, after a breakfast of pork sausage and eggs, they drove toward the border less than five miles south. The two hills were across from each other, separated only by the rutted dirt trail that transected the border some two hundred yards away. Chuy and Solomon parked Solomon's pickup truck behind the eastern hill and walked to the top. There were several mesquite trees for cover. Roy and Joshua parked the BIA police pickup behind the western hill and took cover behind an outcropping of granite topped by a multi-trunked senita cactus. The stench of something rotting assaulted Joshua's nostrils, and he looked around. Ten feet to his left was the maggot-infested carcass of a small coyote. He kicked some dirt over it, trying vainly to eradicate the stink.

They sat for hours on the rocky ground, becoming stiff and cramped, drinking occasionally from canteens filled with now lukewarm coffee. The threat of a torrential rain, so close in the early morning hours, now disappeared, and the relentless sun scorched the earth with murderous heat.

Roy was looking toward the border through binoculars. A thicket of mesquite trees stood just to the left of the road, stretching over the border. Beyond the trees rose a billow of dust.

"There's something," Roy said.

Joshua scrambled to his knees and raised his binoculars. "Sure is," he murmured.

An old Dodge stake truck came into view. As it neared the hills, a gray-bearded man could be seen behind the wheel in the otherwise empty cab. There were a half dozen cattle in the back of the truck.

"Just a little cattle smuggling," Chuy said through the walkie-talkie.

The truck rumbled northward between the hills, leaving behind a fog of dust. It filtered down hazily. Another billow appeared beyond the trees, a rapidly rolling funnel of dust. Joshua squinted through the binoculars.

"Another one," he said.

Roy trained his binoculars on the approaching truck. "A white van."

The van emerged from the blanket of the mesquite trees and passed the border.

"That's him" came Chuy's voice over the walkie-talkie.

Suddenly a pickup truck towing a two-horse trailer crept out of the cover of the dense mesquite trees onto the dirt road. The van stopped across from it. Two men exited the pickup. Manuel got out of the van and walked toward them.

"There's the exchange," Chuy said. "Let's go."

Joshua and Roy ran down the hill to the BIA pickup. Joshua's heart was beating fast, making him almost breathless. He was frightened, he couldn't help it. This was like being in combat again, and the jolting of his mechanical arm on his shoulders reminded him painfully that bravery could exact a terribly high price.

Roy started the pickup quickly and pulled it onto the road with a squeal of the tires, throwing up a shower of dirt. The pickup had a siren and a turning red light atop the cab. Chuy and Solomon were close behind in Solomon's pickup. They closed the hundred yards in seconds.

Manuel had started the van and was trying to turn it around on the narrow road. The two men saw that they could not move their truck on the road, now blocked by the van. One of them pulled a revolver from a hip holster and shot toward the pickup trucks. Solomon skidded the pickup to a halt twenty feet from the two men. The truck fishtailed broadside toward the men. Chuy leveled his .45 Colt Single-Action Army toward the one with the gun and fired two shots.

The man spun backward and flopped to the ground. The other one lifted his arms high in surrender.

Roy blocked the van's movement with the BIA pickup. Joshua leaped out of the truck and ran toward the van door, his pistol drawn, and pointed at the driver. Manuel turned the key off and raised his arms.

Manuel came out of the cab, and Joshua gestured him to lie spread-eagled on his stomach. Manuel quickly did so, his eyes flickering around to the man lying a few feet away with no face left, just bleeding mush that two .45-caliber slugs had created. The other man knelt at the dead man's side, holding his hand and weeping.

Joshua patted down Manuel for weapons. He had none. Roy ordered the other man to his feet and searched him. He found a snub-nosed .38 revolver in his hip pocket and a long hunting knife in a belt sheath. Roy handcuffed him and told him to get into the bed of the pickup. Roy laid the rear gate down. The man struggled to sit on it, then swung his legs into it. Roy ankle-cuffed him on one ankle and secured the other cuff through a small steel ring welded into the side panel. Chuy and Roy then lifted the dead man like a sack of wheat and threw him into the bed of the pickup.

Solomon put Manuel in the cab of his truck and handcuffed him to the door handle. Chuy and Roy searched the van and the pickup. The registration papers for both trucks showed that they were owned by Cooperativa Agricultura Mexicana and leased to Commodity Importers, Inc., in Nogales, Arizona.

Chuy held up the van registration. "That's the phony address in Nogales that's an empty lot on a hill."

Roy nodded. "Same for this one," he said.

Joshua opened the side sliding door of the van. Inside were fifty packages, the size of bricks, wrapped in white butcher paper and taped with masking tape. Joshua picked up one.

"You know heroin?" he asked Roy.

Roy took the package, took a penknife out of his

pocket, opened the blade, punched it through the package, and withdrew some brown powder on the blade.

"Mexican brown," he said. "Looks like fifty kilos. A lot of money. Let's get it to Dr. Wolfe for testing."

They loaded the heroin in the bed of the BIA pickup. Roy and Joshua drove back to the Santos Ranch in Topawa and told Magdalena that it was over, that she could take Hanna and Adam back to Tucson. Hanna was delighted. Adam was disappointed. He was dying to ride that fancy saddle again.

▲✦▼✦▼✦▲

Solomon and Chuy placed Manuel between them in the cab of the truck, his hands cuffed behind his back. They drove to the Indian police office in Sells, and Chuy told Henry Enos to take two men down to New-field, get the trucks, and bring them to the federal impoundment lot across from the federal building in Tucson.

"What do I pay two guys with?" Henry asked.

Chuy thought for a moment. "There's two horses, saddles, and bridles, in the trailer. Each of them can have one."

Henry nodded. They shook hands.

They drove Manuel to the detention center on Mount Lemmon. It took over three hours. Solomon kept up a constant conversation with the boy, trying to get information on the smuggling ring. The conversation was one-sided. For the entire three hours the boy said nothing. They processed him into the detention center and had just finished when Joshua and Roy arrived.

The tall, skinny man with them was Harry Gallegos, a Mexican American from Nogales, Arizona, nick-named "Long Ears," due to an obvious anatomical anomaly. Harry Long Ears was talkative, having rid-den with the destroyed body of his friend Jaime Ver-dugo for two hours, until it was very unceremoniously hauled out of the bed of the pickup and into the coroner's office in Tucson. He was anxious not to meet the same fate, and neither Roy nor Joshua treated him in a way that was reassuring. He started babbling as soon as they came out of the coroner's office, after carrying in the fifty heroin packages. Roy unlocked the ankle cuffs and put Harry between Joshua and himself in the cab of the pickup. Harry babbled for an entire hour up to the detention center, but apparently he knew nothing. Jaime had been the contact man.

Harry Long Ears's usual job was as lookout along with Jaime, to make sure the loads were getting across the border all right. Last month there had been several killings. Harry had seen four of them. Gringos killing each other. Why? He shrugged his shoulders. "Gringos."

Then the stuff had been sent up through the Nogales border crossing again, but that had lasted only a week. Eight trucks had been seized, hundreds of pounds of shit, eight drivers arrested. Two days ago, Jaime told him that the "boss" wanted them to go back to Newfield, pick up a load that would come over in a white van, and deliver it to Tucson. Where? To a crossroads on the northwest side, in the Tortolitas Mountains, Silverbell Road and Sunset. To whom? He shrugged. "*No se.* Just sit there. Someone will come."

Roy processed Harry Long Ears into the detention center. Then Roy, Joshua, Chuy, and Solomon stood in the parking lot and discussed what to do next. Harry Long Ears was a dead end. He probably was telling the truth, and he knew nothing. They already knew about Fat Henry from Manuel, and it was almost certain that he was only a middleman. They needed to find out who the organizer was on the Mexican side. Manuel was the key. He had been recruited on the Mexican side. Even if he didn't know much more than who had recruited him, he was a grave threat to the organization if he became a government witness. His testimony was sufficient to arrest and convict Fat Henry and destroy the American-side distribution system. And maybe he could do much more damage. But even if he couldn't, the "boss" might not be sure how much he knew, and this would throw the organization into turmoil. Turmoil created mistakes. And mistakes created the opportunities to discover and destroy the smuggling operation.

Manuel had been recalcitrant, and Solomon had known that he would be. But they all believed that in a couple of days, his outlook on life would be changed. There was nothing to do but wait for the inevitable to happen.

▲+▼+▼+▲

Three days later, nothing had changed. Manuel spoke only Spanish, according to Solomon, so Chuy tried to interrogate him at the detention center, but the boy was still stone-faced. He looked none the worse for wear, and he wouldn't say a word. Chuy telephoned Joshua at the BIA and told him the bad news. Joshua got into his car and drove to the detention center. Chuy waited for him.

Joshua went into the visitors' area to talk to Charlie Isaiah.

"Is there any talk among the prisoners?" Joshua asked.

"Yeah, sure," Charlie answered. "The kid used to sell his ass to gringo fags who came across the border looking for little boys. Nothing these guys up here do to him is any worse. He knows if he becomes a snitch he's dead." Charlie shrugged.

Joshua walked back to the parking lot, where Chuy was waiting, and told him.

Chuy shook his head in frustration. "Damn kid's a hard case. What now?"

Joshua pursed his lips, frowning.

"Maybe Linda can help," Chuy said.

"By doing what?"

"I'll ask Solomon to bring her up here to talk to him, see if she can convince him to cooperate. Otherwise we have to prosecute him."

"Solomon's going to love that."

Chuy frowned. "What the hell else do we do?"

Joshua shrugged. "Damned if I know," he muttered. "But I don't feel right about bringing her up here. There are too many eyes in there, too many tongues."

"Yeah, I know," Chuy said. "But I'm out of ideas."

They got into their cars and drove back to the BIA. It was one o'clock in the afternoon. Chuy called Henry Enos in Sells and told him to go to the ranch in San Miguel and ask Solomon to bring Linda to the BIA. They could stay in Chuy's house until they returned to the ranch. Then he called Roy Collins and asked him to clear a visit between himself, Solomon, Manuel, and his sister at the Mount Lemmon Detention Center tomorrow morning.

▲✦▽✦✦▽✦▲

The next morning Roy Collins drove Linda up the Santa Catalina Mountains. Solomon came along for encouragement. Chuy went with them to translate if necessary. Linda had had years of contact with Americans, but they didn't do a lot of talking, so her English was minimal.

At the detention center, they had to wait for the visitors' area to clear. Harry Long Ears was meeting with his attorney. Roy had run into the attorney several times before, in the federal court in Tucson. He was a Mexican American lawyer from Nogales, Arizona, who regularly represented people charged with smuggling narcotics. When the lawyer finished the interview and walked through the gate, Roy greeted him frigidly. Roy noticed that the lawyer stared curiously at Linda and then lingered in the parking lot, watched her and Roy and the two Indians enter the visitors' area, and waited to see whom they were visiting.

It made Roy suddenly uneasy. But then Manuel came into the visiting area, and when Roy looked toward the parking lot a few minutes later, the lawyer was gone.

▲✛▽✛▽✛▲

Roy and Solomon dropped Linda off at Chuy's house on the reservation and took Chuy to the BIA. Then they drove to the U.S. attorney's office across from the federal building to talk to Tim Essert.

They told him that Linda had convinced Manuel that if he talked, he wouldn't go to prison. The boy had finally agreed. He had told them about getting the job riding atop the trucks from Ricardo Fuentes, the owner of the Waikiki Ballroom and two other whorehouses. Juanito Coronado was a regular at the Waikiki, always treated like royalty by the owner, and Manuel had seen Juanito give large amounts of money to Ricardo. How much? He really didn't know. For what? He didn't know that either. Maybe for the girls he and his pals used. Maybe for dope. Who knows?

Roy carefully repeated Manuel's description of the other guy who was often with Juanito. He was a gringo, maybe twenty, twenty-one years old, fair hair, good-looking, medium height, real loud clothes, black shirts, yellow ties, bold checked sports coats and shoes with gray fabric covers with buttons.

"Spats?" Essert said, looking doubtfully at Roy.

Roy nodded.

"Who the hell wears spats anymore?" Essert asked. "And racer's checks and black shirts and yellow ties. It's straight out of a gangster film."

"He swears it's true," Solomon said.

"Do the gringo and Juanito Coronado ever talk together?" Essert asked.

"Many times," Roy answered. "Once the gringo gave him a little suitcase. Once he gave him a big, full brown paper bag."

Tim Essert listened closely to Roy's and Solomon's recitations of the boy's information. If Manuel Rodriguez would testify to a grand jury, they would have most of what they needed to charge Juanito Coronado and Fat Henry and the movie gangster with conspiracy. The grand jury could issue a John Doe arrest warrant for "Spats." And if Solomon or Chuy hung around the Waikiki for a while, he was bound to turn up. They could follow him back over the border, see where he went, go back to the grand jury for a search warrant, and then arrest him and search wherever he was living. Odds were strong that "Spats" was the dealer on the U.S. side, maybe even the head man, and Juanito was the Mexican supplier.

"There's a grand jury called for this afternoon at two," Essert said, glancing at his watch. He looked at Roy. "I need you to hearsay the boy's information. The grand jury will issue a subpoena for him. I'll talk to Judge Buchanan and set up a hearing for tomorrow morning. Solomon will pick Manuel up tomorrow morning and bring him to Judge Buchanan's chambers. The boy will say that he's going to refuse to testify about anything because it will incriminate him. Then Judge Buchanan will immunize him, and he'll be able to spill his guts without being prosecuted."

"And we have your word that he won't be prosecuted for the heroin smuggling four days ago?" Solomon asked.

Essert cast him a sour glance. "Yeah, sure. My word, *amigo*." He settled back in his chair and stared at Roy Collins. "By the way, I hear some scuttlebutt that you put out a TWIX on Joshua Rabb's mystery witness."

Roy nodded.

"What'd you do that for?"

"Because he asked me to."

"What the hell kind of crap is that?" Essert's face was turning red. "Some two-bit defense attorney asks you to fuck up my murder conviction, and you jump right to it?"

"It's not for anything but to make damn sure we convicted the right guy."

Essert leaned forward over his desk, and his face was ugly. "You help that scumbag Rabb, I'll have your fuckin' ass."

"I cleared it with my field supervisor in Phoenix, and he okayed it with Washington. You unhappy, make whatever complaints you want to. Issuing search warrants is your call, you're the prosecutor. Looking for potentially critical witnesses is my call, I'm the cop." Roy spoke blandly. He stood up slowly and said, "See you over at the grand jury room at two." He and Solomon walked out of Essert's office.

"The guy loves you," Solomon said quietly as they walked into the boiling sunshine.

"Yeah, he's a real charmer. Loves everybody." Roy chuckled. "Come on, the Bureau will buy you some fried chicken over at McClellan's counter. It's twenty after one, not enough time to take you back to San Xavier."

▲✦▽✦▽✦▲

It was after four o'clock when Roy drove Solomon to the BIA and dropped him off. Chuy had left, out on a call somewhere. Joshua Rabb had also left for the day. Solomon's pickup was parked at Chuy's house, and Linda would be waiting for him there.

Solomon walked down Indian Agency Road to the irrigation ditch. He walked down the sloped side, across the desiccated bottom, and up the other side. He walked absently through the fallow, half-mile-long field behind Mission San Xavier and turned right on the dirt road in front of the mission, past the rectory and the elementary school and the cemetery about a mile to the west, where the road forked, one fork going to Tucson, the other deeper south into the reservation. Chuy lived in a small yellow brick government-built house about another mile south where the graded dirt road turned into a rutted path. It was well after five o'clock when Solomon got to it.

The front door was ajar, and the jamb was splintered where the door had apparently been forced open. Solomon was suddenly chilled. He ran into the house. The living room was empty. In the bedroom where he and Linda slept, blood was everywhere. She lay naked in the middle of the bed, a kitchen knife embedded in her sternum. He ran to her, shook her shoulders as if she might awaken, and put his ear to her chest to listen for her heartbeat. She was obviously dead. He doubled over and vomited explosively on the floor, then fled the room and the house. He stumbled down the wooden porch steps and sprawled on the ground, vomiting again.

He stood up, disoriented, not knowing what to do. He had to call somebody, the FBI, yeah, that's it, got to call the FBI. The only telephone on the reservation was in the rectory, where Father Boniface and two Franciscan friars lived. He had been to mass with his mother enough times to know all three of them. He got into his pickup and pressed the gas pedal while he fumbled with the key. Finally he got the key in the ignition and turned it, but the engine cranked without starting. He smelled the strong odor of gasoline and took his foot off the gas pedal. Too late. He had flooded the carburetor and it wouldn't start.

He got out of the truck and started walking toward Mission Road, then running. In this heat he could only run a mile. He slowed down, wheezing and breathless, and walked the rest of the way as quickly as he could. He banged on the rectory door.

A friar in a brown linen cassock answered the knock. He looked at Solomon in shock. For the first time Solomon realized that he was covered with Linda's blood.

"Can I use your phone, Father Simpson?"

The friar nodded reluctantly and opened the door wide.

Solomon walked in. He dialed the operator and got the telephone number for the FBI. He forgot it as soon as he began to dial and had to call the operator again. He dialed the number and let it ring again and again. No one was there. He called the operator for the BIA telephone number and dialed it. Again no answer.

"What time is it?" he asked the wary-looking friar.

"Almost six."

"Shit," Solomon muttered. He left the rectory and stood outside, wondering what to do. Joshua Rabb. He lived just across from the irrigation ditch. Get

Joshua Rabb, he'd know what to do. Solomon began running, half stumbling, across the rocky field behind the mission. He could see Joshua's yellow convertible and two other cars parked in front of the Rabb house. It took him ten minutes to reach it. He was breathless and almost voiceless.

▲+▽+▽+▲

Joshua was sitting on the sofa with Barbara Dubin. Adam and Magdalena were on the floor in front of the big radio. Hanna was sitting on the overstuffed chair telling a funny story when the banging on the front door stopped her short.

Adam jumped up and opened the door. Solomon was standing there, wheezing, his clothing and face and hands splattered with blood and bits of vomit. Adam backed away. Joshua stood up abruptly and went to the door. He opened the screen and walked onto the porch.

"What the hell happened to you?"

"Not me, not me," Solomon stammered. "Linda. It's Linda. She's in bed at Chuy's house, a knife sticking out of her chest."

Joshua's mouth dropped open. "What?"

"I tried to call Roy Collins. I tried to call Chuy. Too late."

"Okay, come on," Joshua said. "I'll be back late," he called through the screen door.

They ran to the yellow convertible. Joshua jumped in the driver's side, snapped his pronged hand on the specially designed knob on the wheel, and sped away down Indian Agency Road to Valencia, west to the Mission Loop Road, and south to Chuy's house. When they got there, Roy Collins was just getting out of his car next to Chuy's BIA pickup. Solomon remained sitting in Joshua's car, his face buried in his hands.

Joshua ran into the house behind Collins. Chuy was standing in the bedroom staring at the body. Joshua and Roy stood on either side of him. The smell of the blood and entrails was nauseating.

"Same as Jennifer Carter," Chuy said.

Joshua nodded. "Have you checked her closely?" he asked, his voice tight in his throat.

"Yeah," Chuy said. "I can see three other stab wounds, chest and neck. Maybe one more in the abdomen. Too much blood, I can't tell."

Joshua breathed shallowly. "It's not Charlie Isaiah."

"Father Simpson called me at home, told me Solomon was acting real weird, covered with blood."

"He didn't do it, Roy. He just found her."

Collins nodded. He walked up to the body and looked closely. He walked around the bed slowly. He studied the handle of the knife protruding from her chest. Then he walked into the living room. Joshua and Chuy followed him.

"Looks to me like the same M.O. as the Carter girl. Except Linda was actually killed in bed."

Both Joshua and Chuy nodded.

"I want Dr. Wolfe to check her out here before we move her. He may be able to see more than we do." Roy went outside to his car to use the radio.

"We killed her," Solomon said, walking up to Chuy and Joshua. "We killed her," he gasped.

Chuy gritted his teeth and nodded his head slowly. "We all showed up at the detention center like the cavalry. Might as well have put up a sign."

They stood silently, grim-faced.

Roy came back into the house. "Stan is on his way."

"It was us up at the detention center," Chuy said, his voice gravelly. "That's how they got to her. Kill her, Manuel never opens his mouth again. And we're telegraphing it like goddamn hick cops." He swallowed hard.

"Why not just kill Manuel?" Solomon said, his voice almost wistful.

"Too few possible suspects up at the detention center," Roy said. "Who else would it be but Harry Long Ears? Or at least he's the one that would get prosecuted. But out here there's a zillion could have done it. We'll never find the killer."

They stood glumly, minute after minute, waiting for Dr. Wolfe to arrive.

"Yes, we will," Roy said slowly. "That lawyer from Nogales, Arthur Sanchez, he's the one who spread the news."

Chuy looked at Roy and nodded. "Right. This happened too fast for the word to have gotten out from the prisoners. It had to be Sanchez."

"So what?" Joshua said. "Even if you beat his brains out and he tells you who he told, where are you? You keep sweating guy after guy until one of them confesses?"

Roy frowned and sighed deeply.

"Fucking crooked lawyer," Solomon muttered. "It ain't right."

"Lots of things aren't right," Joshua said. "But we've got to get to the bottom of *this,* not just cowboy around like gangbusters."

Roy looked quizzically at Joshua. "That's it, gangbusters. I'm telling you, this whole thing is Bonanno. It's got to be. Nobody in Arizona has the kind of money to throw around on heroin that's necessary for the loads that have been coming up. That's hundreds of thousands of dollars. The only money like that is the Mafia. And the only markets for hundreds of pounds of pure Mexican brown in so short a time have to be back East, New York, Philadelphia, Boston. When it's cut, it's a couple of thousand pounds of H. There aren't enough junkies in all of Arizona to use that much shit in years. I'm telling you, it's got to be Bonanno, because the Mafia couldn't do an operation around Tucson without him. They couldn't. It's got to be him. I feel it in my bones. And what Manuel told us about the white guy who's been dealing with Juanito Coronado, it has to be one of Bonanno's boys. The guy's straight out of a gangster movie."

"Maybe that's exactly how it's supposed to look," Chuy said.

Roy shook his head. "No, no. It's for real. The meetings take place in a Mexican whorehouse. No chance of getting hassled by American cops, no chance of being busted. They wouldn't even expect any surveillance in a place like that across the border. I'm telling you, I feel it in my guts. 'Spats' is for real, and he's working for Joe Bonanno.''

"So what do we do?" Chuy asked. "Go roust Bonanno?"

Roy frowned. "That'll get us nowhere. He's not going to talk no matter what we do. I think what we've got to do is put a twenty-four-hour surveillance on him. Identify everybody who comes to his house, everybody he meets in church or on the street. Check them out. Eventually we'll get there."

Joshua nodded. "But you're the only FBI agent in Tucson."

"I'll get a few guys to help," Chuy said.

"Listen, Chuy, no offense meant," Roy said, "but Indians parked around that neighborhood aren't exactly going to blend in with the scenery. I better ask Phoenix to send down a couple of guys. We can take eight-hour shifts."

"You know," Joshua said, "what I don't get is why in hell Charlie Isaiah would make up a whole cock-and-bull story about Jennifer and her father and brother. If he just woke up next to her and she was dead, why would he invent all that bullshit?"

Roy shrugged. "Scared. Frantic. Say anything he could think of. Not the first guy who's done it."

Joshua rolled his eyes and wrinkled his brow. "But the story's so damn elaborate. It just doesn't make sense that a nineteen-year-old Indian kid invented it."

"Maybe Charlie Isaiah did kill Jennifer," Roy said. "Maybe Linda was just by weird chance murdered in the same way. Or maybe it was meant to look the same to confuse the hell out of us."

Joshua frowned. "It worked. It's confusing the hell out of me."

Dr. Stanley Wolfe arrived and examined the body. "Four stab wounds," he said. "The fifth in the sternum with the knife still in. No prints on the knife handle. Too much blood."

"Is it the same killer as Jennifer Carter's?" Joshua asked.

The coroner sucked in his cheeks and rubbed his chin hard. "Obviously it could be the same. But there's really no way of knowing. One stabbing is just like any other stabbing, no real physical linking evidence except method, and that's really just conjecture. But I'll look her over closer when I get her downtown. She's got what looks like epidermal skin under her nails on the right hand. She probably scratched the assailant. She may have semen in her, or pubic hair. I'll see."

"Jennifer had none of that," Joshua said.

"Right. And no skin under the nails."

▲✛▽✛▽✛▲

Joshua returned home a little after eleven o'clock that night. Barbara and Magdalena were sitting in the living room, talking. The radio was playing quietly. They could read the horror of the evening in his eyes.

"Where are Hanna and Adam?" he asked.

"Sleeping," Magdalena said, pointing at the closed bedroom doors.

"Good," Joshua said. He sat down heavily on the sofa next to Barbara. "Linda Rodriguez," he said. "She was murdered the same way as Jennifer Carter." His voice was a little lispy.

Magdalena crossed herself. "How is Solomon?"

"Chuy and I took him over to a bar, got a few drinks. He had enough to make him sleep for a few hours."

"Why was she killed?" Barbara asked.

"Because of her brother. He was going to testify at the grand jury tomorrow about the heroin smuggling. They killed her to shut him up."

She swallowed. "Who?"

Joshua shrugged. "The FBI thinks Joe Bonanno is behind the whole thing."

Magdalena sighed deeply. "Is Chuy okay?"

"Yes. A little drunk like me, but okay."

"I'm going to go see him," Magdalena said. She got up and left the house.

Joshua slid more deeply into the sofa. He was wearing his aluminum arm, and until now he had not felt it. But his shoulder ached. Sixteen hours in one day were too many.

"You okay?" Barbara said, looking at him with worry.

He nodded. "Just everything hurts."

"Come on," she whispered.

"Where?"

She pulled him up, and they walked into the bedroom. He slumped down on the edge of the bed. She unbuttoned his shirt and helped him off with it. She unbuckled the two straps of the leather harness and took his arm off and propped it against the wall. Then she took his face gently in both her hands and kissed him on the tip of the nose, on both cheeks, on his forehead, and he pressed his face into her bosom. They hugged for minutes.

"You feeling better?" she whispered.

"Yes." He lay back on the bed and swung his legs onto it. She pulled off his loafers and his socks. She unbuckled his belt and unbuttoned his pants and pulled them and his underwear off. She undressed, walked around the bed, and lay beside him. She held him tightly to her and kissed him softly on the cheek, and he fell asleep.

▲✛▽✛▽✛▲

Joshua's first phone call in his office the next morning was from Roy Collins.

"I got an answer back on the Danson girl," Roy said.

"That's great. Where is she?"

"Santa Monica, California. It's on the coast near Los Angeles."

"You have any more?"

"Yeah, the agent even went to see her."

"She say anything?"

"She said she knew Charlie Isaiah and Jenny Carter. And she said Jenny went out on a date with him a couple of times that she knew of. Once Cindy dropped Jenny at Armory Park to meet Charlie. Once she drove her out to the reservation to his house."

Silence for a moment, then, "Hallelujah," Joshua said.

"The agent even profiled her, said she appeared to be telling the truth. She's a secretary in an elementary school. She was shocked about Jennifer's death, couldn't imagine why Charlie would do it. But she was pretty sure they had only had two dates. And she said that Jennifer was so afraid her father would find out that she doubted that Jennifer would have had the courage to see Charlie more than a couple of times."

Joshua breathed deeply and thought for a moment. "Can you meet me over at Essert's office?"

"Yeah, sure. Want me to bring a whip and a chair?"

"I'll be there in twenty minutes."

Joshua drove to the U.S. attorney's office. Roy was waiting in the lobby. They walked down the corridor and into Tim Essert's office. Essert looked up, annoyed.

"So nice to see you boys again," he said. "Have a seat."

Joshua and Roy sat on the chairs in front of the desk.

"I don't like coming here any more than you like seeing me here," Joshua said. "But this is literally a life-or-death problem."

"Let me take a little of the wind out of your sails, Mr. Rabb. You're here to tell me that the whore who was murdered on the res yesterday was cut up the same way Jennifer Carter was, and since Isaiah is cooling his heels up at the Mount Lemmon Detention Center, even a moron could figure out that he damn well couldn't have done it, and therefore he probably didn't do Jennifer Carter either, so I ought to move to set aside the conviction. How am I doing?"

Joshua nodded.

"What about Solomon Leyva?"

Joshua looked at him oddly. "What about Solomon?"

"One of the friars over at the Mission San Xavier rectory told Father Boniface that Solomon Leyva was covered with blood. Father Boniface reported it to me. I guess he thought it was a fact I ought to be aware of."

Joshua shrugged. "Solomon found the body, checked to see if she was alive."

"Maybe it's much more significant than that, Mr. Rabb. Solomon Leyva picks up a whore in Nogales, brings her up illegally, and murders her the same way Charlie murdered the Carter girl. Charlie gets off." His voice was harsh and loud.

Joshua looked back, astonished. He looked at Roy, and saw the surprise in his face. He turned back toward Essert and ignored the outburst.

"Roy's TWIX located Cynthia Danson in Santa Monica, California. She says that Jennifer Carter and Charlie Isaiah dated at least twice. One time she went out to his house on the reservation."

Essert looked at Roy, who nodded.

"So what?" Essert said. "So they went out twice."

"It confirms Isaiah's story, or at least it provides some confirmation. Now we need the search warrants I asked for."

"Why, because they had two lousy dates? That doesn't prove a goddamn thing."

Joshua's anger boiled up and spewed out. "Are you so full of hate for these people that you can't even imagine that any of them could be innocent? How the hell did a bag full of pus like you ever get this job? You're supposed to *prosecute,* not *persecute.*"

He stood up and walked menacingly toward Essert. Roy Collins rose quickly and put a restraining hand on Joshua's shoulder.

"Come on now, let's get out of here. Nothing good is going to come of this," Roy said.

Essert stood up slowly. "My job is to protect society from pieces of shit like you."

"Come on," Roy said, pulling on Joshua's shoulder.

CHAPTER SEVENTEEN

There was nowhere to bury Linda Rodriguez. She was not a Papago or the wife of a Papago, so the San Xavier cemetery was not available. Neither Chuy nor Solomon had three hundred dollars for a burial at Evergreen Cemetery in Tucson. They could have put her in a pauper's grave at the foot of A Mountain, but it was too cruel even to consider. So Solomon put her in a plain pine casket in the back of the pickup truck and drove her to the ranch in San Miguel. Chuy and Joshua went with him. They dug a grave on a small hill of wildflowers overlooking the Baboquivari Valley. Solomon wept as he hung her rosary on the small cross of mesquite branches that was her headstone. Maria Leyva and her sons chanted a short song in Papago, and they recited the Lord's prayer in Spanish with brimming eyes.

They drove back to Chuy's house at San Xavier. He had bought two bottles of Bacardi rum to help them through the day, and the three men passed the first bottle around in silence. And then the second. Chuy crossed his arms on the kitchen table and laid his head on them and slept. Solomon walked to the tattered sofa in the tiny living room and lay down. He covered his eyes with his forearm and began to cry.

Joshua stood up from the table shakily and steadied himself. He walked out to the porch, and the sun low in the west burned his face and made him dizzy for a moment. He was too drunk to drive. He would walk home. It was only a couple of miles, and he could walk off some of the booze. He went inside the house, splashed water on his face at the kitchen sink, didn't dry off, and left the house. As he walked and his face dried, he began to feel better and his head cleared. He looked for a shortcut, through the fields to the mission, rather than walking the whole mile up to the fork and then walking the whole mile to the mission.

The brush and dried grass were low and mostly dead in the scorching heat of July. Occasional clumps of lavender Mexican primrose and red hummingbird trumpets alleviated the drabness of the rocky gray-tan ground. He could see the towers of the mission straight ahead, perhaps a mile. He passed a few adobe houses, several corrugated tin and tar-paper shacks, and a couple of the old traditional little wigwam-like huts, *olas kihs,* where few Indians lived anymore.

He passed a small adobe house with the front door ajar, and he recognized it. Charlie Isaiah's house. He could get a glass of water in the kitchen. He walked inside, into the kitchen, and opened the only cabinet on the wall. There were a few plates, some bowls, no glasses or cups. He looked around. There was no other storage space, just the cabinet under the sink. He opened the saguaro rib door and knelt down to look inside. It was quite dark. There were several cups and glasses. He reached in for a glass that appeared to be unchipped, and he thought he saw a folded set of papers tucked into the rear corner of the small cabinet. Absently he reached farther back and pulled them out. They had a backing sheet of blank blue stock paper. He unfolded the document and blinked at the typewritten heading on the first page: COOPERATIVA AGRI-CULTURA MEXICANA DE SONORA, S.A. The four-page typewritten document was in Spanish. The last page bore two signatures, one for the agent of Cooperativa Agricultura, the other for Commodity Importers, Inc. The line above it bore the signature CHARLIE ISAIAH.

Joshua stared at it, uncomprehending, feeling the rum cloud his perception and his thinking. He stood up slowly, folded the document again, and put it in his back pocket. He opened the faucet, let the hot water run out of the pipes, then cupped his hands and drank the cooler water. He splashed water on his face, swallowed back the feeling that he was going to vomit, walked to Chuy's house, and drove home very slowly.

▲✦▽✦▽✦▲

When there was a war, when some upstart soldier or power-hungry lieutenant wanted to take over the family, you did not simply have a chat with him over the telephone or have a friendly drink at his home. You surprised him wherever you could find him, and you brought along enough friends to control the situation as much as possible. And you tried to talk sense to him.

Joe Bonanno had seven men living at his home with him. Lorenzo Viti and Michael Luna were the leaders. They lived with Bonanno, wherever he might be. The other five were longtime soldiers from Brooklyn. Donatello Luna, Michael's brother, was not known to Alfredo Maggadino. Bonanno had sent Donatello out to El Rancho del Cerro three times, once for dinner in the exclusive dude ranch's small, fancy restaurant, twice for a quiet couple of drinks in the adjoining, elegant bar. There were few guests at the dude ranch in July. Aside from an elderly couple with white hair and new cowboy boots, Donatello counted six men. They were all young, in their early twenties. He didn't recognize any of them save one: Alfredo Maggadino. He had closely studied the photograph of the adopted son of the Buffalo father. The photo was taken last year. Alfredo and Bobby standing together, smiling broadly, arms on each other's shoulders, in bathing suits, on a white sand beach near Castellamare, Sicily.

Alfredo dressed most of the time like a movie gangster, like George Raft or Edward G. Robinson. He looked ridiculous to Donatello. He wore gaudy sports coats and dark shirts, and there was always a bulge under his left arm. And he never went into the restaurant or the bar without his five pals.

The only pattern that Donatello's three trips to El Rancho del Cerro and twenty bucks slipped to the bartender showed was that Alfredo and his soldiers would go to the restaurant every evening at six-thirty when it opened, and then into the bar until it closed at ten. Occasionally they would all be gone for an entire day and evening. And since the bartender always left by ten-thirty, he didn't know if they returned to the guest ranch on those occasions. They had three rooms by the swimming pool with sliding glass doors opening onto the flagstone pool deck. Rooms 4, 5, and 6, the bartender thought. They were all on the south side of the pool.

It was Tuesday night. Bonanno thought that it was the right time. He and his men drove to the dude ranch in two cars and got there at nine-thirty. Donatello Luna remained with Joe in the touring Packard, parked a hundred yards from the ranch house on the shoulder of the access road. The only light was from a weak semicircle of moon. The other car parked behind the Packard. The six men in it got out and walked into the darkness.

A half hour passed. Forty minutes. Forty-five. Out of the thick blackness emerged a man. He walked up to the rear window of the Packard and lit a match to show his face. Donatello put down the revolver he was holding. Joe Bonanno rolled down the window. Michael Luna spoke to him quietly and rapidly in Sicilian. Joe said a few words. Michael walked back into the night. A minute later, two men dragged another man between them to the back door of the Packard. The man was gagged with adhesive tape across his mouth. His hands were tied behind his back. His ankles were tied together. The two men pushed him to his knees beside the door. Joe opened the door

two inches to switch on the pale dome light. Alfredo
Maggadino's eyes opened wide in terror as he stared
at his uncle.

"You have dishonored me, Fredo," Joe said in Sicilian, his voice low and heavy. "You have dishonored
our tradition and ignored the fathers on the Commission, even your own father."

Alfredo's eyes opened even wider.

"Two of your *assassini* have met a tragic fate tonight, Fredo. They will disappear from the face of the
earth without a trace, their souls will roast in purga-
tory, their mothers will wail for them and not even
know where to go to place a lily and a rosary."

Joe's voice became hard and rasping. "For your father's sake, Fredo—for my cousin Stefano's sake—I
do not send you with them. But you must leave this
place, Fredo. You must leave my home and go back
to yours. Otherwise you will join your two compan-
ions, and your father and mother and I must go to
the big church where you received your first commu-
nion, and we must say a novena for you."

Joe closed the car door. The two men dragged Alfredo back into the darkness.

▲✦▽✦▽✦▲

In the morning there was rain, too much to drive
up the mountain. But by eleven o'clock it was clear.
Joshua drove to the detention center on Mount
Lemmon.

He unfolded the contract on the table in front of
Charlie Isaiah and said nothing.

Charlie looked at it, flipped through it, and
shrugged. "So?"

"I know what it is," Joshua said. "Chuy translated
it for me."

"Yeah, so what?" Charlie wrinkled his forehead in
perplexity.

"These are the vehicles used in the smuggling."

Charlie stared at him. "Smuggling what?"

"Quit playing dumb with me, damn it!" Joshua exploded. "Now tell me what role you played in this."

Charlie shook his head slowly. "What's with you, man? You crazy or something?"

"Listen, Charlie," Joshua growled. "A girl was murdered a few days ago because of this. The same way Jennifer was murdered."

"What?" Charlie looked at Joshua in genuine confusion. "They gonna charge me with that murder too?"

Joshua breathed deeply to calm himself. He lowered his voice. "What's this contract for?"

"For Ed Carter, man. He sold a bunch of used trucks to a Mexican company in Sonora and had me sign some papers about being a general partner in an American produce company in Nogales, Arizona, Commodity Importers. But it didn't even exist. I'd just go down to Nogales, Sonora, every couple of weeks and deliver a truck to this old guy on Calle Obregon. The only reason Ed Carter needed me was I was the only salesman he had could speak Spanish."

Joshua sat back and was totally perplexed. "I don't get it," he said.

Charlie shrugged. "I don't know. Carter said it had something to do with taxes and import duties and all that kind of shit. I don't know nothing about that stuff. What I figure he was really doing is he was fencing stolen cars into Mexico, then making it look like they were clean because they got new Mexican registrations from that company and then could be leased to a phony American company, Commodity Importers, get Arizona plates, and be used legally to transport produce into the States again. I figured the owners of the vegetable warehouses were paying about half price for their trucks that way."

"Well, that's not what happened," Joshua said.

"What happened?"

"They were used to smuggle heroin."

Charlie shook his head vigorously. "Hey, man, I don't know shit about that. I swear it."

"What were those snakes on your arms in the photograph?"

Charlie threw up his arms. "Hey, come on, Mr. Rabb. They weren't snakes. What you said in court was exactly right. I was all covered with blood and vomit."

Joshua sat studying the Indian. Once again he believed him. It was uncanny how convincing Charlie Isaiah was.

"Would you be willing to testify against Edward Carter?"

Charlie looked back at Joshua, his eyes narrowing a bit. "In exchange for what?"

Joshua shrugged. "I don't know if I can make any kind of deal."

"Then why the hell should I help the government? I'll get a snitch jacket and die up here before they can execute me down there."

Joshua nodded. "Okay, I'll see what I can do."

▲✦▼✦▼✦▲

"You guys are out of your fucking minds," Edward Carter snarled.

Joshua and Roy Collins sat in front of his desk in his office at the Ford dealership.

"Knock off the shit, Carter," Roy said, putting on the ugliest look he could muster. "We got the contract signed by Charlie Isaiah. Chuy Leyva took his picture down to the Mexican company in Nogales, and the guy said that's who was coming down selling the trucks."

"So how's that got anything to do with me? So Charlie's into selling stolen trucks. He's a fuckin' killer too. Where's the great surprise?"

Roy looked at him disgustedly. "We're all sorry about your daughter. That's the truth. But we got ten of the Commodity Importers trucks in the impound lot across from the federal building. Not one of them was reported stolen by anybody. Most of them had the identification number filed off the engine block, but two didn't."

Carter winced.

"We traced both of them to the wholesale auction up in Phoenix." Roy fished in his seersucker jacket pocket and made a big production out of pulling out a small notepad and slowly turning the pages. "1946 Dodge deuce and a half, sold to Carter Ford on April 17, 1947. 1946 Ford van, sold to Carter Ford a month ago." He flipped the notebook closed.

Carter sagged back into his chair. His jowls hung heavily down his neck. "They were stolen from me, they were both stolen." He turned toward Joshua, then slowly back to Roy Collins. "I reported them stolen."

"There are no reports," Roy said. "We checked with the police and sheriff's departments."

"Well, I told one of my guys to do it," Carter said angrily. "I don't know if they reported it or not. How the fuck would I know? All I know is I told 'em. Fuckin' help today, you know. Can't get no fuckin' help. Everybody's on the GI Bill studying to be a damn sixth-grade teacher. I'm telling ya." He threw up his arms helplessly.

"Who did you tell to do it?" Roy asked.

"How the fuck do I remember?" Carter blustered. "Ask 'em, I got ten of 'em out there sitting on their asses, collectin' pay checks, a bunch of lyin' sacks a shit. Maybe it's that greaser I hired a couple months back."

Roy breathed deeply and gritted his teeth. "Listen, Carter, I don't have enough hard evidence right now to burn your ass, but I will. Soon I will."

He and Joshua left Carter's office. They got into Roy's car.

"Well, we still have Charlie to testify," Joshua said. "He'll swear he got all of the vehicles from Carter and was instructed by him to sell them to the Mexican company."

"Where's Isaiah get us? He'll only talk in exchange for a deal on the murder sentence. And then nobody's going to believe him anyway. A guy sentenced to be executed would snitch off his own mother to save his life."

▲▽✦▽✦▲

When it was just getting dark, Ed Carter drove to El Rancho del Cerro. He had met Alfredo Maggadino three times. The first time had been about six months ago, when Al had first come to Tucson from Buffalo. He had looked up his father's old friend, Ed Carter. He had come to the Carter home in the evening and was obviously real taken with Jennifer. The second time had been right after that. Al had bought a car at the dealership and invited Ed and Jennifer out to the dude ranch for dinner. Jennifer had had a date that night and refused to come. The third time had been about two or three months ago when Al had returned from Buffalo, preparing to stay in Tucson for several months. Those three meetings had been social. This was different.

Carter was afraid to use his telephone, afraid that it was being tapped by the FBI. So he drove out to the dude ranch unannounced, not knowing whether Maggadino would even be there.

He was. He was sitting grim-faced in a dark corner of the bar with three other equally unhappy-looking men. Carter stood in the doorway of the bar and caught Maggadino's eye. The young man gestured him to the table.

"I don't wanna talk in here," Carter said quietly.

"Why not? Bartender ain't even here. He's sick. Just the waiter coming in from the restaurant once in a while."

Carter looked around the empty bar suspiciously. Then he sat at the table across from Maggadino.

"I got a visit today."

"Yeah?" Maggadino said.

"Listen, Al, this is serious. Fuckin' FBI came to see me, and that kike lawyer Joshua Rabb, the asshole who defended Charlie Isaiah."

Maggadino's eyes visibly darkened. His look hardened. "What'd they say?"

"They're on to the Cooperativa Agricultura Mexicana scam."

Maggadino sucked in his cheeks and bit his lip. "How'd they do that?"

"Found some papers at Charlie Isaiah's house."

The young man breathed deeply and expelled the air slowly. "How much they know?"

"They got it pretty well figured out."

"Shit," he muttered. He thought for a moment. "But not good enough to arrest you. That means all they got is a theory, no hard evidence."

"Charlie'll talk," Carter said.

"Nobody'll believe him," Maggadino said.

"FBI agent says he's gonna push till he gets my ass."

"That's what he gets paid to say."

"What about that little bastard Mex they got up at the federal detention center, Manuel Rodriguez?" Carter asked.

"What about him?"

"What's he know?"

"He seen me down there with Juanito Coronado," Maggadino said. "He can prob'ly put two 'n' two together."

"He's gonna spill his guts. He's just a kid."

"He ain't gonna do jackshit," said Maggadino nonchalantly. "I took care his sister. He ain't gonna open his mouth."

"You did that?" Carter looked at him in surprise.

"Who you think, the tooth fairy? She seen me fifty times down in Nogales with Juanito. How long you think it would take her to put the bite on me?"

Carter's face became red, the veins in his nose purpled. "The papers said it was the same way Jennifer got killed," he said slowly. "They said it looked like it could be the same killer." He stared at Maggadino.

"Get outta here with that bullshit. Total bullshit, y' hear me? It's like I tol' you, just like everybody knows. Charlie Isaiah killed your daughter. He must've got hold of some heroin, had a bad hit, went fuckin' nuts. I didn't have nothing to do with it. I just done the Mexican whore the same way to fuck up everybody's mind, man." He studied Carter's face. "I guess it worked good, huh?"

Carter narrowed his eyes and stared at him.

"On my mother's life," Maggadino said, crossing himself and looking earnestly at Carter.

Carter swallowed.

Maggadino gritted his teeth. If this mick lush ever finds out the truth, he thought, he will be too dangerous to let live. Got to be damn careful.

"Okay, okay," Carter said slowly. He looked intently at Maggadino. "I wanna get paid."

"What's that mean?"

"It means you got thirty-five thousand dollars worth of trucks from me. I'm supposed to get ten percent of the action. But there ain't no action. The stuff keeps getting seized and my trucks are all confiscated. You owe me thirty-five grand."

"Who you think you talking to?" Maggadino's eyes twitched. His nostrils flared like a blue tick hound's on a scent.

Ed Carter leaned forward over the table. "Listen, I'm doing this for your old man. Stefano helped me plenty back in Buffalo. I had a little problem during Prohibition. They thought I was runnin' whiskey, Stefano helped me. Hell, it was his whiskey! He got the cops off my ass. When I moved out here, he helped me again, loaned me a couple guys to convince old man Stokes to sell me his dealership. And I paid your old man for it. I paid him real good. But I'll be goddamned if I'm gonna let you steal from me, you little queer bastard."

Alfredo's eyes were bloodshot with rage. "Wait till I tell him about you," he muttered through clenched teeth. "He'll cut your fuckin' throat."

"Don't gimme that shit, Al. Your old man's from the old tradition. He don't do dope. This game is all you." Carter slammed his hand down on the table in front of Maggadino. "I want my fuckin' money."

The guy's gotta go now, Alfredo thought. *Morto.* No

more time. He's suspicious about how his cunt daughter really died. And now he wants money, *my* money.

No one saw the knife until Alfredo Maggadino brought the stiletto blade slashing down through the top of Ed Carter's beefy hand and embedded the point in the table. Carter let out a gargled scream that was immediately smothered by the hand of the man sitting next to him at the small bar table. Alfredo stood up calmly, walked around the table, pulled away the man's hand, and stuffed a cloth napkin in Carter's mouth. He rocked the stiletto and pulled it out of Carter's hand. Carter whimpered and hugged his bloody hand to his chest. Alfredo shoved the stiletto blade through Carter's ear into his brain.

Two of the men at the table got up quickly and held Carter's arms, keeping him from sliding to the floor.

"I can't take the knife out here," Alfredo said. "His brains'll leak all over the floor. But I want my fuckin' knife back. Take him out that way." He pointed at the rear door of the bar. "Take him to that lime pit out Silverbell Road by the abandoned mine. He'll dissolve in two days."

The two men carried the body like a drunk out of the bar. The third man went behind the bar counter and got a wet towel. He wiped the blood off the table. Alfredo sat down and poured himself another drink from the J&B bottle.

"Fuckin' micks," he said. "More guts than brains."

The other man sat down across from him. "Now how do we get trucks?"

Maggadino waved away the problem. "The asshole has a son. I read about him in the papers. He's a hot-shot football star at the university. He'll be taking over the business, and I'll be talking to him. Don't worry. We'll get our trucks."

▲ + ▼ + ▼ + ▲

Alfredo knocked over the lamp on the bed table groping for the phone. "Hello," he said groggily. It was four in the morning.

"You awake to listen?"

The gravelly voice was very familiar to Alfredo. "Yeah, Padre, sure."

"You call me ten minutes, pay phone, President 63508."

Alfredo leaped out of bed, pulled on a pair of pants and a shirt, slipped his loafers on bare feet, took a handful of quarters out of the bed-stand drawer, and ran to his car. He sped to Silverbell and Grant, to the nearest filling station with a pay telephone outside. It was pitch black. He fumbled with the dial and called the operator, then deposited ten quarters.

"Yeah?"

"What's up, Padre?"

"Couple days ago you whacked an old friend, the biggest car dealer in Tucson. You fuckin' *pazzo*?"

"How'd you find out?"

"You forget who you working for, and all your boys?"

"Okay, okay. Nobody'll never find out."

"You better hope not."

"The FBI was on to him. And some lawyer, guy named Rabb, they was all over him, found out about the trucks and how the shit was being sent up here."

"So you pay the FBI a few bills. He walks away like all the other agents we bent. And you whack this lawyer. Gone. All over. But you damn sure don't waste the guy supplying trucks for our whole deal."

"The guy was getting crazy on me. Accusing me of all kinda shit, demanding money. What I'm supposed to do?"

"You supposed to use some brains."

"I got it under control."

"You got nothing under control. You ain't handled the FBI. You ain't shutting this lawyer up. But they ain't nothing compared to Bananas. Bananas is something. Joe's gonna shove a broomstick up your ass into your brains. He's gonna ruin my whole setup, millions of dollars."

"No, he ain't. No, he ain't. I'll take care of it, Padre."

"You can't even take care of yourself. *I'll* take care of it. Four guys comin' in on American Airlines next Tuesday, three o'clock. You hear me? Tuesday, three o'clock. You pick 'em up. *You* go. They'll recognize you. You don't fuck this up, you hear me. They'll take care of Bananas. They'll take care of this lawyer and the FBI asshole too, if it needs to get done."

"Yes, Padre. Yes. I hear."

"You better hear me good, you *pazzo* bastard."

CHAPTER EIGHTEEN

It was Saturday, and Bobby Bonanno was going to meet Hanna at Armory Park at noon. There was a little carnival there again. Bobby took a shower and shaved and put on some of his father's Bay Rum aftershave and pulled on a tight-fitting yellow polo shirt that showed off his big chest and arms and a pair of cream linen slacks and beige suede loafers, clothes he had gotten at Saks Fifth Avenue a couple of weeks ago in New York. You couldn't find stuff like this in Tucson. He combed back his wavy brown hair and shook his head so that a few strands of it fell over his forehead just right.

His father and mother were in the living room listening to the radio. Little Sal was on the floor playing with a toy truck. There were seven men in the house with them, taciturn men who did not chat together affably or wear conspicuous clothing. Three of them sat on the patio porch playing cards. Another was dozing on a chair in Elizabeth's room while she read a book. Another was out front mowing the lawn. Donatello and Michael Luna were in the living room with Joe and Fay and the baby.

"Where you going?" his father asked.

"Downtown to the carnival."

"Mike, go with him," Joe said.

"Aw, come on, Dad. I don't need Mike."

"I say you need Mike, you need Mike. That *stronz'* [shit] Alfredo maybe is still around. Mike will drive you.

"Alfredo wouldn't do anything to me. We're like brothers."

"And me, I'm like his own father. But he has turned into a *mascalzone* [scoundrel]."

Bobby shrugged. Michael took the keys to the Cadillac off the hall table, and they went outside.

▲ ＋ ▼ ＋ ▼ ＋ ▲

Big Julie Lovello sat in the window of a second-story room in the Arizona Inn, down the street and across from the Bonanno house. He sat still behind a translucent lacy curtain that gave him a full view of the front of the house. He had been in this room since four o'clock yesterday afternoon, when he and Micky Mara had joined the two soldiers who had been watching the Bonannos. Pity he couldn't go sit by the pool out back and watch the broads sun themselves. But later, after all of this was over, the Padre would surely give them all a bonus so that they could spend a few days chasing pussy in the sunshine. The Padre was good about that.

Bobby Bonanno came out of his house followed by Michael Luna. Big Julie picked up the walkie-talkie on the dresser and spoke into it. From the small parking lot directly across the street from the hotel, a black Chevrolet sedan with two men in it pulled out behind Bobby's Cadillac as it passed.

Big Julie pulled a .38 revolver from the shoulder holster under his beige Acapulco shirt and swung the cylinder open. Always check to make sure you're ready, he had been taught years ago. He closed the cylinder, put the gun back into the holster, and left the room. Another black Chevrolet sedan waited for him at the curb in front of the hotel, the engine running.

Julie got into the passenger seat. "You got 'em?" he asked the driver.

"Yeah, yeah. They just turned left up on Campbell."

The walkie-talkie on the seat squeaked. Then a scratchy voice said, "They turned right on Speedway, heading downtown."

▲ ✦ ▼ ✦ ▼ ✦ ▲

Hanna didn't used to feel bad sneaking out when her father wasn't around, telling him little white lies about where she had been and what she had done. But that evening sitting on the hill with him had changed something in her. Suddenly she felt guilty. She had realized for the first time that it was her welfare that her father was interested in, not just being a stodgy old man or showing her who was boss. No, it was much deeper than that. He loved her so much and felt so protective of her that he couldn't imagine letting her do anything that had the tiniest possibility of bringing her harm. She understood it when his teardrops had fallen on her hair. She had realized that her father was crying about her, for her, from tenderness, from frustration, and she had also cried.

But about Bobby Bonanno he simply didn't understand. Sure, you wouldn't want your daughter to go out with the average Mafia boss's son. That was natural. But Bobby was so different from what you'd expect.

Hanna studied herself in the bathroom mirror and approved. She had borrowed a little tube with a mascara brush in it from her best friend, Tracy, and it made her eyelashes really look long. She had saved for two weeks to get up enough money for blue eyeshadow, like a lot of the girls were wearing, and she didn't think that she had applied too much. Just enough to heighten the hyacinth tint in her gray eyes.

Daddy had gone to pick up Adam at the Fox Tucson Theater downtown. Adam still went to the "Kiddie Show" that played every Saturday morning from ten to noon. Hanna was too old for Buck Rogers and Ma and Pa Kettle and The Three Stooges.

She dressed in a yellow sundress and sandals and walked out of the house, fighting her guilt. Well, she wasn't going to do anything terrible, just meet Bobby at the carnival in Armory Park, spend a few hours with him and some of the other kids. Just a normal Saturday afternoon, except that Bobby Bonanno just happened to be there.

The bus was as slow as a centipede. A half hour ago she had seen her father and Adam in the yellow convertible pass by on South Sixth Avenue going back home. She had left a note for her father that she was going to the carnival and then maybe over to Tracy Stiller's house for dinner.

Finally the bus stopped in front of the Carnegie Library and Hanna got off. It was almost one o'clock. Her breasts jiggled a little in the sundress, but it didn't embarrass her, because in dresses like this nobody expected you to wear a bra. She walked into Armory Park and it was crowded with people. She wandered around for a few minutes looking for someone she knew and spotted Tracy and Jean and Doug Marks sitting on a bench eating popcorn. She walked over to them and sat down.

"Bobby's over at the Strong Man tent," Tracy said. "He won a dime lifting those big weights last week. He says he's been practicing all week."

"I'll go watch," Hanna said.

She went through the milling groups of people on the narrow walkways between the closely spaced tents: baseball throw for kewpie dolls, duck shoot, ring toss for little pottery elephants, a hot dog stand, various other tents. She waited in line five minutes for a candy apple. Her lips were bright red from the candy when she got to the Strong Man tent. Some grotesque-looking man with a huge body and shaved head was swinging a big wooden sledgehammer on a thing with a round steel base on springs and a pole up the back of it with ascending numbers. The huge man sent a little ball way up the pole to the number eleven. He handed the sledge to Bobby Bonanno.

Bobby had taken off his shirt, and he had a beautiful chest and arms, strong and shapely. Hanna walked up close to the small stage in the open tent.

"Good luck," she called out.

Bobby looked up and smiled happily. He walked up to the contraption, hefted the wooden sledge, and loosed a roundhouse blow at the round pedestal. The ball zoomed up to slightly over eleven. The huge man handed Bobby two dimes and announced to the dozen or so spectators that the next round was worth a dollar. Bobby walked over to Hanna.

"I won forty cents so far," he said, beaming proudly.

"My hero," she said.

He laughed. "The next one's for a dollar."

"That guy looks awful strong."

He rolled his eyes. "Yeah, I think I can't do much more than that eleven. But I don't think he can either."

She shrugged. "In for a dime, in for a dollar, my dad always says."

"If I beat him I'll be the most famous guy in all of Tucson."

"Yeah, for about half a minute."

He chuckled. "Well, it's only a buck."

Three other men had put up a dollar. Bobby handed the huge man a dollar. The huge man walked up to the pedestal, swung easily and effortlessly, and sent the ball to fifteen.

"I've been suckered," Bobby said to Hanna under his breath.

The three other men managed to whack two tens and a nine. Bobby got a twelve. The huge man laughed. Bobby and Hanna walked out of the tent.

"There's one born every minute," Bobby mumbled.

"I just counted four," Hanna said.

They laughed.

"I hope that wasn't all the money you have," Hanna said. "I didn't have any lunch. I have to have a hot dog before I starve to death, and I just spent my last nickel on a candy apple."

Bobby pulled a crumpled dollar bill out of his pocket and held it up victoriously. "My stash."

They went to the hot dog stand and stood in a long line for ten minutes until they finally got hot dogs and Cokes. They walked over to a park bench and were joined a moment later by Tracy and Jean. There wasn't any room on the bench for Doug, so he sat on the grass beside it. He ate a box of Cracker Jacks. Tracy was eating cotton candy. Jean had a small box of popcorn.

"Want to go to a movie?" Jean said.

"What's playing?" Tracy said.

"*Gentleman's Agreement* over at the Fox."

"What's it about?" Doug said.

"Some Jewish guy who gets discriminated against, something like that," Jean said.

"Are you kidding? Who wants to see that?" Doug turned up his nose. Then he suddenly caught Hanna's eye and said, "Oh, sorry. I didn't mean anything."

Hanna nodded.

"It's got Gregory Peck in it," Jean said. "He's beautiful."

"*Farmer's Daughter* is over at the Lyric," Bobby said. "It's got Loretta Young."

"Yeah," Doug said.

"I don't want to see Loretta Young," Jean said.

"Well, while you children squabble," Bobby said, "Hanna and me are going to see *Farmer's Daughter*." He looked at Hanna. "Okay?"

"Sure," she said.

They got up from the park bench, threw their empty cups into a trash barrel, and walked to Bobby's car.

"Don't sit in the back," Tracy called out and giggled. She and Jean were still on the bench. Doug Marks remained sitting on the grass beside it. They talked for five minutes about what to do and finally decided to go see *The Farmer's Daughter*. The girls got up and started walking to Doug's car. Doug got up off the ground.

"Whose is this?" Doug called out to the girls. He pulled a slender pink leather purse from under the bench.

"Oh, it's Hanna's," Tracy said. "She must've forgot it."

She grabbed the purse and went running after Bobby and Hanna. The Bonanno Cadillac was still parked a block away on South Sixth Avenue, but she didn't see Bobby or Hanna anywhere. Odd. She strolled back to Doug's car.

"Bobby's car's down there, but I didn't see either of them."

"We can give it to her at the movie," Jean said.

"Yeah, if we can get her and Bobby apart for long enough," Tracy said.

Jean giggled.

▲✦▼✦▼✦▲

When Hanna did not return by six o'clock, Joshua became worried. He knew that Hanna had planned to meet Tracy Stiller downtown and go to the carnival and maybe to her house for dinner. He called the Stiller home and her mother answered. Tracy hadn't returned yet either. But she had said they were going to a movie and might eat supper at Georgette's Diner. Joshua was somewhat mollified, though miffed at Hanna for not calling him.

Magdalena had made a big dinner. Chuy came over at about six-thirty, and Barbara arrived a few minutes later. Frances and Edgar Hendly came over a little before seven. Adam was at Chris's house for dinner. Solomon was at the ranch in San Miguel.

"I have a little announcement to make," Chuy said as they sat at the table in the kitchen. "Magdalena Antone is changing her name to Leyva."

Barbara clapped.

Joshua smiled and nodded his head. "It's about time. It's sure about time."

Edgar beamed at Chuy. "Yer smarter'n ya look,

Jesus my boy. This is the finest girl on the whole damn res, no doubt about it."

"One of the finest girls in the whole world," Joshua said, his face serious. "To your enormous happiness." He held up his can of Tecate beer for the toast. They all toasted with whatever was in front of them.

"Jesus and Magdalena gettin' married," Edgar drawled. "Somehow it just seems sacrilegious."

They all laughed except Frances. She shook her head and frowned. "Eddie's got a mouth on him that don't know no limits. I'm sorry, dear." She patted Magdalena's hand.

"Actually, we've been married by Indian custom for a few weeks now," Chuy said.

"That's where ya just go under the nearest tree and fuck, ain't it?" Edgar said, straight-faced.

Joshua burst out laughing.

"See what I mean?" Frances said, looking disgustedly at her husband.

"You going to live in that same tiny little place?" Joshua asked, looking at Chuy and then at Edgar. "Maybe we ought to give Solomon a badge and put him in your place and give you two the place across from the school." The government had built a large three-bedroom yellow brick home for Macario Antone when he was chief. He had preferred to live where he always had, in his adobe house across from the mission. The new house simply remained empty.

Edgar looked askance at Joshua. "You guys been conspirin' against me?"

"Damn right!" Joshua said.

"We'll see," Edgar said. "Maybe we oughta put that big place to good use. It'll hold a lotta kids."

"I'm getting married, but I'm not pregnant yet," Magdalena said, smiling.

"Well, I'm shocked to hear it," Edgar said, looking with mock surprise at Chuy and then back at Magdalena. "If ya need help, just call me. Look what I done fer Frances." He patted her belly.

Frances smirked scornfully at Edgar. "Yeah, you old fart. You sure it was you?"

Everyone roared with laughter.

The telephone rang. Joshua got up from the table, laughing so hard his eyes were tearing. He walked into the living room and picked up the receiver.

"Hello."

"Mr. Rabb. This is Tracy Stiller." Her voice was subdued. "I just came home and my mom said you called. She wanted me to call you."

"Yes."

Hesitantly. "Hanna wasn't with me this afternoon or for dinner. We ran into Bobby Bonanno over at Armory Park, and she was going to go to the movies with him. But she didn't. I don't know where she went."

Joshua was so angry he could hardly speak. "You know I told her to stay away from that boy." His voice cracked.

"I know, Mr. Rabb," she replied weakly and sniffled.

"Do you have his phone number?"

"No, I don't."

Joshua slammed down the phone. Barbara came out of the kitchen and walked up to him, a look of concern in her eyes.

"She went out with that Mafia boss's son," Joshua growled. He picked up the telephone and dialed the operator. "Number for Joseph Bonanno, please."

A few seconds later, she said, "That number is unlisted sir. I can't give it out."

Joshua slammed down the receiver and stood glowering at it. He picked up the telephone and threw it into the wall, shattering it.

"I've got to go over there," he muttered. "This shit's got to stop."

Everyone had come out of the kitchen now and was watching uncomfortably.

"What are you going to do?" Chuy asked.

"I don't know."

"You can't just barge in on Joe Bonanno. You'll get killed."

"I don't care."

Joshua strode to the front door, opened it, and went out to his car. Chuy came running after him and got into the passenger seat. Joshua hardly noticed. He started the car and drove recklessly to the Bonanno house. By the time they were there, Joshua had calmed down considerably.

"You okay?" Chuy asked.

"Yeah. Much better. I can handle it."

"Just stay cool."

"Yes, sir," Joshua said.

▲＋▼＋▼＋▲

A black Chevrolet sedan with its lights off drove up in front of the Bonanno house. It was dark, almost eight o'clock. A man got out of the passenger seat holding a large cardboard box. He laid it carefully on the welcome mat and rang the doorbell. He walked quickly back to the car, and it sped away.

The front door opened, and Donatello Luna switched on the porch light. He was holding a small revolver. He stuck it into the waistband of his pants and picked up the box.

"What?" Joe Bonanno asked. He was sitting on the sofa watching TV with Elizabeth. Fay was already in the bedroom asleep.

"I don't know. It ain't ticking."

"Be careful," Joe said. He got up and went into the kitchen with Luna. The dark spots that looked like grease stains in the poorer light were clearly fresh blood in the fluorescent light of the kitchen. Joe was paralyzed with foreboding. Luna put the box in the sink. He took a kitchen knife off a holder on the wall, quickly cut the hemp rope, and opened the flaps.

Donatello groaned and staggered against the counter. His brother Michael's face stared out at him from the box.

Joe stepped to the sink and closed the flaps. The greatest pain that he had ever known welled up in his chest and constricted his throat. "They got Roberto," he choked out.

There was a loud knock on the front door.

Joe opened a drawer and took out a .38 revolver. He stood in the doorway of the kitchen and called out, "Harve, Tonio." A door opened at the end of the hallway and a light showed. The two men walked into the living room.

"We got trouble. Michael Luna is dead. They got Roberto."

Another knock on the door.

"Maggio. Take Elizabeth," Bonanno called out.

Harve took a gun out of his trousers pocket and pointed it at the door. Tonio did the same. Three more bodyguards came into the living room, all holding guns. One of them, Maggio, turned off the TV set, took a very frightened Elizabeth by the hand, and led her quickly to her room.

Another knock on the door, louder than the first two.

"Harve," Bonanno said, gesturing with his gun toward the door.

Tonio switched off the table lamp. Donatello came out of the kitchen and stood in front of Bonanno, shielding him.

Harve switched on the outside light and opened the door slightly.

"I want to see Mr. Bonanno," Joshua said.

"Who are you?"

"My name is Joshua Rabb."

Harve looked toward Bonanno.

"Not now," Bonanno growled. "Not now."

"Mr. Bonanno no here," Harve said, pushing the door closed.

Joshua put his foot in the door. "I heard his voice."

"Take out your foot, I blow you toes off," Harve said, pointing the gun at Joshua's foot.

Joshua snapped his steel-pronged hand around Harve's wrist and squeezed. The man let out a wail of pain and the revolver clattered to the floor. Chuy picked up the gun, and Joshua pushed open the door, still holding onto Harve's hand.

Joshua and Chuy pushed into the living room. Tonio

switched on the light. Another man closed the door. Six guns were pointed at them. Joshua let go of Harve's wrist. Chuy placed the gun carefully on the floor.

"You crazy, Mr. Indian lawyer," Bonanno seethed. "You crazy, break into my house."

"Where's my daughter?"

"Your daughter. Whatta you, a lunatic? I don't know where your daughter."

"She was with Bobby all day."

Bonanno flinched. He lowered his gun slowly. "Sit down on the couch," he said.

Tonio gestured with his gun. Joshua and Chuy sat stiffly on the edge of the couch.

"Dino, go in the bedroom with Fay," Bonanno said. The man walked quickly down the hallway.

"Georgio, go in back," Bonanno said. The man walked into the kitchen, carefully opened the door onto the patio, and slipped into the darkness.

"What the hell is going on with you people?" Joshua asked. This wasn't just a father waiting with his poker buddies for his son to return home from a date.

"How you know your daughter is with Roberto?"

"Her friend called me. She was with them at the carnival at Armory Park." Joshua paused and looked around. "What the hell is happening here?"

"You come," Bonanno said to him.

Both Joshua and Chuy got up off the sofa.

"No, just you, Indian lawyer."

Tonio stepped forward quickly and pushed Chuy back onto the sofa.

Bonanno gestured with his gun toward Joshua to come into the kitchen. Donatello stepped out of the way. Joshua was becoming frightened. All of the adrenaline of a half hour ago had worn off and drained him, and he felt very weak and confused. He hadn't even thought about what would happen when he got to the Bonanno home, but he hadn't expected an army of Mafia gunmen to be looking very grim and training their guns on him. He walked slowly toward

Bonanno. Bonanno backed into the kitchen and gestured with the gun toward the box in the sink.

Joshua walked to the box, opened the flaps, and blinked in shock at the severed head. He backed away from it, looking with horrified eyes at Bonanno.

"He was driving Roberto today" came Bonanno's hoarse, low voice. Joshua heard the agony in the man's voice. Bonanno slowly lowered the gun. His shoulders slumped.

The telephone rang. There was one on the lamp table, one hanging on the kitchen wall. Donatello took the receiver off the kitchen phone.

"Yes," he said. He listened, and his eyes grew wide. "*Sporco* [filth]," he muttered. His eyes were bloodshot with hatred. He held the telephone toward Bonanno. "Lovello," he said.

Bonanno swallowed. He took the phone. "*Si,*" he said, making his voice calm.

He listened. His lips twitched. Then he stared at the phone and handed it back to Donatello.

"They want me to come alone," he said to Donatello, "to the bar at the dude ranch. Alone or Roberto's head comes to me in a box." He turned to Joshua, and suddenly his face lost its rancor. "And your daughter too."

Joshua's eyes opened wide. He had no voice.

"Get Maggio," Bonanno said to Donatello. "Get Dino and Georgio. Get them all in the living room. Take Elizabeth and little Sal into Fay's room, and give Fay your gun."

"*Si, Padre.*"

Joe Bonanno and Joshua Rabb stood motionlessly in the kitchen for moments while the men assembled in the living room.

"What are you going to do?" Joshua asked.

"I'm gonna get my son back. And your daughter too. If they are still alive." He looked at Joshua, and his face blanched. "We cannot be sure."

"Who is it?"

"Alfredo Maggadino. My cousin Stefano's adopted son from Sicily. Alfredo's real father was a close family friend of Stefano's and mine who died valiantly in his service. Stefano and I took Alfredo in, treated him like our own son. But now he loves heroin more than he loves his fathers. He has no respect, no honor for our tradition." Bonanno swallowed and pursed his lips. "But he is only twenty-two years old. He is too young to have done this all by himself. Julie Lovello would not work for a twenty-two-year-old boy."

"Padre Giuseppe," Donatello called out from the living room.

Bonanno walked out of the kitchen, Joshua followed him. Four Bonanno soldiers stood in the living room.

"We are at war," Bonanno said, his voice calm. He looked around at his men. "They want me to come to them so that they can kill me. They take this man's daughter. They take my son to lure me." His voice broke, and he breathed deeply with anger.

"We must take them back." He looked from man to man, and each one nodded.

"Jesus!" Joshua blurted out. "They have my daughter. You go in there with guns and both of them will die."

"You have a better idea?" Bonanno looked hard at him.

"You just can't rush in like—like gangbusters, goddamn it. Let me call the FBI. Let me call the sheriff's department."

Bonanno's face soured. "Roy Collins is one man. There are more?"

Joshua shook his head.

"He's supposed to go to the place and show his badge, and they will all shit their pants and throw up their arms in fear?"

Joshua gritted his teeth in frustration.

"And you have met the sheriff, Patrick Dunphy?"

Joshua nodded grimly.

"You will trust *him* to save your daughter's life?"

Joshua was silent.

Bonanno turned back to his men. "Alfredo and Julie Lovello wait for me in the restaurant. I must go alone. Alfredo learned from Stefano. That means that he will have at least two more *assassini* in the restaurant with him. He will also send at least two men here to kill my family once we have all left. That means there are two men in a car out there somewhere, the same two who delivered Michael's head, or maybe they are now in a room at the Arizona Inn, and they are watching to see us leave, to count us, to know our cars." He paused and looked around.

"There is no one here who was not in upstate New York a year ago, when Don Vittorio thought that he should be the father of the Maranzano family."

They all nodded.

"You remember how that last day happened, in the farmhouse in the hills?"

They nodded and looked knowingly at one another.

"Maggio, Tonio, and Harve will leave first and take the Ford. There are four gas cans in the trunk. Fill them at the station at Speedway and Campbell. Wait for me at the intersection of Silverbell and Grant, behind the gas station there. It is closed at night. Donatello and Georgio and Dino will take the Chevrolet. Do the same.

They nodded.

"Then I will come in the Packard."

They all nodded.

"I'm going too," Joshua said.

"No." Bonanno shook his head. "You do not have the skills for this, Mr. Indian lawyer."

"I was a major in the army," Joshua said, holding up his steel-pronged hand. "I can't let anything happen to my daughter."

"This is a different kind of war, Mr. Rabb. This is not your nice little war where you get medals on your chest." Bonanno stared hard at him. "But I got a very important job for you and the Indian cop." He looked from Joshua to Chuy. "I need all of my men with me. We are going to burn the *animali* out like rats from a haystack. It is the only way. But there will be at least two *assassini* come here after we leave. It is the way. They will look to kill my wife and my children.

You and your cop friend will kill these men. You will not let harm come to my family." Bonanno's voice was sepulchral. "You understand, Mr. Rabb? You understand me? It is on your head."

Joshua nodded, his face mordant.

"My family will stay in Fay's bedroom, our bedroom. It has bulletproof glass on the windows. The house will not burn—it is brick with an asbestos roof, only the doors will burn. There are only three places they can come in: through these glass doors to the patio"—he pointed—"through the patio door in the kitchen, and through the front door. You can cover them all from here in the living room." He jutted his chin at Donatello.

Luna walked to a closet and took out two .45 Colt automatics with long silencers screwed onto the barrels. He brought one over to Chuy and laid it on the couch next to him. He laid the second pistol on the lamp table in front of Joshua. He walked over to the closet, took out a metal can filled with at least a dozen loaded clips, and put them on the lamp table. He put a clip in Joshua's pistol, retracted the slide, let it slam closed, loading the first cartridge, and reseated the hammer carefully. He handed the gun to Joshua.

The other men took various rifles and handguns out of the closet. There was no more talk. The first group hid their weapons under sports coats and left through the front door. Bonanno cut the telephone cord in the kitchen, then the one in the living room. The second group left through the kitchen door to the patio. The Chevrolet was parked behind the gate in the six-foot masonry wall surrounding the patio. Bonanno waited ten minutes, turned off the lamp, the light in the kitchen, and the porch light, nodded grimly at Joshua, and left.

The house was dark and still. Chuy loaded a clip into the .45 pistol. He turned the overstuffed chair by the sofa around so that he could sit in it with a view of both the sliding glass doors and the kitchen door. Joshua sat on the floor against the living room wall, facing the front door. The can of clips was next to him, the pistol held loosely on his lap.

He was terrified for Hanna, afraid to think about what they would do to her. Would they fondle her, rape her? The next time Joshua saw her, would it just be her face staring up at him from a cardboard box? He fought back the intense feeling of nausea that overwhelmed him and tried to keep from thinking about anything but the gun in his hand.

▲✦▽✦▽✦▲

A half hour later, three cars parked behind the gas station at Silverbell and Grant. It was an overcast night without the moon or stars for illumination.

"There is a little hill at the entrance to the access road," Bonanno said. "Donatello, you and Harve and Tonio go, no lights, stop a couple hundred yards from the hill. Go take care of whoever is up there. Then come back."

The three men drove slowly away from the station. The others waited restlessly. Twenty minutes, thirty, over an hour. The black sedan rolled into the back of the station.

"Okay," Donatello called out of the driver's seat.

"How far you go?" Bonanno asked.

"All the way up to the front of the ranch house."

"How many?"

"Two."

"*Fantastico!*" Bonanno said. "How many more can there be? They send two to my house. Two more stay with Roberto. Three with Alfredo. Sound right?"

"*Si, Padre,*" Donatello said.

"Let's go," Bonanno said.

They drove to the access road, parked, and walked to the ranch house. Four of the men had full five-gallon cans of gasoline. They crept around the exterior of the main ranch house, the lobby, restaurant, and bar, and doused the wooden walls that sat on the building's ornamental stone foundation. Bonanno, Donatello, and Tonio continued past the main house to the guest rooms by the pool and braced themselves against the front wall of the three rooms facing the pool, the center one of which had a light on in it. They sidled past the first dark room and heard nothing. They stopped beside the second sliding glass door. Through a crack in the curtain Bonanno could see Bobby lying on the bed. He was bound and gagged. Hanna was slumped in a chair beside the bed, also tied with hempen rope and gagged with a broad strip of adhesive over her mouth.

In the reflection of the mirror on top of a chest of drawers, Bonanno could see two men sitting on a small sofa watching a television set. One of them had a Thompson submachine gun slung on his shoulder. Bonanno couldn't see any other guns.

He tapped Donatello on the shoulder and signaled him to go around to the other side of the glass door. "They are just to the right, here," he whispered and pointed. Donatello tiptoed to the other side. They both flattened back against the wall, and Tonio took the submachine gun out from under his jacket and stood directly in front of the glass doors. They waited until they saw the flames start leaping up above the stone foundation of the main house. In seconds it was an inferno. Tonio opened fire with the Thompson, spraying dozens of .45 rounds through the right-side glass door into the right side of the room.

Bonanno and Luna burst through the demolished glass door past the two gunmen, who lay in widening pools of blood on the floor. Bonanno ran to his son. Bobby had oozing bruises on his forehead and cheek, and blood was matted in his hair above his ear. Joe pulled the tape off his son's mouth. He took out a pocket knife and cut the rope on his hands and feet. The boy's eyes opened and he tried to focus. He groaned. Joe ran into the bathroom and wet a washcloth and washed Bobby's wounds tenderly.

Donatello Luna cut the rope binding Hanna to the chair. She pulled off the tape on her mouth. Her eyes were glazed with fear. She wept uncontrollably. A cut on her bruised cheek dripped blood slowly down her chin and onto the bodice of her sundress.

"Are you all right?" Donatello asked.

She blinked away her tears and nodded, shuddering uncontrollably.

Bobby was standing up beside the bed now, his arm around his father's shoulders. Joe held him around the waist, and they walked outside. Donatello helped Hanna up, steadied her, and they followed.

Flames had devoured almost the entire main ranch house. They began to leap toward the rooms behind. Large cinders and sparks were exploding up and to the sides from the burning roof.

"Pull the two out," Joe said to Tonio.

"Si, Padre." He ran back into the room and dragged the two bodies out, one by one.

"Get all the bedding, towels," Joe ordered.

Tonio ran back into the room.

Harve walked up to Joe. "It's done, Padre Giuseppe. They came running out. They're lying outside the rear door of the bar."

"Wrap them up. Take them and these two to the old mine. There is a huge pit beside it. Donatello, you know where it is. You take them. Except for Alfredo. Donatello, *porti mi suo capo*. Tonio, you help the girl."

"Si, Padre," Donatello said, smiling for the first time. *"Piacere* [with pleasure]."

Donatello handed Hanna gently to Tonio.

Tonio and Bonanno slowly walked Hanna and Bobby to the Packard parked on Silverbell Road.

Tonio drove. Hanna was in the passenger seat next to him, crying gently now. Joe and Bobby sat in back.

△✦▽✦▽✦△

It was eerily quiet at the Bonanno house. Joshua and Chuy sat in the coal blackness of the living room, and even though their eyes had adjusted, they could barely make out each other's forms from twenty feet away. The drapes on the patio door were closed.

"A nice little war," Joe Bonanno had called it. A nice little war. Joshua sat on the floor, and the only sound was the slight buzzing of an evaporative cooler vent. It must be a little loose, Joshua thought absently. The air current is making it buzz like a bumblebee. That's alliteration, he thought inanely, all those B's: buzz, bumble, bee. It began busily buzzing like a big bad beady-eyed bumblebee.

His mind began to drift. He could still smell the bodies from the nice little war.

He stands behind the four barracks of the concentration camp just outside of Medzibiez, Czechoslovakia, and he stares with horrified eyes and a gaping mouth at the huge piles of corpses. They are seventy- or eighty-pound bags of skin enveloping bones. And the vision that most appalls him, that will flash through his mind's eye at least once a day each day that he lives, are the faces. Huge open eyes, staring at nothing from cadaverous faces, the mouths open like the ricti of baby birds waiting to be fed. And the smell of death, the cloying odor of rotting, decomposing human flesh, so overwhelming and dizzying that it is beyond description, beyond capturing with mere words. The stench nauseates him.

He gagged and vomited on the floor beside him. His feeling of nausea abated for a few seconds, and suddenly he realized that the stink was not in his memory, the nausea was not two years ago. It was now. He was so dizzy that he could hardly stand. His eyes were tearing, and he felt as though he was about to have uncontrollable diarrhea. He stood up with an immense effort of will. There was a sound on the roof, creaking, then rapid footsteps. He squinted over at Chuy. He was slumped in the chair. He appeared to be sleeping.

Joshua's face was directly in the air flow from one of the cooler vents, and the stink was overwhelming. He whirled away from the rushing air, staggered to the sliding glass patio doors, braced himself face into the wall, and smashed his steel hand as hard as he could into the glass. It shattered explosively. He snapped the prongs of his hand high on the curtain and ripped it down. Fresh air from outside began to revive him.

A bullet took off one of the prongs of his hand. Two more pierced the hollow aluminum cylinder that was his arm. He spun around and flattened against the wall. Suddenly he remembered the .45 automatic. He ran to the hallway, picked it up off the floor, turned toward the patio door, and began shooting rapidly at two forms as they burst into the living room. In seconds they lay motionless in front of the sofa.

Joshua forced himself to stand still and try to hear noise above the buzzing of the cooler vent and the blood squishing in his own ears from the wild pumping of his heart. He heard nothing. He switched on the wall switch and two ceiling lights went on. He rubbed his tearing eyes harshly with the back of his hand and staggered toward the smashed patio door. The fresh air revived him again.

The cooler switch. Where is the cooler switch? He squinted around the living room. Nothing. He ran shakily into the hallway and found it next to the bathroom door. Two switches. He turned them off and the cooler clattered to a standstill.

Oh, my God! Bonanno's wife. His children. They were in one of the bedrooms, sealed in tightly. A literal gas chamber. He tried the doors down the hallway. One was locked. He stood back from it and kicked it. Once. Twice. On the third kick the thin doorjamb splintered and the door opened. He ran inside and switched on the light. The stink was suffocating. His eyes teared and nausea enveloped him again. He slumped dizzily to his knees.

Someone else was there. He dragged Joshua out of the room and down the hallway to the patio door. Then he ran back down the hall. Joshua vomited several times and began to feel better.

Chuy dragged an older woman next to Joshua. He ran back down the hall and came back with a baby in his arms. He put the baby on the sofa.

Joshua got up and ran down the hallway into the

bedroom. He lifted the unconscious teenage girl off the bed, carried her to the patio door, and laid her on the floor next to her mother.

There was a pounding on the door. The bell was ringing. More pounding.

Chuy picked up his .45 pistol. He went to the door, switched on the porch light, and opened the door a crack. A sheriff's deputy looked at him. He unsnapped his holster and drew his weapon, pointing it at Chuy.

"We got a call from one of your neighbors, pal. What's the ruckus?"

Chuy backed into the house. The deputy followed cautiously. He saw the bodies on the floor in front of the sofa. Joshua was sitting on the sofa holding a baby who was vomiting. Chuy went to the older woman lying in front of the patio door. She was struggling to stand up, and he helped her. The deputy ran back outside.

Two minutes, four minutes, five. The sounds of sirens rent the arid, hot night. Two sheriff's cars sped down Elm Street and parked at the curb by the first one. The three deputies spoke together for a moment. Two of them went into the house, guns drawn. The third one got back into his car to use the radio.

Chuy walked Fay Bonanno out onto the back porch and helped her into a metal spring chair. He went back into the house and picked the girl off the floor. He carried her to a chair next to her mother. As he lowered her into it, she vomited violently all over the front of Chuy's shirt.

Joshua switched on the rear porch light by the side of the sliding glass door and walked up and down on the porch, holding the baby as though he were burping him. The girl started weeping hysterically. Fay stood up, steadied herself, pulled her daughter Elizabeth out of the chair and hugged her closely.

Another siren wound down. Chuy went into the bathroom, turned on the shower, and stood under it fully clothed to wash off the vomit. He came back dripping into the living room, his boots soaked and squeaking.

Sheriff Pat Dunphy came into the house. He looked

a little like a dissolute Edgar Hendly, portly and bald-
ing. He blinked and squinted when he saw Chuy.

"What the hell you doin' in Joe Bonanno's house,
boy?" Dunphy asked.

Chuy looked back at the sheriff blandly.

Dunphy looked around. The deputies were examining the bodies. Dunphy saw Joshua Rabb burping the
baby on the back porch and the two women hugging
each other and weeping.

"That Jew bastard back 'ere," Dunphy muttered.
"What's he doin' in Bonanno's house?" He looked acidu-
lously at Chuy. "I ast ya what the fuck's happenin', boy."

Chuy stared back at the sheriff, saying nothing.

Dunphy backhanded him in the face. Chuy wiped a
trickle of blood from the corner of his mouth.

Roy Collins walked into the living room. He looked
around slowly. "Well now, Patrick," Roy said, "you
got a little excitement going on?"

Dunphy nodded. "What're *you* doin' here?"

"Well, I was out to Davis Monthan Air Force Base
at the officers' club having a couple of drinks, and I
heard the traffic on my radio on the way home. Figured I'd come on over and take a peek, it being Joe
Bonanno's house and all."

"Just stay the fuck outta the way," Dunphy
growled. "This ain't yer jurisdiction."

A deputy walked up to Dunphy. "Two empty gallon
jugs of chlordane on the roof next to the cooler, Sheriff. Been poured all over the pads."

"Bug killer?"

"Yip."

"What in the hell is goin' on?" Dunphy said, looking hard at Chuy.

Joshua handed the baby to Fay Bonanno. She sat
down in the spring chair and began to rock it gently.
Joshua walked into the living room. Roy Collins studied his face. He saw the holes in Joshua's aluminum
arm and the missing prong.

"You okay?" he asked Joshua.

At that moment Joe Bonanno came into the house.
His eyes showed dread.

"They're all okay," Joshua said to him. "Hanna?"

"In the car," Bonanno gasped. He went out on the back porch.

Bobby Bonanno walked through the door, looking bewildered. He also went out on the back porch.

Joshua turned to leave the house. Sheriff Dunphy grabbed his good arm and restrained him. "Where ya think yer goin', Jewboy?"

"Let him go," Collins said.

Dunphy held on. He turned hotly toward the FBI agent. "You ain't the law *here,* sonny."

Collins pulled his revolver out of his shoulder holster and held it down at his side. "You are restraining the movement of two federal officers," he said evenly, "the BIA legal officer and the BIA chief of police. On what basis do you arrest them?"

"On the basis there's two dead fuckers in the living room, you asshole," Dunphy growled.

Tonio came to the front door carrying Hanna in his arms. Joshua pulled his arm away from the sheriff and ran to the door.

"Stay here!" Collins ordered, looking hard at Sheriff Dunphy.

"She's all right, Mr. Rabb. She's all right. Just frightened," Tonio said.

Joshua took Hanna in his arms, and she buried her face in his chest and wept.

Chuy went outside and took the car keys out of Joshua's pocket. They walked to the convertible, and Joshua laid Hanna in the backseat.

"No, Daddy, stay with me," she gasped and sat up.

Joshua got into the backseat with her and wrapped his good arm around her shoulders. She huddled against him, crying quietly.

▲+▼+▼+▲

The telephone rang next to Meyer Lansky's bed. He jerked his head up and rubbed his eyes. It wouldn't stop ringing. He lifted the receiver.

"Yes?"

"Meyer. Do you recognize my voice?"

Lansky sat up in bed and switched on the lamp. It was five o'clock in the morning, two o'clock Tucson time. "You're up very early."

"Yes, or very late, Meyer. The matter of which we last spoke."

"Yes."

"You tell me it was Frank. It seems to me that it was Stefano."

Meyer paused. "I will tell you again: Frank. Stefano has nothing to do with it."

"How can that be?"

"I only know what I know. Frank and Charlie. It is no longer merely a guess."

Meyer heard the tiredness in Bonanno's voice, the resignation.

"Thank you," Bonanno said.

△✦▽✦▽✦△

The morning newspaper carried a short epitaph for the grand old El Rancho del Cerro that had burned down the night before:

Not until flames leaped forty feet in the air was the Rural Fire Service even notified, since the nearest neighbors to the old dude ranch are almost five miles away. By the time the fire trucks reached the scene, there was nothing left to save. Luckily, it appears that no one died in the blaze. George Maxon, the longtime owner of the ranch, who has been confined to a wheelchair for the last two years, was at his daughter's home in Phoenix.

No bodies have been discovered. The employees had all apparently left for the night. The chief of the Rural Fire Service speculates that the fire may have been caused by a lightning strike igniting the old split-shingle wooden roof of the main ranch house. "These roofs are no longer permitted under Pima County fire code regulations," Chief Elmer Rogers said, "and for good reason. After baking in the sun in Tucson's heat all day long, this is what can happen."

Albert Anastasia brought a large box into Frank Costello's bedroom. It was seven o'clock at night, and Frank was sitting in a silk smoking jacket, drinking a martini, watching television. Albert's face was drawn and ashen. He put the box down on the table in front of Costello.

"This came by special messenger." He folded back the flaps, which he had already opened outside. He removed the package of dry ice and tilted the box toward Costello.

Costello gritted his teeth. A cloying odor made his nostrils quiver involuntarily. He breathed shallowly.

"Call Joe," he said, his voice thin. "Tell him the war is over. No more in Arizona. On my honor."

△✢▽✢▽✢△

There had been no detectable heroin smuggling across the border for over two months. The FBI field offices in New York and Philadelphia reported a drastic reduction in the supply of Mexican brown. In its place, white Asian heroin was showing up in large quantities. Roy Collins walked to the U.S. attorney's office to talk to Tim Essert. It didn't take long for the shouting to start.

"So what if Manuel Rodriguez refuses to talk?" Essert said. "He doesn't have to talk. He confessed to you."

Roy Collins stared back at him. "You mean out of this whole deal, only the kid gets prosecuted? Not Juanito Coronado, not Fat Henry? They just walk away and the kid gets ten years in Terminal Island?"

"I don't have enough to charge them. The boy won't open his mouth to the grand jury. I have no evidence without him."

"You promised us you wouldn't prosecute him."

"You arrested him in the act of smuggling heroin. He's going down," Essert said.

"He's only sixteen."

"He'll be tried as an adult."

"Only if Judge Buchanan orders it," Roy said.

Essert squinted at him. "What the hell are you pulling here?"

"If I testify at the transfer hearing that he ought to be tried as a juvie, you can't indict him as an adult. And if I testify that you promised him immunity for his information, the judge'll throw out the whole damn case. He won't even allow the confession into evidence. What do you have then?"

"I have you and two Indians and Joshua Rabb testifying you arrested him smuggling over a hundred pounds of heroin across the border in a van. I don't need his confession."

"Yeah, but you need me, or Solomon Leyva, or Chuy Leyva, or Joshua Rabb."

"What the hell's that mean?"

"It means I don't like the way you do business, Mr. Essert. I think you're a bigger asshole than a lot of the guys you prosecute."

"You'd lie for that maggot?"

"He's a poor kid from the wrong side of the border. His sister had to suck cocks to get him a pair of shoes. She gets murdered because he has the guts to wear a snitch jacket and testify for us. And now you tell me because he clammed up to save his life, you're going to put him in the joint." Collins swallowed back his anger. "Fuck you, Mr. Assistant U.S. Attorney."

Essert stood up abruptly and his chair spun back into the wall. "Who the hell you think you are? I've had enough of you, Collins. You don't belong in the Bureau. I'll have your fucking badge."

Collins stood up. "Listen, you lowlife. I was a lawyer before I joined the Bureau. We're all lawyers or accountants, or haven't you heard? I know the difference between how it's supposed to be done and how *you* do it. You start screwing with me, I'll rip you a new asshole."

Essert's mouth gaped open.

For punctuation Collins spat on the floor of Essert's

office as he walked out. He went across the street to his office and called Joshua Rabb.

"Tell Solomon Leyva I'm having the boy released," Roy said. "There won't be any charges filed against him. And after what happened to his sister, it would be unfair to try to force him to testify."

Joshua was surprised. "You serious? Essert's going to let you do that?"

"Tell Solomon to be up there tomorrow at ten. I'm going to Judge Buchanan's chambers to get a release order right now. Solomon can stop over here tomorrow on the way up to the detention center and pick it up."

"Essert know about this?"

"Sure. It's his idea."

Joshua laughed. "Yeah, right. You'd better keep looking behind you, pal. Those footsteps you hear aren't a herd of elephants looking for a place to take a nap."

"No. It's Essert looking for a place to take a shit."

Both men laughed.

CHAPTER NINETEEN

When Joshua had left Brooklyn a year and a half ago, everyone had told him that Arizona didn't have any winter. It was always summer, spring, or fall in Arizona, they said. But they obviously weren't here this December. When Joshua got up many mornings there was frost on the plants outside, and he had to throw a potful of hot water on the car windshield to melt the ice. The mud puddles from the winter rains were often frozen over with a thin sheet of ice. And it didn't warm up until about ten or eleven in the morning. Then it would usually be between fifty-five and sixty-five degrees for the rest of the day. That was the part New Yorkers heard about.

It was a particularly cold night. At ten o'clock Joshua put on his black wool overcoat—they had told him in Brooklyn that he'd never need it in Tucson—and walked to Edgar's house. It was about thirty degrees, and the blowing wind knifed through him.

Almost as soon as he knocked, Edgar opened the door and came out. He was wearing a plaid wool mackinaw. His face lacked its usual overlay of frivolity. They both got into Edgar's car and drove silently toward Florence. The route took them down Oracle Road to the Oracle Highway, then thirty miles north of Tucson to the Junction, and another forty miles north. The road was narrow and wound sharply through rough hills most of the way. Near Florence was a wash made notorious by Hollywood's most famous silent movie cowboy, Tom Mix, who had too much to drink one day in 1940 and plowed his car much too fast into the wash. Neither he nor his car had survived. Edgar drove carefully through the wash.

The men were silent. Joshua stared glumly out the side window into the darkness. Things had quieted down in Tucson. Joe Bonanno had sent his son off to boarding school far from Tucson. Joshua had grounded Hanna until her twenty-fifth birthday. But then Mark Goldberg had come back from the Catskills, and Hanna no longer thought about Bobby. Joshua liked Mark. He liked him a lot. He was a freshman at the University of Arizona. And when Joshua saw him and Hanna together, there was no mistaking this for kid stuff. They were young adults, and they were in love.

There had not been enough hard evidence to win a writ of habeas corpus for Charlie Isaiah. Edward Carter, who Joshua was sure was the killer, had disappeared right off the face of the earth. His son was running the dealership now and had the bravado and callousness of a much too young man suddenly being thrust into a much too high place much too early. He wouldn't even meet with Joshua. Joshua had gone to Santa Monica to talk to Cindy Danson, but her affidavit was hardly sufficient to win freedom for Charlie. She had known of Jennifer Carter seeing Charlie Isaiah two years ago, early in her junior year, when Charlie was a senior. But she had not seen them together since then. Jennifer had been going steady with Jerry Hawkins for over six months. She had even gone all the way with him twice, Cindy confided to Joshua. She didn't think that Jenny would have been going out with Charlie Isaiah at the same time she was going all the way with Jerry. That wouldn't be like Jenny.

Joshua had submitted a clemency petition to the governor's office ten days ago, but it still had not been acted upon. The execution was at 12:01 A.M. on December 10, 1947. Until the handle was pulled and the cyanide pellets dropped into the bucket of hydrochloric acid between Charlie's feet, every eye would be on the telephone in the gas chamber.

Florence, Arizona, was a quaint old town harking back to the pioneer days of Arizona. Only a couple of thousand people lived there. They were either farm workers at the many farms around the valley, or employees at Arizona State Prison. The prison administration building was a simple and unimposing structure of wood and brick. The prison itself was decidedly different, a forbidding monolithic three-story cement box with little grates in it at measured intervals. Even if it had not been surrounded by a ten-foot chain-link fence topped with six strands of barbed wire, it would not have appeared inviting.

The guard at the wooden shack pushed the swing arm up, and they parked in the lot in front of the administration building.

Deputy Warden Higuera, his name tag said, was dressed in a too-tight brown uniform shirt. His stomach bulged the buttons. He wore a soiled pair of tan trousers. He was assembling the spectators in the conference room on the first floor and showed Edgar and Joshua into the room. Edgar, by law, attended all executions of Indians from the Papago reservations, a rare event among these gentle people. Joshua was there as Isaiah's defense attorney. The chairman of the Board of Pardons and Paroles was there as the governor's representative. Reporters from the Tucson and Phoenix newspapers were there. They all sat silently around the conference table. The last one to arrive was the warden.

"Gentlemen," he said, "let me briefly explain what we will do. We will go over to the gas chamber in a few minutes. You may take any seat you wish in the viewing theater. You can see through the glass into the chamber itself, but the inmate inside cannot see you. I will call the governor's office at a few minutes before midnight and we will coordinate our watches. The governor has until 12:01 to grant clemency. After that time I will signal the executioner to drop the pellets. Once that has been done, the execution cannot be stopped. It usually takes ten seconds for death to come. It has taken as much as four minutes for inmates who hold their breath. Death this way is not an attractive sight. If you get sick, please feel free to leave. If you must vomit, you will find a bag on the seat of each chair in the viewing theater. Please use it. Are there any questions?"

Nobody had a question.

"Is Mr. Rabb here?" the warden asked.

Joshua raised his hand.

"Mr. Rabb, as his attorney, you have the right to spend these last moments with your client in the holding cell behind the chamber. He also has a priest with him."

Joshua nodded and stood up, feeling very weak. The warden stared at him.

"I'm sorry, Mr. Rabb. You'll have to take off your prosthesis. We can't allow anything in there that could be used as a weapon."

Joshua took off his coat, his suit jacket, his tie, and his shirt. Edgar unstrapped his harness, pulled the arm off, and put it beside his chair. The other men stared. Joshua put on his shirt, jacket, and overcoat, stuffed the tie in his pocket, and followed the deputy warden out of the conference room.

They crossed the yard to the prison building and walked down the stairs into the basement. The death cells were here, single cells for the prisoners awaiting execution, a dozen of them. The condemned men stood at the barred gates of their cells, staring hatefully at the two free men. The cell at the end of the corridor was the holding cell that opened directly into the back of the gas chamber. It was the only cell with a solid steel door.

The deputy warden knocked. A slide opened in the center of the door, then closed. The door cranked open, and Joshua went inside. A prison guard was there. Father Boniface from San Xavier Mission was sitting with Charlie Isaiah on the bunk bed. The priest had come up early that morning and spent all day with Charlie.

Charlie was crying. Joshua put his hand on the Indian boy's shoulder.

"We still have a chance," Joshua said. His voice was thin and hollow. He tried to make it sound stronger, hopeful. "The governor's still studying the petition."

Charlie sniffed. "I didn't do it, Mr. Rabb. I didn't do it. Call the governor. Please," he pleaded in a weak voice. "Tell him I didn't do it."

Joshua sat down next to Charlie. He was impotent with grief. He held Charlie around the shoulders.

A buzzer rang on the wall. The back door to the gas chamber opened. Two men in full black fabric masks and guard's uniforms came through the door. Father Boniface stood up. He made the sign of the cross over Charlie. Charlie began to weep violently. The guards pulled him off the bunk as gently as possible. He was handcuffed, belly-chained and ankle-chained. They half carried him into the gas chamber.

Boniface put his arm around Joshua's trembling shoulders. Joshua was crying. He helped Joshua out of the cell and through the door beside it into the viewing theater. The theater was semi-darkened, and the spectators in the thirty-seat arena were blurs to Joshua.

He and Boniface stood next to the chamber window and watched the guards strap Charlie into the big chair. They covered his face with a black mask. One of them put a bucket between his feet. He placed a small device with electric wires attached to it on top of the bucket. Both of the guards left the chamber.

Minutes passed interminably. Joshua watched numbly through tear-filled eyes. He heard a buzzer and glanced at the warden standing by the telephone on the wall, pushing a button by it. Oh, thank God, Joshua thought.

But the warden didn't pick up the telephone.

Joshua looked back at Charlie, struggling violently against his restraints. Fumes were rising out of the bucket. Joshua sagged to his knees weeping, covering his face with his hand. Boniface knelt down beside him, his arm around Joshua's shoulders.

Unmeasured moments passed. There was activity. Joshua did not see it. After some time he stood up slowly. Boniface stood with him.

The viewing theater was brightly lighted and empty. The gas chamber was empty. A guard in a gas mask was hosing it down.

Joshua staggered to a chair and slumped into it. He wiped his eyes roughly with the sleeve of his overcoat. "I can't ever do this again," he murmured. "Ignacio. Charlie." He looked at Father Boniface and shook his head.

"You must not stop helping these people," Boniface said gently. "You are all they have."

Joshua grimaced. "I do a hell of a lot for them, don't I?" He began to cry again softly.

Boniface stood directly in front of him and whispered, "I am not supposed to do this, Mr. Rabb. A confession is sacred. But I can reveal a confession to save another person's life."

Joshua squinted up at him.

"Charlie Isaiah murdered Jennifer Carter," Boniface said. "He made his confession to me this morning."

Joshua stared at him. "What?"

Boniface nodded. "He had been chipping on heroin all that day with a friend of his named Maggadino. Charlie had used it before, but never so much. This Maggadino and Charlie were bragging about girls. Maggadino asked him if he knew Jennifer Carter, since Charlie worked at her father's dealership. Charlie said that he had dated her a couple of times, but then she had refused to go out with him again. Maggadino said that she had snubbed him, that she was a stuck-up bitch, that what she needed was a real man. Charlie was crazy out of his mind on heroin. He kidnapped her and brought her back to his house on San Xavier and raped her. She tried to run away, and he caught her and killed her. He couldn't even remember why."

Boniface paused and looked intently into Joshua's tortured eyes. "You must keep on with what you are doing for our people, Mr. Rabb," he said gently. "We need you."

CHAPTER TWENTY

Joshua was sitting in his office finishing preparing the Office of Land Management contract for repairing a stretch of storm-damaged road near Sells. The telephone rang on his desk.

"Hello."

"Hello, Mr. Rabb. This is Buck Buchanan."

"Yes, sir," Joshua said, straightening a little in his chair. "What can I do for you, Judge?"

"You planning to come downtown this afternoon?"

"If there's something you want to talk to me about, I will."

"Well, I think there is. I got a criminal case here, a man named Pablo Mariscal."

Joshua sucked in his cheeks. "You mean the Indian who made the front page of the papers this morning? Murdered a rancher and his wife down by Tubac?"

"Yep, that's the one. Allegedly. The grand jury just indicted him on armed robbery and murder charges. He needs a lawyer, and he's indigent."

"Are you crazy, Judge!" Joshua slammed down the phone.

▲ + ▼ + ▼ + ▲

Ten minutes later he put his pen down, sighed deeply, and stared hostilely at the telephone. He picked up the telephone receiver and dialed.

"Hello, Mrs. Hawkes. This is Joshua Rabb. Judge Buchanan in?"

"Yes, Mr. Rabb. He's been waiting for your call."

Joshua winced.

A moment later, the judge came on the line. "Yes, Mr. Rabb," he drawled casually.

"I'll be over in a half hour, Your Honor."

"I told Ollie Friedkind to give you as much time with him as you need."

"Thanks." Joshua hung up. He pursed his lips and grimaced. He picked up a blank legal pad and walked slowly out of the BIA to his car.

We invite you to preview
Richard Parrish's
new Joshua Rabb suspense novel,

WIND AND LIES,

forthcoming from Dutton/Signet

CHAPTER ONE

Even though it was just late April, it was over a hundred degrees, and heat shimmered off the asphalt highway making the road appear to have liquified under the blowtorch sun. The great saguaros were in bloom with their waxy white blossoms, and the unusually long and heavy winter rainy season had resulted in an explosion of wildflowers on the huge Papago Indian Reservation west of Tucson. Bell-shaped scarlet penstemon, red skyrockets, and white thistles called eryngo, grew thick along the road. The hills were studded with clusters of brittlebush that looked like small black-eyed susans. It was a sight that Joshua Rabb never tired of seeing. Before coming to Tucson almost two years ago with his daughter, Hanna, and son, Adam, he had lived his entire life in the asphalt and concrete of Brooklyn, New York, except for the war years spent in Europe. The Papago Reservation was about a million miles away from Crown Heights, and in Europe he hadn't noticed much of the scenery. He had been too preoccupied just trying to stay alive.

He slumped in the passenger seat of Edgar Hendly's spiffy 1946 Ford sedan, kind of a celery-green color, and stared out the side window.

"Looka them clouds over there," Edgar said, jutting his chin toward the Baboquivari Mountains just a few miles to their left. "It'll be pourin' by the time we start back."

Joshua shrugged. The car hit a pothole in the narrow asphalt highway, and both men bounced high on the front seat.

"I'm more worried about getting there alive than a little rain," Joshua mumbled. "I thought this road was getting resurfaced last month."

"Couldn't get it done. Rained so damn much in March and the first part of April that the bed never dried out enough to put the blacktop down."

The Ford hit another pothole and Edgar fought the wheel to keep the car from swerving. Joshua looked at him and frowned. "Better slow down or we'll end up in a ditch."

"Naw," Edgar said. "That stretch was the only real bad part. I wanna be able to start back by four o'clock or we're liable to be pinned down by the storm that's comin'."

Joshua slumped deeper into the car seat and tried to stretch out some of the stiffness from the long drive. He was tall and strongly built. His left arm was missing, and the stainless-steel prongs of his mechanical arm emerged ominously from the sleeve of his tan linen suit. His hair was straight and brown except for patches of gray at the temples, and he usually combed it straight back from his widow's peak. Today, however, in the scorching heat, it hung limply over his forehead. His bright blue eyes studied the Sonora desert.

He had come to Tucson back in June 1946 because the doctor at the Veterans' Hospital in Brooklyn had told him that the gunshot wound to his lung had healed but left potentially troublesome scar tissue. New York weather was giving him bronchitis which would probably become chronic. But even more debilitating than his physical wounds had been the emotional ones. His wife, Rachel, had died in an auto accident in December 1944, but Joshua hadn't even been aware of it as he lay in an Army hospital in Antwerp recovering from wounds he had suffered at the Battle of the Bulge. He had been a captain with the 109th Infantry Regiment in Diekirch, Luxembourg, pinned down by a machine-gun battery and what seemed to be the entire *panzer korps* of the Nazi Army. For reasons he would never fully understand, he had crawled over the snow to within forty feet of the battery at the edge of the skeletal winter-ravaged forest and hurled a grenade into it. Then he'd sprayed the three German soldiers with the entire clip of his Thompson submachine gun. When he became fully conscious again, he was lying in a bed in the Army General Hospital in Antwerp, Belgium, with a bullet wound in his left thigh and the four small toes of his left foot frostbitten so badly that they were shriveled and discolored like tiny prunes.

It was not until weeks later that they had told him of his wife's death. But the war was still on, and he was still mobile, so the hospital commander had given him a wooden cane and pinned a silver star on his chest and gold-colored oak leaves on his epaulets, and he had been attached as JAG officer to a rear unit of Patton's 3rd Army as it swept through Germany into Czechoslovakia. He was already almost crippled by fear for what Hanna and Adam were going through, trying to cope with the death of their mother while their father was off in Europe getting shot. But the prison camp at Medzibiez, Czechoslovakia, had really crushed his soul. It was a concentration camp with piles of emaciated dead behind four barracks filled with the cadaverous bodies of hundreds of once-people only barely clinging to life. Shards of charred bones of his own people lay in heaps in front of a line of ovens in a small cinder-block building next to the camp headquarters.

A few days later, on a patrol for SS troops in the forest, Joshua had been shot in the chest and the left arm. These wounds were not so quickly repaired as had been his leg and foot. By the time he got out of the Veterans' Hospital in Brooklyn, the war had been over for several months. He still vividly remembered the frightened gray-hyacinth eyes of thirteen-year-old Hanna and the terrified blue eyes of ten-year-old Adam when they came with Grandpa and Grandma Rabb to the hospital to pick him up.

So much had happened since them. He had accepted a job as part-time legal officer for the Bureau of Indian Affairs, and as Chief of the Federal Office of Land Management in Tucson. It was a fifteen-hour-a-week job which paid only $129 a month, but it came with a little adobe house right across from the San Xavier del Bac Papago Reservation six miles south of Tucson, and he was permitted to use his office in the BIA to attempt to create a private law practice.

Four months ago, Joshua and Hal Dubin's daughter Barbara had set their wedding date for June 20. They would move into a house owned by Hal near downtown Speedway. But at least, for the time being, Joshua hadn't given up his job with the BIA and the OLM, partly because he needed the money, and partly because he had grown deeply attached to Edgar Hendly, the superintendent of the BIA, and to the Indians who came to him for help. In fact, he had come to the poignant realization as the months passed that perhaps even more than the Indians needing him to help them, he needed them to help give his life some meaning, other than just the quest for money and things which inevitably became the major motivating factor in the lives of most men.

It wasn't that he was altruistic. That had a false ring to it, like the pronouncements of Dewey and Truman running for president. No. From his own experiences, he had simply come to understand people's pain. *"Haud ignara mali, miseris succerere disco,"* a Poor Claire nun had once said to him. "Not a stranger to misfortune, I have learned to succor the downtrodden."

"Ya sure ya got alla the papers we need to serve on that asshole?" Edgar asked, looking at Joshua for reassurance.

Joshua stirred and straightened up slowly in the

seat. "We've got everything but legal jurisdiction," he said. "Quit worrying."

"When ya see this guy, ya'll start worryin too. He's right outta *Moby Dick*—Ahab, ya know, the crazy ship captain who cain't think a nothin but killin a big white whale."

Joshua grinned. "Why Edgar, I didn't know you were so literary."

Edgar was short and portly. He combed a few strands of gray hair across his bald pate with his fingers. Despite the heat, he was wearing a rumpled gray-wool suit and an oft-washed white dress shirt with a frayed collar which made his neck bulge. He chuckled. "Well, actually I ain't real literary. I read the Classic Comic Book version a *Moby Dick*. Frances bought it a year ago fer Jimmy to do a book report."

Joshua slapped his knee and laughed. "Well, this guy isn't after white whales."

"Ya don't think so?" Edgar frowned histrionically. "Wait'll ya take a gander at his number-one wife, Miriam. If she ain't a white whale, I don't know who qualifies."

Joshua laughed again. "You ought to go on the road with Abbott and Costello."

"When ya see em, ya'll know I ain't jokin," Edgar said. "They came to my office 'bout three months ago, when they first started buildin out here. They called theirselves 'Sister-wife Miriam and the Prophet Josiah.' They didn't bother to tell me at the time about all the little girl wives. Alls they said was they wanted to put up a Mormon meetin hall so's they could minister to the Indins' souls. Well, hell, I didn't see nothin wrong with that, and the BIA don't interfere with the buildin a churches on the res. But that ain't what these folks're about. It ain't *souls* that ol' Josiah's after."

A crack of thunder turned both of their faces toward the rapidly gathering slate-gray cumulus clouds to the south.

"Shit," Edgar grumbled. "Don't know if we're gonna be able to beat this som bitch."

Joshua hadn't used a cane in a long time. His left foot had long since lost its tenderness, and he had learned to walk evenly and without a limp. But today he had brought along the gnarled mesquite limb cane that Adam had so carefully carved as a gift for his thirty-ninth birthday last year. He used the cane now on those rare occasions when there was a possibility of trouble. Usually someone looking for a fight would be daunted by Joshua's size and stainless-steel hand. But at times it was advisable to have the cane along as well. This was one of those times.

He was worried that the BIA probably lacked "standing" to be the plaintiff in a trespassing action without the Papago tribe being co-plaintiff. But this was a very touchy matter involving Mormons, and the tribe might well balk. So Joshua and Edgar had decided to try it this way first, hoping that the cult would just put its tail between its legs and fade into the sunset without a court fight.

They drove slowly through Sells, sixty miles west of Tucson on the Big Res, and the tribal headquarters of the Papago Reservation. Actually there were two Papago Reservations in Southern Arizona. The "Big Reservation" was almost three million acres, a hundred miles east to west at its widest point and reaching north from the Mexican border almost eighty miles to below the town of Casa Grande. The other reservation was San Xavier del Bac, below Tucson and just seventy-one thousand acres. Over ten thousand Papago Indians lived on the reservations.

Sells was little more than a shantytown, small adobe and saguaro rib and tin and tarpaper shacks with a few yellowed stucco government-constructed buildings and the small redbrick BIA in the center. Edgar turned south on the dirt road toward the Mexican border. The road skirted the small peaks that formed the Artesia Mountain range, and Edgar pointed at the half dozen wooden buildings that had recently been erected a hundred yards west of the road.

"That's them," he said.

The car rumbled jerkily over the rocky ground.

Other vehicle tracks in the mud had dried and formed hard ridged ruts in the otherwise barely discernible trail to the settlement. Behind and beside the buildings were huge fields. Indian boys were plowing furrows, pulling hand plows strapped around their shoulders as though they were oxen.

"It's the big one," Edgar said, pulling the car in front of the longest of the six buildings. "Josiah Porter has his office in here next to the meetin hall."

They got out of the car and walked into the meeting hall. There were two women sweeping the crude wooden floor in front of a raised platform at the rear. They were both wearing long dresses of coarse gray homespun cotton and large bonnets of the same material.

One of the women looked up, startled, and ran to the side of the room. She knocked on a door, and a voice from within boomed, "Come!" She went inside and closed the door behind her. The other woman continued sweeping.

Joshua and Edgar walked to the door of the side room. It opened forcefully as they reached it, and a huge man stood framed in the doorway, filling it almost completely. He looked to Joshua like what he had always imagined an Old Testament patriarch would be: in his mid-sixties, a curly gray beard reaching all the way to the middle of his chest, thick black eyebrows over deep-set imperious eyes, a barrel chest. Amos the prophet chastising the people for their sins, Micah excoriating them for their waywardness. The only thing that differentiated the Old Testament patriarchs from this man were the clothes: a black suit grayed by time and desert dust, a once-white heavily starched shirt buttoned at the collar, a vest of the same grayed-black wool stretched tautly over his ample girth, and mud-caked black brogans.

"Why do you come here?" the man asked, his voice a deep stentorian rumble. He fixed Edgar with a hard frown. "I have told you twice to stay off my land."

"This isn't your land, pal," Edgar said, assuming an air of authority, and his speech lost the easy western slang he usually used. "This is Papago land under the supervision of the BIA, and you're trespassing."

Joshua handed the papers he had prepared to the man, but the man's arms remained at his side, and he made no move to take them. Joshua dropped them at the man's feet.

"As legal officer for the Bureau of Indian Affairs, I am serving you with a notice to quit the Reservation. A civil trespass case has been filed in Federal District Court in Tucson requiring you to appear and show cause why you shouldn't be compelled to remove yourself and your followers from Indian land."

"It's God's land."

"Well, right at the moment it belongs to the Papago Tribe," Joshua said. "You have no permission to be here."

"I have God's permission."

Joshua smiled benignly. "You have the absolute right to assert that in your defense at the show cause hearing. I'm sure that Judge Buchanan will consider it."

"God is my judge."

Edgar's drawl returned. "Cut the bullshit, ya old fart. Yer out here turnin Indin boys inta slaves and fuckin the girls. God aint got nothin t'do with what's goin on here."

The man's eyes opened wide and reddened noticeably. His nostrils pulsed, and he looked like a bloodhound sniffing the wind. His hands became fists and he stepped toward Edgar.

Joshua placed his rubbed-tipped cane in the man's chest and stopped him with it. The man looked at Joshua, surprised, and visibly assessed him. He lowered his fists and glowered at Joshua and Edgar.

"Thou sons of Satan!" he bellowed.

Joshua couldn't fully suppress a smile. "Listen, pal," he said, "you are so clearly full of shit that it's hard to imagine anybody buying into your crap. But that part of it isn't my business. This reservation is my business, and you have no right to put buildings on it and farm it. That OSC on the floor there"—he pointed with his cane—"says for you to either get off the reservation within ten days or tell Judge Buchanan why you won't leave."

Edgar was staring at one of the woman sweeping. His face became sour and turned to the old man.

"Who's that?" he said. "One a yer daughters?"

The man gritted his teeth.

"She's one a yer wives, ain't she, ya old pimp? She caint be more'n twelve years old."

The man again gathered his hands into fists. Joshua stepped closer to him. The man slowly relaxed his hands.

"It is an abomination to look lustfully upon the countenance of a married woman," the man thundered. He lifted his arms above him in a hieratic gesture and looked toward the ceiling. "May the Lord of hosts strike down those who transgress His ordinances."

Edgar breathed deeply and shook his head. "Let's get outta here," he said to Joshua. "This fucker's crazier'n a rabid skunk."

They got back into Edgar's car, looked at each other, and laughed.

"Was I tellin ya a lie about that asshole?"

Joshua shook his head. "Hard to imagine anyone believing that *he's* a prophet."

"Yeah, it's damn sad," Edgar said. "These people out here are so damn poor and uneducated that they'll follow anyone who gives em a few bags a groceries and promises em it's all gonna get better."

"Where's he from?"

"Way up north just below the Utah border, a little town called Short Creek. Joseph Smith, the founder of the Mormon Church, had a revelation a hunnerd years ago that the good ol' boys oughta have as many wives as they could afford. So bein faithful followers a 'the Prophet'—that's what they call Joseph Smith— a lot of em jumped on the idea. But when Utah couldn't get statehood without guaranteein the gov'-ment that there wouldn't be no more polygamy, the church president at the time, whoever he was, suddenly had a revelation that the good ol' boys could only marry one woman from then on. Some of em didn't take too kindly to the new revelation, so they moved to godforsaken isolated little farmin villages and kept their way a life. A few like this asshole Porter marry girls no older'n ten, eleven." Edgar shook his head. "It's downright sick. He calls his outfit the 'Church of the True Vision of the Latter Days.' But the only vision he's after is some little girl squattin on his pecker."

Joshua grimaced. A clap of thunder reverberated against the hills and echoed several times.

"I've had the missionaries over to my house several times," Joshua said. "Persistent young men. Real true believers."

"Yeah, there are plenty a them. 'Round these parts, the Mormons sent missionaries to the Indins and the white folks both. I've listened to em a few times. The mainstream ones mean well, they got a lotta faith. They believe that Jesus came to North America after he was crucified and rose again, and converted the Indins. The Indins are supposed to be the descendants of Lehi and his family who came here from Jerusalem hunnerds a years before Jesus. One a Lehi's sons was named Laman, and he was some kinda bad guy, so God cursed him by makin' his skin dark, and from then on all the dark-skinned natives a North America are called Lamanites. So these Lamanites are the modern Indins, who are also descendants of the Israelites, and the Mormons think it's their duty to bring em all back to the fold."

Joshua shrugged. "Well, I guess everybody has a right to believe anything he wants."

" 'Cept'n if it causes other folks harm," Edgar said. "And this nutcase Josiah Porter is doin a lotta harm."

The rain started with a crash of thunder. It pelted the windshield and soon overcame the capacity of the windshield wipers.

"Damn," Edgar said. "It done got us." He stopped his car two miles east of Sells and headed back to the tiny town.

Joshua always brought along his shaving kit and a change of clothes when he went to Sells, because more often than not he was forced to stay overnight in the BIA office. It was either the weather or the condition of the highway or car trouble or you name it. And it was never a pleasant experience, but at least it wouldn't be so boiling hot in the office after this rain. He had also taken to carrying along the latest novel he was reading, just in case. But this time, it wasn't a novel, it was a collection of plays by Tennessee Williams. Joshua had seen an off-Broadway production of *The Glass Menagerie* a couple of years ago, and it was terrific. Now he was reading Williams's current Broadway hit, *A Streetcar Named Desire,* and he found it mesmerizing.

They parked in front of the BIA and ran under the porch overhang onto the wood-plank sidewalk. Water was dripping through leaks in the overhang everywhere, but at least it protected them from the torrent of rainfall. Edgar found the key and opened the door. It had cooled off to about eighty degrees and was almost pleasant inside the office. Joshua sat down on the sofa against the wall and immediately started reading. Edgar paced and stared out the window. By five-thirty, the rain began to slacken slightly. Edgar stood moodily looking out the window at the drab, bedraggled town. "I reckon I'll go on over to the Tribal Headquarters, see if I can stir up a game of checkers with Francisco or one a the boys. I'll be back when the rain stops."

"See you next month," Joshua said sourly.

Edgar chuckled. "Yeah, 'pears to be a permanent condition." He ran outside, got quickly into his car, and drove away.

▲▼▼▲

The Church of the True Vision of the Latter Days had three meetings each week. The regular church service was on Sunday. On Tuesday and Thursday evenings beginning at about seven o'clock, there were special prayer services which all potential converts were urged to attend. There were always several cartons of old clothes and canned food in the meeting hall, and the only requirement was that they were distributed after the services to Indians who had been there from the start. Sunday's service went on literally all day, punctuated only by an austere lunch served at noon. But the weekday sessions were usually only a couple of hours. So many more Indians attended weekdays than Sundays.

At eight-thirty, Edgar parked in front of the meeting hall beside several old pickup trucks and a few horse-drawn wagons. It had stopped raining an hour ago, and the clouds had dissipated. Out here where there were almost no electric lights to dull the sky, the myriad stars flickered brightly like guttering candles which appeared close enough to pinch.

Edgar opened the door of the meeting hall just a few inches and peeked inside. Two bare bulbs hanging over the stage illuminated the young Papago man who was gesturing with both arms over his head, looking toward the ceiling, speaking Papago in a prayerful voice. Darkness shrouded the forty or fifty people sitting cross-legged on the floor in front of the stage. Edgar crept into the hall and sat down quietly on the floor next to the door.

The Papago man slowly dropped his arms and bowed his head. Then he stretched forth his arms, intoned some kind of benediction over the audience, and left the stage. Two young white girls carried a wooden box to the stage and laid it down in front. It was two feet square and a foot high and was painted with gold leaf. On the front of it facing the congregation was a carefully painted picture of a coiled diamondback rattlesnake.

The Prophet Josiah came out of the side room followed by Sister-wife Miriam, and they mounted the stage. He was dressed as always in the once-black suit and vest and white shirt. Miriam was almost as tall as her husband. She wasn't wearing the sun bonnet that had almost hidden her face the other times that Edgar had seen her, and he was startled at how strong her face appeared. Her gray hair was pulled tightly to the back of her head and plaited in two thick braids which were pinned around the sides. She wore no makeup, and her skin had the color and texture of wrinkled parchment. She was almost as heavy as her husband, and she wore an unbelted long white robe which emphasized her stoutness. But rather than ugly or ungainly, she appeared commanding, even regal, like one of those bigger-than-life Brunhildes in the German operas.

Josiah ceremoniously took off his suit coat, folded it neatly, and laid it on the floor. He rolled up his sleeves. Then he looked around the congregation of his wives, children, and Papago Indians.

"If you believe not in signs, then you are not a Christian," he bellowed.

The abruptness of his expostulation, the loudness of it, riveted all eyes upon him.

"Once I did not know the true God," he continued, his voice now resonated and softer. "The devil had seized upon me to drag me under. But, exerting all my powers to call upon God to deliver me out of the power of this enemy which had seized upon me, and at the very moment when I was ready to sink into despair and abandon myself to destruction—not to an imaginary ruin, but to the power of some actual being from the unseen world, who had such marvelous power as I had never before felt in any being—just at this moment of great alarm, I saw a pillar of light exactly over my head, above the brightness of the sun, which descended gradually till it fell upon me."

Josiah's face was bathed in the light of the strong bulbs suspended from the ceiling. He appeared genuinely kind, Edgar thought, the first time he had seen him this way, like a saint with a halo around his head in one of those old paintings that hang in churches. Josiah got down now on his knees behind the box, his arms extended heavenward.

"It no sooner appeared that I found myself delivered from the enemy which held me bound. When the light rested upon me I saw two personages, whose brightness and glory defy all description, standing above me in the air. One of them spoke unto me, calling me by name, and said, pointing to the other— *This is My Beloved Son. Hear Him!*"

Josiah began to sway, and strange sounds came from his mouth, words with no meaning, gibberish, cries of anguish and exaltation. It was absolutely electrifying. Edgar was fascinated, as was everyone in the meeting hall. The sounds stopped, and Josiah lowered his arms to his side and fixed his kindly stare above the congregation.

"Thus did our Prophet Joseph Smith tell us of his revelation, and thus have I told you of the selfsame revelation that has shown God and His Son to me. I have seen a vision, and who am I that I can withstand God, or why does the world think to make me deny what I have actually seen? And for any of the unbelievers who might yet doubt that I am the successor to the revelator of the one true Church, God has bestowed upon me the gift of the words of his only begotten son, as preserved for us by the Apostle Mark: 'And these signs shall follow them that believe; In my name shall they cast out devils; they shall speak with new tongues; They shall take up serpents; and if they drink any deadly thing, it shall not hurt them.' "

Again he began to sway, and he sat back on his haunches and uttered sounds of no meaning and spoke rapid words. His eyes were glazed over with detachment, and he was in the throes of new tongues. It went on for fifteen minutes, like an opera in a language Edgar had never heard, and the rich bass voice of Josiah the Prophet mesmerized them all. And then he leaped to his feet and stretched his hands up to touch the hem of God's garment or His outstretched hand or to caress His feet, and it startled everyone. They watched now in awe as the Prophet leaned over, threw off the top of the box, reached in seemingly carelessly, and withdrew a three-foot-long diamondback rattlesnake in each hand.

Edgar stared in wide-eyed fascination. He had seen

a Penetecostal minister speak in tongues once, but he had never seen anything like this.

Josiah slowly waved the snakes in front of his face like an orchestra director with two batons. He was speaking in tongues again, and he continued babbling and passing the snakes before his face for twenty minutes. Then he placed one back in the box. The other he held a few inches from his face, peering directly into its eyes as though he were trying to hypnotize it. He held it by the neck with his right hand and stretched his left hand to the side, still staring at the snake. Sister-wife Miriam walked up to him, handed him a small drinking glass, and left the stage.

He brought the snake's head slowly down to his left forearm, and in a split second the rattler flashed its fangs into the Prophet's meaty forearm. Everyone in the congregation jumped and gasped, but Porter uttered no sound of pain, and the saintly look on his face did not change. He stretched the snake forward to the audience, milking its venom rapidly into the glass by pressing its upper fangs over the rim for ten seconds. Then he dropped the snake into the box and drank the venom from the glass.

Edgar was almost dizzy with the insanity of it. It was not the drinking of the venom that was so repugnant. Papago healers had long used increasing doses of venom to immunize men and women who came into frequent contact with snakes. It didn't happen in Sells or at San Xavier anymore, because they were too urbanized. But in some of the more remote areas of the Big Reservation, where there were still many rattlesnakes, such folk medicine was commonly employed.

But what so sickened Edgar was watching Josiah Porter intentionally cause the snake to bite him. The only word to describe that was *nuts*! The Gospel of Mark, that "they shall take up serpents," could hardly be conceived by Edgar as a prescription for normal conduct, but rather as a symbol that genuine faith in Jesus would protect you even from a lethal serpent. But Josiah took the words literally. Edgar couldn't observe any more of this lunatic's act. He stood up quietly and left the meeting hall.

He sat impatiently in his car, waiting for her to come out. It had been too dark inside to see if she was there, but she usually came here on Thursday nights. At least she had told him that she did.

A half hour later the door opened, and a small boy switched on a yellow bug light over the door. The people filed slowly out of the hall, and he saw her.

His eyes narrowed, and he gritted his teeth.

THE DIVIDING LINE

The crimes are ugly—not your ordinary killings. First, three kids are found in an irrigation ditch, and within days, a dead nun is discovered. All were brutally raped and murdered. Brooklyn-born attorney Joshua Rabb, who became the lawyer for the Bureau of Indian Affairs in Tucson, Arizona, after barely surviving World War II, is obsessed with learning the motives for such unspeakable violence. Although he's teetering on an emotional precipice himself—his wife dead, he has two children to raise alone—these horrific events give him the shove and stamina he needs to defend an innocent and powerless Indian man arrested for the killings. To keep ahead of the prosecution, Joshua digs deep into layer upon layer of deceit and corruption, moving dangerously closer to shocking secrets—and a killer. But who in this vast reservation and its bordering locales would be capable of such murderous extremes? With is life on the line, as well as the lives of his children and the woman he has come to love, Joshua Rabb is about to learn the lethal answer. . . .

VERSIONS OF THE TRUTH

Law school didn't prepare Joshua Rabb for this. Even battlefield combat didn't. In a brutal Southwest courtroom trial, he has to use every trick of the legal trade and come up with a few new curves to try to get a man from the local Indian reservation accused of rape and murder off the hook. In a bitter battle for a multi-million-dollar government contract, Rabb has to keep a cool head, even though he's having an affair with the daughter of a bidder. In a nest of vice and corruption south of the border, he must stay out of the hands of a Mexican cop with with a taste for cracking heads and breaking bones.

With the corpses piling up around him and those he loves, Rabb finds that questions of guilt and innocence have turned into a matter of life and death.